LONGING

This Large Print Book carries the
Seal of Approval of N.A.V.H.

LONGING

KAREN KINGSBURY

THORNDIKE PRESS
A part of Gale, Cengage Learning

GALE
CENGAGE Learning

Detroit • New York • San Francisco • New Haven, Conn • Waterville, Maine • London

GALE
CENGAGE Learning®

LIBRARY OF CONGRESS CATALOGING-IN-PUBLICATION DATA

Kingsbury, Karen.
    Longing / by Karen Kingsbury.
        p. cm. — (Thorndike Press large print Christian fiction)
    (Bailey Flanigan series ; bk. 3)
    ISBN-13: 978-1-4104-3901-7 (hardcover)
    ISBN-10: 1-4104-3901-1 (hardcover)
    1. Large type books. I. Title.
PS3561.I4873L66 2011b
813'.54—dc23   2011038326

Published in 2011 by arrangement with The Zondervan Corporation, LLC.

Printed in the United States of America
1 2 3 4 5 6 7 15 14 13 12 11

DEDICATION

To Donald, my Prince Charming . . .

Tyler is gone to Liberty University and Kelsey is more than half finished with college, but here's what's amazing: God continues to take us on one adventure after another! A move to Nashville? Who could've seen that coming? So many exciting transitions ahead. It hit me the other day just how much I really love you. We've been busy with kids, but at the end of a trip or a day or an afternoon . . . I look across the room and see you and I know that God has given us the greatest gift of all in each other. You constantly tell me I'm beautiful or that you wish we were together more. In every way you make me feel like a princess living out a fairytale that is more wonderful with every year. Thank you for that, Donald. Thank you for being so steady and strong and good and kind. Hold my hand and walk with me through the coming seasons . . . the graduations and growing up and getting older. All of it's possible with you by my side. Let's play and laugh and sing and dance. And together we'll watch our children take wing. The ride is breathtakingly wondrous. I pray it lasts far into our twilight years. Until then, I'll enjoy not always knowing where I end and you begin. I love you always and forever.

To Kelsey, my precious daughter . . .

Only one year left of college, and I am amazed at how far you've come, Kelsey . . . how much you've grown. Your time in California — though some of the most painful days in your life and mine for reasons we both understand — was a time God used to raise you into the strikingly beautiful young woman you are today, inside and out. Your commitment to living for Him even in your loneliest days stands as an example for teenage girls and young women everywhere. I have watched you learn to love serving and listening and helping others — more than you care for yourself. I remember one day not long ago when you were still in California — alone and heartbroken — and you called. "Listen to this!" Hope filled your voice. "Some great Bible verses I found today. They're perfect for where God has me." You didn't know this, but your dad and

6

I were in our room, and you were on speakerphone. The two of us exchanged a look — the sort of look that could only be shared between two parents who have prayed a lifetime for a child, only to see God's answer in a single moment. I'm so glad that hard year is over . . . and that God has brought friends into your life who know your heart. Really know it. Friends who make you laugh and dream and believe what only yesterday felt impossible. Like I told you, sweetheart, God cleared away the old and wrong to make way for the new and right. Whoever he is, honey, God is preparing him for that time when the two of you will be together forever. Until then, you keep being the light of our family, the laughter in our hearts . . . and that one-in-a-million girl who inspired an entire series. My precious Bailey Flanigan, I pray that God will bless you mightily in the years to come, and that you will always know how He used this time in your life to draw you close to Him, and to prepare you for what's ahead. In the meantime, you'll be in my heart every moment. And wherever you sing and dance and act for Him, we'll be in the front row! I love you, sweetheart.

To Tyler, my lasting song . . .

You're gone to college and the house is quieter for the change. But even so I can't begin to express how proud I am, how happy my heart is that you are at Liberty University singing for Jesus. I guess I knew deep down you'd end up at LU ever since we toured it a year ago. "If heaven had a university," I said that day. And right now it feels that right for this season of your life. You're not too far away now that we're in Nashville, and very soon you'll wind up back in our new home. I believe that. Still, I thank God for Skype and school breaks, when we'll see you in person again. In the meantime I believe with all my heart that God has you right where He wants you. Learning so much — about performing for Him and becoming the man He wants you to be. I feel a little like I did when you left for kindergarten. Like I want to line up your professors and mentors and friends and let them know that you're not just any fresh- man. You're that rare guy with a most beautiful heart for God and others. Your dad and I are so proud of you, Ty. We're proud of your talent and your compassion for people and your place in our family. And we're proud you earned a scholarship to Liberty University. However your dreams unfold, we'll be cheering loudest as we watch them happen. Hold on to Jesus, son. I love you.

To Sean, my happy sunshine . . .

How wonderful to see you running and dribbling and dunking on the basketball court again, last year's injury behind you finally and fully. This past summer was a crazy one, picking up and moving to Nashville in little more than a few weeks' time. But God was calling us, and we wanted nothing more than to follow Him. Already I can say I'm so glad we did. Especially as you have started working out with the basketball team at your new school. Basketball is at an entirely different level here, and I know you're having to work harder than ever. But that's been good for you, and along the way you've kept the most amazing attitude. That's the one thing that sets you apart, Sean. Besides your athleticism and concern for people, you have this happiness that defines the joy God must be talking about when He commands it for all of us. Be joyful, He tells us. And so in our family you give us a little better picture of how that looks. On top of that, I love how you've gotten more comfortable talking with me and Dad and Kelsey about your life.

Stay that close to us, Sean. Remember, home is always the place where your heart is safe. Your dream of playing college basketball is alive and real. Keep working . . . keep pushing . . . keep believing. Go to bed every night knowing you did all you could to prepare yourself for the doors God will open in the days ahead. I pray that as you soar for the Lord, He will allow you to be a very bright light indeed. You're a precious gift, son. Keep smiling and keep seeking God's best.

To Josh, my tenderhearted perfectionist . . .

Can it be you're starting your junior year? Our move to Nashville was intended to benefit you and Sean most of all. Because having just two more years of high school left, there was no time like this year to get involved with a school whose bar is exceptionally high at every level. The way we want that bar set for you. I feel this is the beginning of so many exciting times for you, Josh. College coaches looking at your football and soccer skills and the very real possibility that you'll play competitive sports at the next level. But even with all your athleticism, I'm most proud of your growth this past year. You've grown in heart, maturity, kindness, quiet strength, and the realization that time at home is short. God is going to use you for great things, and I believe He'll put you on a public platform to do it. Stay strong in Him; listen to His quiet whispers so you'll know which direction to turn. I'm so proud of you, son . . . I'll forever be cheering on the sidelines. Keep God first in your life. I love you always.

To EJ, my chosen one . . .

EJ, my jokester, this move to Tennessee has been hardest for you, for sure. And yet, even so, from the beginning you have said, "Whatever you and Dad think is right, that's what we'll all do, and God will lead us." You are starting your sophomore year in a new place, and already I can see that with a good attitude comes growth and more opportunity for you. School seems to be your thing, and for that I'm so proud of you. I see you sitting at the counter or at the computer working hard as you can for those *A*'s and *B*'s and I wonder if you know that your effort really will go somewhere. One day not too far off from here, you'll be applying to colleges, thinking about the career choices ahead of you, the path God might be leading you down. Wherever that path takes you, keep your eyes on Jesus and you'll always be as full of possibility as you are today. I expect great things from you, EJ, and I know the Lord expects that, too. So glad you're a part of our family . . . always and forever. I love you more than you know. I'm praying you'll have a strong passion to use your gifts for God as you move through your sophomore year. Thanks for your giving heart, EJ. I love you so.

To Austin, my miracle boy . . .

As you enter your last year of middle school in a brand new place, I see you becoming such a godly leader, determined to succeed for Him, standing taller — and not just because you've grown so much this past year. I love the fact that before we moved you stopped in at one of the baseball games from last year's team and the dads didn't recognize you. They wondered who that man was in the dugout. Not for a minute did they believe it was Austin, eight inches taller than when they saw you last. In the past season I've seen your competitive drive like never before. Some days you come home from training with tears and some days you come home with frustrated silence. Austin, I love that you care enough to be and do your best. It shows in your straight *A*'s and it shows in the way you treat your classmates. Of course it absolutely shows when you're playing basketball. But always remember what I've told you about that determination. Let it push you to be better, but never, ever let it discourage you. You're so good at life, Austin. Keep the passion and keep that beautiful faith of yours. Every single one of your dreams are within reach. Keep your eyes on Him . . . and we'll keep our eyes on you . . . our youngest son. With you come a host of lasts, but I hold on a little longer to every one. I refuse to focus on tomorrow when you're giving us so much to smile about today. There is nothing more sweet than cheering you on — from the time you were born, through your heart surgery until now. I thank God for you, for the miracle of your life. I love you, Austin.

And to God Almighty, the Author of Life, who has — for now — blessed me with these.

ACKNOWLEDGMENTS

No book comes together without a great and talented team of people making it happen. For that reason, a special thanks to my friends at Zondervan who combined efforts with a number of people who were passionate about Life-Changing Fiction™ to make *Longing* all it could be. A special thanks to my dedicated editor, Sue Brower, and to Don Gates and Alicia Mey, my marketing team. Thanks also to the creative staff and the sales force at Zondervan who work tirelessly to put this book in your hands.

A special thanks to my amazing agent, Rick Christian, president of Alive Communications. Rick, you've always believed only the best for me. When we talk about the highest possible goals, you see them as doable, reachable. You are a brilliant manager of my career, an incredible agent, and I thank God for you. But even with all you do for my ministry of writing, I am doubly grateful for your encouragement and prayers. Every time I finish a book, you send me a letter worth framing, and when something big happens, yours is the first call I receive. Thank you for that. But even more, the fact that you and Debbie are praying for me and my family keeps me confident every morning that God will continue to breathe life into the stories in my heart. Thank you for being so much more than a brilliant agent.

Also, thanks to my husband, who puts up with me on deadline and doesn't mind driving through Taco Bell after a football game if I've been editing all day. This wild ride wouldn't be possible without you, Donald. Your love keeps me writing; your prayers keep me believing that God has a plan in this ministry of Life-Changing Fiction™. And thanks for the hours you put in helping me. It's a full-time job, and I am grateful for your concern for my reader friends. Of course, thanks to my daughter and sons, who pull together — bringing me iced green tea and understanding my sometimes crazy schedule. I love that you know you're still first, before any deadline.

Thank you also to my mom, Anne Kingsbury, and to my sisters, Tricia and Sue. Mom, you are amazing as my assistant —

16

working day and night sorting through the mail from my readers. I appreciate you more than you'll ever know. Traveling with you these past years for Extraordinary Women and Women of Joy events has given us times together we will always treasure. Now we will be at Women of Faith events as well. The journey gets more exciting all the time!

Tricia, you are the best executive assistant I could ever hope to have. I appreciate your loyalty and honesty, the way you include me in every decision and the daily exciting website changes. My site has been a different place since you stepped in, and the hits have grown a hundredfold. Along the way, the readers have so much more to help them in their faith, so much more than a story. Please know that I pray for God's blessings on you always, for your dedication to helping me in this season of writing, and for your wonderful son, Andrew. And aren't we having such a good time too? God works all things for good!

Sue, I believe you should've been a counselor! From your home far from mine, you get batches of reader letters every day, and you diligently answer them using God's wisdom and His Word. When readers get a response from "Karen's sister Susan," I hope they know how carefully you've prayed for them and for the responses you give. Thank you for truly loving what you do, Sue. You're gifted with people, and I'm blessed to have you aboard.

And to Randy Graves, a very special thank you. As my business manager and the executive director of my One Chance Foundation, you are an integral part of all we do. What a blessing to call you my friend and coworker. I pray that God allows us to continue working together this way.

Thanks too, to Olga Kalachik, my office assistant, who helps organize my supplies and storage areas, and who prepares our home for the marketing events and research gatherings that take place here on a regular basis. I appreciate all you're doing to make sure I have time to write. You're wonderful, Olga, and I pray God continues to bless you and your precious family.

I also want to thank my friends at Premier (Roy Morgan and team), along with my friends at Women of Faith, Extraordinary Women, and Women of Joy. How wonderful to be a part of what God is doing through you. Thank you for including me in your family on the road.

Thanks also to my forever friends and family, the ones who have been there and continue to be there. Your love has been a tangible source of comfort, pulling us through the tough times and making us know how very blessed we are to have you in our lives.

And the greatest thanks to God. You put a story in my heart, and have a million other hearts in mind — something I could never do. I'm grateful to be a small part of Your plan! The gift is Yours. I pray I might use it for years to come in a way that will bring You honor and glory.

FOREVER IN FICTION®

For a number of years now, I've had the privilege of offering Forever in Fiction®* as an auction item at fund-raisers across the country. Many of my more recent books have had Forever in Fiction characters, and I often hear from you reader friends that you look forward to this part of my novels, reading this section to see which characters in the coming pages are actually inspired by real-life people, and learning a little about their real stories. Then you enjoy looking for them in the coming pages, knowing with a smile how it must feel to their families seeing their names Forever in Fiction.

In *Longing,* I bring you two very special Forever in Fiction characters. The first is Lance Egbers, age sixty, whose friends pitched in to make him Forever in Fiction

---

* Forever in Fiction is a registered trademark owned by Karen Kingsbury.

at the Whitinsville Christian School auction. Lance has been the much-loved principal at the school for a very long time. In addition, Lance has been married to his best friend Roseann for thirty-seven years, and together they enjoy hot-tubbing, sledding, and hiking around their large country house. Lance's hobbies include remodeling furniture, fixing things, and spending time with his three grandchildren. People know Lance for the way he lives his life as a Christian. In *Longing,* Lance is the opposing football coach in the state title game against Cody Coleman and the Lyle Buckaroos. He plays a man known throughout the state for his character, and as such he serves as a role model for Cody.

The second Forever in Fiction character is Bill Dillman, age eighty-one, whose daughter Marcia Ridenour won the right to place him in this book at the King's Way Christian School auction. Bill is a godly man with tremendous history of loyalty and laughter and living the vibrant life. He has been married for more than sixty years to his forever love, Barbara. Before retiring, Bill was a highly successful salesman, even while serving as a deacon at his church and singing in the gospel quartet. His family likes to say Bill could sell snow to an

Eskimo. Though Bill dreamed of spending his retirement years in Florida, he gave up that plan when his sweet Barbara was diagnosed with Alzheimer's Disease. Last year he took a rare trip from her side to accompany his family to the first Baxter Family Reunion. In *Longing,* Bill plays the manager in a jewelry store when a key character is shopping for an engagement ring. Bill's wisdom and conversation that evening have a great impact — as they would in real life.

A special thanks to both of my auction winners for supporting your various ministries and for your belief in the power of story. I pray the donations you made to your respective charities will go on to change lives, the way I pray lives will be changed by the impact of the message in *Longing.* May God bless you for your love and generosity.

For those of you who are not familiar with Forever in Fiction, it is my way of involving you, the readers, in my stories, while raising money for charities. The winning bidder of a Forever in Fiction package has the right to have their name or the name of someone they love written into one of my novels. In this way they or their loved one will be forever in fiction.

To date, Forever in Fiction has raised

more than $200,000 at charity auctions. Obviously, I am only able to donate a limited number of these each year. For that reason, I have set a fairly high minimum bid on this package so that the maximum funds are raised for charities. All money goes to the charity events. If you are interested in receiving a Forever in Fiction package for your auction, write to *office@ KarenKingsbury.com* and write in the subject line: *Forever in Fiction.*

ONE

The rich smell of cooked turkey warmed the house, and for a moment Bailey Flanigan stopped at the base of the kitchen stairs and closed her eyes. Just long enough to take it all in — Thanksgiving at the house where she grew up, her boyfriend Brandon Paul in the next room with her brothers, and the sound of the NFL Lions and Cowboys playing football on TV. Everyone she loved gathered around her. Once in a while God presented a slice of time where Bailey's whole world felt perfect. Or almost perfect. Bailey felt the smile on her lips, the peace and joy in her heart.

This cool, cloudless Thanksgiving afternoon was one of those times.

She leaned against the wall and tried to imagine a year from now. Would Brandon still be in her life? Would she still be part of the Broadway cast of *Hairspray* in New York City? Or would God lead her through still more changes?

"Bailey?" Her mom's voice brought her back to the moment.

"Sorry." She opened her eyes and stifled a laugh. "Just memorizing this, the way it feels right now." She glanced at the stove. The potatoes were off the flame, sitting in a pot of hot water near the sink. "I'll work on these."

Her mom was putting the finishing touches on a deep dish apple pie — the Flanigan family Thanksgiving favorite. She leaned close and peered toward the TV room. "Looks like it's going well."

Bailey smiled and followed her mother's gaze. Brandon was sitting next to Ricky, the two of them laughing about something. "I didn't tell you what happened this morning," Bailey whispered, making sure only her mom could hear her, "what Brandon said."

"About having Thanksgiving with us?"

"Yes. Actually, first he said you and Dad have made him feel so welcome." She bit her lip, as the memory from earlier returned. "But he also said he was a little nervous. You know, about whether he would connect with Dad and the boys."

Her mom's surprise showed in her eyes. "Why would he worry about that?"

26

"Because . . ." Bailey allowed a quick look into the family room, "he knew they'd watch a lot of football today. And I guess because football's not really Brandon's thing."

"Hmmm." Understanding slowly softened her mother's expression. "And of course, last year Cody was here."

"Cody, who loves football as much as Dad and the boys." Bailey pictured Cody in the family room, playing pool with her dad and she felt her heart sink a little. Was that only a year ago? Wherever Cody was this Thanksgiving, he hadn't contacted her or even wished her family a happy holiday. She dismissed the thought. "Anyway, yeah. Brandon was a little worried. Like he might not fit in." She gave her mom a crooked smile. "He hasn't been here in a while."

For a long moment her mom didn't say anything. Then she turned her back on the scene in the family room and studied Bailey. "Have you heard from him? From Cody?"

"No." Bailey's tone made it clear she didn't want to talk about Cody Coleman, not now. "If I hear from him, you'll be the first to know. Like always."

Her mom angled her head. "No need to get upset." Clearly she had picked up on Bailey's irritation. "I just wondered. It seems crazy that none of us have heard from him."

Bailey exhaled and tried to see past her frustration. "He walked away when everything was perfect." She brought her tone back to normal. "I'm sorry for sounding mad, it's just . . . I don't know, I guess his silence today shouldn't surprise us."

A brush of sorrow filled in the fine lines around her mother's eyes. "You're right." She looked over her shoulder to the family room again and back at Bailey. A smile tugged at the corners of her lips. "I'd say Brandon doesn't need to worry."

At that moment someone must've scored, because Ricky shot to his feet and Justin raised his fist in the air and shouted, "That's it, baby . . . tie game."

Brandon high-fived Bailey's other brothers — BJ and Shawn — and the enthusiasm of the moment left the guys too focused to notice the girls watching them from the kitchen. Bailey smiled. "Yes. He'll be fine." She watched him for a moment. "Besides . . . around this family it's impossible not to love football."

The game must've gone to a commercial or maybe Brandon felt her thinking about him, because he looked at her and smiled. Then he stood and came to her. As he did, their eyes held.

"That boy's crazy about you," her mom whispered as she turned her attention back to the apple pie. "No question about that."

"Like a dying man in the desert." Bailey still kept her voice low.

"Yes." Her mother didn't sound as convinced. "It sure seems that way."

Brandon reached the kitchen. "Halftime." He rolled up the sleeves of his white buttoned-down shirt. "Tell me what to do."

Bailey let her eyes linger on his. *Take me for a walk, Brandon,* she wanted to say. *Tell me again that I don't need to be afraid.* Not of falling in love with him or of longing for Cody at some distant point in time. With everything in her she wanted Brandon to hold her hand and tell her that she was right to finally and fully let her feelings for Cody Coleman fade. Because no one would ever love her like Brandon did.

But it wasn't the time.

And anyway, his words could hardly tell her more than his eyes had just said. "Here." Bailey handed him a stick of butter. "Unwrap this and I'll mash."

"Got it." He took the spot beside her, slid the paper off the butter and found a paring knife, which he used to cut butter slices into the potatoes. As he worked, their elbows

29

brushed against each other and Bailey could feel the chemistry between them. Like electricity on a stormy summer night.

God, am I getting ahead of myself? She pressed the masher into the potatoes and tried to gather her feelings. If she let herself fall this hard now, there would be no turning back. They weren't in high school, weren't flirting through freshman year of college or planning a weekend dance date. This was grownup stuff. And the love they shared, the feelings between them were the kind that sometimes lasted forever.

"There." Bailey's mom sprinkled brown sugar crumbs across the top of the pie. "That should do it."

Ricky bounded into the kitchen and leaned on the bar opposite the work area. "Another perfect Thanksgiving dessert." He raised his eyebrows a few times in Bailey's direction. "How does she do it?"

The distraction lightened Bailey's thoughts and she grinned at her youngest brother. "Simple. Mom's the best."

Her mom opened the oven and set the pie carefully inside where two others were already cooking. She glanced at Bailey. "I don't know about the best. There was the time I set the turkey on fire."

"Yeah, before I was born." Laughter rang

in Ricky's voice, but he was serious at the same time. "You're a lot better cook since then." He gave a firm nod of his blond head. "Like Bailey said . . . you're the best."

"Definitely." Brandon breathed in through his nose. "The house smells like heaven." He turned so he could see their mom. "I've looked forward to this day since September."

"Hey . . ." Bailey felt her eyes begin to dance. She put one hand on her hip and faced him. "September? I hadn't even invited you yet."

"I know." He winked at her and caught her playfully by the waist with his right hand. "I was still looking forward to it."

Somehow the way he said the words, combined with the feel of his hand on her waist and the light in his eyes, made her forget everything except him. Had Cody ever really made her feel like this? She pulled slightly away, her tone both teasing and stern. "Mashed potatoes, remember?"

"Of course." Brandon laughed, clearly enjoying the exchange. "I'll get the milk." He hesitated. "We need milk, right?"

"Yes." She laughed. "Good idea."

Bailey watched him head for the fridge, glad he didn't need to linger too close to her. Yes, they had grown very comfortable

31

over the last few months. But they were still — and always would be — careful to keep boundaries in their physical relationship.

Her mom returned with Ricky to the living room to hear the halftime report, and Bailey and Brandon finished mashing the potatoes. She stirred in salt and pepper, took a small spoonful, and held it out to him. "Here . . . taste."

He took the bite. "Mmm. Perfect." They were alone in the kitchen and he kept his eyes on hers. "Like everything about this day."

She felt her heart and soul join hands in a dance that was becoming familiar when Brandon was around. She leaned on the counter and studied him, his tanned face and light brown eyes. "Is this, you know, like Thanksgivings at your house?" The question was a risky one, and Bailey was glad she hadn't asked in front of her family. In case his answer wasn't as wonderful as hers.

No walls flew up around Brandon's heart. Bailey could see that much in his eyes. He nodded slowly, his gaze on the mashed potatoes as he seemed to consider her question. "We celebrated, of course. But not like this. With my parents . . . a sort of tension came with every holiday. Even at Thanksgiving." His smile warmed his expression. "I'm pretty sure this will be my best ever Turkey Day."

"Thanks . . . for telling me." She tucked her hand in his. "I'm glad you're here."

He slid his fingers between hers. "Me too." He grinned. "Let's go watch some football."

She laughed out loud at the change from earlier that morning. "Football fan, are you?"

"Absolutely! You should see this guy throw."

They both laughed and sat together for the second half until the Cowboys had secured the victory. During that time she received a text message from her college roommate Andi Ellison. "Look," she showed Brandon. "This makes me so happy. I haven't heard from her in a month."

"Tell her I said hi." He leaned into Bailey's shoulder and kept his eyes on the game.

Bailey studied the message from her friend. The text wished her a Happy Thanksgiving and suggested they Skype sometime.

Definitely, Bailey texted back. *I might be in LA soon, and when I am we have to get together. So much to catch up on. By the way, Brandon says hi. He's sitting beside me, hav-*

33

*ing dinner with my family here in Blooming-
ton.*

Andi's response took no time. *That's so
sweet . . . I'm happy for you, Bailey. Let's talk
this week and we'll make plans.*

The conversation ended, and after the
game, the family headed to the kitchen.
Shawn and Justin brought the Jell-O salads
in from the garage refrigerator, and Ricky
and BJ set the warm dinner rolls in a linen-
draped bowl their mom had prepared.

Finally her dad took the turkey from the
oven, and he carved it while Connor
scooped the stuffing into a waiting bowl.
Brandon and Bailey helped set the table and
fill the glasses with iced lemon water —
another family Thanksgiving favorite.

With everyone working, steaming hot
serving dishes covered the table in no time.
They took their places and their dad smiled
at them. "Let's join hands and thank God."

Bailey enjoyed the warmth of her family
with every breath. After her time in New
York City, being home again felt wonderful.
Here with her parents and brothers and
Brandon, she knew without a doubt she was
loved. She held hands with Ricky on one
side and Brandon on the other and closed
her eyes as her dad began.

"Lord, we come to You this Thanksgiving

Day overwhelmed with gratitude. We are grateful beyond words for Your gift of salvation, and for the sacrifice of Jesus on the cross. We thank You for bringing our family together this special day and for the presence of Brandon with us this afternoon. Father, the years fly quickly. Kids grow up and leave, and that is right and good and part of Your plan. But we are especially thankful today that family we love can come home again. Bless those who are less fortunate. And thank You for this food and the hands that prepared it. In the powerful name of Jesus, amen."

A chorus of amens followed while Bailey and the others opened their eyes. She loved the way her father prayed, the way he had prayed since she was a little girl. With strength and faith and always with a grateful heart. Her dad was one of the best coaches in the NFL, a man whose great physical strength matched up easily with his character. When sports announcers talked about Jim Flanigan, they saw him in that light. But those who really knew him talked about his tender heart. Bailey loved that most about him. Her heart held onto the moment, because time had taught her this much: They would only have so many Thanksgiving days together.

The boys dished food onto their plates at such speed that Bailey laughed out loud. "Wow." She tossed a helpless look at her mom. "Glad you made a lot."

Brandon shrugged and joined in the rush to fill his plate. "No one has to tell me twice."

But twenty minutes later the meal gave way to more conversation and less eating, and her dad led them in what was an annual tradition. "It's that time," he grinned at the faces around the table and set his napkin down. "Everyone gets to share what they're thankful for."

"Yes!" Justin pushed his chair back slightly. "I'm ready." He raised his hand. "Pick me, Dad. I'll go first."

"I don't wanna go last this time." Ricky looked at Brandon. "We have a rule — no repeats. It's always hardest to go last."

Bailey remembered feeling that way, like all the good answers were taken by the time it was her turn to share what she was thankful for. But leaving home had changed that. Today she had a thousand easy answers for why she was grateful. All around her the boys began talking at once, reminding each other the rules: no easy answers and no answers the same as last year. She set her fork down and leaned close to Brandon.

"This gets complicated."

"I'm getting that." He was still eating, but he gave her a quick look. "I feel like I should take notes."

"It's okay." She loved the way he made her laugh. "I'll help you."

"Listen up." Her dad's cheerful voice cut through the commotion. "Let's go over the boundaries. We know we're all thankful for God's love and for Jesus dying for us and for our family and our home. An answer has to be specific and creative. If not, The Committee can veto it."

"Really?" Brandon raised his eyebrows.

"I told you." Bailey stifled a laugh. "Crazy rules."

"I don't know." Brandon pretended to be suddenly nervous. "You people are serious."

"Yes." Bailey's mom grinned. "Would you expect anything less than a competition from a coach?"

Bailey watched the exchange. Brandon shouldn't have worried about fitting in. He came across fun and affable and kind, and his new faith was deeper than before. He couldn't quite yet take Cody's place among her brothers, but he definitely fit in.

Her dad chose Justin to go first, and Bailey watched her brother sit up a little straighter. "Okay." He grinned, taking his time and enjoying having the floor for a moment. "I'm thankful Connor decided to play football for Clear Creek. I love having my older brother as quarterback." Justin sat back in his chair, satisfied. "How was that?"

Around the table Bailey and her family held up their fingers showing a score for Justin's answer. Everyone had both hands up: perfect tens — even from Brandon, who was picking up on the rules as they went along. "Great answer, son." Their dad looked at Connor. "It's been good for all of us, watching Connor play. Next year, who knows? Maybe he'll try out for *American Idol* and make it to Hollywood."

Connor had planned to try out last summer, but football hadn't allowed him enough time. This was his last year of high school, so their dad was right. Connor was headed for Liberty University to study music, but there was no telling what God had planned for him.

Ricky went next. "I'm thankful Mom still takes time to write notes for my lunch box." He gave her a lopsided smile. "I know I'm getting old, but I still love opening my bag and seeing your note inside."

"Notes?" Brandon's tone softened. "What do they say?"

"She writes them on Scripture cards."

Ricky clearly appreciated their mom's practice. "Verses like, 'I can do all things through Christ who gives me strength,' from Philippians. And then on the back she says stuff like, 'I'm proud of you,' or 'Keep trying because God is working in your life.' Things like that."

"She did those for all of us until we reached high school." Connor smiled at their mom. "Now we eat hot lunch."

"But she still leaves us notes." Shawn looked at Brandon. "On our pillows."

"Or in our gear bag before football." BJ's expression showed that he, too, was thankful for the way their mom made them feel special.

"Okay, so we'll just assume that's a perfect ten for Ricky's answer." Their dad kissed their mom on the cheek. "I'm thankful too. For the way you love our kids."

"Hey, not fair." Justin jumped to his feet. "That's a repeat."

Their dad laughed. "That's not my answer. Just the truth."

They worked their way around the table and when it came to Bailey, her answer was easy. "I'm thankful for the lessons God has taught me in New York." She looked straight at Brandon. "And I'm thankful Brandon could be with us today." She wanted to say she was thankful for his love, but her brothers didn't know how serious things had gotten between them. Yesterday Ricky even asked if Cody might stop by for dessert after Thanksgiving dinner. Bailey needed more time before her family could know how thoroughly her heart had moved on.

Their mom was thankful Bailey lived with an older couple who loved God, and that she'd made a smooth transition to her life in New York City, and her dad was thankful the Indianapolis Colts were winning on the efforts of Matt Keagan, the quarter-back whose faith was legendary in the NFL.

"Didn't you use that one last year?" BJ squinted teasing eyes at their dad.

"Nope. No I did not." He shook his head, trying to look serious. "Last year I was thankful for twenty-five years of marriage to your most wonderful mother." He nodded in her direction. "Isn't that right?"

"Definitely." She tilted her head, enjoying the moment. "I can vouch for that."

"Okay, then." Their dad tossed his hands in the air and smirked in BJ's direction. "Can I get a round of tens on that answer?"

BJ still didn't look convinced, but he gave their dad a ten for his answer, and everyone else followed suit.

It was Brandon's turn to share, and he

took a deep breath. "Wow . . . so many things I could say." He hesitated and Bailey quickly realized he wasn't at a loss for words. Rather he was caught up in the scene, moved by his many emotions. Seeing the confident Brandon Paul this vulnerable — the way she'd seen him only a few times — always made Bailey care for him twice as much. He found control before the moment could feel awkward. "All right." He was still struggling, but his focus was back. "I could say so much. But here you go. I'm thankful to be part of your family this Thanksgiving, and," he raised his brow at Bailey's mom, "I'm thankful for the best turkey I've ever eaten."

A ripple of laughter came from around the table. "Brandon, come on." Ricky leaned around Bailey and met Brandon's eyes. "That sounded like a movie script. You're making the rest of us look bad."

"Just being real . . ." Brandon chuckled and the sound relieved the emotion from a moment earlier. "You guys make it easy."

Ricky thought about that for a long moment. "You have a point." He sat back and lifted one shoulder. "Go ahead then, I guess."

Bailey and her family laughed. "No one does the grateful game crazier than us."

Bailey turned to Brandon. "Are you done?"

His emotions were fully in control now, and Brandon waited for his own laughter to subside. "Just one more thing." He looked at Bailey. "I'm thankful for Bailey, that God has used her to show me what real love is."

Bailey's heart melted, and she held her breath. From around the table she caught the looks from her brothers and even her dad. Only her mom didn't seem surprised by the intensity of Brandon's answer. If her dad and brothers hadn't known how serious things were between her and Brandon, they knew now.

Her mom seemed to sense the mixed feelings in the room. "Brandon . . . we're very happy for you and Bailey." She reached across the table and covered Brandon's hand with her own. "And we're glad you could be with us today."

"Thanks." If Brandon knew the ambivalence Bailey's brothers probably felt, he didn't let on. "Your kindness . . . it isn't something I take for granted."

Ricky grinned at Brandon. "I think I speak for everyone when I say officially that answer was a ten." He pointed at the others. "Yes?"

"Absolutely!" Connor took the lead.

"Brandon loves our sister. That's at least a ten!"

"At least!" Justin clinked his glass against Connor's, and as he did a small wave of lemon water sloshed onto his plate.

Everyone laughed once more as the mood lightened, and the others flashed tens in Brandon's direction. If they felt a sadness in Brandon's declaration, if they missed Cody Coleman, they were nice enough to hide their feelings. They liked Brandon, after all. None of them would've wanted him to feel anything but accepted.

Shawn was last. He stuck his chest out and grinned. "I can handle going last this year, because I have the *perfect* answer."

"This better be good." Their dad crossed his arms, his eyes twinkling.

"I'm thankful Cody is coaching Lyle in the state playoffs, and that the game is tomorrow right here in Bloomington!"

Bailey tried not to react. Cody's championship game was tomorrow? Here in their hometown? She shot a look at her mom, and the glance they shared told Bailey her mom figured she knew about the game. Suddenly Bailey remembered hearing something about it in the last few weeks. But she mustn't have given it much thought because she never planned to stay past Friday morning after Thanksgiving.

"The game's tomorrow?" Brandon looked at Bailey. He seemed unfazed, relaxed as much as before Shawn's statement. A smile warmed his eyes. "I guess I didn't know."

Bailey wanted to pause the moment and explain that she hadn't thought to tell him because she didn't know she'd be here for the game. Her *Hairspray* director had given her the weekend off only at the last minute. But there was no way to explain that. Not right now.

"You're going too, right?" Shawn turned his attention to Brandon. "Everyone's going."

"Actually, no." Again Brandon's eyes didn't give anything away. "I'm flying out after midnight tonight. Meetings in LA tomorrow morning."

Bailey was sure Shawn had come to the table planning to be thankful for Cody's game. Her brother meant no harm to Brandon.

But still, the laughter around the table faded into an awkward silence.

"Shoot. We wanted you to come." Even Ricky seemed to sense that things were suddenly uncomfortable.

"Me, too." Brandon smiled at him, his

mood unchanged. "I'm sure it'll be a great game."

"Definitely." Justin looked at Bailey. "But you're coming, right? You have to."

Bailey uttered an uncomfortable laugh. "Um . . . I guess so." She glanced at Brandon. "I have the weekend off, so sure . . . probably."

A long pause followed, and finally her dad clapped his hands a single time and nodded in Shawn's direction. "Perfect answer. You're right, son. We're all thankful Cody's doing so well. And what a great way to end the Thank You game for another year."

A chorus of agreement and flashes of ten scores came from the others around the table, and Bailey's mom stood. "Let's clear the table." She sounded almost too happy, but she was doing her best — trying to move past the moment and onto anything other than tomorrow's football game. "Hot apple pie coming!"

Her pronouncement set everyone in motion — even Brandon. Without looking at Bailey, he collected his plate and silverware and walked alongside Ricky to the kitchen. For the next few minutes Bailey's youngest brother regaled Brandon with highlights from previous years of the Thank You game. Bailey was glad for the time. She needed to

45

talk to Brandon, needed to explain the situation so he wouldn't think she'd hidden this from him.

But that didn't come until after dessert, when her family had cleared their plates once again and this time migrated to the family room to play Pictionary. Until that moment, Brandon had come across happy and unmoved by news of the game. But after dessert they were the last to get up from the table, and as they headed for the kitchen she caught up to him and gently touched his elbow. "Hey . . ."

"Hey." He kept walking, but at least their eyes held longer than a few seconds. He rinsed his plate and set it in the open dishwasher and she did the same. He dried his hands on his dark jeans and smiled at her. "I love your family . . . if I haven't already said so."

"Brandon . . ." His pleasant tone and expression didn't hide the questions in his eyes. She knew him too well. "Can we talk? Outside?"

"Sure." Again he was pleasant, but now she knew for sure that he was being guarded. He took hold of her hand. "Out back?"

"Perfect." Bailey had spent far too many nights talking to Cody on the front porch.

The few times Brandon was here they usually stayed in the backyard. This time was no different. "Let's light a fire."

"Okay." Bailey followed him out past their family swimming pool to the fire pit. She sensed Brandon wasn't in a major hurry, though he had a car picking him up in an hour or so for the ride to the airport and his private flight back to LA. He got the fire going and then turned to face her. For a long moment he slid his hands in the pockets of his jeans and stared at her, his kind eyes searching hers. Finally he drew in a full breath. "I'm listening."

"Brandon." Bailey patted the spot beside her on the double rocking chair. "Sit by me. Please . . ."

He wasn't angry, she could tell that much. Just confused, maybe. Which made sense. Again he took his time, grabbing a nearby stick and poking the fire, stirring up the flame before setting the stick down and finally taking the place next to her. He turned so he could see her and the light from the fire reflected in his eyes. He waited, giving her time to say what was on her mind.

"I didn't know about the game." She didn't rush her words. There was no need to defend herself. The relationship she

47

shared with Brandon had been rooted in honesty from the beginning. "I didn't think I'd be here past Friday. I guess I just . . . I forgot about it."

Brandon lifted his hand to her cheek, his fingers soft against her skin. "You're going . . . right?"

Her silence was answer enough for both of them. The breeze danced icy cold above them and Bailey was glad for the fire. She slid closer to him. "Yes. I'll go with my family." She shivered a little, doubting herself and her motives and every feeling she'd been so sure of just an hour ago. "You want me to stay home?"

"No." His answer was as quick as it was kind. He still had his hand alongside her face. "Your family's going. You should go too. It would mean a lot to him."

But wouldn't it mean something to Brandon . . . if Bailey found anything else to do tomorrow besides going to see Cody Coleman? Bailey couldn't look into his eyes another moment. She let her head fall slowly against his and for a long minute neither of them said anything.

"Don't feel bad." Brandon drew back first. "It's okay, Bailey. Maybe . . . maybe if you see him you'll have answers." His voice was a whisper, a caress against her soul. "I'd rather have you know."

Bailey looked at him, studying him. Brandon clearly understood that this was about more than a football game. Brandon wanted her to go to Cody once and for all, to prove to herself that her feelings were for Brandon. His eyes told her all of that.

"I'm not afraid." He smiled and the love in his eyes was so real, so pure it almost hurt to look at him. "I love you." He leaned in and gently touched his lips to hers. The kiss grew and Bailey brought her hands to his shoulders.

After a few seconds she eased back, trembling. "I love you, too."

He searched her eyes, her heart. "I trust you. What we share . . . it's something neither of us has ever felt. I believe that."

"I know." She slid closer still and leaned her head on his chest. "It's just a football game."

"Right." Brandon chuckled quietly and wrapped his arms around her. "Let's believe that." He kissed the top of her head, his breath warm in her hair. "And we'll be back together in New York on Tuesday."

They stayed by the fire, talking about his Friday meetings in LA and refusing to revisit the issue of tomorrow's football game or the fact that Bailey was bound to see

Cody for the first time in months. Bailey was grateful for Brandon's confidence, but long after his ride picked him up for the airport, Bailey couldn't deny the obvious: She wasn't only thinking about Brandon and the way her heart connected with his. She wasn't only consumed with his gentle touch and his deep belief in her and the love they shared. If she was completely honest with herself she was thinking of something else too.

A state championship high school football game she hadn't known she was attending until just a few hours ago.

Two

Cody Coleman drove by himself to Memorial Stadium, the place where for years he'd dreamed of playing, the football field where the Indiana University Hoosiers played. And now he was about to coach against one of Indiana's legends — Coach Lance Egbers of Whitinsville Christian School — a winner in life and football, a man who headed up a program that was consistently a powerhouse in the single A football class.

The 37 South was free of traffic at four in the afternoon, and Cody kept his eyes on the school bus ahead of him. The team wanted to ride together, but Cody needed this time alone. His mind could barely get a grip on his feelings.

He was headed back to Bloomington, and despite every other crazy emotion fighting for position in his heart, that fact was at the top of the list. He was headed toward his past. The Flanigans knew about the game, and Cody was sure Jenny and Jim would attend. The boys too. Whether Bailey was in town or not, whether she'd even want to be at his game — he wasn't sure.

He just knew he couldn't stop thinking about it.

Beyond that there were other layers, other realities that complicated the way Cody felt. This evening's game was the last for his seniors — including DeMetri Smith. Smitty still lived with Cody, but he'd made a decision about his future. He'd come to him just this morning with the news.

"Coach, I know what I wanna do. I made up my mind." The kid had wide eyes, and he looked more nervous than before game time.

A few Division II schools were talking to DeMetri, so Cody waited, wondering what the announcement was. "Wherever you go, you'll do great." He gave DeMetri a light slap on his shoulder. "You're ready, Smitty."

"It's not what you think." The kid gulped and wiped small beads of sweat from his brow. "I'm . . . I'm going to Liberty. I wanna be a pastor, Coach. More than I wanna play football. I have to tell people about Jesus."

The news had worked its way through Cody's being, and he felt his heart respond. "That's amazing, DeMetri. You're sure?"

"So sure." He laughed, and his nervousness seemed to dissipate. "I'll suit up for Liberty, but I'm more excited about the mission trips." His smile lit up his face. "I'm going to Kenya, Coach. To tell kids about Jesus!"

"I love it." Cody patted the kid on the back. "And hey, after the game, remind me to introduce you to Connor Flanigan." Cody was touched that two kids who meant so much to him would attend the same school next fall. "He'll be a Liberty freshman too."

DeMetri grinned. "Maybe he'll go with me to Kenya."

"It wouldn't surprise me."

Cody replayed the conversation as he drove. The decision was more than Cody had hoped when he allowed DeMetri to move in with him. The player's mother was still in prison, his dad long gone. Whether DeMetri ever played a down of football for Liberty University didn't matter. The kid had made up his mind . . . he was ready to move on — in his life and in his faith. Tonight would be more than a championship game for Smitty: It would be the last time anyone would define him by his skills on a football field.

Cody thought about the other layers,

Cheyenne and her health. She would be there tonight, but with their dear friend Tara Collins — in case she needed to leave early. Her rehab was nearly complete from the car accident that had almost killed her. But she still suffered headaches. Sometimes so severe she couldn't function. If that happened tonight, Tara was ready to take her home.

"You don't need to spend all this time with me, Cody," Cheyenne had told him last night. "I'm sorry . . . I'm so sick lately."

His feelings for Cheyenne Williams were never easy. Complications were the norm. But one thing was certain, and Cody reiterated it to her. "We've been over this, Chey. I told you I'm not leaving. You're my girl . . . I'm here for you."

But now, as he pulled into the stadium parking lot, he wasn't sure what those words even meant. Not that he was afraid of her headaches or her poor health since the accident. They were dating, after all. But there were days he couldn't quite define what he felt for Cheyenne. Whether it was love or the deep care of friendship.

Cody blinked and let the thought pass. Cheyenne was his girlfriend, and that would be true for as long as Cody could see into the future. She was wonderful, and she needed Cody the way no one had needed him in a very long time. Maybe ever. No matter his feelings for her, they were current. And maybe that was all he needed to think about. Especially tonight.

Kickoff wasn't for another three hours, and this early the parking lot was still empty, the media and reporters from across the state only barely setting up their camera crews and news feeds. Cody followed the bus to the back lot and the locker room facility. Whatever thoughts crowded his head, however his heart was being stretched . . . it was time to focus.

He and the Lyle Buckaroos had a game to win. One last game.

The team emptied into the visitors' locker room. Both Lyle and Whitinsville came to the game undefeated, so officials had flipped a coin last week to determine the home team. Whitinsville won the honor, but the distinction meant very little. Come game time they'd both be on a neutral field, the best field in Indiana.

Cody let his team settle into the locker room, waiting while the initial hype of being in the Hoosiers' stadium wore off a little. As the guys began suiting up, Cody set out to find Coach Lance Egbers. Tens of thousands of fans were expected at the game;

whole towns would fill the stands. The chance of having an actual conversation with the legendary coach later was slim. Cody had emailed him earlier in the week, and both of them decided to talk early, before the game.

By the time Cody reached the home locker room, Coach Egbers was exiting the facility and headed his way. The man's smile was genuine enough to warm the entire stadium. "Cody Coleman!" He held out his hand as he approached. "It's an honor."

"Sir," Cody felt the man's presence as the two shook hands. He was larger than life, no doubt. Cody tried not to feel nervous. "The honor's mine, sir."

In a flash everything Cody knew about the legendary leader came to mind. The man wasn't only the Crusaders' coach . . . he was their principal. A favorite among the kids and a mastermind at the game of football. Articles had been written about the man and Cody had read more than one including a feature that ran in the *Indianapolis Star*. Lance had been married to his wife Roseann for thirty-seven years. When he wasn't coaching, Lance liked to hike and sled and hot tub with his wife and grand-kids. But more than the recreation of his off-season or the excellence of his coaching,

Lance was known throughout the world of football for his faith.

The way he lived out the message he so deeply believed in.

No question the Crusaders had an edge tonight. They'd won the state title three out of the last five years, and local media sports experts favored Whitinsville tonight by a couple touchdowns. But with all that, Lance had only one agenda for this private meeting between the two of them. He crossed his arms and squared his stance as he faced Cody. "I've read a lot about you, Cody. You're very young to have this kind of success."

Cody thought about his days as a prisoner of war in Iraq. "I don't feel young."

"But you are." Lance's eyes sparkled in a knowing way. "You're the next generation. I can't do this forever."

His words seemed strange in light of the fact that the man had just coached his team to another undefeated season. Cody laughed lightly. "I'd say you have a lot of years left, sir."

"A couple maybe." The man angled his head. "Kids are different these days . . . they need someone they can relate to." He hesitated and pursed his lips. "God wants to use you, Cody. Let Him lead you where you can make the most difference. Let that guide you always."

Cody felt privileged beyond words, that Lance Egbers would take a few minutes to share with him. "I'll do that, sir. I can only imagine having the impact you've had on kids."

"It's not just me." The coach's eyes softened. "It's Jim Flanigan and Ryan Taylor and so many other Christian coaches like them around the state. Men changing the lives of today's youth."

Impressive, Cody thought . . . that Lance knew the names of Jim and Ryan, two coaches who'd worked with Cody when he was younger.

"But even then there aren't enough guys who love God and the game." Lance winked at him. "You're one of the few, Cody. Stay with it. Fall in love with the game. Let it be your platform again and again, every year, every season. The kids need you." He gave Cody a pat on his shoulder. "Now go get your team ready."

"Yes, sir."

"I'd wish you good luck, but I don't believe in it." Lance's smile filled his face again. "I'll *pray* for you." He tipped the bill of his baseball cap. "Besides, even if luck mattered you wouldn't need it." He raised

58

one eyebrow. "You belong here, Cody. You're a gifted coach and teacher. Your reputation is well deserved." He shook Cody's hand and took a step back. "Don't forget that."

"Sir . . . thank you, sir." Cody watched the man turn and head back to his locker room. When he pictured this contest against Coach Egbers' Crusaders, Cody never imagined a meeting like the one they'd just had. He was speechless, certain he'd remember everything Lance Egbers had shared with him in the last few minutes. God had just used the legend to confirm the dreams Cody had allowed to form this season. If a bigger school asked Cody to join the staff, he'd at least have to consider the possibility. Especially with DeMetri heading off to Virginia. In some ways — no matter what happened tonight — his time at Lyle was no longer certain. It was a long commute and maybe his purpose with the program had been fulfilled.

Cody returned to the locker room and called the guys into the meeting space. As they gathered around him Cody could practically feel their fear. He could see it in their eyes and sense it in their quiet shiftiness. Cody squared his shoulders and looked them in the eyes. Each of them.

Okay, God, give me the words. They look like they've already lost.

You are not alone, my son . . . I go before you . . . I will never leave you nor forsake you.

Peace and strength coursed through Cody's veins and he drew a determined breath. "We have ninety minutes before kickoff." He paced a few steps and then stopped and turned to them again. "Ninety minutes before we play our last game of the season." He hesitated. "A perfect season." Cody watched a few of the guys sit up a little, watched the fight in their expressions catch fire. "We didn't get here on our own. You know that, and I know that. God brought us to this point." His voice grew louder. "And God will get us through this final game. Play by play . . . quarter by quarter. So that we go out there tonight and play Lyle football . . . so we leave it all out there on that field."

The air in the locker room began to feel lighter . . . a sense of electricity working its way through the heart of the team. Cody continued, "We did not let fear have a voice before tonight, and we will not let it speak now. We are Lyle." Passion rang in his tone. "We are undefeated and we are His."

Slowly the guys began to nod. DeMetri punched the palm of his hands a few times.

60

"Coach is right . . . we can do this. God'll lead us same as before."

A murmuring of "yes" and "amen" came from the team and Cody felt a rich sense of accomplishment. God was meeting them in the moment right here when they needed it. He would meet them along the way too. Cody had no doubt. He told the guys how the next half hour would go. They would finish suiting up and then find a quiet place to stretch and pray. Then they would visualize playing their best game ever. The game of their lives.

"Now listen . . . the stadium will be packed. And yes, we're playing at Memorial Stadium. Media will be here — everywhere you look. It's the sort of Friday night lights moment most guys only dream about. But in the end it's just another football game, men. Another chance to show the world who you are. And whose you are."

With that, a few of the players hit their feet and urged the others into a spontaneous huddle. "You heard Coach!" one of them yelled.

"Whose way?" DeMetri led the familiar chant.

"His way!" The chorus of voices was strong and united, without a trace of the fear that had been evident just a few minutes ago.

"Whose way?"

"His way!"

"Okay!" DeMetri patted the backs of the players on either side of him. "Let's get ready. Let's do this!"

And with that the guys dispersed to follow Cody's instructions. He watched them go, satisfied. His players would be fine. Now he had to meet up with Hans Tesselaar — the writer from *Sports Illustrated.* The reporter had followed the Buckaroos' success and he planned to run a story on the team sometime next week. Cody left the locker room, and as he rounded the corner toward the field, he could already feel the energy. The stands were filling, and marching bands from both schools were in place and warming up.

God, You brought us this far . . . let us play our best. Please, Lord.

There was no immediate answer, but that was okay. Cody didn't need answers or even a win, necessarily. As long as his players gave it everything they had. Besides, Coach Egbers would pray a similar prayer now. Whichever team won, God would get the glory.

"Cody?" Hans came up and touched him

on the shoulder.

"Hey!" Cody turned.

"This is something else." Hans chuckled, and for a moment the two of them looked around, soaking in the atmosphere.

Hans smiled and shook his head. "It's gonna be a great one. I can feel it." He held a notepad and he had a camera slung over his shoulder. "We'll run the story regardless of the outcome. It's too good to pass up." He pulled an envelope from his bag. "By the way, this is the official request from a buddy of mine at ESPN. They want you in the New York studio for an interview."

New York.

Cody felt his heart skip a beat as he took the envelope. Bailey Flanigan's new hometown. "Did they mention when?"

"It's all in the request." Hans grinned. "But I think the first week of January. During NFL playoffs. Oftentimes the network runs a feature looking back at the previous high school and college football season. It'll make for a good story around that time."

"Right." Cody nodded. New York City in January. He narrowed his eyes, squinting against the glare of the setting sun. "I'm honored. Tell your friend thanks. And tell him I'll be in touch."

He talked to Hans for the next few minutes, filling him in on the team's preparations leading up to the championship game and sharing the news about DeMetri's decision to attend Liberty University and become a pastor.

Hans shook his head. "Like a movie script . . . seriously."

Cody blinked and in the fraction of an instant when his eyes were closed he was suddenly not on the plush artificial turf of Memorial Stadium. He was back at Clear Creek High, suited up to play quarterback against Bloomington, and Bailey . . . Bailey was in the stands cheering him on. The moment passed and a chuckle worked its way from Cody's heart. "Yeah, like a movie. Almost." He scanned the stands. If the Flanigans were coming, they would be here soon. Jim Flanigan would never be late to this game.

Instead he saw Tara and Cheyenne making their way up the home bleachers. They didn't see him, and Cody didn't have time to make a trek over to talk to them. He'd see them later, when the team took the field for warm-ups.

Hans thanked him for his time and pointed to a spot near the end of the bench. "I've got a quick appointment with Lance Egbers." He nodded at Cody. "Good luck tonight, Coach."

"Thank you." Cody was about to head back to the locker room when he spotted them: the Flanigan family entering the stadium halfway up the structure. Again he was back at Clear Creek High, back when he could always sense her arrival at any game. He froze and watched them file in. Jim and Jenny, the boys trailing behind them. And beside Connor near the end of the line . . . yes, it was her.

Bailey had come.

Cody shaded his eyes, watching them make their way along the cement aisle, searching for seats in the Lyle section. Cody let his eyes settle on Bailey. The other Flanigans, the faces in the crowd, every sound . . . all of it faded. There was only Bailey, the way there hadn't been for too long.

Even from here he could see she was more beautiful than ever, her long layered brown hair and the graceful way she walked alongside Connor. She stopped, and he could tell she was searching the sidelines, looking for him. And just like that, it happened. She froze and their eyes found each other. The look on her face had a way of erasing the distance between them, even from twenty yards, way up in the bleachers.

"Cody!" The voice was familiar, but it

took Cody a few seconds to pull himself from Bailey's gaze, to look away when all he wanted was to freeze time, run up the stadium stairs, and take her in his arms.

"Cody . . . over here!" The voice was Tara's. Cody blinked and turned toward the sound. And there she was with Cheyenne at the edge of the railing, only a few feet above the sidelines. Tara waved, a grin stretching across her face, her big sunglasses still in place. "Can you believe this?" She couldn't keep the enthusiasm from her voice.

But Cody could hardly focus on Tara. He was too busy noticing the direction of Cheyenne's gaze. She wasn't looking at him the way Tara was. She was looking at whatever had held Cody's attention for the last few seconds. In the exact direction of Bailey Flanigan.

Cody glanced that way once more, but Bailey was already seated, talking to Connor, and caught up in whatever conversation her family was sharing. There was no way to tell if Bailey had seen Cheyenne and Tara. But one thing was certain: Cheyenne had seen Bailey. He quickly headed toward the spot where Tara and Cheyenne still waited. "You're here early!"

"Of course." Tara took the lead. She was dressed in Lyle blue, and she carried a cardboard sign painted with the words *Lyle Buckaroos All the Way.* She waved the sign in his direction. "Whooo-wooo! Biggest game ever!"

Cody smiled, but his eyes found Cheyenne. Her expression told him everything he needed to know. She wasn't angry or upset, not jealous or insecure. But he had no doubt she'd seen the exchange between Bailey and him, and now her soft smile held a knowing, a walls-up sort of understanding. As if she understood how Bailey might've captured his attention, and in some sad sort of way she expected it.

Cody felt uncomfortable. Cheyenne deserved to be first place in his heart. The place he thought he'd reserved for her. "How's the team?" Tara still seemed oblivious to the silent exchange happening between him and Cheyenne.

"Good." He shouted his answer, so she could hear him. Then he gritted his teeth. He couldn't do this. Couldn't make casual conversation. Not now. "Gotta get back to the guys." He smiled, waved big at both of them, turned, and jogged back to the locker room without checking the stands again to see Bailey, to satisfy his curiosity about whether she was watching him again or not.

He didn't need to look. He already knew

she would watch him tonight, same as he would be keenly aware of her position in the stands, her presence behind him. He would be focused on the game, for sure. But he felt certain about how the next few hours would play out. No matter what else consumed his heart and mind, one thing was certain. And it continued to trouble him deeply as he rounded up the guys and brought them out onto the field for warm-ups.

Regardless of Cheyenne's presence, as long as Bailey was here, a part of him would be only hers.

Always hers.

THREE

Brandon hadn't heard from Bailey all day, but then he'd been busy — his phone off most of the afternoon. His meetings that day had blended together, one into the other. A handful of producers and directors all linked to the biggest studio in the country, meeting around an impressive table in a boardroom where some of the biggest movie deals in history had gone down.

His manager and his agent sat on either side of him.

Since ten that morning a dozen projects had been laid out, any one of which would advance his career in the direction everyone saw him headed — a move from teen heartthrob to serious actor. Already Brandon had agreed to a couple pictures, films that would be shot in Los Angeles and wouldn't take more than eight weeks a piece. But the movie he was looking for still hadn't crossed the table: "What about a love story?"

The team surrounding him nodded thoughtfully, and his agent turned slightly to face him. "There's a love story element in just about every one of these pictures."

"I know." Brandon pictured Bailey. "I mean a love story. Something people will remember forever."

"This is about your *Unlocked* co-star, right?" His agent sounded slightly irritated.

"Her name's Bailey." Brandon sat back in his chair, calm in the face of whatever resistance came from the people around him. "And, yes, I want to do another picture with her. I think the fans want that too."

"Listen, Brandon . . ." His manager leaned onto his forearms and folded his hands. "We all like Bailey Flanigan. But she's a little . . . I don't know, a little whole-some, to be honest. Some of these projects," he waved his thumb toward the pile of scripts, "they demand an actress with a little more of an edge."

"An edge?" Brandon shifted in his seat. "Maybe I don't want edgy."

"That's why we're having this meeting." One of the studio execs cleared his throat. "We're trying to make decisions that are best for your career, Brandon."

"Not what's best for your relationship with Bailey." His agent muttered.

"Listen. We have a few girls coming in to meet with us . . ." His manager swapped looks with the producers at the end of the table. "Just to see your thoughts . . . initial chemistry . . . that sort of thing."

"Why isn't Bailey one of them?"

"We already know Bailey . . ." His agent used that irritated tone, the one that bordered on patronizing. "We're looking for fresh talent, someone a little racier."

Anger blew hot against Brandon's understanding. He nodded slowly and then pushed his chair back from the table. "I'm taking five. We can talk after the break."

Out in the hall he turned a corner and found a quiet stairwell where he could sit and think. Too wholesome? Wasn't that what people wanted these days? Films that gave people a message of hope and faith? A renewed purpose in life? Then how come the people around him thought he should do edgier projects with edgier actresses? He reached into the back pocket of his jeans, pulled out his cell phone, and found Bailey in his favorites. A single tap and her phone began to ring.

Answer, Bailey . . . please, answer.

"Hello?" She was there . . . but the noise in the background was so great, her voice was barely audible.

71

"Bailey?" He checked the time on his phone. Nearly four o'clock. Almost kickoff in Bloomington, Indiana, where Bailey was at the game. He covered one ear, and tried to make himself heard above the commotion. "Hey, can you hear me?"

The noise grew louder. "Brandon?" She shouted his name, but clearly she couldn't hear him. She was trying to say something about the game when the call failed. Something that he knew happened often in this part of the building.

Brandon thought about trying again, but why? The noise was too much and the cell reception too sketchy. They'd have to talk later, when the game was over. He hung his head for a moment.

What do You want me to do, God? Why can't Bailey be in one of my films? I want to be with her . . . not some other actress.

The answer came readily to his heart:

I know the plans I have for you, my son. Plans to give you a hope and a future . . .

The verse was from Jeremiah 29:11, one of Bailey's favorites. He exhaled slowly. God would lead him. As long as he didn't compromise his faith by taking the wrong role; if this wasn't the time for Bailey and him to star in a picture together, then maybe later. He stood and moved easily back down the stairs and into the hallway.

All he wanted was to finish the meeting and the dinner with his manager and agent after that and get home before eight o'clock. If there was time he wanted to Skype with Bailey. So he could look in her eyes and be absolutely sure that no matter how the evening at her old boyfriend's game had gone, everything was still okay between them.

The way he was sure it would be.

He couldn't see a day ahead without her. She had worked her way into the fiber of his being, and he would fight to hold onto her, to never let her go. Forever wouldn't be long enough to love her, Brandon was convinced. The idea of that stayed with him as he finished his meetings and headed to dinner with his team. Lately when it came to Bailey he didn't wonder so much about the answers, but about the question, no matter how far off.

One question.

The first two quarters of the championship game flew by, and after a blur of the most intense football they'd played all year, Lyle ran off the field at halftime down twelve points, 18–6. Cody trailed his players, not sure what had happened, what had gone wrong.

Yes, Coach Egbers' Whitinsville Christian team was strong at every position. But his guys seemed like they were going through the motions — as if they were happy just to be here. Nothing about their offense even remotely reminded Cody of the team he'd coached all year. Whether it was the roar of the enormous crowd or the reality of playing in Memorial Stadium, Cody wasn't sure. But if something didn't change at halftime, the outcome was easy to predict.

Not only that, but the physicality of their opponent had taken its toll. Larry Sanders limped on a sprained ankle, and Josh Corothers was out with a knee injury. Cody knew they could do this; they could rally their efforts and talents and come out with a winning second half. But he wasn't sure whether his guys actually believed that.

Around them the crowd was on its feet cheering as they ran off the field, and even before the noise died down, as soon as they rounded the corner into the locker room, DeMetri jumped onto the nearest bench and glared at his teammates. "No!" he shouted at them. "No, we did not come this far to hang our heads and let that team get the best of us!" He wasn't angry, just intense. Blazing from a fire that burned deep within him. "Come on, guys, get in here. Get close."

Cody watched his players respond. They were sweaty and exhausted, still breathless from the action in the first half. But the fire in DeMetri was contagious. Cody could see it in their faces.

"Come on . . . we're gonna cry out to Jesus, y'all. You understand? Cry out to Him . . . because I will not go out my last game a loser. I wanna hold my head high and know I gave everything . . . everything for this team and for Coach and for God who brought us together."

In all his days as a player and coach, past and future, Cody knew he would always remember this moment, the passionate confidence of a player who only six months ago had been sleeping in the school weight room, without a home or a family, without a hope. The changes God had brought about in DeMetri were proof of His existence all by themselves.

"All right." DeMetri's voice still filled the locker room, a fierce cry louder than the packed stadium on the other side of the brick wall. "Let's pray. Because that's when we're strongest . . . when we're laid bare before Him, no hope but the hope we have in Him."

The others nodded, pressing in closer, closing their eyes and hanging their heads. A few of them raised their hands, the way they might do during a church service. Cody felt a chill run down his arms.

God, they're getting it . . . they know how badly they need You.

He held his breath, watching . . . waiting.

Meet us here, Father . . . please meet us.

"Lord, we are nothing without You. All season we've relied on You. Every touchdown, every tackle, every play by every man here. You've brought us together and given us a strength beyond ourselves." DeMetri's voice held a cry, and sure enough two trails of tears made their way down his cheeks. "We haven't given everything out there, God . . . we've been playing in our own strength . . . like maybe we think we're all that." He sniffed and kept his words steady, strong. "But we're nothing without You, God. Go with us onto that field in the second half. Every man here including myself . . . Lord, we cry out to You. Not that we would win the game, but that we'd play beyond what we've played so far. Because after this, we're done. This Lyle team will only be a memory. That's the point, God . . . that we would be remembered not for what we did, but for what You did through us." He was breathless, nearly overcome. "In Jesus' name, amen."

A resounding *amen* followed, and for the remainder of halftime the guys were quiet. They tightened wraps on their ankles or sat quietly, stretching their legs, heads bowed. For all the ways they'd come together over the season, Cody had never seen them like this, so focused and intent on the task ahead. He had a feeling God would indeed meet them on the field in the minutes to come and that the result would be something the people of Lyle would remember for a very long time.

Before halftime was over, the team came together one last time for the battle cry that was now as familiar as their uniforms.

"Whose way?" Again DeMetri led them, and Cody held onto the moment, convinced that someday — not too far from now — DeMetri wouldn't only become a pastor. He would become one of the best.

"His way!" The chorus of their voices was deafening, louder than any time they'd done this in the past.

"Whose way?" It was a fierce shout of determination, an insistence that the guys believe in the mission ahead.

"His way!" A few more times back and forth and the frenzy was in full force. When they ran back out on the field Cody wondered if the fans would even recognize them. Sure enough Lyle had the ball in the opening drive of the third quarter and after seven solid plays, quarterback Arnie Hurley connected with his best friend, Joel Butler, for a touchdown that brought the Buckaroos within five.

In the back of his mind, Cody was aware that Bailey and Cheyenne were there, but all he could think about was the matter at hand: stopping the Crusaders. "I need you to dig down, guys," he yelled at his defensive unit, struggling to be heard over the sound of the crowd. "Remember DeMetri's prayer. Don't hold back. Give Him your best."

The guys responded at a level Cody hadn't seen before, and with seven minutes left in the half, Whitinsville remained scoreless in the second half. Lyle had the ball again, but they were struggling to advance when Larry Sanders found Cody. "I can do this, Coach. If my sister can battle cancer, I can play on a sprained ankle. I mean it." Fierce tears cast a watery layer over his eyes. He blinked, his jaw set. "I can do this."

Cody nodded and slapped Larry on the shoulder pads. "All right then . . . go get 'em."

The marching band played the Lyle fight

song and the entire town sang along as Cody watched Larry take the field. The first few passes his direction fell flat, but on third and ten he ran for the end zone and looked back just long enough to catch the best pass Cody had ever seen his quarterback throw — and, like that, Lyle had a two-point lead.

But, with four minutes left in the game, Whitinsville marched down the field, chewing up half the remaining time before kicking a forty-three-yard field goal. Down by one, the Buckaroos had a final chance. One drive to play out of their minds and find the most unexpected ending to the most unexpected season.

As his team took the field, Cody felt a quiet even at the center of the screaming crowd. They didn't need a win tonight to prove what God had done among them, to put an exclamation mark at the end of the miracle the Lyle football team had been a part of. But, even so, Cody believed in one as he stood with his toes against the sidelines calling in the plays and willing the guys to do the undoable one more time.

A few yards forward, a few back, a breakaway run and another set of downs, and suddenly there were nine seconds left and Lyle was against the wall. Fourth and two on the Whitinsville forty-five. Too far out for a field goal. Cody didn't have to look at the huddle, didn't have to catch the eyes of DeMetri Smith to know who was getting the ball. The kid had led the team from the beginning. Cody could remember his first day at Lyle, walking out of the gym and certain he wouldn't consider taking the job. It had been DeMetri praying in the far end zone of the Buckaroos practice field, one knee in the snow, that had changed his mind. DeMetri who had jogged past him and casually explained that if he were the new coach, the prayers had been for him.

Sweep right to DeMetri. He called the play in to Arnie and settled back on his heels. The play took shape in slow motion, the sound of the crowd, the chaos of media and marching bands quieted completely until there was only the sound of his heartbeat and the ticking of the clock. Seven . . . six . . . five . . .

DeMetri took the handoff and darted between two defenders.

Instead of sweeping right he spotted the slightest sliver of daylight and ran for it as if his life depended on it. And just like that he pierced the defense straight up the middle and in the most unexpected ending possible, with four seconds on the clock, DeMetri had nothing ahead of him but open stadium grass. The Lyle bench was on its feet, the screams of the crowd once more thunderous around him.

"Run, Smitty!" Cody ran along the sideline with half the players, all cheering and shouting and doing their best to keep up with DeMetri. But on this night he was faster than anyone in Memorial Stadium. Faster than Coach Egbers' award-winning defense, faster than any of his teammates, faster than he'd ever run in all his life. Several strides before he crossed the finish line, the clock ran out, and as the referee signaled the touchdown, as the buzzer sounded bringing an official end to the game, the players of Lyle High School stormed the field and surrounded DeMetri. Cody joined them, but as the group reached the end zone his players didn't jump into a celebratory pile.

DeMetri was on one knee, and now, one by one, the others did the same thing. And there it was — a picture for the newspaper, the shot for *Sports Illustrated,* proof that long after tonight, this Lyle Buckaroos championship team would be remembered. Not for who they were.

But for whose they were.

Tears and shouts of praise filled the moment, and then the guys stood once more and circled DeMetri in a group huddle. Only after they celebrated the moment together did the guys jog back to the fifty-yard line, where a throng of media and fans awaited them. They had done it. His players had allowed God to change them, allowed Him to work miracles in their lives and through them. And now God in His strength and for His glory had given them this:

A place in history.

They had done it; they had beaten Whitinsville Christian for the state title. Cody exhaled, soaking in the moment. Memorizing it. Then just as quickly his thoughts shifted. And even as he began answering questions from reporters, he caught himself distracted, scanning the audience. Because with the game behind him, he could finally think of the reality: Bailey Flanigan here with her family.

And whether in the coming minutes they might finally see each other face-to-face.

FOUR

Bailey was on her feet like everyone else in her family, everyone in the stands. He'd done it! He'd taken the winless Buckaroos and won state. They'd gone from last place in their league to state champions — something no one in Indiana had ever done before. She clasped her hands and brought them to her face. Her brothers jumped around, high-fiving and hugging their dad and each other.

But Bailey felt a quiet come over her. She watched Cody and him alone. Earlier she had seen Cheyenne, of course. And again Bailey was struck by her beauty, how she looked striking in a tailored pea coat, so different from the badly injured victim she'd been in the hospital bed the last time Bailey saw Cody. Cheyenne had come for him, no question. But in those early moments after the Flanigans had first arrived at the field, Bailey was aware of just one thing.

Cody's presence. And it had been the same way for him, aware of only her.

No matter how strong her feelings for Brandon, the intensity of her emotions here tonight caught her off guard and took her by surprise. Every few seconds throughout the game she'd catch herself looking at him, watching him. Wondering at her feelings and remembering all they'd shared over the years. The journey they'd been through. For years she had longed for him, and now . . . now she wasn't sure what she felt, but whatever her feelings, they were stronger than she'd expected. Being here, breathing the same air, made her miss him like she hadn't missed him in a year. In the quiet of her inner thoughts, and with the celebration swirling around her, Bailey tried to analyze all this, but she couldn't put her emotions into words.

"Let's go see him!" Ricky stayed worked up, celebrating the victory. "Come on, Dad." He reached for their father. "Let's go."

"Hold on." Jim laughed and folded his arms. "We need to wait. Let the reporters get what they want, let the crowd die down."

Ricky thought that through, and he nodded fast. "Good idea. Then we get Cody to ourselves."

84

Bailey heard the conversation, but she was still lost in the moment, watching Cody field requests from the media and smile for dozens of photos. He hadn't really been a true friend to her, right? So why was she missing him so much, now? She narrowed her eyes, wishing she could see into his heart. Had he really moved on so easily?

"Hey." Connor leaned close to her. "You look like you're in a trance."

"I feel like it." She turned to him. "I mean . . . I don't get it. Why Cody walked away."

An alarmed look came over Connor's expression. "Bailey . . . you have a *boy-friend*."

"I know." She pictured how wonderful she'd felt last night, sitting next to Brandon near the fire. The way he'd surprised her, the way he'd treated her like a gentleman should. Brandon communicated like no guy she'd ever known and he was always aware of her feelings. "I love him." She searched her brother's eyes. "I do. He's amazing."

"Yeah." Connor glanced at the field, where the crowd around Cody was finally thinning. "Remind yourself of that in a few minutes."

"You like Brandon better than Cody?" Bailey was surprised. Cody had coached

85

Connor. He'd been part of their family for years, after all.

"It's not that simple. I love Cody. We all do." Connor raked his hands through his dark hair, confusion clouding his eyes as well. "It's just . . . he walked away, Bailey. After how Brandon looked at you yesterday at dinner, what he said . . . I don't know, I have a feeling he would never do that."

She nodded slowly, thoughtfully. "I agree."

The stadium emptied all around them and before Connor could respond or continue the conversation, their dad stood. "Okay, let's head on down."

Bailey's heart pounded harder than it had at any point during the game. As they stood to leave, her mother hung back and walked beside her. "How're you doing?"

She could never hide her heart from her mother. "I'm good." She smiled, not wanting her deeper thoughts exposed for now. "I'm happy they won."

"Bailey . . ." Jenny slowed and looked straight into her eyes. "I know you better than that."

Bailey looked down, not sure what to say or how to say it. She stopped and faced her mom. "I couldn't take my eyes off him."

The rest of the family headed up a concrete flight of stairs toward a tunnel that would take them to the field.

"I know." Her mom brushed her fingers briefly against Bailey's cheek. "I watched you." Sadness lined her face.

"But remember this." Bailey felt the fight return to her. "Cody walked away. It was his decision."

Her own words spoke strength to her soul, strength and resolution. Cody was no longer part of her life. He would only be a friend who had willingly walked out of her life. An old friend. The guy who held her yesterdays.

They reached the field, but as they headed toward Cody — now only fifteen feet away from them — Bailey saw something out of the corner of her eye. As she turned she saw Cheyenne and a joyful looking pretty black woman headed straight for Cody. Bailey stopped short and put her hand on her mother's shoulder. "Go ahead. Give me the keys and I'll wait for you in the Suburban."

"Bailey, maybe it'd be better if you met her." Her mom wanted only the best for her, but the idea sounded crazy.

"I don't want to see him with her." Bailey felt panic rise up within her. She wanted to be gone before Cody spotted them, before he could look at her again, and take her breath the way he had earlier. "Please, Mom."

Her mother sighed and reached into her purse. Once she had the keys she handed them over to Bailey. "We'll be there in five minutes."

"Take your time." Bailey didn't mind her family maintaining their friendship with Cody. But she couldn't possibly stand with them and pretend to be happy about Cheyenne's presence. Not when she had no closure over why he'd walked away and chosen someone else. Which was maybe why she had reacted so strongly to seeing him again tonight. No closure.

But before she could turn away, Cody looked over his shoulder. Almost as if he could sense her running. The same way he had run a year ago. Once again, their eyes met, like magnet and steel they found each other. Bailey broke contact first. Cody's girlfriend waited a few feet away. And her boyfriend was at home waiting for her call. She had no business being here looking at him, let alone talking to him. Without waiting another moment she turned and headed up the tunnel.

She walked to the SUV, slid into the backseat, and stared at the black sky over Bloomington. Her family joined her ten minutes later, and Ricky squinted his eyes at her. "Why didn't you stay? Cody wanted to see you."

"He was busy." She worked to sound lighthearted about the matter.

"What?" Ricky was completely baffled. The struggles between Cody and Bailey had gone unnoticed by Ricky — other than the obvious: the fact that Bailey dated Brandon now. Ricky took the spot beside her and made a confused face. "He kept looking back at the tunnel. Like he was waiting for you." Ricky sounded upset. "You didn't even tell him congratulations." He shook his head. "That's crazy."

The boys climbed in, filling every empty seat. In the front, her parents took their places and after a few seconds her dad looked at her in the rearview mirror. "Ricky's right." His tone was kind, but he also seemed confused by Bailey's actions. "People kept coming up and saying hello, telling him what a great game it was, but it was like he couldn't focus." He paused, his eyes on hers. "Clearly he wanted to talk to you, honey."

Bailey shrugged one shoulder. "I didn't want to be in the way."

Her mom glanced back, as if she didn't buy the argument.

On the way home, the conversation shifted when Ricky launched into a replay of the game. The chatter gave Bailey a chance to analyze her behavior. She probably should've walked up and talked to him like everyone else. That shouldn't have been too tough, right? The fact that she couldn't stay had to mean something.

Bailey just wasn't sure what.

When they were home, her mom pulled her aside. "He might come over. I wanted you to know."

"Who?"

"Cody." Her mom's look almost pleaded with her. "He talked to me before we left. Asked if it would be okay if he stopped by . . . if it would be crossing any lines."

"Mom!" Bailey felt immediately frustrated. "It crosses every line." She sighed out loud. "You should've told him no."

"Honey . . ." Jenny looked over her shoulder. "The boys don't know. This is between you and Cody, but I really think you need to talk."

"Why?" Like yesterday, she hated being short with her mom, but somehow it seemed like her mom would only be happy if she and Cody got back together. "Mom, we're dating other people. I don't see the point."

"Even as a friend . . . if he wants to talk to you, I think you should hear him out."

Bailey forced herself to relax. "You mean

well." She allowed a weak smile. "If he comes by, I'll talk to him. But I really wish you would have discouraged it."

"I'm sorry . . . I did what I thought was best." Her mom smiled, her eyes deep. "Maybe this will be the closure you're looking for."

"Maybe."

For a long while her mom looked at her, loving her, caring about the hurt in Bailey's voice. Finally she gave Bailey a quick hug. "If he comes . . . I'll be praying. For both of you."

"Okay." She smiled again. "I'm going out front now. So I can call Brandon."

The boys were congregated in the TV room to catch the local news and the highlights from Cody's title game. Bailey squeezed her mom's hand and then headed for the porch. She dialed Brandon as soon as she was outside.

"Hey . . ." The joy in his voice made her heart dizzy. Brandon cared. He loved her like no one ever had. "How was the game?"

"Great." Her answer was quick and a little too upbeat. "Cody's team won by a touchdown."

"Really? That's awesome. He's got to be one of the only coaches to take a high school team from winless to an undefeated state title."

"Yeah. The only coach in Indiana history."

"That's fantastic." Brandon's confidence was attractive. He simply trusted that her feelings were for him. Period. "Did you congratulate him?"

"No. He was busy." She hesitated and squeezed her eyes shut. "But my mom told him he could stop by later. So, yeah . . . we'll see." There. She'd said it. Because she wouldn't lie — not now or ever. Honesty was the glue in any relationship.

"You think he will?"

"Probably. We haven't talked in forever."

His silence lasted ten seconds. "Okay."

"I think it's good. The two of us never really had closure."

Brandon could've said a lot of things in that moment. From the beginning he had teased Bailey that Cody didn't exist. Cody who had never come around the set of *Unlocked,* never showed his face at the premiere, or at Bailey's house the times Brandon was over. He could've said some quick remark about how the two of them hadn't only missed out on closure — they'd missed out on the kind of relationship that might actually require it. But instead he kept his tone even, kept it rich with assurance and faith that she was telling the truth.

"Then you go ahead and talk to him, Bailey."

"It's nothing." Her heart hurt with the depth of Brandon's kindness. "You believe me, right?"

Brandon chuckled. "If you're asking me whether I'm crazy about the idea that my girlfriend is about to have a late-night talk with her old boyfriend, then *no*. I'm not crazy about it." He waited, until the easy laughter faded from his voice. "But if you're asking whether I trust you, the answer is *yes*. I absolutely trust you, Bailey."

"Thanks." Her voice sounded more somber than she meant it to. "That means a lot." Guilt ran a quick course through her veins. She had no ulterior motive, no plans to do or say anything that would betray Brandon. But if he could've read her heart during the game — when she couldn't take her eyes off Cody — she might have some explaining to do. Not only to him, but to herself.

"Well, then . . . I'll let you go."

No, she wanted to say. "I don't want you to." Her tone lightened and grew serious all at the same time. "Please don't let me go."

"I won't, baby." No doubts lived in his answer. None at all. "Go have your talk. Text me tomorrow when you wake up."

"Okay." She felt lost and unsure. If she were stronger she should've told her mother to call Cody and stop the visit. She wouldn't talk to him, wouldn't meet with him if she had a backbone. Not after how he'd walked away. Not when she had a boyfriend who deserved her undivided attention. She exhaled and her shoulders slumped forward a little, like someone was pressing down on them. "I'm sorry."

"Don't be." His smile sounded in his tone. "Hey . . ."

She hated this, hated how she felt. "What?"

"I love you."

Hearing him say the words . . . knowing he'd never said them to anyone but her made her even more conflicted. "I love you too."

The call ended and Bailey sat in silence, staring at the long dark driveway in front of the house she grew up in.

What am I doing, God? Why am I allowing this talk?

No answer drifted across her heart except one. A Scripture she'd read that morning in her time with God. Romans 8:28:

I work all things to the good for those who love me.

Bailey thought about that. *All things.* That

94

meant the conversation with Cody would somehow wind up being a good thing. Because there was nothing inherently wrong with it, and Brandon had even given his blessing. So she had nothing to feel guilty about. They would share a conversation, nothing more.

But if that were true then Bailey had no explanation for one thing.

The way her heart reacted when Cody's truck came over the hill.

FIVE

Bailey felt the temperature drop the moment Cody parked along the circle in front of her house. Even in the dark of night, she could feel him watching her, sense his eyes on hers the way she'd sensed them on her at the football game. He climbed out of his truck, slipped his hands into the pockets of his hooded jacket, and made his way up the walk. Everything about the moment, every mannerism of Cody's, the sway of his body, the easy athletic way he had about him even after his devastating injury in Iraq — all of it was so familiar.

She stood and waited, holding on to the feeling of seeing him here again, like a vision from some not-quite-forgotten time. He came to her slowly, his eyes on hers right up until he stood a few feet away.

She had wondered about this moment since the last time she saw him, up at the hospital with Cheyenne. Should she hug him or shake his hand . . . or should she just keep her distance the next time they might meet? But she had never quite made up her mind, and now he decided for her.

"Bailey." Her name was little more than a whisper on his lips. And without hesitating he pulled her close, held her in a way that was familiar. The brotherly sort of hug he used to give her when she was in high school, when neither of them had been ready to admit their feelings for each other.

The hug lingered, the way it might at a homecoming or a reunion. But the feeling of being in Cody's arms strangely didn't stir her heart the way being there once had. As nice as it felt to be hugged by him again, the change, the way this was only a friendship hug, hurt. As if the Cody who had once fallen for her was as gone as those long ago days. Bailey eased away first. She crossed her arms and tried to hide the shiver that ran down her back. He was still looking at her, and she realized the comfort level between them was maybe the one thing that hadn't changed. "Hi."

He stopped a few feet from her, his chest rising, his breathing harder than usual. "Why?" He sounded angrier than he looked. "Why did you run?"

She forced herself to stay calm. Her eyes

held his and she didn't blink. Instead she looked at him a long time before she answered, her voice quiet and sure. "Why did you?"

He opened his mouth to say something, to rebut her response and probably demand she stick to his question. That she might give him a reason for turning around and leaving instead of walking up to him and congratulating him back at the stadium like the rest of her family. "Can we sit?"

Bailey nodded and she led him to the swing, the place where they'd talked so often before. They took opposite sides, in a way that left no danger their elbows or knees might brush against each other. The swing stayed still.

Cody looked up at the sky. Like maybe he was searching for the right words, the right way to begin. "I've wanted to do this ever since that night in the hospital."

A pang of frustration slapped at Bailey's heart. "You have?" Her laugh held no level of humor. "Then why haven't you?"

"Because." His tone rang slightly indignant. "You have a boyfriend, Bailey." He tossed his hand and let it fall on the arm of the swing. "What's the difference? You moved on."

"You did too."

"I didn't mo—" Whatever he was going to say he stopped himself. "Forget it." The muscles in his jaw flexed, and he looked at the ground for a long moment. When he looked up resignation shadowed his expression. "Okay. We both moved on." He looked defeated, like he didn't want to fight. "But I thought about this conversation every day, Bailey. Every night."

Bailey caught something in that last sentence, something in his tone. Like maybe Cody had doubts about his relationship with Cheyenne. Either way, Bailey didn't want to talk about Cody's girlfriend. Instead she let his words wash over her again: *He'd thought about having this conversation every day . . . every night.*

"Bailey . . . say something . . ."

"You thought about this . . . and not once did you call or text me? Nothing?" She wanted to cry. How could he think about her for such a long time and not call?

"Again . . ." He gave a sideways nod, as if his response should be obvious. "You're in a relationship. I wouldn't have come tonight if your mom didn't give me the okay. I don't go around calling other guys' girlfriends."

She was on her feet, and she could feel anger light up her eyes. "Wait a minute." She spun around and faced him. "I'm not just some guy's girlfriend. Remember me, Cody?" She spread her fingers over her heart. "Remember how it was before you went to war and how it was when you came home?" She hesitated, finding a level of control again. "How it was a year ago summer?"

"Of course." His voice fell and he dropped his head into his right hand. For a few seconds he massaged his temples with his thumb and forefinger. "Bailey." He looked up and for a second she thought he might take her hands in his. Instead he crossed his arms again. "Don't say that. Don't be angry at me. If I had it to do over again . . ."

"You don't. *We* don't." Only then — in a sudden rush — did she realize he was right. She'd been angry from the moment she saw him earlier at the game, and in this moment her anger seeped through every response, every question or comment. She leaned back against the porch rail and closed her eyes.

Okay, God. I need You. I'm angry, I am. I don't want to be nice to him. Help me, Lord . . . give me the control of Your Holy Spirit.

And in the still of the night she heard His response.

I am with you, daughter. Be honest . . . be kind.

Be honest and kind. Bailey thought about that and instantly the idea stilled her anxious heart. She opened her eyes and looked at him. "I'm sorry. For arguing." She sat back down on the edge of the swing and looked straight at him. "The truth is, Cody, I'm angry. Really angry at you."

He slid back a few inches, clearly surprised by her answer. "*You're* angry?"

"Yes." She folded her arms and resisted the way her teeth wanted to chatter together, resisted the cold that ran through her. "You and I shared the most amazing summer ever, and a few weeks later it seemed like you fell off the earth. Like you and I never existed."

"You were with Brandon."

"I was *not* with him." She wanted to raise her voice, but she kept control. "I was supposed to be with you, to be honest." She uttered a single, frustrated laugh. "I told Brandon I had a boyfriend, and he used to tease me. He didn't believe you were real, because you never came around."

Regret flooded his eyes, his expression. For a while he didn't respond, but then he hung his head before he looked at her again. "I'm sorry. I have my reasons."

"Your mom?"

"Yes." Cody sounded more serious. "She

was involved with some, well, some very dangerous people, Bailey. At the time I was afraid." Cody's eyes begged her to understand. "Afraid you'd get hurt. I couldn't take that."

"But, Cody, don't you see?" She didn't want to cry, but this was the hardest part. "Your actions . . . the way it came across . . . it did hurt me. Like you didn't care at all."

"Of course I cared." He looked broken. "I ached for even a single minute of this, being with you again."

"Then why did you get serious with Cheyenne?"

Cody set his jaw again.

Bailey waited. "Cody?" She wasn't letting the conversation move on from here until she had an answer. Her voice quieted some. "Why did you turn to her?"

"She needed me." He looked like maybe those were three of the most difficult words he'd ever said.

A cool wind picked up, and Bailey felt colder than before. But she kept her distance. They were finally getting somewhere. "Because of her accident? She needed you because of that, or just *she* needed you . . . and I didn't?"

"You didn't." Defeat sounded from the most private places of his being. "Your life is magical, Bailey." He turned to fully face her. "What could I offer a girl like you?"

"What you offered me that summer . . . a love that watched me grow up, that knew me for who I was and cared about my family." She took a breath. "A love like I'll never have again, not exactly like it, no matter who God brings into my life." The cold made her teeth chatter a little. "That's what you had to offer."

For the first time since he pulled up, the conversation between them wasn't one of questions and explanations. In light of what she'd just told him, for a few precious seconds Cody looked at her the way he had that summer. Back when it felt like they might have found forever. But he kept the distance between them. "So . . . what happens now?"

The answer was as easy as her next breath, even if she felt a little sad saying it. "We move on." She placed her hand on his shoulder for a brief moment. "Back at the game I had this . . . I don't know, this physical reaction to seeing you. Like an ache in my heart." She hugged herself, still cold. "I wasn't sure what I felt."

He didn't have to say anything. His eyes told her exactly how his heart was reacting to that. That maybe if he'd believed how strongly she felt for him . . . maybe neither of them would be where they were today.

"But I was mad. I figured it out." She felt herself relax, felt her control return a little more. "Angry about the past . . . but not anymore." The image of Brandon's face, the sound of his voice filled her heart. "Having a reaction . . . feeling something about the past . . ." She shook her head. "It's not enough. What I have with Brandon is real." In all her life she never pictured saying these words to Cody, but it was time. "I love him . . . I really do."

His eyes gave him away at first, about how hard her statement hit him. But then he seemed to find a place of understanding as well. "I get it." He breathed in deep and sat up a little, distancing himself even more. "I'm not asking you to walk away from Brandon." He raked his hand over his short hair. "I just . . . I wanted to explain myself. Why things went the way they did."

She nodded. "I appreciate that." The truth of what she'd said, the depth of her feelings for Brandon were still finding their way to the control center of her heart. But as they did, they felt real and right and true. She couldn't be mad at Cody. Like he said, they had both moved on.

"Anyway . . ." He seemed to catch himself,

seemed to remember there was no point to furthering the conversation. Not late at night out here on her parents' porch. "I can't stay long. DeMetri is out with the guys, but he'll be home soon."

"DeMetri Smith? Your running back?"

"Yeah." Cody smiled, the familiar smile that instantly recalled the close connection they would always share. "He lives with me . . . Long story." Cody glanced at her house, at the sound of the boys' voices beyond the front windows. "Let's just say God allowed me to do for DeMetri a little of what your parents did for me."

Suddenly Bailey remembered the game. "Congratulations, by the way. On the win."

"Thanks. We had a lot of help, I know that. DeMetri's touchdown — not possible without divine intervention. It's been great . . . just being a part of it all."

This was something she would always love about Cody: his humility. She only wished it had been mixed with the sort of confidence Brandon had. At least where she was concerned. "I'd say God used you in the lives of those players . . . they'll never forget Him or this night . . . or you."

"I pray that's true." Cody looked more at ease, despite the falling temperature. "De-Metri wants to be a pastor. He's going to

Liberty University, same as Connor, right?"

"Right. Cody . . . that's wonderful." She couldn't help but make the obvious connection. Her parents had taken him in and he'd gone into a line of work that might help people. And now he'd helped DeMetri, and the guy wanted to be a pastor. "I guess it's true, what my dad always says: You never touch just one heart. Because once someone is loved like that, they'll go on to touch countless hearts. And with God the chain reaction never ends."

Cody laughed softly and looked off again. "I remember him saying that. He'd tell us players to walk the halls of school and spread kindness." He allowed a light bit of laughter. "That didn't come naturally for most of us. Not back then."

"For you it did." Bailey smiled. If they only had a few minutes left together, she wanted to find her way back to a place of friendship with him. The way she felt when he first got here. "Remember? You wanted to know about that Bryan guy I liked, how he was treating me? You were like the perfect older brother."

"Mmmm." Cody stared straight ahead for a long beat and then found her eyes once more. "The perfect older brother."

Bailey realized how that must've sounded.

But she didn't care. "That's what you were back then." She smiled and gave a light shrug. "Of course, I had a fierce crush on you the whole time, so yeah . . ."

The depth in Cody's face, his eyes told her he was struggling. "Bailey . . ."

Whatever he wanted to say he must've changed his mind. What could he tell her at this point? That he still had feelings for her? It was too late. That was the sad truth. No matter how long she had loved Cody and no matter what they'd found together once upon a long ago summer, time had moved them to different places. And here . . . now maybe he was right to keep his feelings to himself.

Or maybe not.

She leaned closer, no longer shivering. "Say it, Cody . . . what were you going to tell me?"

For a long time he only looked at her, as if by doing so he could will himself back to those summer days, back to the time when it seemed nothing could ever come between them. He reached out like he might take her hands in his, but then he seemed to change his mind again. Instead he let his eyes do all the holding either of them were willing to do on this November night. "Like I said . . . if I could do it over . . ."

Her anger from earlier was gone. "We had something very special."

"We did. . . ." He looked up, clearly desperate for answers. He found her eyes again. "I didn't know how to hold onto you. You're so good, Bailey. I wasn't sure I could . . . I could be everything you needed." He clenched his teeth and breathed in sharply, the sound a reflection of the way his words grated on his heart and hers. He allowed a quick shake of his head. "It wasn't the drug dealer. I mean . . . deep down, I wasn't really worried about your safety." He exhaled, and the look in his eyes, the ocean of caring and loving was finally, *finally* the look Bailey remembered. "You were off and running, Bailey. Finding your life. Filming a movie with Brandon Paul, of all people."

"You weren't afraid for my safety." It wasn't a question because she understood now. Like never before until this moment, she understood. "I get it. You were afraid for your own."

His expression told her she'd hit the reason exactly. "Yes. Losing you . . . I wasn't sure I could survive it. So . . . I told myself it could never work. I walked away instead of believing in us."

"Because that was easier?"

"No." Cody sat up a little and his strength was palpable. This was the soldier who had survived Iraqi captivity and later saved a whole platoon. "I wasn't looking for the easy road. I was looking to survive. Blame it on the Army training. When a direction is certain death, we go the other way. Survival, Bailey, that's all."

She wasn't sure what to feel. Yes, she understood now. But that didn't make his decision right. It didn't change the fact that they'd both lost in the process. Bailey drew back, putting enough space between them so she could think clearly, so she could remember once more that they'd moved on. This wasn't that summer, and Cody wasn't her boyfriend. She closed her eyes and focused on God, the plans He had for her, the fact that He worked all things to the good for those who loved Him.

But what about this, Lord? What I am supposed to do now?

"Talk to me . . . please, Bailey."

Cody's voice seemed far away. She pictured Brandon, the sincerity in his eyes and smile, the way he loved her with everything in him. Cody had been honest . . . now it was her turn. "About Brandon . . . I love him, Cody. I didn't mean to fall for him. I never imagined it when we were filming

Unlocked." She wanted him to understand completely. "Back then you alone had my heart."

Her words seemed to hit him like so many knives. "I . . . believe you."

"But since then . . ." She placed her hand over her heart again. "Brandon and I have gotten very close. I . . . I can't imagine breaking up with him."

"No." Cody shook his head. "I'm not asking for that." His tone was more guarded. "You had a right to move on. I mean, really, Bailey . . . I want you to be happy." He rubbed the back of his neck, clearly frustrated with himself. "What did I expect would happen? I'm the one who walked away."

"Yes." There. He had said it. Bailey relaxed a little. Their breakup, the silence between them, the missed communication and losses were his fault. Because he had walked away. "Well . . . at least we have closure. So I don't have to wonder forever what happened."

"Yeah." He rubbed his hands together. "And maybe next time you see me you won't feel like running."

"Or maybe I'll run faster." She laughed, and the break from their serious talk felt good. Her smile faded. "None of this is easy, Cody. Not for either of us."

"I know." For the first time since he arrived, he seemed to lose the battle with himself, the battle to keep her from knowing not only the truth about the past, but the reality of how he still felt about her. He reached out and gently touched her cheek, brushing a wisp of her hair from her face. "I'm sorry, Bailey." He looked like he might kiss her, but he kept the space between them. "I guess . . . I'll always regret walking away. But I had to tell you why I did it." His smile didn't hide his broken heart. "At least I won't regret that part."

They stood and he drew a deep breath as he turned to her. "I don't want to go."

She didn't want him to leave either. But she couldn't lead him on, couldn't let him think her heart was free. "Maybe we can talk sometime . . . every once in a while."

"Hmmm." He tilted his head, looking still deeper within her soul. "I never was much good at being your friend." The kindness in his smile allowed her to see the Cody she knew so well, the one she had loved for so many years. "We'll see, okay? That's about as good as I can do for now."

"Okay." She felt the slightest sting, because once again they were saying goodbye. But she understood. "Thanks, Cody. For talking."

He didn't respond, didn't have to. Instead of saying anything more, he simply took her in his arms and hugged her. This time there was more there, more depth and longing. A longing for something they had both walked away from, something they would never have again.

As he pulled away he let his cheek brush lightly against hers. "I love you, Bailey." He whispered the words, and they mixed with the sound of the wind in the barren trees. "I always will."

Bailey sucked in a quick breath, hating the way her heart responded to his so easily. Even now when she loved Brandon Paul. She put her hands on his shoulders and looked at him, straight through to his hurting soul. "You'll always matter to me."

If he was wounded by the fact that she didn't tell him she loved him too, he hid the fact. Instead he allowed a resolute smile and he nodded a few times. "See ya, Bailey." He started to walk away, his eyes still on hers for a few final seconds.

"See ya." She hugged herself tightly and watched him walk away. Long after he climbed in his truck and drove away she sat there, oblivious to the cold all around her. Unable to do anything else, she relived every moment, every line of their conversation.

Her night with Cody Coleman . . . a too-quick hour stolen from yesterday. When she couldn't stand the thought another minute, she headed inside. As she did she realized that watching him walk away hadn't caused the same physical pain in her heart as before. Maybe because she loved Brandon Paul. Here alone she felt God reassuring her that she'd said the right things, made the right choice in loving Brandon. Because the truth was this: After only a day apart she missed Brandon, more than she had been willing to admit.

Even to herself.

Six

Cody couldn't see the end of Bailey's driveway for his tears. Maybe he'd said too much, shown more of his heart than he should've. He definitely hadn't planned to tell her everything, to be so honest. But once he sat across from her, smelling her perfume and the shampoo in her beautiful hair . . . once he was inches from her, he was helpless to do anything but open up about how he felt.

Exactly how he felt.

As he drove home north on Interstate 37, he allowed the conversation to play again in his mind. The look in her eyes, the way he could still read her heart the same way he could read it when she was a high school girl. She still cared, still loved him. But her feelings were different now — that much was clear. She was in love with Brandon Paul now. Cody would respect that. It was why he hadn't called her out on her feel-

114

ings, why he hadn't forced the issue when he admitted how he still loved her and when she couldn't say the same back to him.

If he hadn't been so afraid of losing her, he'd still have her. It was the most bitter irony, and it plagued him, weighed on him. He ran over their conversation again, replayed the minutes. She'd moved on, and she'd accused him of doing the same thing, but then . . .

Then, what?

Suddenly his response was as clear as if he'd just watched a video of himself during that part of their talk. He had actually started to say what? That he hadn't moved on? That he didn't have those kinds of feelings for Cheyenne? Which could only mean that . . . that he still loved Bailey. Still wanted her more than he had known until tonight.

A sick feeling came over him and Cody couldn't go another minute without addressing the issue. He took the next exit, turned left and then right into the parking lot of a closed supermarket. He put his car in park and killed the engine.

If he loved Bailey, then what was he doing with Cheyenne? She'd had a headache tonight. It was why he felt okay about going to the Flanigans' house. Cheyenne wasn't expecting to hang out with him. And the minute he'd known that, he had run to Bailey. Again his words came back to him. *I didn't move on . . .* that's what he was about to tell Bailey. Yes, he'd stopped himself, but the truth remained and it hit him like a sucker punch.

He didn't love Cheyenne . . . he loved Bailey. The way he had always loved her. At least his heart felt that way here . . . now . . . after being close enough to touch her. Maybe he didn't want to explain the situation, because to do so would mean first explaining it to himself. His feelings for Cheyenne had been strong from the moment they met at Tara's dinner more than a year ago. But in light of this new realization, he couldn't have felt love or infatuation or longing.

Rather what he felt for Cheyenne was sympathy and concern, pity even.

The reality of that turned his stomach and made him furious with himself. Yes, he was attracted to her and, yes, he enjoyed being with her. But all of that was still wrapped up in some sad sort of feeling sorry for her. Cheyenne had given him purpose; she'd helped him get past the flashbacks of war and the pointless way his life felt after he'd walked away from Bailey. She helped him feel less lonely, and he helped her get through missing her fiancé and then he'd stood by her during the rehab she'd needed after her car accident.

But that didn't mean he was in love with her.

Not when being with Bailey defined the word.

Cody hung his head. What was he supposed to do now? Already Chey had asked him why he stayed, whether he really loved her. And he'd always assured her that yes, he was falling for her. Because he believed that himself. It was only tonight, after spending time with Bailey, that he knew for sure.

Love? Being in love? That bar was set a long time ago by Bailey Flanigan. He loved Cheyenne, but in a completely different way. If he wanted to face God and the mirror, he would have to set things straight with her as soon as possible.

Sometime tomorrow.

He lifted his head, weary from the realization of what the morning would bring. Then in a rush of anger he slammed his hand on the steering wheel. *Nice work, Coleman.* How could he have let things get this serious with Cheyenne without stopping to examine his real feelings? Now the talk they had to have would hurt both of them, even if Cheyenne wouldn't exactly be surprised by it.

Options presented themselves as he started up his truck. Maybe he could tell her he needed more time, and maybe after a while the concern and caring he felt for Cheyenne would become a love brighter than what he'd once shared with Bailey.

Or maybe not.

No, Cody couldn't ask her to hold onto that hope. He couldn't do that to either of them. Either she would be okay to see him as a friend — nothing more — or they would have to part ways. Another heartache at his hands. The sick feeling remained as he headed out of the parking lot. But before he could pull into traffic his phone rang. *Strange,* he thought. It was nearly one in the morning. No one called him this late.

He grabbed his phone from the seat beside him and glanced at the face of it. The call was from Tara. He wrinkled his brow. Tara was normally asleep hours earlier than this. He took the call and pressed the phone to his ear. "Hello? Tara?"

"Cody." She was crying. The cry of someone heartbroken. "We're at the hospital. I'm with Cheyenne."

His heart stopped and then thudded hard

into a strange rhythm. Cheyenne was at the hospital? "What is it? What happened?"

"Her headache . . . it got worse, and she . . . started getting sick. Really sick, Cody, so I brought her here." She was trying to control her weeping, but she was losing the battle. "The doctors are worried. She . . . she has something on her brain. They're doing tests."

Cody felt the blood leave his face. There couldn't be anything worse wrong with Cheyenne, right? She'd already been through so much. Cody gritted his teeth.

God, You can't let her be sick. Please . . .

"Which hospital are you at?"

Tara explained where they were, at the hospital not far from where Cody lived in Indianapolis. "Okay. Got it."

"Please, Cody . . . hurry. She's in so much pain. I'm so afraid for her." Tara tried again to find control. "She's . . . she's been asking for you."

"Thanks, Tara." He pulled into traffic and headed for the freeway on-ramp. "I'm on my way."

Cody made the drive to the hospital in record time. The whole way he couldn't think even a little about the talk the two of them needed to have. Instead he did the only thing he could do: He prayed for her

119

safety and healing. And that God would give him the strength to help her through whatever season they were about to enter.

Less than an hour later he rushed into her hospital room. Cheyenne was asleep, IV tubing in her arms, her complexion paler than usual. Tara sat beside her, eyes red and swollen, and as she saw Cody she hurried to him. Her fear was like a shield around her. "They gave her something . . . so she could sleep." Tara bit her lip and looked back at Cheyenne. "The test," she turned to Cody again. "They found something on her brain. What . . . what could that mean?"

"First . . . come here." He took the woman in his arms and rocked her, calming her. "God is with us. Whatever this is, whatever's coming . . . He's already gone before us. He won't leave us now." He ran his hand over Tara's back. "God doesn't want us to be afraid."

He felt her exhale, felt a level of calm return. "You're right." She grabbed a few quick breaths, evidence of the sobbing she'd done earlier. "I can't . . . I don't know if I can handle this. I don't know."

Cody wasn't sure either. "Life only comes at us one day at a time. That's where we need to let God meet us." His words weren't quite in sync with his pounding heart. But he was speaking truth. That was enough for now. "Let's ask Him to meet us . . . right here . . . whatever comes next."

Tara nodded, and for the next minute Cody held her and prayed, asking God to go before them and carry them through whatever came next with Cheyenne, with her headaches and the spot they'd seen on her brain. When they finished, he led Tara back to the spot beside Chey, and he took the chair opposite her bed. The moment felt altogether too familiar, the way they'd so often sat with Cheyenne in the days and weeks after her car accident.

"Did they say . . . maybe it was scar tissue? From her head injury." It was something he'd thought about since he took Tara's call. After all, Chey's brain had suffered much trauma in the accident. Certainly that could account for an unusual MRI, and the appearance of something on her brain.

"I asked." Tara folded her hands in her lap and did her best to look stronger. She lifted her chin. "They couldn't tell me. Said it would take an expert to look at the pictures."

Cody was about to ask whether anyone who had tended to Cheyenne after her accident had been called in yet, when a woman walked in. She shut the door behind her, and immediately Cody knew two things. First, this doctor had the test results they were waiting for. And second, the news wasn't good.

"Hello." Her sad smile was another indicator. "I'm Doctor Juarez. I've spent the last half hour going over Cheyenne's MRI and a few other tests."

Cody shot a quick look at Tara and nodded. God knew what was coming next. Cody took the lead. "You know about her accident?"

"Yes." Her eyes were a mix of intelligence and sympathy. "She nearly died from what I read."

"Her head was badly damaged. It was a miracle that she didn't suffer brain damage."

"I saw that." She took a step closer and held the chart in her hands out in front of her. "Sometimes after an accident like that, we see scar tissue. And sometimes scar tissue on the brain can be a troublesome issue. My initial thinking was that the previously injured areas had scarred some, and that this was causing her severe headaches and nausea. But sometimes . . . and there's not conclusive evidence about this . . . a previously injured area of the brain can actually develop a tumor."

A tumor? Cody gripped the edge of his chair and tried not to flinch.

Tara had a hold of the railing of Cheyenne's bed. "No," she uttered the word in a way that was barely audible. "Dear God, no."

If Doctor Juarez heard Tara, she didn't acknowledge the fact. Instead she opened the file and read the contents for a few seconds. Then she looked straight at Cody. "In this case that seems to be what we're looking at. A tumor in the same location where Cheyenne suffered trauma to the brain from the accident."

"Meaning . . . her brain is still recovering?" Cody couldn't let his mind go anywhere else.

"No, I'm afraid what we're seeing is an actual tumor on her brain." She looked discouraged by the news, and she glanced at Cheyenne, then back at Cody. "We need to do a biopsy. But I have a feeling we might be dealing with cancer. An aggressive cancer. That's the way it looks." She paused, letting the shattering news make its impact. "I'm very sorry."

"You . . . you said you can't know for sure, right? Not without a biopsy?" Cody's hands trembled, the news knocking hard against

123

his heart.

"True. We can't be sure until then." She nodded, as if she understood Cody's need for hope. "Still, we need to live with what we do know. She has a tumor at the site of her brain injury. Whether it's cancer . . . that news can wait until Monday. I'd like to keep her in the hospital until then, run some blood tests and find a medication that will help with her headaches and nausea."

The doctor said something else, something about managing pain and being honest with Cheyenne when she woke up. "These cancers . . . if it's cancer . . . can move very quickly." She sounded more serious than before. "It's important that you both help Cheyenne have a realistic approach to this. If that's what we're dealing with."

As she excused herself and left the room, Cody's mind screamed with the doctor's words: *Realistic? Pain management?* It was like the woman had already determined that Cheyenne was terminally ill. The fact made Cody angry . . . at the doctor and the tumor and the looming diagnosis. Maybe even at God. Across from him, Tara covered her face with her hands and started crying again. He wanted to stand, walk around the bed, and go to her . . . be strong for her. But he couldn't. He stared at the hospital floor and tried to believe he was really here again. Sitting at Cheyenne's bedside dealing with yet another impossible situation.

His own words came back to him. God would only have them handle the next thing. And now they knew what the next thing was.

"Cody . . ." Tara's voice was muffled by her fresh tears. "How could this happen?"

Cody wanted to have an answer. The truth rattled down the road of his mind. God was a mystery . . . His ways were good. His plans might be hard to understand, but they could be trusted. Even in the darkest days.

But this?

He swallowed hard, stood, and went to Tara. He took her hands and helped her to her feet. He hugged her for a long time and when he released her he shook his head. "I don't know."

It was all he could say. Because when Cheyenne woke up they'd have to tell her the most impossible news. He had no idea what God was doing. He knew just one very real thing in light of this news: If Cheyenne was fighting a brain tumor, he couldn't possibly leave her.

No matter how he felt.

He excused himself and rode the elevator to the fifth floor, the floor that housed the chapel. Without hesitating he took a spot in the empty room on a pew at the back. Then he pulled his iPod from his pocket and slipped his earbuds in. His new favorite band was Anthem Lights, and every song on their album spoke to him. Sometimes — moments like this — only a song could bridge his heart to God's, filling his senses with truth and hope. He chose the last song on the album. The song was "Where the Light Is" . . . a reminder that darkness didn't have a chance where the presence of God could be found. Where light existed, light would win. It was a truth Cody needed desperately — especially now. When darkness seemed determined to win out.

Cody let the music run through him.

Look in my eyes in the morning . . .

See the hope there and the soul that still remains . . .

Darkness doesn't stand a chance, where the light is . . .

The truth brushed against his soul and spoke promises to his heart. God was in control. He wouldn't take them through a season where He hadn't gone first. He would never leave him or Cheyenne, and He would never forsake them. Not ever. Again and again Cody listened to it, playing the Anthem Lights song until finally . . .

finally, he began to see the one thing he desperately needed in this darkest hour.

The slightest glimmer of light.

SEVEN

Brandon could hardly wait to get out of Los Angeles. First, he was headed to New York City and more than a month in the same city as Bailey, but also being on location would give him a break from the studio and his management team.

He was aboard the studio's private jet, the one he could use pretty much whenever he needed it, and in fifteen minutes he'd land at the private runway at LaGuardia Airport. He turned so he could watch the city come into view through the window of the plane. He was a day early, one more way he could surprise her. One more way he could let her know how crazy he was about her.

How great that he was flying in a day early.

He needed Bailey so badly, he couldn't take another day without her. Talking to her would help him sort through the ultimatums he faced. Because of his faith and the studio's perception that he'd become weak, they wanted an action picture for his next project. So the fans would see him as strong and indestructible — not the Jesus-loving guy he'd become. Brandon closed his eyes. Ridiculous. He sank back into the plush white leather sofa. Hollywood could be so weird. Wanting its leading men bad to the core. But that image wasn't him any longer. And anyway, surveys showed people wanted movies themed around faith and family. Wouldn't it only make sense they'd want movie stars that fit the same mold?

The proposal on the table right now was seven pictures. Seven movies over four years, movies where he'd need a different leading lady for each. And his agent had made himself clear on that subject. "You need love scenes, Brandon. We can't go from *Unlocked* to another sweet picture. It'll ruin you."

Brandon reminded him that the last film involved a leading lady — even if the storyline wasn't exactly a romance. That one had been filmed on a tropical island. A far cry from the high school hallways of *Unlocked*. "How about we do this my way and see if I'm right? I think my fan base will grow if I'm doing films people want to see. Box office numbers already back the idea that rated R movies never perform as well as cleaner pictures. So let's live in that world."

"Let the no-names do those movies." His agent was relentless. "The studio brass knows what it wants. Actors make a name for themselves in this town by doing edgier pictures. You know that."

In the end his manager backed off a little. "Look. We can sign the deal and leave the specifics open." The man seemed desperate for Brandon's cooperation. "Studios don't offer this sort of money, this type of package to anyone anymore. Seven films, Brandon? You'll be set for the next four years. One huge hit after another." He patted Brandon on the back, in a way that was just short of patronizing. "We can do this. I'll make sure there's room for your input when it comes to scripts. That way we'll make the decision about which films, which co-stars, one picture at a time, as the contract plays out."

Still Brandon doubted he'd have that sort of control. His management team was right, of course. No one put together offers like the one the studio had laid out. Eight figures each for seven feature films? The money was so crazy Brandon could only imagine what God would lead him to do with it. How he could help others or give back.

"You'll be the biggest movie star in the world." His agent smiled at him after the meeting. "One day we'll look back at today's bickering and laugh out loud." He tossed his hands in the air. "We should celebrate! The deal is crazy!"

Crazy. Brandon opened his eyes and looked out at the city again. Maybe it was crazy. He wanted to run it by Bailey, because . . . well, he saw his next four years with her. And the next four after that, and the next sixty or seventy from that point. He couldn't make a plan that involved so much of his future without hearing her thoughts. The deal would certainly keep him in LA, close to the studio, to the marketing machine that would kick in once he signed the deal. If he lived somewhere else, he'd forever be flying in for meetings and brainstorming sessions, to discuss plots and scripts and co-stars. It was a part of the business most people didn't understand — the fact that actors didn't live in LA because they loved being chased by paparazzi. They lived there because for every day on set there were ten days in meetings at the studio offices.

And studios were in LA.

He turned off his iPod and slipped it in his bag. His suitcases were in the cargo compartment. Three of them — since he was practically moving here. He even had a private trainer, who he'd work with at a local gym before public hours early each morning and late each night. His manager and agent had set that up. "Can't lose your physique," his manager had winked at him.

"What . . . I'm not as buff as I was?" Brandon laughed and patted his flat stomach. "I think I'm doing okay."

"Well." His agent smiled and tried not to look as condescending as he sounded. "You've lost a little weight. Love's made you a little too busy for the gym."

Brandon hadn't reacted, but he felt his blood simmer. His decision to love God hadn't changed his routine. He still did a hundred pushups every morning and night, still did two hundred sit-ups three times a day. Nothing had changed. It was like his team was looking for reasons to disagree with his decision to date Bailey Flanigan. Like her goodness was making him soft.

He felt a wave of anger hit him. Nothing could be further from the truth. Because of Bailey he felt stronger than he'd been in all his life. He pulled his Bible from the nearby glass table. He'd read it the first hour of the trip and now, before he put it away, he opened it to 1 Timothy 4 again. Verse 8 had caught his attention earlier, and now he read it once more:

Physical training is of some value, but godliness has value for all things, holding promise for both the present life and the life to come.

The words made him feel stronger. Promises for this life and the next. How could his management team think living for God had made him weaker? His eyes moved down the page a few verses.

Don't let anyone look down on you because you are young, but set an example for the believers in life, in love, in faith, and in purity . . . Be diligent in these matters; give yourself wholly to them, so that everyone may see your progress.

Brandon read the words again, amazed. It was like God had written this chapter for him alone. The opening line might as well have said, "Dear Brandon Paul . . ." Even the last verse in the chapter seemed written for him.

Watch your life and doctrine closely. Persevere in them, because if you do, you will save both yourself and your hearers.

If God had been sitting in on the studio meeting, making comments and letting His voice be heard, then the answer would've been obvious. Brandon could only sign the contract if the films were in some way a reflection of his faith, if through his public platform he could set an example for believers, and if he could persevere in a way that would actually lead people into a saving relationship with Christ.

Right? Brandon ran his thumb over the words.

Father, I hear You. Thank You . . . because when I'm most confused You make everything clear. Please . . . guide me through the process. Help me make decisions based on what You want. Not what everyone else is pushing for.

Again, the line from the verses shouted at him:

Don't let anyone look down on you because you're young . . .

A chill ran down his back. If God was talking to him, he understood the message. Everyone else at the table, everyone involved in the negotiation of his next contract was twice and three times his age. But he couldn't let that stop him from taking a stand.

As the plane landed, and as he made his way down the stairs to the waiting SUV, he felt stronger than he had in weeks. Another reminder that Jim Flanigan had been right that night when he'd baptized Brandon. The way to stay connected to God was through

His Word. Sure, he could make time for the personal trainer here in New York City. But more than that he would make time for God. Otherwise he couldn't possibly make the right choice with the major decisions that lay ahead. Not just with his next contract.

But with Bailey.

The producer of the film he was shooting in New York City had set him up in the penthouse at the Ritz Carlton on Park Avenue, right across from Central Park. The SUV had black tinted windows, and no one was expecting him except a few select employees. So when they pulled up, Brandon managed to stay unnoticed as he climbed out and as his bags were brought up to his room.

Everything about the suite was perfect, of course. He had a refrigerator stocked with bottled water and string cheese and Greek yogurt and almonds, diced chicken and vegetables. The foods he lived on. In the bathroom were bottles of his favorite hair and face products. All the comforts of home. Brandon wandered to a desk near the expansive window and the view of the park. An impressive fruit basket held a note that read, "Let the filming begin — you'll make the best spy ever!" Brandon read the message and smiled. He looked forward to this movie — and not just because it put him in Bailey's backyard. He was playing a college kid caught in some minor trouble, and brought in by the FBI to do an undercover job.

He unpacked, changed into one of his nicer pairs of jeans and a fitted caramel-colored buttoned-down shirt and boots he'd gotten from a J. Crew ad he'd filmed last week. By now Bailey would already be at the theater, warming up, getting ready for tonight's performance. Brandon sprayed his neck with a few quick bursts of her favorite cologne.

It had only been four days since he'd seen her, but he missed her with every heartbeat. A quick glance at the mirror and Brandon was satisfied. After her performance, he had a plan for tonight, and he needed to look the part. He buzzed the driver of the SUV once more. The man was at his disposal throughout his time in New York.

Twenty minutes later, after navigating ridiculous traffic on Fifth Avenue, the driver dropped him off at the theater entrance. He'd had his manager call ahead and arrange to let him enter the building early. At this hour — forty-five minutes before show time — there wasn't much of a line outside.

He slipped out of the Navigator and hurried to the entrance and the theater employee standing guard.

"Brandon! Look! It's Brandon Paul!" A group of teenage girls were among the few already in line. In lightning speed the news spread to the rest of the twenty people in line. Brandon didn't stop, didn't turn around and look. Instead he met the eyes of the guard, who must've been expecting him, because he snapped into action and shuttled Brandon through the doors into the empty theater.

He wanted his arrival to be a secret, and the theater management knew as much. Bailey was backstage, so he took his seat in the first row, middle. On either side of him, the theater management would seat stand-ins — actors hired to be on hand in case of an emergency with one of the show's leads. That way he wouldn't be bothered with conversations or picture-taking or autographs while he watched the show. Of course, the staff could promise nothing about what might happen after the show. That was okay. Brandon and Bailey would have to get used to attention if they were going to live in the same city for the next five or six weeks.

As the theater opened, the stand-ins took

their seats. Brandon chatted with them, keeping his head low and trying to appear part of their group. For the most part the ploy worked. That and the fact that the theater stationed a guard halfway down the center aisle.

Once the overture began, the people looking to meet him found their seats and focused on the show. Good thing. Brandon loved the fans, even more since he'd become a believer. But right now all he could see or think about or long for was a certain brown-haired, blue-eyed girl about to take the stage.

She didn't spot him right away. Brandon sat so close to the stage she probably looked past him, which meant he could watch her. Really watch her. She moved like the wind, the way she floated across the stage. And no one lit up the ensemble like she did. Whatever her director was talking about in her poor reviews of Bailey, Brandon disagreed. Bailey wasn't the weak link. She was the reason people kept watching.

Not until the end of the first ensemble number did she spot him. The song raced a million miles an hour right up until the end, when they all struck a pose and froze in place. And at that moment her eyes found his. The surprise on her face became a joy that filled his heart and reassured him. Not that he needed reassuring. But after her talk with Cody he knew the moment he saw her he'd have answers to the questions he didn't want to ask her.

Now he could see the proof in her eyes, on her face. As she left the stage she moved her fingers just slightly in his direction and he did the same. For the rest of the performance, she glanced at him so often, it was like she danced and sang for him alone. As great as the show was, he was glad when the show ended. The rest of the night would belong to them alone.

Before the houselights went up, someone from the theater staff escorted him backstage, and after the final curtain he waited in the shadows until she stepped lightly down the stairs and into his arms. "You're here." She hugged him and held on. "Mmm, Brandon . . . I'm so glad you came."

After she changed they exited through the front of the building to his waiting Navigator. Since the crowd gathered at the back stage door, they managed to get away without walking past even a single anxious fan. "Wow," she exhaled as she buckled her seat belt. "Are you moved in?"

"I am. I feel like I'm home." He took her hand, smiling at her, lost in her eyes. "Now that you're here."

They talked nonstop from the theater to Bailey's apartment building a dozen blocks away, the place where she lived with Betty and Bob Keller. For a few minutes they hung out with the older couple, updating them about his New York movie. But pretty soon Betty winked at him. "You two young people need some time alone. Don't let us get in your way."

Brandon winked at her in return. Bob and Betty had helped set up his next surprise. He looked at Bailey and shrugged. "I don't know . . . what about the rooftop?"

"In December?" Bailey laughed, but her eyes danced with excitement.

"So? Get your coat." He led her to the Kellers' hall closet and found a brand new fur-lined, black wool coat. With ease, he slid it over her shoulders and saw that the store clerk had chosen perfectly. The coat hung to just above her ankles.

"Brandon!" She gasped and brought her fingers to her lips. "Whose is this?"

"It's yours." He pulled her close and hugged her, but only briefly. "Hey look, here's another one." He took the coat that hung beside it — a three-quarter length, wool-lined military-style jacket, something fashionable and warm at the same time.

He'd bought both coats over the phone the day after Thanksgiving and had them delivered here.

For this very purpose.

"Brandon . . . how?" She giggled. "This coat must've cost a fortune. And yours . . . you look amazing in that. It . . . it fits you perfectly."

"Thank you." He took her hand. "Now that we're warm, come on . . . the night's waiting."

They'd met up on the rooftop a number of times. The place was at the top of Betty and Bob's building, and no one seemed to use it. Every time they'd been the only ones here, their private hideaway. A spot where no one would recognize them or follow them or take their picture.

"Let's take the elevator this time." Bailey laughed. "Remember . . . that first time when we walked up?"

"At least we were committed." Brandon still had her hand, and after they stepped off the elevator, the night opened up before them. Despite the cold air, the sky was clear and — even competing against the lights of the city — the stars shone through.

"It's beautiful." Bailey slowed her pace and slipped in close by his side. Then she looked at him, her eyes bright with happiness. "You planned this?"

"Of course." He walked her slowly toward the other side of the roof, along the path lined by potted shrubs and low-level lights. When they neared an open patio area, he eased her into his arms. "I got to thinking the other day, after our talk Saturday."

"When I told you about my talk with Cody?"

"Right." He leaned in and touched his lips tenderly to hers. As he eased back, he searched her eyes. "And it occurred to me that you and I never went to the prom."

"We didn't."

"And that coat," he glanced down at it, "is long enough, beautiful enough that it might . . . well, it might as well be a prom dress."

"It's more beautiful than any prom dress."

"And warmer. Which is the main point."

"Brandon, you're amazing. How did you set all this up?"

"Really, Bailey?" He brought her hand to his lips and kissed her fingers. "I take you to the top of the Empire State Building for a Skype date? Certainly I can find a way to take you to the prom."

She looked dizzy with it all, and he wondered if he'd ever been this happy. He led her onto the patio, and waiting there was a portable speaker with an iPod connector. And next to it was a small table set with two full fluted glasses and a half-full bottle of orange soda nearby.

"Your favorite and mine." He smiled at her. "But then you already knew that."

"I did." Her eyes welled up, despite the smile that filled her face. "I can't believe this . . . all of this."

"I want to make a toast." He made a funny face. "Not sure they make toasts at proms. But at this prom we do."

He swore off drinking after finding faith in God, not because there was anything wrong with having a glass of wine here and there. But because he couldn't afford for his witness to be affected by the appearance of partying. He'd already lived that life, and now . . . with his very public faith he needed to make sure the paparazzi never snapped a picture of him drinking, never gave him a reason for someone to mock his beliefs.

"Hold on." He took a glass and gave her one. "Okay . . . here's the toast." He looked straight into her eyes, to the newfound pathway he'd worn to the depths of her heart. "To the next five weeks . . . and the next five years . . . and every day God gives us together after that. That you would know even partly how much I love you."

This time her tears got the best of her. They filled her eyes and spilled onto her cheeks. "Brandon, I . . ." She shook her head, trying to find control. "I don't know what to say."

"Baby, that's easy . . ." He held the glass out to the side and touched his forehead to hers. "Tell me you love me."

"I love you." She didn't hesitate, didn't look away. "I love you so much."

"Okay, then." He held the glass up and clinked it against hers. "A toast to today and tomorrow . . . as long as God gives us."

"Cheers." She smiled, her cheeks already dry from the cool winter air.

They both took a long sip and he held onto the moment. The night was perfect, and the coats had made it possible. "Now . . . some dancing." He made a funny face, one that elicited a quick laugh from her. "A prom isn't a prom without dancing. Even I know that much."

He took his iPod from his jeans pocket and hooked it to the top of the portable speaker. The playlist was something he'd worked on late last night. It started off with Taylor Swift's "Sparks Fly." Brandon waited until the music was playing, then he swept into a graceful bow and grinned at her. "My lady?"

"My prince . . ." She took his hand and they swayed to the music. Their coats allowed them to keep a little distance between them. They laughed and danced and talked and swayed through the entire playlist, a series of songs by Adele and Owl City and Michael Bublé. The last song by Lady Antebellum was "Just a Kiss." The lyrics talked about how they only needed a kiss — nothing more — because this love might be the kind that lasted forever.

"I love this." Bailey whispered near his ear as they danced. "It's exactly how I feel." She smiled at him. "About you."

"The perfect song."

The cold night hadn't even been a factor while they danced, and Brandon silently thanked the Lord for letting every detail work out so smoothly. When the song ended, Brandon framed her face with his hands. "Your cheeks are cold."

"But my heart is warm." She searched his eyes. "I didn't see this coming. Everything about the night . . . it's been perfect."

"One more thing." He took his phone from his other pocket and switched it to camera mode. Then he held it out at arm's length. "A quick picture."

She snuggled up beside him and with their cheeks touching Brandon took the picture.

Then he tapped a few buttons and typed out a quick message. "For Twitter." He held the phone up for her to see.

"Went to prom tonight with the prettiest girl in the world!" She tapped the attached link and up came the picture they'd just taken. "Brandon!" She turned to him. "That's the nicest thing ever. Your fans are gonna be brokenhearted."

"No other girl matters, Bailey. When I'm with you . . ." his voice grew softer, "I want to tell the whole world. And since we can't dance in front of them, I can at least do this."

They hugged again, and he led her back across the roof and down to the front door of the Kellers' apartment. "My ride's waiting for me."

"Wanna come in? Watch TV or a movie?"

"I meet with my trainer at five in the morning." He grinned. "Maybe next time."

"Okay." She looked shy, her eyes still bright from all that had happened that night. "Then I guess I'll see you tomorrow."

"You're a very, very good dancer, Bailey." He put his hand up alongside her face again. "Not just here, but onstage. I could've watched you forever."

She lowered her chin, and her expression told him she was too full, too moved to say much. After a few seconds she managed a quiet: "Thank you."

Then in the sweetest moment of the night, he drew her close and kissed her. "Sleep well." He whispered. "I love you, Bailey."

"The prom was lovely." She returned his kiss and this time they lingered in the moment a little longer. When she drew back, the longing in her eyes was enough to make his knees weak. She broke the moment with her smile. "Absolutely perfect, Brandon. Everything about tonight."

He studied her, his heart at peace. "We didn't talk about Cody."

"No." Her answer came easily, same as her smile. "It's a closed door."

"Good." He had no reason to push her, no doubts. "You can tell me details later if you want."

"Yes." Her eyes shone, happier than she'd ever looked. "Not on prom night."

They said one last goodbye, and Brandon walked out of the apartment building barely feeling the floor beneath his feet.

He looked into the night sky as he walked out the front door and jogged down the steps to his waiting SUV. The driver closed the door behind him, and then climbed in the front seat. "A good night, Mr. Paul?"

"Definitely." Brandon settled into the seat,

still warm from being with her. "I went to the prom."

Surprise flashed on the driver's face. "The prom, sir?"

"Yes. With the most beautiful girl in the world."

EIGHT

The magic of Brandon's first night in New York City stayed with Bailey for the next several nights. He managed to be in the audience for each of her performances that week, and on Thursday after the show they stayed at the apartment and watched *Tangled* with Bob and Betty. The Disney animated movie was a takeoff on the old fairytale about Rapunzel.

When the movie was over, Bob and Betty said their goodnights. As soon as they were alone, Brandon led Bailey to the sofa near the glass wall in the Kellers' living room, the one that overlooked the park and the city. "I loved that movie."

"Really?" Bailey was glad. "I wasn't sure. It's sort of a chick flick."

"Not at all." Brandon looked indignant, and his expression made her laugh. The way he always made her laugh. "The chameleon, the horse, the chase scenes. Come on,

Bailey, it was an action movie."

She laughed harder, and then remembered Bob and Betty. They didn't want to keep the older couple awake. "You crack me up."

"Honestly . . . what I loved most was that one line." He turned and faced her, in no hurry. He brought his fingers to her hair and played with a single strand. "The part where she was a princess worth waiting for."

"I liked that part too." She felt her eyes getting lost in his.

"That's you, baby. A princess worth waiting for."

How did he do this, always say exactly the right thing for every moment? "That . . . that means so much."

"It's true." He kissed her forehead, and then leaned back and took her hands in his. His expression grew more serious. "Hey . . . I got a call from my agent today. He's pressing me about the contract."

"Hmm." Bailey didn't want to feel worried, but the look in his eyes told her he was concerned. And if he was even a little bothered by the deal, she would be too. "You were going to tell me details, but we ran out of time the other night."

"The prom was too special for contract talks."

"Contracts and dancing . . . nope." She

laughed a little. "They don't go together."

"But tonight . . ." His smile eased off. "I want your opinion."

"So . . . tell me about it."

Brandon took a long breath, like he was trying to figure out where to begin. "It started with the studio. They offered me a contract for seven movies."

"Seven?" The number was so high. "That's crazy . . . how would they even know what movies you'd want to do that far out?"

"Exactly." He went on for the next fifteen minutes explaining how they struggled with his good-boy image and how they expected him to do edgier movies, pictures that weren't PG or even PG-13. "They think R-rated films win bigger awards and make an actor more legitimate."

"People don't want R-rated movies."

"I told them that. It isn't about what people want." He looked out the window at the city. "It's about what the studio wants, who they want me to be. The image they want me to fit."

"Wow." Bailey felt her heart sink. Was he even entertaining playing a bad boy to please the studio? A sense of panic took hold of her. "You'd think they'd be happy with your image." She gave him a crooked grin. "It's better than it was."

"Exactly." He laughed, but his shoulders slumped forward a little. "It's insane, really. Like they'd rather have me smash drunk with a different girl every night than going to church and dating you."

Something in Bailey's heart bristled. "Is that really how they feel?"

"Pretty much."

Bailey needed a moment to think about that. Now it was her turn to stare out the window. What was she doing in an industry where people looked down on a person's faith and purity? Was she really a light here if that's the way the entertainment world viewed her? She turned back to Brandon, still lost in thought. "I never thought about it before, but maybe that's why Francesca doesn't like me." She lifted one shoulder and let it fall, fighting the defeat welling inside her.

"Maybe." Brandon ran his thumbs along the tops of her hands. "It's certainly not because of your dancing. I've watched you every night this week. You light up the stage more than any dancer out there."

"Really?"

"Definitely."

"Hmm." Bailey settled into a deeper place. "So interesting. The journey of life."

They were silent for a moment, and Bailey

pictured the years ahead. She held a little tighter to Brandon's hands. "Makes me wonder."

"Bailey . . ." He seemed to sense that her thoughts were taking her places he couldn't follow. "There's a point to you being in this business . . . if that's what you're thinking."

"You know me." She looked into his eyes. "Maybe I should go back to Bloomington. Teach at the Christian Kids Theater and forget about New York."

He hesitated just long enough to show his concern. "Teach them for what? So they can grow up and find their way to LA or New York only to walk away because it's tough?" His voice was soothing, without any sort of confrontation. "So they can walk away from an industry that needs them."

"But does it? If the people in charge think less of us because we believe? If they insist on making edgier projects? Do they really need us?"

"Yes." Brandon chuckled, but the sound held no sense of humor. "Don't you see? We need more people like you, more light in this business. Then maybe the tables would turn and the world would know . . ." He paused and released one of her hands. He touched his fingers to her face. "That only when a person's soul is full of God's light can true brilliance happen on the screen. The way it happens when you're in front of an audience or a camera."

She loved him for his response. Without saying a word, she released his other hand and slipped her arms around his neck. "Thank you." She allowed her face to brush against his for a few heartbeats. "I needed that."

"I know." He pressed his forehead to hers and made a silly face. "You were about to pack your bags and run for Indiana."

"Hey." She gave him a sheepish smile. "How do you know me so well?"

"I pay attention." He touched the side of her face again. "Love does that."

They talked a little longer about the movie choices his management and production team had presented him in the last week. He was ten minutes into the discussion again when his eyes darkened some. "They want me to read with a group of girls when I'm back in LA next." He made a frustrated face. "A check on whether I'd have chemistry with any of them."

Bailey's confidence took the hit like a ship tossed against a craggy reef. Moments like this she remembered again that her boyfriend wasn't just any guy pouring out his love and attention on her. He was the nation's top heartthrob, the actor everyone talked about. After Brandon tweeted the other day about taking the most beautiful girl to the prom, Bailey checked the responses. It felt like most of his eight million followers weighed in that Bailey Flanigan was certainly not the most beautiful girl in the world, and that Brandon would be better single. The marriage proposals alone were daunting.

Still, none of that really bothered her. He loved her, she was sure about that. It was this part of his life that was hardest to live with. The fact that the people he trusted, his management team and the studio execs, wanted to pair him up with girls he might have chemistry with. The perfect scenario was the actor who every season, every film, might have a steamy romance with his co-star. That sort of marketing was a studio's dream.

"You're quiet." Brandon studied her, as if he understood what she was feeling. "That bothers you? The girls . . . the chemistry?"

She smiled. "Yeah . . . a little." This didn't surprise her. "It's like your team is setting you up."

"Only if I let it be like that." He took her hands again, his voice strong and sincere. "That's business . . . it's pretend."

She watched him, searching his eyes. "I believe you." And she did. Brandon had no interest in having an affair on set — she knew that. Bailey took a settling breath through her clenched teeth and willed herself to look relaxed, confident.

Bailey had chosen Broadway, but right now she wished she might be asked to the table, as one of the possible leading ladies for Brandon. Again he seemed to know what she was thinking. "Babe, I told them I wanted to do another movie with you. They promised me . . . they're looking for the right script." Nothing about this conversation ruffled him. His eyes danced. "I told them it had to be the perfect love story."

He'd talked about this before, and always Bailey had laughed, not really taking him seriously. But this time she nodded, weighing the possibilities. "I'd like that."

"It'd be amazing." He leaned in slowly and kissed her. "And think . . ." He brought his lips to hers again. "About the hours of rehearsal."

She loved this, the way it felt here beside him on the sofa, here in the late-night peace and sanctity of Bob and Betty's home. But the unsettled pieces of his future stopped her from enjoying the moment completely.

"Bailey . . ." He looked deep into her soul.

"I feel you, baby. Your heart. You don't have to worry. I promise . . ." He framed her face and wove his fingers into her hair. "I won't take a picture that disappoints you . . . or God." He kissed her once more.

Her words didn't come quickly, but they came. "I believe you. I do, Brandon." Her hands were on his shoulders, his muscles taut beneath her fingertips. They shouldn't spend too much longer here. "Thanks for talking . . . for sharing with me."

The fact that he wanted to talk to her about his professional life made her feel closer to him. Like they'd moved past mere magical moments and were headed toward a real connection. A lasting relationship. The feeling both exhilarated and terrified her.

She eased back, and as she did she realized how badly they needed space between them. "I'm getting water." She felt him get up and follow her.

"Me too. Then I should probably go."

This was another thing she appreciated about him. The fact that he knew when it was time to go. She never had to remind him or have that awkward conversation where she stepped back and asked him to respect her. He simply did. It was further proof of the change in him, the way he wanted this relationship to be different than those he'd experienced in the past.

They drank their water in silence and she walked him to the door. "When do you have to let them know? About the contract?"

"Soon." He bit his lip, less confusion in his eyes. "I'll make sure the creative clause gets in there. Where I have final say on the projects we green-light." He stroked her hair lightly, letting his hand rest on her shoulder. "One movie at a time, babe . . . nothing that would hurt me or us." He came closer, his voice quieter. "I promise."

Their goodbye didn't take as long as usual, and after he was gone Bailey could practically feel herself pulling away. What in the world was she doing, dating Brandon Paul? Every movie would involve some girl, some beautiful actress whose chemistry with her boyfriend would have to be practically explosive before the studios would agree to it. That, combined with their efforts to see him be edgier, less faith-driven — who could stand up to that kind of pressure?

She went to her room, dropped to the edge of the bed, and closed her eyes.

I'm in over my head, Lord . . . maybe I shouldn't be dating him.

My daughter . . .

The words were quieter than any she'd

ever heard, but they were spoken and she had to believe this was a direct answer.

Do not fear . . . remember, perfect love drives out fear.

God was reminding her not to look down, not to base her decisions on worldly wisdom. She felt peace settle over her heart and she breathed in.

You're right, God. One day at a time. I can't leave Brandon for something that might happen, for something he might do. After all, that's what Cody did. Walked away over what-ifs and fears.

The answer came in a Scripture she had loved since she was little:

I am with you, daughter. You are never alone. Do not worry about tomorrow . . .

She didn't need to worry because today had enough trouble of its own. She thought about the *Hairspray* production, and the Bible study she still led with several of her castmates . . . the rumors that the show was doomed, Brandon's contract, or the fact that the two of them had to work harder all the time to stay out of the tabloids, to find even a few hours alone each week. Yes, each day had enough trouble of its own. Worrying about tomorrow was pointless.

She crossed the room and sat at the desk opposite her bed. Her laptop was open and she was still signed on to Facebook. Which meant she hadn't been on the computer since she'd returned to New York. Not since her talk with Cody.

With a few clicks she checked posts her Bloomington friends had left in the last week, liking their comments and commenting back to several of them. One comment was from Katy Hart Matthews — her long-ago drama teacher. Katy was married to the Baxter family's oldest son — Dayne Matthews — one of the most famous actors to ever grace the big screen. Her comment was sweet and timely. "Hey girl, when are you going to make a visit to LA? We have a guestroom waiting for you whenever you're out this way next!"

Bailey smiled and liked the post. She thought about the uncertainty of the *Hairspray* show, as beneath it she wrote, "It could be sooner than you think! Keep the room open for me . . . miss you and love you!"

Most nights when she checked Facebook, she didn't think about going to Cody's page. He usually updated it every day or so, but most of the time his words gave very little window to his heart. It was why she hadn't felt closure before their conversation. Nothing he ever said in person or on

Facebook gave her any idea what he was feeling.

But tonight she couldn't stop herself. She typed his name in the search window and in seconds his Facebook profile appeared on the screen. For a long time she only looked at it, stared at his photo. It was an older picture, one from a month ago moments after a big win. Cody was hoisted on the shoulders of his team, all of them gritty with mud and grass and sweat, their smiles brighter than the Friday night lights. Cody Coleman was definitely changing lives at Lyle High. She looked closer, into his eyes. He didn't look miserable, right? Didn't look like he was thinking about her. He'd gotten by without her just fine.

Especially with Cheyenne around.

The other night, Cody seemed ready to deny falling for her, as if he and Cheyenne never had anything serious between them. He'd stopped himself, of course. But whatever their relationship, Bailey couldn't see it lasting. He wasn't in love with the former fiancée of his Army buddy Art. Bailey checked his status update and the posts on his wall. There were dozens of comments after Friday's game — parents and Lyle townspeople congratulating him. But after Monday the posts quieted down. Other than a few comments from students or reporters looking to interview him, his wall hadn't been very active in the last few days.

So what did that mean? Had he really bared his heart that night and then blithely gone back to Cheyenne to continue things with her? Bailey pressed her teeth together and tried not to be frustrated. She had no right wondering about him. She loved Brandon — that was the truth. Cody belonged to her past.

As she clicked back to her own profile page, her phone buzzed. A quick glance and she felt her face light up. The text was from her mom: *You still up?*

Bailey's fingers flew across her phone's keyboard. *Yes . . . hi, Mom. What's happening?*

Nothing . . . her reply came immediately, as if there weren't a thousand miles between them. *Just finished writing an article and I wondered if you were awake. Wanna Skype?*

The idea sounded wonderful. Her mom was just the person she wanted to talk to, and Skype would make it feel like they were together in the same room. She responded in all capital letters: *ABSOLUTELY!!!*

A few seconds later the sound of an incoming call came through Skype. Bailey clicked the Video Chat option and — just like that — her mom appeared on the screen, grinning at her. "I love this."

"I know . . . it's the best thing ever." Bailey was careful to keep the sound turned low, careful to talk in a hushed voice. "The Kellers are asleep."

"It feels like forever since you were here."

"Like Friday was a month ago." Bailey propped her elbow on the desk and leaned the side of her head against her hand. "Brandon's here."

"Right now?" Her mom's eyes sparkled as she pretended to be shocked. "I hope not."

"Not here." Bailey laughed. "He went home half an hour ago."

"You're serious?" She looked surprised. "So he was there till midnight."

"Every day this week." She loved the honest relationship she had with her mom. She would tell her the truth always, even if what she had to say wasn't exactly what her mom wanted to hear. She laughed louder this time. "Don't worry . . . the Kellers have been here."

"With you?" her mom raised an eyebrow.

Bailey laughed. "Most of the time."

"Most?" Now her expression became wide-eyed. Then as if she knew better than to make the matter too lighthearted, her smile faded except in her eyes — where it firmly remained. "I know you, honey. You're being careful . . . I'm sure."

"We are." She leaned back in the desk chair, her eyes never leaving her mom's. She had nothing to hide. "We kiss sometimes, mostly goodbye when he leaves. But he's the first to remember when it's time to go. He won't cross those lines, Mom. He cares too much."

"Good." She didn't look overly relieved. Their relationship had always been this open, and so the news that Brandon respected her came as no real surprise. "Just realize that being together more often makes it easier to let the lines blur."

"Yeah, I felt that tonight. How easy it would be to kiss longer or hang out alone more." She tilted her head. "I feel comfortable around him."

Her mom smiled. "I'm glad. And I'm glad you're both being careful . . . mindful. No one's beyond that sort of temptation if the situation allows it."

Bailey agreed, and she told her mom about Brandon's contract, how he was being urged to sign a major deal and to allow for the possibility that the studio might want him to play darker roles, parts that would curb his good-boy Christian image.

"I'm glad he can talk to you." Her mom

didn't look worried. "Have you prayed for him?"

"About the contract? Yes . . . God keeps telling me not to worry about tomorrow."

"Hmm. So true." Her mom's smile relaxed the fine lines around her eyes. "Today has enough worries of its own."

Bailey wished for a moment she could climb through the screen and be right across from her, the two of them sitting on the living room couch talking. New York was so far away from Bloomington. But this was better than a phone call or a text conversation. "Did I tell you he took me to the prom?"

"I follow him on Twitter . . . so I saw your picture. How did that work out?"

Bailey was glad for the chance to relive the magic of that night. She told her mom about the coats and the sparkling cider, the playlist of songs. "We danced on the roof and it was like . . . I don't know, like a scene from a movie, I guess."

"Very appropriate." Her mom smiled. "I like him, honey. He really cares about you."

"He does." Bailey still had the feeling her mom cared more for Cody. Which was frustrating but understandable, since he'd been a part of their family.

"Have you heard from Cody?"

Bailey grinned and gave a light shake of her head. "Am I that easy to read? Brandon was doing that all night — knowing exactly what I was thinking."

"For people who know you, yes. You're pretty easy to read." A sense of pride shone in her mom's eyes. "But only because you're so honest, Bailey. You are guileless, and so what you think and feel shows up pretty much immediately in your eyes."

"Thanks . . . I think." Bailey laughed. "Anyway, to answer your question, no. I haven't heard from him."

"Which shouldn't surprise you, I guess. You told him you were in love with Brandon."

"I did." She nodded, checking her heart at the same time. "I am."

She and her mom talked a little longer about the past week, how the boys were doing in school, and the way her dad's team, the Colts, were excited about making the playoffs.

"If they keep winning, you'll have to come home again and catch a game."

"I will." She yawned, and after a few minutes they wrapped up their conversation.

Her mom ended the Skype session by going back to the things Bailey had started with. "Listen to the Lord, honey. Don't worry about tomorrow. God will make it all clear." Her smile reached across the internet lines and warmed Bailey's heart. "He always does."

When they hung up, Bailey brushed her teeth and climbed beneath the covers. In the dark, the answers seemed even clearer. She pictured Brandon and felt herself smile as sleep came over her. Because the picture was this:

Brandon and her, dancing under the stars on a New York rooftop, at the best prom a girl could ever wish for.

Nine

The diagnosis filled the room like a black cloud, reaching into every corner, sucking the oxygen from the four walls and dimming the sunlight streaming through the window. Cody wanted to run from the place, find some solitary spot on the trail around Lake Monroe, and cry out to God. How could this happen? Why would He allow Cheyenne to go through yet another trial? And how was he supposed to breathe while the news suffocated him minute by minute?

Cheyenne's tumor was cancerous. The diagnosis was a part of them all now.

He sat beside her in the hospital room, her hand in his. She was awake, staring at the ceiling, weighed down by the same reality that pressed in on him. He leaned against the railing of her bed and watched her, studied the way her eyes looked flat since she'd received the news.

"Chey?" He spoke softly, his voice filled with the question he wanted to ask every few minutes. "You okay?"

"Hmm?" She turned to him. A smile tugged at the corners of her lips, even though it clearly stopped short of reaching her heart. "Yes, Cody. I'm fine."

She wasn't fine. They all knew that much. "How's the headache?"

"Better." A calm resonated from her, one that could only come from the faith still rooted deep within her. "Whatever they're giving me," she looked at the IV pole on the other side of her bed, "it's working."

"Good." Cody shifted, not wanting to let go of her hand, but desperate to be anywhere but here. Anywhere but seated beside the beautiful girl fighting for her life. "Do you need anything?"

"No." Her eyes found his again, and her look was pointed. "You should go . . . get some rest. Take a walk." She hesitated. "You don't have to be here."

"I know that." They'd been over this. "I want to be here."

Tara was at work, where she struggled to get through a day without breaking down. Cody wasn't surprised. Tara hadn't come to terms with the situation. She wanted answers and a cure. Losing Cheyenne after losing her son, Art? The possibility wasn't something she could even remotely believe. Not yet, anyway.

But sooner than later, Cheyenne's diagnosis would catch up with them. The tumor was rooted at the site of Cheyenne's brain injury, but from there it had cast out tentacles, finger-like tumors that over the last month or so had silently taken a sickening hold on her brain stem.

Surgery was scheduled for tomorrow, but Dr. Juarez had been honest: "We won't be able to get the whole tumor." The news came last night. "We'll take what we can, and we'll follow up with large doses of chemotherapy and radiation. There is no cure, so our treatment at best buys us a little time."

She went on to explain that sometimes with a tumor like this, the fingers of the mass were nonresponsive to any treatment. "Six months to a year — that's the best I can give you." She hesitated. "For some people it goes much more quickly."

Six months to a year? Possibly faster? The reality played over in Cody's mind again and again, making him long for something to say, some way to change the conversation or lighten the mood. But there was nothing. The diagnosis said it all.

"I keep thinking about what the doctor said." Cody sighed, and the sound gave a clear picture of his tortured heart. "She said six months to a year was the most she could give us."

"Yes." Again Cheyenne was calm. She looked at Cody again. "That's if the treatment goes well."

"Yeah, but she can't make that determination. I mean . . . I don't like how she said it, you know? How that was all *she* could give." He sat a little straighter, the fight still breathing inside him. "But God is greater than the doctors or the evidence or the research, right? The question isn't how much time the *doctor* can give you, Chey . . . it's how much time *God* will give you."

She didn't respond, didn't add so much as a nod of her head. Instead she looked off toward the window and after a long time she drew a shaky breath. "Do you think I'll see Art first? When I get to heaven?"

The question ripped at Cody's soul. Art had been Cheyenne's fiancé, but the guy had been Cody's best friend during their days in Iraq. A big black guy with massive muscles and a smile that could cut through the desert sand. Art had loved Cheyenne with every breath. Getting home to her, marrying her was the single thing that drove him to fight hard, to keep his head low during every battle.

Tears stung Cody's eyes. "I . . . I'd like to think so." He couldn't stand this, couldn't handle sitting here and watching her give up. "But that doesn't mean you need to go now." He tightened the hold he had on her hand. "You have to fight this, Chey. You're too young . . . you have too much to offer to leave us now."

Cheyenne nodded slowly and turned her eyes to him again. "Thank you, Cody." She looked at him for a long time. "Tell me about your talk with Bailey Flanigan . . . that night, when Tara brought me here."

They'd managed to stay away from that conversation. Cheyenne was in and out of consciousness for the first few days while the doctor tried to regulate her pain medication. Then there'd been the biopsy and the test results. Discussion about Bailey had been the least of their concerns. But here . . . in this moment . . . the fact that Cheyenne wanted to talk about it told him the issue had been on her mind.

"It went well." Details weren't important. The fewer the better, Cody figured. Cheyenne was fighting for her life. She didn't need to know exactly what was said between him and Bailey that night. "We both needed closure . . . about how things ended between us."

Cheyenne smiled, and though she was weak from the medication, she released his hand and brought her fingers to the upper part of his arm. "That night . . . I saw for myself."

A sick feeling filled Cody's gut. "That night?"

"At the game." Her smile warmed, and it was clear that her words were not anchored in jealousy, but rather she seemed to feel an understanding, a sense of peace. "I watched you . . . how you looked for her. When . . . when your eyes met it was like you were the only two people in the stadium." She ran her fingers down his arm in a show of deep friendship rather than anything romantic. Then she took hold of his hand again. "You still love her."

"Cheyenne, that's ridiculous."

"Cody." She shook her head. Her brown eyes radiated a calm that defied logic. "It's okay. God has a plan. He's letting me find my way back to Art . . . and one day, He'll let you find your way back to a love like that."

"That's —"

"Please . . . don't argue." Her smile grew sad. "I'm right." She waited, searching his eyes. "You love me . . . I know that. But not like you love her."

With everything in him Cody wanted to disagree with her, to tell her she was crazy for thinking such a thing. He wanted to remind her that his heart beat for her alone. But he couldn't lie. If things had gone differently this week, by now he might've had this conversation with her — rather than her having it with him.

He hung his head and felt fresh tears again. He didn't want to cry, didn't want to give her even the slightest sign that she was right. But he couldn't stop himself. As he looked up, he blinked away the wetness that blurred his view of her. "I do love you, Chey . . . I'm not going anywhere." He gritted his teeth, summoning his determination like never before. "We're going to pray and believe and you're going to fight this cancer. You're a fighter, Chey." He felt a single tear slide down his left cheek. "Look at the battles you've already survived."

"Yes." She nodded and her eyes welled up too. "But don't you see, Cody? No one . . . no one on earth will ever love me like Art Collins loved me. And now," she smiled despite the tears that fell onto her cheeks. "Now God's going to let us spend eternity together. Working for Him . . . worshiping

Him. How could I argue with that plan?"

Again he wanted to fight with her, correct her, and tell her that she was wrong about this, that God would never intend for her to be gone from this earth so soon when she had so much to give. But he couldn't argue with one point: how much Art had loved her. And that in heaven, at least the two of them would be together forever.

The way they had missed out on here.

He hung his head once more, too overwhelmed to speak. The sadness of the situation — the whole situation — was almost more than he could bear. Tomorrow Cheyenne would have brain surgery so they could remove a part of the vicious tumor. He still didn't understand how a person could develop cancer at the site of an injury without the two being connected. But Dr. Juarez was right — Cody had googled Cheyenne's type of cancer. Science had yet to prove a connection. "For now we have to consider it a coincidence." She had given them a skeptical look. "But it's a coincidence we see a little too often."

It didn't really matter.

Chey had incurable cancer, a terminal illness that would cut her life short unless God granted them a miracle. And in the midst of it all she was thinking about him and Bailey, how he'd given himself away at last week's football game. He'd done her more harm than good by sticking around when he still had feelings for Bailey. She didn't need to feel like anyone's pity project. Cheyenne was far too valuable for that. He lifted his head and found her looking at him.

"Don't, Cody . . . don't be hard on yourself." Her kindness was otherworldly, as if it came from a place beyond herself. "I'm not hurt by the way you feel for her. Any more than you should be upset with me for the love I still have for Art." Her serene expression said she had already resolved this. "Life's like that sometimes." She withdrew her hand and folded her arms over her chest. "We came into each other's lives for a reason; I have to believe that. Maybe so we could heal after our previous losses. Or maybe so God could build our faith stronger in light of the struggles we had to face together."

Struggles that were only now beginning, Cody wanted to say. But instead he nodded. "I believe that, too. I know God brought us together."

A knowing look cast shadows in her eyes and Cody could practically read her thoughts. Because at this point all that mattered was the obvious battle that lay ahead.

"You don't have to stay." A flicker of hurt flashed in her eyes and then was gone. "I have Tara. This isn't your problem."

The embers of anger fanned into flames within Cody's soul. He pushed back from the bed, stood, and walked to the door. For a long time he stared at the exit, wanting desperately to take her up on her offer, to leave and not look back and thereby somehow avoid the pain ahead. But he didn't have it in him. He'd walked away before — where Bailey was concerned. Walked as a way of surviving what seemed like certain defeat.

He wouldn't do it again.

With every bit of strength he possessed, he turned and walked slowly back to her bedside. "I don't know what God has ahead." He pressed his lips together, fighting a wave of tears that could've dropped him to his knees. "And the love we have for each other might be different from the way we've loved before." He shifted, struggling. "But I'm not leaving you, Chey. This battle . . . this cancer . . . we'll fight it together."

She waited, watching him, and then finally, almost imperceptibly, she nodded. "Okay. As long as you know you can leave. Any time."

It was something she couldn't do — leave the battle ahead. "I told you . . . I'm not going anywhere."

This time she didn't argue. She only smiled and closed her eyes. "I'm tired, Cody . . . if it's okay, I'm going to sleep."

He lowered himself to the chair by her bedside again. "That's fine . . . get some rest. You'll need it so you can fight." He hesitated. "And you will fight it, Chey."

Her response never came. She was already asleep.

TEN

Ashley had fifteen minutes before the family would arrive for their annual Christmas celebration and she couldn't move fast enough — setting the table and moving dishes from the oven to the stovetop. Cole vacuumed the living room where baby Janessa had just spilled a cup of dry Cheerios, and Devin busied himself stirring the banana cream pie filling on the other side of the kitchen.

Landon had been in his room for the past hour, and in his absence a slight bit of frustration crept in and colored Ashley's Christmas spirit gray. Yes, Landon was struggling. That much was obvious. But God provided him purpose a little more every week. Even in the face of the lung disease, he would battle the rest of his life.

At least he hadn't been given a terminal diagnosis. The fight wasn't against polymyositis, but rather against COPD — constrictive obstructive pulmonary disease. But even so, the illness would prevent him from doing the thing he loved most about work — fighting fires. So yes, Ashley understood when Landon was quieter than usual, when he wasn't his usual cheerful, helpful self.

But this was Christmastime. If he couldn't help, he could at least keep her company. Something moved behind her, and she turned around. "Devin, I still need you to —"

Suddenly he stood before her: Landon. The man she had loved as long and far back as she could remember. "Hey."

"Hey." Her frustration eased.

"I thought maybe you could use some help."

She set her pot holders down beside the stove and came to him, slipping her arms around his waist. "I was just thinking about you."

"The house looks amazing." The look in his eyes was familiar, the look of confidence and love and assurance. All of which had been missing in varying degrees since he began struggling with his lungs.

"Thanks. The kids helped." She allowed no accusation in her tone, but she looked deep into his eyes, wondering. "You've been gone for awhile. Everything okay?"

"I was reading the Bible. The story of Job."

"Nice." Ashley smiled. "Especially at Christmas."

"Yeah, I know." He chuckled easily, and again he seemed more himself. "But I needed to read it. I think God had a Christmas present waiting for me between the lines."

"Hmmm." Ashley understood. "We haven't had things as bad as Job. That's for sure."

"Right. And if Job could thank God and look for God's plans even in the ashes of his life . . ." Landon gave her a crooked grin. "I guess I can be finished moping around and believe the same thing."

"So you're back . . . is that what you're saying?" She kept her tone light, flirting with him, teasing to keep the moment from overwhelming her.

"Yes, Ash . . ." He ran his hands along her back, his eyes locked on hers. "I'm back, and I'm sorry. I'm ready to live. I promise."

Hope soared through her. Every day she had prayed that though a lung disease had taken Landon's ability as a firefighter, it wouldn't take the beauty of his soul, the man God had made him to be.

She pulled herself close to him and gently laid her head on his chest. His heart beat strong and steady, the way he had always been before this season in his life. And now . . . now he was back. The Landon she loved and longed for. "That . . ." She lifted her eyes to his and saw that his were watery, same as hers. "That is the best Christmas present ever."

The doorbell rang and from the other room Devin cried out. "They're here, Mommy . . . everyone's here! It's Christmastime!"

"Get the door, sweetie . . . I'll be right there." She kept her eyes on Landon, seeing him the way he had been and wanting this moment to last longer because of it. She ignored the sounds of her sisters coming through the front door, as she worked her hands into Landon's hair and pulled him to her. It didn't last long, but their kiss was rich and passionate, filled with promise. Ashley smiled. "I'm glad you're back."

"Me too." He kissed her this time, and they were still standing in each other's arms when Kari appeared in the doorway of the kitchen and cleared her throat. "I guess you two are in charge of the mistletoe."

Ashley and Landon laughed as they separated. Ashley hugged her older sister and Landon shook hands with Kari's husband, Ryan. "Another Christmas," he glanced at

Ashley, the moment between them still unbroken. "Maybe the best."

"Definitely." Ryan held a box of sparkling cider bottles. He moved past Landon to set it down and at the same time, the doorbell rang again. Over the next ten minutes everyone arrived.

The old Baxter house practically sang with the sounds of the family all gathered under one roof again. Ashley worked with her sisters and Luke's wife, Reagan, along with her dad's wife, Elaine, to get dinner on the table. As she did she remained mindful of how precious this time was. Nothing about life could be taken for granted.

If her mother had lived, this would've been her favorite day of the year, coming back to the Baxter house for a Christmas gathering that included every one of her kids and their spouses and families. Even Dayne and Katy had made it back in time, and they arrived with little Sophie well before dinner was served.

"Getting out of LA could almost kill the Christmas spirit in anyone." Dayne laughed as they took off their coats and rolled up their sleeves. "But I would've walked to find my way back here."

Katy grinned at him. "Sophie kept saying how we were flying away to find Christmas."

"I like that." Cole walked through the kitchen with Janessa on his hip. "When we're all here . . . in this house . . . we can always find Christmas. No matter what." He looked at Landon. "Right, Dad?"

His question brought instant tears to Ashley's eyes. Kids understood so much more than they let on. In the months of Landon's discouragement, Cole had said very little about the health concerns his father faced. He didn't complain at all about the change in Landon's personality. But here, in the heart of December, he sensed something had happened to restore Landon to his old self.

That somehow his dad had found Christmas.

Finally they reigned in the kids, whose laughter made the perfect backdrop to the night's beginning. As they sat down, Brooke was in the midst of telling a story about a patient who came in for routine blood work, scared to death something was wrong.

"His results were perfect, so I called him myself, rather than wait for the lab. Just to set his mind at ease — especially at Christmas." Brooke spoke loud enough to be heard above the hustle of people moving in and taking their seats. "So I call the guy — and remember he's like eighty-five — and I get his voicemail."

Ashley loved how Brooke could tell a story. She had a way of getting the whole family laughing. Brooke helped her youngest daughter Hayley slide into the seat beside her, never losing a beat in her story. "So I'm talking to his answering machine, and I tell him his test results were perfectly normal and that he should have a good Christmas and not worry, and then just before I finish leaving the message, the girls walk in and they're trying to talk to me about what to wear for tonight's party, and Peter yells from the other room that he can't find his dress pants, and all of a sudden I hear myself finish the message by saying, 'All right, well I love you. Talk to you soon.' "

"What?" Luke looked like he might fall out of his chair. "You said that?"

"Yep." Brooke gave a confident nod. "To a patient."

"The poor guy probably had to take an extra nitroglycerin pill when he listened to his messages that night," Peter laughed. "I mean, you get a beautiful young doctor saying she loves you? Come on . . . talk about your Christmas presents."

They all laughed again, and Devin raised his hand, his expression as earnest as it was confused. "So Aunt Brooke, does that mean you really love him?"

A few of the older kids laughed, but Cole took the lead. He was thirteen now and more patient with Devin. "Buddy, that's the point. Aunt Brooke doesn't really love him. She was just distracted because of Uncle Peter and Maddie and Hayley, and she accidentally said she loved him."

"But . . ." Devin still looked baffled. "If you tell someone you love them, doesn't that mean you have to love them always?"

Ashley swapped a look with Landon, and the tenderness of the moment wasn't missed between them or among the other adults at the table. Cole looked at Ashley's dad. "Papa . . . you wanna help me out here?"

Their father, John Baxter, stifled a laugh and then cleared his throat, his eyes intent on Devin's. "You're right, Dev, but here's the thing. Aunt Brooke didn't really mean it. She said it on accident. See?"

It took a few seconds, but then Devin's eyes lit up. "Ooooh. Like a 'stake."

"Yes." Landon added his voice to the mix. "Like a mistake."

"Which is why," Ashley's dad smiled at Devin, "we never want to tell someone we love them unless we really mean it."

"Because love is forever and always."

186

Devin gave a firm nod. "Right people?"

A chorus of affirmations came from around the table.

The conversation hit a natural break, and Ashley sensed Landon sitting up a little straighter. "I have some good news . . . I thought I'd share it with everyone . . . since we're all together."

Ashley met his eyes but his look told her she didn't need to worry about whatever was coming. The others leaned in — listening, waiting.

"Did you save more people in a fire, Uncle Landon?" Luke's son Tommy asked the question innocently, his eyes wide and round.

Ashley felt the loss of Landon's position with the fire department sharper than she'd felt it in months. An awkwardness came over the room, as if everyone knew he was feeling the same way. But he only smiled at their young nephew.

"Not this time." He looked around the room. "The good news is that I've been asked to lead a task force helping kids stay away from drugs. It's an aggressive approach." He grinned at Tommy. "And yes . . . your Uncle Landon will be saving lives again, buddy. Real soon."

"Landon . . ." Ashley forgot about her

family all around them. "You didn't tell me . . ."

"I know." His smile was more genuine than it had been in months. "I wanted it to be a surprise."

"That's the best Christmas present ever." She turned and threw her arms around his neck. "Seriously, Landon."

Around the room the others clapped and cheered and Cole and Devin and Tommy ran up and joined the group hug.

Across the room Ashley caught her dad wiping at a few errant tears. "Merry Christmas, indeed." He grinned at Ashley. "God is good."

The rest of the night seemed a little brighter, a little more meaningful. The Baxters had always been open about their love for each other, and this Christmas celebration was no exception. In fact, when Devin opened his present from his Uncle Ryan and Aunt Kari, he ran up to them and looked them straight in their eyes. "Thanks, guys. I love you." Then he'd follow that up by saying, "I mean it for real." He did the same after opening every gift that night.

When the presents were opened, Ryan brought out the newest *Sports Illustrated*. "I never thought I'd see our own Cody Coleman on the cover of *SI*." He held it up for the others. "The reporter did a phenomenal job capturing small town football and Cody's heart." Ryan looked at the cover, his face basking in pride. "I feel honored to know Cody — the man he is and the distance he's come since his days at Clear Creek."

"Why don't you read it to us?" Their dad sat beside Elaine, his arm around her, contentment filling his eyes. "I used to read you kids a story every time we gathered for Christmas. Maybe you could do the honors this time, Ryan."

The others added their agreement, and Ryan grinned. "I'd love to. Any time the Christmas story involves football count me in." He held up the article and found the beginning. Then he read about the trials and struggles of the Lyle Buckaroos, a small town football team down on its luck, coming off a handful of winless seasons.

"Before Cody Coleman, the prayers of the players and families and townspeople had grown cold. All except the prayers of one high school junior, DeMetri Smith." Ryan took his time, telling the story the way it deserved to be told. "Not a day went by through three losing seasons when DeMetri didn't pray for his team, for God to work a miracle among them.

"The answer began to come into focus one day last spring. The day Cody Coleman showed up for the assistant coach's position."

The room fell silent, adults and children alike hanging on the story. The children too young to understand were cuddled up close to their parents, so that only the sound of the crackling fire and Ryan's voice filled the room. He went on to read about Cody's decision to coach at Lyle and his discovery that the team faced many struggles. Big struggles. "The cancer battle of one player's sister, the loss of homes for other players, kids struggling with grades. And of course DeMetri's struggle."

Ryan continued, reading about DeMetri's homelessness and Cody's intervention. "The team came together at camp, and one by one the boys found strength and faith to help each other, to tackle their troubles. DeMetri called it a series of miracles."

Ultimately the quest for greatness in the strength of God led the Buckaroos to the state title game and the most storybook finish ever: a winning touchdown by DeMetri Smith. "By the way," Ryan continued as he finished reading the story, "Smitty, as he's known by the team, won't be running touchdowns next year. He'll be touching hearts in his new role: that of a Bible student on a quest to be a pastor, so that he might spread the hope and kindness that Cody Coleman brought to him in this, the most unlikely season ever."

For a solid minute after Ryan closed the cover and lowered the magazine, no one spoke. Ashley could see why. Like her, they were all fighting tears, wrapped up in the emotion the article stirred in them all. Ryan was the first to talk, and then only through a voice strained with unshed tears. "That . . ." He hesitated, holding up the magazine once more. "Is why I coach football. So that somewhere along the way I might have the privilege of making an impact on one or two Cody Colemans . . . and in the process, watch that player grow into a man who will make the same difference in the life of a group of kids like the Buckaroos."

"It's why any of us do anything." Ashley's dad slid to the edge of the sofa and looked around the room. "It's why Katy and Dayne make films with a message of faith and it's why Brooke and Peter practice medicine . . . why Kari spends her days homeschooling and being a team mom for the kids at Clear Creek." He took his time. Over the years Ashley's dad had done this, found a reason to single each of them out in front of the group. His words were a gift more precious than anything they could wrap and put under the tree. "It's the reason Ashley paints and the reason Landon has accepted a new position helping out with drug intervention at the local schools." He smiled at Landon. "Because all of you want to touch lives somehow, because you hope you'll impact a Cody Coleman along the way."

Ashley could've jumped up and hugged her dad. His words were exactly what Landon needed to hear, and they would only serve to validate Landon's determination to be joyful in light of his new life and new limitations. Her dad looked across the room at her sister Erin. "Changing lives is the reason Erin and Sam put their family first, and the reason Luke practices law, the reason all four of them believe in adoption. All so that we might make a difference." He sat back and smiled at Elaine and then the others. "The way Cody made a difference this year."

Again the group was quiet, caught up in the gift their dad had just given them, the gift of his powerful affirmation. But the silence didn't last long. Janessa pointed to the kitchen. " 'Nana pie, Mommy. 'Nana pie?"

"Banana pie," Devin patted her tiny wrist. "It's called banana pie."

The adults gathered everyone back to the table. Erin and Brooke had each brought something to share for dessert. Erin made her mother-in-law's famous chocolate cake, and Brooke pulled a huge casserole of deep-dish apple pie from a warming bag. "Mom's favorite."

There was a time when a statement like that might've caused an awkward silence, a moment when people might look at Elaine and wonder if she was bothered by the reminder of Elizabeth Baxter. But they had moved past that sort of moment years ago. Elaine moved toward the dish with a pie server. "Your mom would slice apples all day, removing every bit of peeling." She smiled at Brooke. "Perfect choice, sweetheart."

By the end of the night, they were caught up on everyone's lives and happy to have spent this Sunday before Christmas with each other. Each family packed up their presents and empty dishes, and after a long round of hugs and picture taking, the house was finally quiet again. Landon helped Ashley tuck the kids in, and sat with her while she gave Cole a brief backrub during their goodnight prayers. This time — for the first night in a long time — Landon led the prayer. The way he used to.

"Lord, thank You for this Christmas celebration. The chance to get together with our family and remember once again the love of the Baxters and the way it has changed all of us over the years." He opened his eyes just long enough to swap a look with Ashley. "Thank You that Christmas has come again, and thank You for being in our midst. We know that the greatest gifts of all are those that cannot be wrapped, cannot be placed under the tree. And so we thank You for life and second chances and healing." He paused, his tone rich with emotions that knew no end. "Thank You for love. In Jesus' name, amen."

When he opened his eyes he told each of the kids that he loved them, and Ashley did the same. As they left the boys' room, Devin said one last thing.

"I love you too, Mommy and Daddy. I mean it for real."

Landon smiled at Ashley as he looked back at their youngest son once more. "Thank you, buddy. I love you for real too."

They put Janessa into bed in her room down the hall and walked back to the family room a few minutes later. Ashley held tight to Landon's arm, pressing in against him as they headed for their room. For a long moment she wished she could go back in time and thank Job — a man she hadn't thought much about before today. For the truth was, Job's faithfulness in the face of utter devastation had given them all hope this special Christmas season. And that hope had given them love.

As real as it had ever been.

ELEVEN

His work on the set of the new movie was better than anything Brandon had ever done. He could feel the difference with every scene, every take. As if God had allowed him to raise his game despite the fact that his image remained squeaky clean. If his management team thought he needed the bad-boy reputation to be taken seriously, then God would help him prove otherwise.

The days blended one into the other, and the nights were a string of beautiful moments with Bailey until finally it was Christmas Eve. Neither he nor Bailey could get away to celebrate. Bailey had a show every night including Christmas, and his shooting schedule allowed only Christmas Day off. Since they couldn't be back in Bloomington with her family, the two of them made plans to spend Christmas dinner with Bob and Betty.

Brandon wrapped up the last scene of the day, a chase through the streets of the financial district. Police had closed off Wall Street just after three that afternoon so they could film without distraction. By then most of the business people had gone home to celebrate Christmas Eve. Brandon's workouts with his trainer had been intense, but good for him. He could see the difference in the definition of his arms, and he could sense it in the way he could run faster without getting winded.

The way he had to run for this scene.

"Okay, let's go through it one more time." The director was a perfectionist, a man who typically got what he was looking for from his actors without having to do a dozen takes. This shot was no exception. They'd run it three times, and already Brandon felt like they'd gotten amazing footage. The director clearly agreed. Through the megaphone he shouted, "I think we have what we need, but I'd like to be sure."

Brandon loved this role. A college kid who has the chance to turn his life around by helping the government bring down a terrorist cell in the heart of New York City. He was the last guy they would've expected to be spying on them, the last person any terrorist would've thought might be relaying information back to authorities. He was too young, too fresh looking. His smile too sincere.

But that only gave him greater permission to be where he might never otherwise have been. In this scene he had information that needed to get in the hands of the government, but finally one of the terrorists was onto him. It was one of the final scenes of the movie — something they'd shot out of order because this was the best day to close down Wall Street.

"Places!" The director held up both hands. "Quiet on the set." He laughed into the speaker. "As quiet as we can get it."

The sounds of city traffic never let up, but people found their places and at the director's cue, Brandon began running. He looked over his shoulder — first one way, then the other, running faster, faster . . . until suddenly one of the terrorists stepped out right in front of him and grabbed his shoulder. "Not this time." The man gave Brandon a violent shake. "You know what happens to people who tell on us?"

Brandon looked like he might give up, but then at the last possible moment he kneed the bad guy in the crotch and sped off even faster than before down a side street. When he was out of sight the director yelled again.

"Cut! Best take yet." He paused. "Okay, everyone. Go celebrate whatever it is you celebrate."

A smile flashed across Brandon's face. The director was a self-proclaimed atheist. But around Brandon he seemed softer toward the idea of God. Especially since it was Christmas.

He said goodbye to the cast and decided to walk back to his place at the Ritz. The beard he sometimes used as a disguise would work as long as he could slip out the back of the trailer and into another couple trailers before heading toward Central Park. Fans had gathered around the movie location most of the day, but Brandon made his move to the food trailer quickly and hung out there for a while before slipping into the beard and a ratty jacket. He topped off the look with a worn derby hat, something actors from the forties might have worn.

"That should do the trick." Dennis Sceptor played the lead FBI official. Dennis had been a much sought-after actor back in the day, and even still he had the ability to draw screams from the crowd in New York City.

"I hope so." Brandon grinned at him and tugged on the beard. "As long as no one does this to me."

"Here." Dennis stood and led the way to

the door. "Get your things. Leave with me. They'll figure you're an assistant producer or a grip. Someone behind the scenes."

Brandon loved the idea. He gathered his things and slung his bag across his chest. "Let's do this."

The gruffness of Dennis Sceptor gave way to a lighthearted chuckle. "You make the rest of us feel young again."

"Come on, Dennis. What are you? Like twenty-nine? You're one of the youngest guys here."

"Yeah, Merry Christmas to you too." He laughed again and with that they walked out of the trailer.

The key to making this work was Brandon's ability to carry himself confidently, not like someone slinking off down a side street. He held his head high, the beard tickling his neck. As they came into view, a couple dozen diehard fans let up a murmur, and then in a sort of chain reaction they recognized Dennis and began calling his name. The actor made a big show of stopping to shake Brandon's hand, pat him on the shoulder and wish him a loud Merry Christmas. "Back at work on the twenty-sixth. You're the best editor in the business . . . better get ready for some major editing!" Dennis practically shouted as he took a few steps away from Brandon and toward the crowd.

Brandon laughed to himself as he waved. "I'm ready!"

With that he moved easily toward the street and the sidewalk, his pace even and unrushed, head high. For the first ten yards he held his breath, wondering if they would actually buy the act. But with Dennis headed their way and ready to sign autographs, the crowd didn't look back at the guy they assumed was an editor.

Brandon would have to thank his friend later.

For now the ruse allowed him the freedom to walk along the streets of New York City like any other business guy or tourist. Someone walked past without so much as a second glance. Brandon breathed deeply, loving the anonymity. As much as he enjoyed acting, as greatly as God had blessed his time in Hollywood, he hated that he couldn't go anywhere unrecognized without a huge effort. It was part of his life, but even so he relished moments like this.

The solitude allowed him to think about the one thing that was never far from his mind: his feelings for Bailey Flanigan. Lately he'd taken to using a phrase when it came to their time each night, the way they kept in touch through the day. They were *doing life together.*

The most normal things — having lunch and talking about his contracts, getting together for dinner after her show, or watching a movie. These were the details that made up other people's relationships. But they hadn't been possible until now for him and Bailey. All of which led him to think even deeper as he walked toward Central Park this Christmas Eve.

In a few weeks the movie would wrap and he'd head back to California. And what then? Would Bailey's time on Broadway continue or would the show run its course and close down? Whatever happened, Brandon knew this much. He wanted to do life with Bailey long after he went back to LA.

Father, I love her . . . I want her to be a part of my life forever.

The prayer lifted from his heart, and Brandon waited. But no answer spoke to him. None except a sudden crazy impulsive idea. It was Christmas Eve, after all. He'd bought Bailey a diamond bracelet — something simple and classy and understated — perfect for her. But that didn't mean he couldn't buy her another gift, right?

He picked up his pace and dug his hands deep into the pockets of the raggedy jacket.

They were old enough. The love they shared was something they both felt strongly about. So why wait? Why put themselves through years of dating and struggling to find times on the same coast? He could ask her tonight and then sometime next summer they could get married.

Is there a reason, God . . . a reason why I shouldn't ask her to marry me tonight? On Christmas eve?

Again he waited, and again there was no response. But as Brandon walked a light snow began to fall. He stopped and looked straight up. The snow had to be a sign. God was blessing his idea, setting the stage for the most amazing night ever. The night he would ask Bailey Flanigan to be his wife.

It wouldn't be hard. He could go to Tiffany's on the way home, look for their most beautiful ring — the only one fitting for a girl like Bailey. He would use his debit card and then if it wasn't what she wanted, they could come back and pick out what she liked better. He could get a horse-drawn carriage and take her to the Empire State Building again. And this time instead of talking about the view he would wait until they were alone on the top floor and he'd drop to one knee.

A hundred years would never be long

enough with her, so why would he consider leaving New York without asking the question? The one question that had drifted through his mind nearly every time they were together lately. Especially now, after she'd had her big conversation with Cody. If she could do that, and if she could still return to him completely sure of her love, then she had to be ready. She was twenty-two and he was twenty-four. The perfect age to make this decision — perfect for the two of them, anyway.

His heart pounded to the rhythm of his feet against the wet pavement. The snow wasn't sticking yet, but it would. The temperature was supposed to drop into the twenties tonight, making the promise of a white Christmas all but guaranteed. He didn't notice anyone who walked past him, barely noticed the stoplights and street signs. Instead he saw only the colors of Christmas — the displays and brilliantly decorated trees and sparkling garland — as if all of New York City was throwing a Christmas party to celebrate his decision.

He walked quicker than before. Tiffany & Co. was just a block ahead. The timing was perfect. He would carry the ring with him to her show and afterwards . . . well, afterwards every moment would be like something from the best love story ever filmed.

He pressed ahead and then just when the plan seemed beyond destined, he reached the front door of Tiffany's. It took a minute to understand why the lights were off, why the door was locked.

"No!" He groaned the word out loud. "Come on!" He knocked on the window. "You can't be closed. Not tonight . . ."

In the movies, of course, Tiffany & Co. would stay open until midnight on Christmas Eve. But here on Fifth Avenue, the staff clearly had real lives. The place must've closed at four o'clock, like most boutiques on Fifth Avenue. He slumped against the door and peered through the darkened glass. The place was empty.

"Really?" He gave the door a final single knock. "It isn't supposed to work like this." He stepped back and looked up into the snow, into the darkening sky. "What next, God?"

He leaned his back against the pale brick that made up the outside of the jewelry store and waited. This time an answer formed deep inside his soul, an answer that seemed to come up time and again in his Bible reading lately.

Be still, my son . . . be still and wait on me.

Brandon felt the disappointment to the

depths of his heart. He didn't want to be still and he certainly didn't want to wait. As he slipped his hands in his pockets and as he started out, a noise sounded at the door behind him. He turned, and from the dark store came a handsome, elderly man. The scene felt almost surreal, snow falling on the empty New York City Fifth Avenue, the kind-looking man stepping out of what moments ago had seemed like a deserted Tiffany's.

"Hello." The man's eyes were full of light. He studied Brandon, shielding his face from the falling snow. "Were you the one knocking?"

"I was." Brandon hesitated because this was about the time when most people would recognize him and react. Even before now. But the man seemed to see him only as an unfortunate customer. Brandon exhaled. "You must work here?"

"I do." He smiled, unhurried. "I'm the assistant manager." He looked over his shoulder and then back at Brandon. "You were looking for a Christmas gift?"

Brandon enjoyed this, the chance to be like any other customer. "An engagement ring."

"Hmm." The man's eyes sparkled. He reached out and shook Brandon's hand.

"I'm Bill Dillman. The guards have gone home. I've locked everything and set the alarm. Otherwise I'd let you take a look."

"Brandon," he introduced himself in return, skipping his last name. "And that's okay." Brandon leaned his shoulder into the brick wall, and brushed the snow off his arms. "It was sort of an impulsive decision."

"Ahh, yes." Bill nodded, his expression more lit up than before. "Do you love her? The young lady?"

"I do." Brandon didn't need to think about his answer.

"Then God will let you know when the time is right." The man looked well beyond retirement years. He had a head of white hair and weathered skin, but he was the picture of health. Vibrant and sharp as anyone half his age. "Love is an amazing thing, young man. I've been married to my bride Barbara more than sixty years now. We've followed God from one season to the next." He winked at Brandon. "Now that I'm off work, I suppose I can say that."

"I'm a Christian also. So's the girl I love. Her name's Bailey."

"Bailey." Bill smiled. "Pretty name."

"She's a pretty girl. Inside and out." Brandon wasn't in a hurry either. Besides, how often did he have the chance to talk to a man married six decades, a Christian man? "So . . . what's your secret? Being happily married so long?"

The man leaned on the point of his umbrella, using it like a cane. "Keep Christ at the center." His eyes grew distant, like he was seeing the love of a lifetime play out in his mind. "I've always been in sales." His smile warmed his face again. "Barbara used to say I could sell snow to an Eskimo."

Brandon laughed quietly at the picture, appreciating Bill Dillman more with every passing minute.

"But it was never the sales that made life beautiful. It was serving as a deacon at church and singing in the gospel quartet. Sharing Bible studies with my dear Barbara and standing beside her when . . ." His smile waned. For a long moment he was quiet and in the fading snowy twilight tears gathered in his eyes. "When I began to lose her." He found Brandon's eyes again. "Alzheimer's struck early, but she's still my love. As long as God gives us today."

"I'm sorry . . . about Barbara." Brandon felt the rest of the city fade away. All his life he would remember this chance meeting with the godly assistant manager of the famed New York jewelry store. A man too far along in years to know about Brandon's fame or maybe even to care. "So . . . maybe you could do me a favor."

"I'd love to." Bill's smile was back, laced with the sort of sadness that came with great reflection and long-ago Christmas memories.

"Can you pray for us . . . for Bailey and me?" He felt his own smile turn a little sheepish. "Tonight would've been impulsive, for sure." His hesitation allowed a depth to fill his tone. "But I do want to marry her."

Bill nodded. "I will. In fact, I'll do that right now." He came closer and put his hand firmly on Brandon's shoulder.

The man couldn't know the gift he was giving. Brandon closed his eyes and felt a rush of peace. As if the Holy Spirit's presence was as real around them as the snow.

"Father, You brought Brandon and me together this Christmas Eve and we acknowledge that no appointments are by accident. I ask a special blessing on Brandon and his girl, Bailey. If marriage is in Your will, Lord, then show Brandon the timing. And grant him a magical night . . . even if it doesn't include a proposal just yet. Stay in the middle of them, dear God. Thank You for being gracious enough to listen. In the name of Jesus, amen."

"Amen." Brandon opened his eyes, and

took the slightest step back. "Thank you, Bill."

"Well," he looked at his watch. "I need to get home to Barbara. The staff where she lives . . . they're expecting me."

Brandon was touched to the depths of his soul. "Yes . . . you better get going then." He took a step back and waved. "It was an honor meeting you."

"And you." He winked once more. "I'll be praying for you and Bailey." With that he opened his umbrella, waved in return, and headed down Fifth Avenue in the falling snow.

Brandon drew a long breath and thought about what had just happened. He wouldn't have been surprised if he stopped in at Tiffany's tomorrow only to find that there never had been a Bill Dillman at all, that the gentleman had been a Christmas angel instead. The impact of their conversation was that strong. Bill Dillman and his precious Barbara . . . years in a home for Alzheimer's patients — her memory gone, but not the love of her life. He would stand by her until he drew his last breath. Brandon had no doubt.

Because it was the sort of love he wanted to have one day. The kind he wanted to share with Bailey.

He wouldn't ask her to marry him tonight, but after talking to Bill, he had a peace about the timing . . . and whatever lay ahead. He dug his hands deep into his pockets and trudged back toward Park Avenue and his room at the top of the Ritz. Fine. If the Lord wanted him to wait, he'd wait. But not for long. He had no intention of heading back to LA without at least a plan — a way and a when as to how he was going to ask her the question burning in his mind.

He changed clothes and called for his ride so he could get to her show early — the way he always did. And again she gave a tremendous performance. Brandon watched her, mesmerized by her. Bailey defined beauty, not just because of the way she looked dancing across the stage, but because of her heart. The way she loved.

After the show and after they signed autographs at the stage door, the cast shared an impromptu Christmas party in the green room, where even Francesca Tilly, the show's director, joined them. "Best to enjoy our time together," she said with a broad smile. "You never know if we'll have another Christmas together."

Brandon shared a quick look with Bailey. The woman always found a way to put a damper on a moment. But being with Bailey, sharing Christmas Eve with her, meant that even Francesca's splash of reality couldn't darken the moment.

After the party, several of the cast asked to join Brandon and Bailey for the Christmas Eve service at St. Thomas Episcopal Church ten blocks away, back on Fifth Avenue. Bailey's castmates Gerald and Stefano especially wanted to go. "I've never set foot in a church." Gerald uttered a nervous laugh. "I figure this is as good a night as any to give it a try."

Brandon knew about Bailey's Bible study with her cast, how they met at Starbucks every Wednesday morning, and how they tackled topics most people feared to touch: issues about sin struggles and finding freedom in Christ. He couldn't have been more proud of her, the fact that her life and her love for Jesus had reached these two men and three of the women in the cast so strongly that they actually wanted to attend a Christmas Eve service.

At eleven-thirty, when there wasn't a single fan left milling outside the theater, Brandon took Bailey's hand in his. "Let's start walking." The two of them wore their "prom" coats, and the rest of the cast was prepared as well, dressed warmly enough to handle the walk, regardless of the winter night.

Outside the theater, the snow fell heavier than before, and the streets were emptying fast. A perfect setup, Brandon reminded himself. It would've been a great night to ask Bailey to marry him. But instead they would spend their evening with Gerald and Stefano and the other dancers. The way God clearly intended for this night.

Along the way they laughed and remembered funny moments from the night's show. And halfway to the church Gerald fell quieter than the rest. "I wish . . . I wish Chrissy was here."

Brandon held tighter to Bailey's hand. "I'm sure . . . you all wish that."

"Yes." Bailey's eyes glossed over a little. "She would've been with us tonight."

Chrissy had been a dancer on the cast, and late last summer she'd collapsed during a performance and died later that night. Too many years of crash dieting, too many pills to maintain an energy level she simply didn't have. Brandon looked at Bailey and spoke to her in a whisper. "You okay?"

"Yes." She smiled up at him through sad eyes. "I miss her . . . but I learned so much from her, Brandon. You know?"

Again Brandon felt the pride in his heart

well up. The girl beside him understood God so much better than most people. She wasn't perfect, but she was perfectly committed to living her life for the Lord. Sharing her heart and soul with people so that they might find a saving faith. The way she had shared with him during the filming of *Unlocked.* He slipped his arm around her and walked close beside her the rest of the way.

St. Thomas stood like a beacon in the snow as they rounded the corner from Forty-Second to Fifth Avenue. Snow clung to the myriad of tiny architectural details in the breathtaking structure, and Brandon knew he'd remember this Christmas Eve forever. Even if it wasn't playing out the way he had hoped.

Once they were inside, he remembered the other cast members — most of whom had never been in a church.

Please, God, use this service. Speak to them and to us. Speak to me.

They settled into a pew halfway toward the front and in no time the choir took the stage and began to sing a haunting rendition of "Silent Night." The group sat shoulder-to-shoulder, Brandon on one side of Bailey and Gerald on the other. Whatever happened, this group of dancers was connected to Bailey. That much was clear.

Then, as if God wanted to make sure that this different sort of Christmas Eve had true purpose for the moment, the pastor took the pulpit and gave them a message that he and Bailey could've written for these new friends.

The message was on longing.

"This time of year people are longing." Kindness emanated from the pastor's tone, his body language. "We long for love and relationship and healing and hope." He smiled, and the warmth of it reached to the back row of the enormous old church. "But this Christmas God wants us to long for so much more."

He spoke then about longing for holiness, for a closer walk with Jesus, for God's truth to speak louder than the noise of the world. "When we long for the right things, we find a different sort of love. The kind of love that will never let go of us, never let us down. Never walk away or disown us. A love that knows us and our flaws but stays anyway." He paused. "For us . . . to long for God is to long for a perfect love."

Brandon glanced down the row and saw Gerald wipe a tear. His story was something Bailey had shared with him because there were similarities between Gerald's upbringing and Brandon's. In both cases their fathers had accused them of being gay because of their love for the arts. With Brandon the accusation made him distant and reckless, far from God and impulsive with any girl he came in contact with. But for Gerald the disapproval of his father must've been at least a part of the struggle he now faced: the struggle with homosexuality.

He watched Bailey reach over and take Gerald's hand. Again, Brandon's heart swelled with pride over Bailey's ability to love. He faced the front of the church.

Keep working on his heart, Lord . . . lead him to that perfect love. Please, Father.

The sermon wrapped up with the pastor urging them to never settle for the longings of the world. "Some of you here tonight have never been in a church, never considered longing for a God who knows you by name, who knit you together." He smiled big. "If that's you, then welcome home! This is the night, friends. The time when you can choose to change your life once and for all. It doesn't matter who you are or where you've been. Your soul has been longing for God the whole time."

Gerald's tears came faster and he still held tight to Bailey's hand. Down the row the rest of her castmates were glued to the sermon, each of them clearly moved by the message.

"Give yourself the gift of God's love this Christmas. God's Word promises if we start longing for that perfect love, everything . . . absolutely everything will follow that longing." He held out both hands toward the people scattered throughout the pews. "Remember, God created our ability to long for love. But He wants us to long for His perfect love. And what in all the world could be a better Christmas gift than that?"

Brandon thought about the gift he'd wanted to buy, the one he had wanted to give Bailey later on tonight. But in light of the changes on the faces of Bailey's friends, Brandon had to agree with the pastor's message. On this Christmas night if five people who had run from God were suddenly willing to long for His truth, His love . . . then there could be no better Christmas gift.

As the service ended, Gerald pulled Bailey into his arms. In muffled words Brandon heard him tell her that he wanted that perfect sort of love. "I can't run from God anymore. He loves me, even if my family never did."

They stayed in the pews long after the other congregants had filed out, and Bailey and Brandon took turns talking about God's power, His truth, and how it had the ability to set people free from whatever bound them. Brandon still wished that tonight might have been the night he could've proposed. But as they left the church, he felt certain God would show him the perfect timing for him and Bailey, for their love and the forever he was sure they had ahead of them. A forever like Bill and Barbara Dillman. In the meantime this Christmas Eve was about something else.

Longing for an eternal sort of love.

TWELVE

Cody had never experienced a sadder Christmas. Cheyenne was tired — just through with four weeks of chemotherapy and radiation. She'd lost eighteen pounds and most of her hair — especially where it had been shaved for surgery. Chey's doctor wanted her to stay in the hospital through the aggressive treatment, but she'd begged him to be home. Tara would take care of her, and Cody could help. So, even though she was very sick and often too tired to get out of bed, she had been home for the last week.

Tonight, though, she was worse and Cody could do nothing to help her. Once Cheyenne was comfortable in Tara's guestroom where she lived now with Tara, Cody sat for awhile with Tara. The woman was still devastated by Chey's diagnosis, but she'd come to accept it. She no longer seemed on the verge of collapse or hysterics at the thought of losing Cheyenne.

They were all realistic about the battle. God could work a miracle, but short of that Cheyenne was losing the fight. Tests would determine exactly how badly next week, but they didn't need official results. Chey was wasting away, her headaches stronger every day. Cody hugged Tara for a long while before he left. "We'll get through this." His words were as much for him as they were for her. A reminder of the truth they were anchored in. That with God all things were possible. Even surviving a season like this.

"She's so sick." Tara looked over her shoulder back at the room where Cheyenne spent most of her time. "I can't watch her suffer." Peace soothed her expression. "If God's gonna take her home, then He can do it." Tara nodded. Quiet tears fell from her eyes as she smiled at Cody. "I won't leave her until then."

"Me either."

"But you need to, Cody. Go home tonight. Pray . . . think about your life. God's doing something in both your hearts. Sometimes you have to get away from here to know what He's trying to tell you."

Cody agreed, even though he hated leaving Tara alone with Chey. If something happened . . . if tonight were the night . . . he would never want Tara to be by herself. "Call me. If anything changes."

"I will." She found her smile again. "And hey . . . Merry Christmas, Cody. God's still in control. Just like He was two thousand years ago."

"He is." Cody kissed Tara's cheek. "Call me."

She nodded and stepped back, waving. He headed through the front door, down the stairs, and into his truck. He both hated and loved the freedom that came over him as he drove away. He rolled both his windows down and let the cold Christmas air fill his truck. For the first time that night he felt like he could breathe, like he'd been given a pass to leave the valley of the shadow of death — even if just for a little while.

Tara's words gave him the comfort and assurance to keep driving. He needed to talk to God, to see what he was supposed to take from this sudden tragedy that had taken over all their lives. With everything in him he wanted to give Cheyenne a cure. No, he wasn't in love with her. But he still loved her, still wanted life and hope and a future for her. She had so much to offer.

Tears blurred his eyes and he blinked, working to see the snowy highway ahead of him. Very few people were out tonight, and suddenly he thought about swinging by the Flanigans' house. He glanced at the time on his dashboard. Just after eight o'clock. By now they'd be finished with dinner. Probably playing Catch Phrase! or Apples to Apples . . . something where the family would be gathered around the living room fireplace, laughing and enjoying another unforgettable Christmas.

At the last moment, just before Cody could've taken the exit that led to their house, he changed his mind. It would take an hour to get there, and by then they'd be headed for bed. Jenny and Jim, at least. The Colts had been knocked out of the playoffs last week, but that didn't mean Jim wasn't busy. And whether the season was underway or not, Jim always turned in early and woke with the sun. So he could get up and pray for his family, read his Bible, and jog a few miles. The things that kept Jim Flanigan the strong man of God he had always been. The man he would always be.

No, he wouldn't go to the Flanigans.

But Tara was right. He needed this time to think about his life, to refocus. He reached his apartment, parked on the street, and shivered as he unlocked the door and headed inside. There had been no time to buy a tree or decorations. He'd been gone so much, that DeMetri had taken to staying with his teammate Larry Sanders' family. At least while Chey was sick. Otherwise the poor kid would've been here alone most of the time.

Cody fell into the nearest dining room chair and planted his elbows on the wooden table. Cheyenne's illness had come up out of nowhere, and every moment since then had been a whirlwind of sadness and shock and survival. For Chey and Tara and himself.

He closed his eyes and allowed a helplessness to weigh in around his shoulders. Like a rising river it reached his neck and then his mouth and nose — practically suffocating him. Was this really how life was going to end for Cheyenne? With a sudden, intense, and losing battle to cancer? He raised his hands to his face and hid behind his fingers, as if by sitting here this way, motionless, he could will it *all to be nothing more than a bad dream.*

I don't get it, God . . . it's not fair. She's so young . . . she's been through so much.

The cry came from the most terrified place in his soul, the place where his faith was being rocked one hour at a time by the battle Cheyenne was fighting. He was a soldier, after all. A fighter. If he could've taken this war on himself, he would have. But instead he was helpless to do anything but stand by and encourage her. Encourage her while she lost weight and threw up the small bits of food she managed to eat. While her hair fell out and her clothes started falling off her.

It was enough to make him scream.

Cody had no idea how long he sat there, but long enough so that finally the waters of helplessness began to recede. Until his mind cleared enough to think about something other than Cheyenne and her terminal illness. When that happened, the first image that planted itself in his mind didn't surprise him.

The picture of Bailey.

Of course Bailey didn't know about Chey's cancer. Not Bailey or her parents or any of the team. It had only been weeks since they'd won the title. Most of the guys were still walking on clouds, still fielding congratulations everywhere they went. The heroes of Lyle, Indiana. Even so, he would've told them — so they could pray and so they might know what he was going through, the reason he wasn't around much. But Chey didn't want anyone to know.

"Whatever time I have left, I want to

spend it with you and Tara. Not with a stream of people coming by, feeling sorry for me."

Her response made sense, but still Cody thought they should be entitled to pray for her. The more people praying, the better. But she only refuted by saying that she had her church praying. People who didn't know her connection to Cody or Lyle High. That way the town could carry on with their celebration. Cody stared out the window at the dark of Christmas night.

After awhile, he left his spot at the dining room table and found his laptop. He settled in on the worn sofa and found Bailey's Facebook page. She was probably having the best Christmas of her whole life. Brandon was filming his most recent movie in New York City, which meant the two of them were together every night. Cody felt the familiar ache at the thought, the jealousy that didn't take root, but reminded him how he felt about her.

How he would always feel.

There was nothing new on her Facebook, but with Bailey there was always a way to find out what she was up to. When a girl dated Brandon Paul, Google would have plenty to say about what they were doing and where they'd been. He typed in her name alongside Brandon Paul's and hit enter.

Sure enough, pictures of the two of them instantly covered the screen. The most recent headline showed a picture of Bailey and what must've been some of her castmates working alongside a young bearded guy. The headline read, "Disguise Doesn't Hide the Truth: Brandon Paul and Bailey Flanigan Serve Up Christmas Dinner at a New York City Mission."

The guy seemed almost too good to be true. Whatever ugly details remained about his past, they were no uglier than the ones that made up Cody's yesterdays. In Bailey's presence Brandon was clearly a new guy. A guy sold out to God and to the work the Lord called him to do. At least it seemed that way.

He clicked through other pictures. Bailey and Brandon holding hands as they left St. Thomas Episcopal Church after a midnight Christmas Eve service, and the two of them sitting on a New York City bench during a break from his filming. The paparazzi were relentless. If Cody wanted to, he could literally follow Bailey's every move — as long as Brandon was in town.

"Are you happy, Bailey . . . really happy?" He whispered the question aloud. "I miss you. I wish . . . I just wish I could hear your voice."

The thought faded in the silent room, but as it did, a memory filled his mind. The box of belongings Bailey had given him at the hospital a year ago. He had brought the box home and looked through some of the contents. But not all of them. The box had been full of letters from Bailey, notes she'd written to him while he was in Iraq. Wasn't that what she'd said? But last year when he brought the box home he hadn't had the strength to look through them. He was still doing his best to run from her, to avoid the pain of losing her — strange as that all felt now.

So maybe that's how he could spend the rest of this Christmas night. Since there was nothing he could do for Cheyenne, no one to visit, and since he couldn't celebrate Christmas with his mom in prison until their visit tomorrow afternoon — this was the perfect time to find Bailey's letters and read them.

He set his laptop down on the couch beside him and walked to his room. He didn't have to wonder where they were, now that the idea had hit him. He remembered hiding them at the top of the closet like it was yesterday. He found the box easily and carried it back to the dining room table. The feel of it in his hands reminded him again of that day in the hospital, when he could've said something. Could've stopped her from leaving and told her how he felt about her.

But instead he watched her go. Let her leave him with a life-time of memories and regrets . . . and this: the box of her letters.

He opened the lid and sifted through the contents. It felt almost eerie the way the contents smelled like her, the way they made him feel like she was sitting beside him, sharing this Christmas night with him like she might've been if he hadn't freaked out. If he hadn't run for his life instead of talking to her and hearing her heart when she set out to film *Unlocked* with Brandon Paul.

A few of the letters were handwritten, notes that were never sent his way — probably once she knew he was missing in action. Others were copies of what looked like pages of her journal. He took one from the box and opened it.

September 28, she'd scribbled at the top of the page. There was no year, just the month and day. He let his eyes find the first line, let her words fill his heart as surely as if she were speaking them to him this very moment.

I've thought about Cody all day long, and now I can only do one thing. Write about him here, in my journal. He's gone of course. Off fighting the bad guys in Iraq. But I keep asking myself why he had to leave. Didn't he understand what I was feeling that day when we took the walk through the woods? Before he left?

Cody's hands began to tremble. She'd felt that strongly for him back then? Before he left for war? The idea shocked him enough that he lowered the piece of paper and reminded himself to breathe. She never told him . . . but then, of course she didn't. She was barely out of high school back then. It wouldn't have been her place to tell him what she was feeling. Rather it should've been him who talked about it with her, who had that conversation before he set out for Army training.

He clenched his jaw and brought the journal page back up so he could see it. He found his place and began reading again. *Sometimes I think Cody left so he could fight that battle, instead of fighting for me. I know . . . he's already made it clear. He doesn't think he's good enough for me. But that's crazy. No one could ever care about me the way he does. Even when he thinks I don't know how he feels about me, I do know. But now he's gone and I can't talk to him. I might not ever get to talk to him again. So all I can do is pray. I pray that God will protect him and bring him home safely and that somewhere down the road Cody will talk to me and tell me how he feels.*

I pray that God teaches him to be open with me — and not afraid. Until then I will picture how it was that day, the last walk we took together before he left. I wanted him to kiss me so badly, but it wasn't God's timing. It might never be God's timing. If that's true, then I have one more prayer. That God will help me learn to let go of him. Because right now letting go of Cody Coleman doesn't even seem possible.

Cody read the last two paragraphs three more times before folding the piece of paper and setting it off to the side. He hadn't learned much over the years, had he? When he left for Iraq Bailey knew him well enough to know he was running, that he was afraid to face his feelings for her. And now here he was . . . in the same exact situation.

Bailey's prayers tugged at his heart and made him love her more . . . miss her more. God had answered every single one. He had kept Cody alive, brought him home as safe as possible, and led him to that wonderful

July day when he'd finally told Bailey how he felt.

Cody read another few letters, before he couldn't take another minute and had to put the box away. He pictured the paparazzi pictures of her and Brandon and it occurred to him that God had even answered Bailey's last, most desperate prayer: That where Cody was concerned, since he hadn't found a way to stop running from her, she might somehow learn to let go of him.

The way she most definitely had.

THIRTEEN

Katy Hart Matthews hadn't only come to accept her life in Los Angeles alongside her movie star husband, Dayne. She had come to enjoy it. She wiped the peanut butter off their daughter Sophie's face and glanced out the window of their Malibu beach home. The sun was heading toward the horizon, the few clouds in the sky promising a sunset fitting of the last day of the year.

"Can we take a walk, Mommy?" Sophie loved the beach. Her white blonde ringlets only accentuated her tanned cheeks and bright blue eyes. She was almost four, but she talked like a child twice her age. Dayne liked to tease that he was easily outsmarted by the two real talkers in the family.

"Yes, baby girl . . . Daddy's changing clothes so we can take a walk."

Dayne had met with a couple top actors earlier that day, trying to work out another movie deal. Faith-based films continued to gain popularity, and Dayne was convinced God had exciting projects ahead. Though she still sometimes missed their days in Bloomington, Katy wasn't in a hurry to go back. Especially on a gorgeous afternoon like this one.

Katy smiled to herself. Brandon and Bailey were flying in right about now. They'd get a ride over, and tonight would be very special, indeed. The four of them had more to celebrate than even her husband knew. At least for now.

When Sophie's hands were clean, the two of them linked fingers and walked back toward the bedroom just as Dayne stepped into the hallway. He wore khaki shorts and a white T-shirt. Never mind his passion for making movies, Dayne could still star in them if he wanted to. He was tall and muscled and his eyes shone from across the house. She was in love with him, more than she dreamed. Today and every day.

"Sophie wants to take a walk."

"Me too." He hurried to them and swept their little girl into his arms. "Ready for an adventure, sweetie?"

Sophie giggled and put her hands on her daddy's face, messing up his hair and making silly faces at him. "You always have an adventure for me, Daddy."

"Yep." He bounced her onto his hip and pulled Katy close for a quick kiss. "Life with you girls is always an adventure." He kissed her again, longer this time. "You look stunning . . . if I haven't told you."

"You did." She returned the kiss. "This morning. Remember?"

"Well then it's about time I told you again."

"Hey . . . no kissy face." Sophie let her head hang back as she laughed out loud. "Come on, Daddy! We have to have our adventure."

Dayne gasped and tickled Sophie a few quick times. "You're right! I almost forgot!" He put his arm around Katy and the three of them headed for the back door. "We can't miss our adventure."

Katy felt the butterflies in her stomach. Dayne had no idea just how much of an adventure they were about to take. They walked down the back steps toward the shore. The paparazzi almost never bothered with them these days. Dayne wasn't an actor now. He was a producer and director and there was nothing remotely scandalous to create about his life. The paparazzi had other more popular faces to catch. Faces like Brandon Paul's. If he and Bailey didn't make a clean getaway from LAX in the next hour, the photographers were bound to follow them here. Which would cast a serious shadow on the evening.

"We need to pray the media doesn't follow Brandon and Bailey." Katy loved the way it felt walking through the chilly ankle-deep surf with Dayne and Sophie beside her. The sun warmed her shoulders and ahead was nothing but shoreline as far as she could see.

"I've prayed. It's tough, where they're at right now."

"Yeah." Katy laughed. "I remember. It was like yesterday." She paused and looked at Sophie. Their little daughter seemed content in her father's arms, her head on his shoulder. "So what do you think?"

"About Brandon and Bailey?" Dayne still read her mind as easily as he'd done when they first started out. He smiled, the bright sky reflecting off his sunglasses as he turned to her. "Together, you mean?"

"Yes. Do you think they can do this? Are they right for each other?"

"We made it work." He leaned in and kissed her lightly as they walked. Passion was always at the surface of their relationship. "What do *you* think?"

"I'm not sure. I talked to her a week ago.

235

She loved having Brandon in New York these last few weeks, so I asked her if it was serious. She told me it was as serious as it could be with their careers in different parts of the country."

"Which means . . ." Dayne looked slightly confused.

"It means she's sure about today. But that's as far as she can see." Katy smiled. "She loves him . . . she was clear about that."

"And what about Brandon?" A pair of seagulls squawked as they fought for something in the water a few yards away. "Does he think it's more serious?"

"I'm not sure." She shrugged and felt her face take on a nervous look. "I think we'll know more after this visit."

"Good that they could both get a little time away."

"Yes." She breathed deep, loving the ocean air all around her. "They need this time for sure. All couples do."

He stopped and adjusted Sophie, who had fallen asleep in his arms. "It never gets old, the sunset here on the beach."

"With you . . . nothing ever gets old." She still faced him, but now she turned and looked out at the water. For a while they stood like that, mesmerized by the display

God put on in their backyard day after day after day. Finally she turned to him again. "Too bad about Sophie's adventure. She slept through it."

"Mmm." He reached for her hand with his free one and eased his fingers between hers. "I'll guess she'll have to wait until tonight. The noisemakers you bought for our New Year's Eve party will make for a pretty fun adventure."

"True." She laughed, and the sound mixed with the crashing surf not far from where they stood. There was no gradual way to say this. She exhaled, steadying herself. "Anyway . . . I was thinking about adventures. How our life has been one ever since we met."

"That day in the Bloomington Community Theater . . . when you were onstage directing *Charlie Brown*."

"Yes." She smiled, and even though they both wore sunglasses, she could feel his eyes looking straight into her heart. "Since then."

"You're big on adventures today." He released her hand and slid his fingers through her hair, alongside her face. "Is that your tender heart . . . evaluating the end of another year?"

"Ummm, well." She felt a shiver pass over her arms. "More like evaluating the year we're about to have."

"Oh. Definitely." He nodded and looked out to sea again. "With us we never know what sort of adventure God's got planned for us."

"Except," Katy started to giggle. He wasn't picking up on her clues whatsoever. "Except this time we do sort of have at least a little idea." She put her hand over her stomach. "A very little idea."

Dayne looked at her. He started to say something but then stopped himself. He looked from her face to the place where her hand remained over her middle. "A *little* idea?"

"About the adventure coming our way in July." She laughed out loud, loving this, holding onto the moment. "The end of July to be exact."

"What?" He shouted the word so loud that Sophie lifted her head and looked around, all sleepy eyes and curly blonde hair. He patted her head. "Sorry, honey. Go back to sleep, sweetheart." As soon as she lay her head back down, Dayne moved slowly in toward Katy and took her in his arms. His sunglasses couldn't hide the tears suddenly sliding down his face. "We're having a baby?"

"Yes." She made a sound that was more

laugh than cry.

"We are?" He studied her, loving her more than she had ever dreamed anyone could. "We really are?"

"Yes." She grinned, blinking back her own tears. "Life's just one big adventure."

"But when . . . how did you find out?"

"I went in this morning." She laughed and dried her cheeks at the same time. "Dr. Baker met me even though he didn't have office hours today. The test was positive. Just like I guessed."

If Dayne hadn't been holding Sophie in his arms he would've let out a shout the whole beach could hear. Katy could read that much in his face. But since he couldn't shout out loud, he drew close to her again and kissed her. The sort of kiss she would remember long after this day was a part of their history. "I've . . . I've asked God for this. For His timing, of course. But . . . that there would be another baby someday."

"Me too." They had talked about it. Katy didn't get pregnant easily, and so there were no guarantees. No promises that she and Dayne would ever have another child. And in that case they were at peace with the fact that they might only have Sophie. But now . . . now their prayers had been answered so completely she could do nothing but cling to him and to their little girl. "Congratulations, Dayne . . . you're going to be a daddy again."

When he looked at her this time, he was crying in earnest. He put his hand over her stomach and looked long at her, as if he never wanted the moment to end. "I love you, Katy."

"I love you too. Always and a day."

It was something they said to each other often since they were married. *Always and a day.* As if no amount of time here on earth would ever be enough to share the love they'd found together.

"Pray with me, Katy." He closed his eyes and sniffed a few times, finding control for the moment. "Thank You . . . dear God, thank You. We commit this baby to You, every day, every month, every season of his or her life. Because You are a great and mighty God, and we want our whole family to serve You all the days . . ." his voice caught and she could feel him trembling, "all the days of our lives."

"In Jesus' name, amen. Hey . . ." She kissed the tears off his cheeks. "It's a happy adventure, remember?"

"Yes. Crazy happy." He laughed and dragged the back of his hand over his face. "Those are the only ones that make me cry."

■ ■ ■ ■

Bailey's heart raced as they stepped off Brandon's private jet and climbed into yet another black SUV, this one driven by one of his personal staff. They'd already gotten word that the paparazzi were circling LAX. Someone had spotted them leaving La-Guardia, and their destination was obvious.

With a four-day break listed on the shooting schedule, the couple had to be flying back to LA and Brandon's hometown for a New Year's celebration and a break from the cold and snow.

"It's okay." He stayed a foot in front of her, in case anyone with a long lens was shooting them even now, on the private runway. "I've got you, Bailey."

"I know." She exhaled, willing her heart to slow down. "I'm fine. Really." The paparazzi didn't exactly frighten her. They were just so much more intense here in Los Angeles. After all, this was where Dayne Matthews had been nearly killed being chased by photographers. One reason she had never seen herself moving here, being a part of Hollywood.

Brandon's driver motioned to them. "Get inside. I'll get your bags."

"Thanks." Brandon waited for her. "You first, baby."

"Okay." She still couldn't shake the uneasiness of the circling paparazzi. "I have a bad feeling about them . . . the helicopters. Reminds me of Dayne and the accident."

Brandon's frustration showed in his face. "My driver won't let that happen." His gentle tone encouraged her to relax. "Come on, it's okay."

"I'm sorry . . . it's weird. I guess it's just . . . it's more intense here." Bailey slid across the leather seat of the SUV and buckled herself in. Not until they were on the road and Brandon's driver, Seth, outsmarted half a dozen photogs chasing them, did Bailey finally catch her breath.

"You sure you're okay?" He looked worried. "Come on, Bailey, we've done this."

"I know." She laughed, but it sounded nervous and forced. "I'm sorry. It's just . . . maybe it's because we're dating . . . but they never sent helicopters before." She managed a nervous smile. "Doesn't it bug you?"

"I don't think about it." He reached for her hand. His frustration about the paparazzi faded and his attention was hers alone. "Let's think about tonight instead . . . this is supposed to be fun, remember?"

"You're right." She nodded, trying to

242

convince herself. Maybe it wasn't only the photogs that had her on edge. They were having New Year's Eve with Dayne and Katy and something about the trip felt more serious than anything they'd done before. Like they were playing the same roles their friends had played six years ago. Hollywood star and small town girl trying to find sanity in the world of moviemaking.

Living here, married to a celebrity like Brandon Paul? It wasn't a role she ever pictured herself playing in real life. She'd assumed she'd marry someone like her dad and live in Bloomington when the time came. But here she was, driving down Pacific Coast Highway in Brandon Paul's hired car, ready to spend New Year's Eve with him — if only their driver could dodge the next set of paparazzi trailing their car and circling overhead.

Brandon's playlist kicked into action, and the first song came on — their favorite by Lady Antebellum, "Just a Kiss." The song was the last one they'd danced to at their rooftop prom.

"There." Brandon searched her eyes after the song played for a minute. "You're okay now. I can see into your heart."

"I'm better. Yes."

He put his arm around her and eased her

close, gently pressing her head to his shoulder. "Rest, baby. Everything's going to be fine."

He was right. Of course everything was going to be fine. She told herself that several more times on the drive and as they made a mad dash into Katy and Dayne's house avoiding a rush of three paparazzi cars who pulled up at the same time.

"They know we're here." She was breathless as they darted inside. "Now we'll have to stay inside. They won't leave us alone."

"They will." He pulled his cell phone from his pocket. At the same time he yelled for Dayne. "Hey, guys, can you pop the garage door for us?"

"Sure thing." Dayne didn't need to ask why Brandon and Bailey were in a rush or what the hurry was about the garage door. He'd lived this life once too. The driver must've answered because Brandon wasted no time. "Seth, I need you to circle around the block and then pull into the garage. Wait half an hour and then leave in a hurry. They'll think we stopped by for a quick visit, and we can lose them."

It was a good plan, and thirty minutes later after they'd chatted with Dayne and Katy and played with little Sophie, and after they'd learned the family's exciting news about expecting another baby, Seth called Brandon. The report was a good one — the plan had worked. Seth had led the paparazzi on a chase to an ice cream shop drive-thru, and then to the private backside of a popular Malibu area restaurant — giving the impression that they'd celebrate the New Year there. Brandon hung up and grinned. "We're okay. They think we're out to dinner."

This was the first time Bailey had been here without her parents — another reason she felt the presence of the paparazzi more keenly. If they could find a way to make it seem like Bailey and Brandon were spending the night somewhere, they would do it. Of course, she was staying with Katy and Dayne — no matter what the paparazzi might report in the days to come. And Brandon was staying at his own house. But that might not be enough to stop the tabloids. Bailey was glad they'd have some time apart. She wanted to talk to Katy, wanted to share the thrill of her relationship with Brandon, every wonderful thing he'd done to show his love for her. But she also wanted to share her concerns about the future.

When they were certain no paparazzi remained, Brandon took Bailey's hand. It was nearly dark by then, the sunset casting a brilliant range of orange and yellows across the Pacific. "Come on." He led her to the back door. "Let's take a walk."

Bailey looked back at Katy, and her friend nodded. "Go ahead. It's fine."

"I told you, baby. I've got you." He chuckled as they headed through the back door. "I've been looking forward to this all day."

The beach was empty except down to the right a ways, toward the public stretch. The two of them walked to the surf and then turned left.

Bailey settled into the moment. "Did I tell you? I'm meeting Andi on Monday for coffee. At her parents' house." She raised her brow. "Where no one can take pictures."

He smiled. "Good idea. I'm glad the two of you made time for each other."

"I know. I miss her a lot." Bailey had visited with Andi on Skype a few times, long enough to know she was doing well, taking small acting roles, and helping her dad with his production company. Andi explained how she still thought about the little boy she gave up for adoption, but she was at peace with her decision. Bailey smiled. "God has her in a great place. Makes me happy."

Their pace slowed, and Bailey felt safe beside Brandon. He kept his arm around her shoulders and he seemed to relax a little more with every few yards of sand. "I love the snow . . . on Christmas Eve and all." He leaned his face upward toward what remained of the heat from the sun. "But you can have your New York winters." There was a smile in his voice. "I'll take the beach."

"It is amazing." She loved the sand between her toes, the warm breeze even at this hour. Hard to believe just hours ago they'd been caught in the dead of winter. But a part of her wanted to say she'd take Bloomington. She missed home more than she had in a long time.

Brandon grew quiet for a while, but when they were a ways from Katy and Dayne's house, he walked with her up onto the dry sand and they sat down. Bailey pulled her knees up to her chest and looked out at the night as it grew dark over the water. He turned to her and for a long time he only watched her, looking at her as if whatever he wanted to say was too serious to rush. Finally he put his hand on her back and soothed his fingers along her spine. "Can I tell you something?"

She felt her heart skip a beat. Things had been so good between them. Maybe too good. Because for some reason she had a feeling wherever this was headed it was more serious than she had expected. "Of course." She kept her smile easy, her tone light. "Anything."

"So . . . on Christmas Eve. Before I met up with you at the theater . . ."

She turned slightly so she could see into his eyes better. "You filmed that day, right?"

"I did." He nodded, remembering his beard and his co-star's help. "I walked home and along the way it started to snow. And, I don't know, maybe because it all felt so wonderful I got this crazy idea."

Her head felt lighter, not sure where he was headed with this. "How crazy?"

He didn't blink, didn't look away. "Tiffany's crazy."

Again her heart hesitated before thudding into a faster rhythm. She smiled, and the good feeling coming from her heart took her by surprise. "Tiffany's?"

"Mmm-hmm." He shifted so he was facing her directly. Then he took her hands in his, his fingers cool between hers. "I figured I'd go in and buy the prettiest ring I could find and take you to the top of the Empire State Building and ask you."

She couldn't breathe, couldn't make herself believe what he was saying. Was this why she'd felt so uneasy? Because she could sense where their relationship was headed?

How serious things had gotten between them? "Brandon . . . you were . . . You really thought about that?"

"Definitely." He chuckled, the lighthearted sound of it soothing any uneasiness between them. "I went there . . . to Tiffany's. But it was closed." He made a face. "I tried to think of some way inside, some connection I might have. But it was too late. The last employee — an assistant manager — actually gave me this great lesson on married love. Told me he'd been married sixty years, of all things." He gave a slight shrug of one shoulder. "But he couldn't open the door."

They both laughed, and again the sound helped lighten the mood.

"So we went to St. Thomas with your friends instead. God reminded me that there was more than one kind of forever love."

His beautiful words hit her straight in the heart. How great that Brandon understood what was more important that night. But the truth remained and it screamed from everything within her. "You mean if . . . if Tiffany's had been open . . ."

He hesitated, studying her, the longing in his eyes desperately clear. "I would've asked." His smile faded, and he had never looked more serious in the time she'd known him. "I want forever with you, Bailey." He stopped and lifted his eyes to the distant moon. "Since then I've felt God tell me to wait, to listen for His leading." He slid closer to her, so they still faced each other, but now their legs were touching, their faces closer together. "I figured maybe part of the process was talking to you . . . letting you know how I feel."

Bailey nodded. Was this really happening? Was she dreaming? "That's . . . that's a good idea. Talking about it."

"So, are you surprised?"

She wasn't sure what to say, how to respond. Everything about the last year had been unforgettable, and the past few weeks together in New York were like living out her own personal fairytale. Every moment. But she hadn't thought seriously about marrying him, about living in LA together.

A host of thoughts hit her all at once.

She figured she'd feel scared if he brought up something as serious as marriage. Just because they'd shared a wonderful month or so didn't mean she was ready to make a decision about marriage, right? They should wait another six months or a year, maybe? See how things went and how their lives gelled . . . or didn't gel. That's how she thought she should feel.

But instead a new sort of happiness filled her and consumed her, coursing through her heart and mind and soul like electricity.

At first, in the face of her silence, Brandon didn't seem worried. But the longer she stayed quiet, the straighter he sat, and his eyes grew wide. "Bailey, talk to me."

"I'm sorry." She giggled and held tight to his hands. "I'm . . . I'm so happy, Brandon. I mean, I guess I can't believe the way I feel. Or that . . . that if Tiffany's had been open . . . you would've asked me to marry you on Christmas Eve."

His smile reached through the night air. "I'd ask you now if I thought you'd say yes."

"I might." She laughed. "Do you have a ring?"

"Let's see." He patted his jeans pockets and then looked at the sandy beach around him. He found a stray piece of dry seaweed, tied it carefully in a small loop, and held it out to her. He conjured up a mock look of romance, every word and movement exaggerated. "Bailey, nothing would make me happier than if you'd marry me. If you'd give me your todays and trust me with your tomorrows."

"Hmmm." She held out her left hand and watched while he threaded the seaweed ring onto her bare finger. "I have to admit . . .

that sounds nice." She admired the work he'd done, the handmade seaweed loop on her ring finger. Gradually the teasing dissipated and their eyes met and held. Even by the light of the moon she could see the way he looked at her, how he was no longer teasing.

Gradually everything about the moment changed. The sound of the gentle surf faded and there was only the two of them. What was this feeling coming over her? A chill ran down her arms and legs and she tried to imagine for a single moment how she'd feel if this were real. If he'd really just proposed to her. In a rush she knew the answer. It was as easy as the air between them.

She would feel amazing.

The truth caught her by surprise again, and Bailey wondered if he could hear her pounding heart above the rhythmic sound of the surf a few feet away.

"Bailey." Brandon sat up on his knees, facing her, and she did the same. "I'm only teasing for one reason . . . because I'm not sure what you'd say if I was being real. If the ring wasn't seaweed . . . but gold."

In this moment Bailey was convinced what she would do. She looped her arms around his neck and he eased his around her waist. "I know what I'd say."

"What?" He breathed the word against her face, her skin. "What would you say?"

She didn't have to think about her answer. It came from deep inside her and no longer surprised her. "I'd say yes. I'd give you my todays and trust you with my tomorrows." Nothing she'd ever said had been truer, and Bailey trembled with the realization. Because up until five minutes ago she would've thought a proposal from Brandon might terrify her. But suddenly under the Malibu night sky, his eyes lost in hers and their hearts beating in time with the future, Bailey had no doubts.

He took her hand, lifted it slowly, tenderly to his lips, and kissed the place where the seaweed ring sat. Then with all the controlled passion he seemed even remotely capable of, he took her face in his hands and kissed her. "You know what I wish?" He kissed her again and another time after that.

"What?" She felt like she was floating, like there could be no more right place in all the world for her to be right now than in his arms, here on his private stretch of beach. "What do you wish, Brandon?"

"I wish I had a gold ring."

She thought about telling him it didn't matter. That for all intents and purposes he had just proposed to her and she had just said yes. But she didn't want to cheat him of the real thing. Especially when this moment had started out as a silly joke, a way to break the ice on the topic of taking things to the next level. "You know what *I* wish?" She touched her nose to his, and their cheeks brushed against each other.

"What?" He leaned in closer to her, his body trembling, his voice a breathy whisper. "What do you wish?"

Bailey felt the intensity of the moment, too. She leaned back slightly. "I wish you had a ring too."

This time he put his hands on her shoulders and searched her eyes. "Really?" He looked like he might cry, like the moment was more than he had dared hope for. "You really wish that?"

"I do. Because then we wouldn't have to think about it or analyze it or wonder if it was the right thing. We'd . . . we'd be engaged and there'd be no looking back."

His breathing was heavier than before, more because of what his heart must've been feeling than because of the closeness of their bodies. He took her left hand and ran his finger gently over the seaweed ring. "I'd ask you . . . to let this hold you over until we could get to a jewelry store." He swallowed hard and studied her, their connection so strong nothing could've broken the moment. "But you deserve more than that."

"Thank you." She meant what she'd said, that she partly wished this were the real thing and that by now they could be past the asking, past the wondering. But she appreciated his wanting to wait. They needed time to think about this beyond the impulse of a perfect New Year's Eve. "I think I'd be ready, Brandon . . . Soon. Really."

The words seemed to be all he needed to hear. He hugged her again, the passion from earlier gradually becoming a more tender moment, a time between them Bailey was sure they would both remember always. "That's what I hoped you'd say."

She smiled. "I do have one question." She held up her left hand, admiring the makeshift loop around her finger. "Can I keep the ring?"

"I hope so." Laughter came easily for both of them. He helped her to her feet. "I'd be crushed if you just, you know, threw it on the ground or dropped it in the ocean."

"Never." She admired it again as they started walking back. "Not every day a girl has Brandon Paul make her an engagement ring out of seaweed."

"Not every day we do a dress rehearsal of the biggest moment in our lives." He raised his brow and allowed a nervous laugh. "That was crazy, right?"

"Right. But think about it. That would only be the *next* biggest moment of our lives." If he was thinking about marrying her, then she would think about it too. After how she'd felt kneeling there on the sand, she wasn't afraid.

"Of course. Because with us . . . we have big moments all the time."

"Exactly." She grinned at him, reaching for his hand and swinging it between them as they walked. "Like this New Year's Eve party."

"And the next time I get to watch you perform in *Hairspray*." He pointed at her, as if the idea had only just come to mind.

"Right. And dancing on the rooftop with you."

"In a winter coat. Don't forget that."

"Yes," she laughed out loud. "In a prom dress that *looked* like a winter coat." She stopped and hugged him, not too long because they needed to get back. But she wanted him to know she appreciated him, appreciated his depth and ability to communicate. The way Cody never could. She looked deep into his eyes once more. "Too many big moments to count . . . you know why?"

"Why?" He looked lost in love, mesmerized by her nearness. The result made him irresistible.

"Because . . ." She took a step back, giggling and dragging him along the sand with her. "Everything about loving you is crazy and different and amazing." She held both hands high in the air. "One big unforgettable moment."

He swept into a grand bow, grabbed her left hand, and held it high over her head. With a grace she hadn't known he was capable of, he twirled her and then pulled her close, waltzing with her across the shoreline.

"What's this . . . another prom?"

"What? I didn't tell you?" He laughed as they held hands and started running along the shallow surf toward Katy and Dayne's. "Proms are every few weeks for us. From now on."

She was laughing, too, but she wouldn't have minded it.

"Actually," he slowed down, out of breath more from the sheer joy of their time together than from their short run. "It's a long story, baby."

But before he could launch into it, they

heard the sound of pounding feet behind them in the distance. Bailey turned and saw the shadowy figures of several men running toward them, the outline of their oversized cameras clearly visible.

"Brandon!" She screamed without meaning to. The men were maybe twenty yards away and closing in fast. Which meant they'd been shooting pictures from some hiding place for who knew how long. Bailey felt suddenly sick to her stomach as she turned her back to them.

"Come on," he grabbed her hand and they ran up the sandy beach as fast as they could.

The entire time Bailey couldn't tell the pounding of her heart from the rapid fire clicks of the cameras behind them. What pictures had they caught? The two of them kneeling in the sand? The exchange of the ring? In pictures it would seem like Brandon had actually proposed. "Wait!" Adrenaline coursed through her and she couldn't draw a full breath. Panic surrounded her. "I can't . . . keep up."

He slowed a little and put his arm around her waist, protecting her from the cameras as best he could. They ran up the stairs and burst through the back door of Katy and Dayne's. Bailey paced to the kitchen, back to the door, and to the kitchen again.

Brandon bent at the waist and put his hands on his knees.

"They found you?" Katy didn't look troubled by the fact. She was pulling a pan of salmon from the oven. Dayne was in the next room reading a book to Sophie.

"Yeah." Bailey still couldn't catch her breath. What if they'd seen the mock proposal? They would run it on the front page of every rag all across the country. She gasped for air, forcing herself to calm down.

"A crew must've stayed back. Just in case." Brandon turned to Bailey. "Baby, shhh. It's okay." He seemed to know instinctively that she wasn't okay, that the encounter was more than being caught by the paparazzi.

Katy must've realized it too, because she set the dinner down and came to Bailey's side. "Hey . . . it's okay. They can't hurt you. And they won't get any pictures of you in here."

Bailey was still breathing too hard to explain how she felt, how the sound of the men running had freaked her out and how now she couldn't help but replay everything about the last half hour and wonder whether the whole world would see it in the next week or so. Instead she concentrated on exhaling, so she wouldn't hyperventilate and pass out here on the Matthews' floor.

Worry darkened Brandon's face and he turned to Katy. "Get her a cold cloth. Please . . ."

"Hold on." Katy ran back into the kitchen and pulled something from the closest drawer. She returned with the wet cloth seconds later. "Bailey, it's okay. Really, honey."

Control . . . she needed control. Please, God, give me Your peace. Help me catch my breath.

God's peace. That's what she needed to think about.

Do not be anxious about anything, daughter . . . my peace I give you.

More than the cold cloth or Brandon's hand on the small of her back, the sense that God was with her, that He readily extended His peace to her was enough to make her relax just a little. Enough so she could finally draw a complete breath and find her voice. "I'm . . . I'm so-sorry." She coughed a few times, reminding herself to breathe out so she could breathe in again. "That was . . . so weird."

"It was a panic attack." Dayne said it from the next room, quietly but just loud enough to be heard. Beside him Sophie wore a look of grave concern too.

A panic attack. Dayne was right, which could only mean what? After all, the paparazzi didn't normally bring out this response in her. So it had to be the seriousness of things between her and Brandon. The fact that this might not be a passing moment during a red-carpet event or a random moment in New York City.

This might one day be her life.

"Bailey . . . you okay?" Sophie slid off the sofa and danced a few steps in her direction. "You can pray to Jesus."

"Yes." Bailey straightened and allowed herself to lean into Brandon. "That's just what I did, Sophie."

"Jesus always helps us." Sophie nodded big and looked at her mother for approval. "Right, Mommy?"

"Right, baby."

Sophie waited another few seconds, until she was convinced that Bailey was okay. Then she ran back to Dayne and cuddled up close to him again. "Start at the beginning, okay, Daddy?"

He gave Bailey a teasing look. "Thanks a lot, Bailey."

"My . . . pleasure." His comment made her laugh, and for the first time since they'd come into the house, she felt Brandon relax beside her.

"What in the world?" He faced her.

Katy returned to the kitchen, leaving the two of them with at least a little privacy to talk about what had happened. "At first I . . . I was scared to death. But then . . . I started thinking." She ran her hand through her hair and took a full breath. "About the pictures. Everything they might've seen."

The shadows from earlier stayed, but now they weren't so much concern as they were frustration. "You were worried about that?" He laughed but there wasn't much humor in his voice. "What? That people might know we're in love?" The truth dawned on him gradually. "Or that pictures might make people think we got engaged?"

"Well." She felt terrible about the direction this was going. "It . . . could look like that."

He seemed to make a willful decision right there before her. Rather than let her reaction anger or hurt him, he found the teasing place they'd owned right up until the time when they heard the running feet. "Ohhh . . . I get it. Because of the seaweed ring."

"The seaweed —" She switched gears and allowed herself to laugh again. Tentatively at first, and then in a way that was more real.

"What's this?" Dayne called from the

other room. "Brandon gave you a seaweed ring?"

"Daddy gave mommy a ring and that means we're going to have a baby sister."

"Or a baby brother." Dayne corrected her. "We have to leave a little room there, sweet girl."

Everyone laughed, and the awkwardness from a few minutes ago left entirely. Katy cast a quick look at Bailey from the kitchen. Clearly she had overheard more than Dayne. The part about the photographers thinking they'd witnessed a proposal. "I'll say this . . ." She smiled at both Bailey and Brandon. "The two of you are a lot like Dayne and me back in the day." She grinned. "It was insane most of the time, but I came to expect that nothing about loving Dayne Matthews would ever be normal."

"Hmmm." Brandon gave Bailey a sheepish smile and then turned back to Katy. "Like getting a seaweed ring?"

"Yes, like that." Katy laughed and pointed at her husband. "Right, honey?"

"Definitely." He pumped his fist in the air a few times. "Let's hear it for never normal."

The words made Bailey laugh again, and she shared a quick hug with Brandon before the two of them headed into the kitchen to

263

help with dinner. Why had she gotten so worked up? Whatever the paparazzi caught, it didn't matter. Only they knew what their lives were like. The truth behind their relationship. If the rags wanted to run a picture of her getting a seaweed ring from Brandon Paul, so be it. That didn't bother her.

But as the night progressed, she couldn't help but admit that one thing did bother her. The fact that with Brandon, life would never truly be normal. She thought about her family in Bloomington, the love her parents shared, and the easy way they had about life, about grocery shopping and attending church and hosting Bible studies and being in the stands every Friday night for another Clear Creek football game. Sure, her dad was an NFL assistant coach. But their life had been more normal than not.

Late that night, after she and Brandon had said goodnight and he'd headed off with Seth, the driver, to his own house, Bailey stared at the seaweed ring on her finger and tried to imagine never having normal. A part of it sounded exciting. The way Katy had obviously come to see it. That night and later during her coffee date with Andi, she referred to the situation with Brandon this way: Where he was concerned, she had come to ask God for just one thing: If Brandon was the guy for her, that she would learn to live without the very thing that had in some ways defined her childhood.

The ability to breathe in and out.

Like normal.

FOURTEEN

The lunch meeting with *Sports Illustrated* and the interview with ESPN were two hours off, and Cody could hardly believe the drive into the city. He'd never been to New York, never seen the skyscrapers or the high rises that grew from Madison Avenue. Never even imagined the lights of Times Square. But here he was — he and DeMetri Smith — on an adventure he had almost cancelled.

When it first came up a few months ago, he had imagined taking Cheyenne. He would have paid for her hotel room, since ESPN was springing for his, and together they'd take in the sites of the city. But now that wasn't possible, of course. Cheyenne was into another round of chemo. Down another ten pounds and looking worse every day. He almost didn't come because he wasn't sure it was right to leave her.

In the end she was the one who urged him

to go. "I'm fine, Cody . . . I won't be any less sick because you miss this chance." She had a way of moving him to do things he might not otherwise attempt. This was no exception. She even used the DeMetri card. "Neither of you has ever been to New York City. Who knows when you'll have a chance like this again?"

She was right, and Tara also assured him that though Chey was sick, she was stable for now. A few days away wouldn't make a difference.

Cody settled into the stretch limo and smiled at DeMetri. The kid hadn't stopped talking since the car picked them up. "I mean, this is crazy high living, Coach. Traveling by limo." He shook his head as he stared out the window, craning his neck to see the tops of the buildings. "This is sick."

"True." Cody laughed. "It would be sick to get used to it, Smitty. Especially if you want to be a pastor."

"Hmm. You have a point." He settled down for a minute. But then he bounced around on the seat again. "Still . . . I think God would want me to enjoy the ride, right Coach? For now?"

Again Cody laughed and he realized how good the action felt. How long had it been since he'd laughed? Cheyenne was right.

This trip would be good for him. He would meet with a few members of the staffs at both *Sports Illustrated* and ESPN — where he and DeMetri would be interviewed on camera — and then they'd share a night on the town. There had been moments when he thought about seeing *Hairspray* tonight. Smitty would like the show, and, well . . . he'd never seen Bailey on Broadway.

But there seemed no point to it. He would only love her more if he watched her perform. And this week's pictures on the cover of every gossip magazine seemed to suggest that Bailey and Brandon were getting more serious every day. One picture — though it was dark — almost made it look like Brandon had proposed to her. But the magazine stopped short of saying so.

The idea that Bailey could get engaged hadn't even occurred to Cody until then. As if somewhere in the back of his mind he still held out hope that her relationship with Brandon would run its course . . . that Cheyenne would get better and he could be honest with her — that he needed to move on with his life. And somehow . . . some miraculous somehow . . . he and Bailey would find their way back together.

An idea that no longer seemed even remotely possible.

They hit traffic once they crossed into Manhattan, but even still the limo got them to ESPN studios in plenty of time. He and DeMetri slid out of the limo and the driver assured them he'd be with them all day. He gave Cody a card with his phone number. "Call me when you need a ride."

That night they were staying at the Marriott Marquis on Broadway — just three blocks from the theater where *Hairspray* was playing. Now as they headed past security to the elevator of the ESPN studio, De-Metri seemed to remember their plans for the night. "You said we're hitting the town, right Coach? So does that mean a play? Because back before I started football I used to think I wanted to be a singer on Broadway. You know . . . the black Phantom of the Opera. Something like that."

Cody elbowed the kid in the shoulder. "It's not too late. You could put Liberty off for a year or two."

DeMetri thought about it for a few seconds and then shook his head. "Nah, Coach . . . That time has come and gone. God's calling me into the ministry for sure." He waited a beat. "Besides, Liberty has musical theater. Did you know that, Coach?"

"I didn't." The fact that the kid had even

269

taken him a little bit seriously was just one more reason to laugh. "Okay so about tonight. The *SI* reporter has a package for us. Tickets to one of the plays — probably *Mary Poppins.* He mentioned something about that being the hottest show on Broadway right now."

"Aww, *Mary Poppins?*" They reached the right floor and the doors opened.

"Shhh." Cody reminded him as they headed down a plush hallway toward a set of enormous double glass doors.

"Mary Poppins?" He whispered his disapproval. "That's like for little kids. We need something more hip, something with dancing." He did a little dance move as they continued down the hall. "Come on, Coach. Use your pull a little."

Cody ignored him as they pushed through the doors and introduced themselves. The interview would be first, they found out. A taped five-minute session with one of the network's top anchors. A makeup artist powdered both their faces in the half hour before it was time to go on the set.

"If the guys could see me now!" DeMetri closed his eyes and wrinkled his nose as the woman brushed powder beneath his eyes.

"It's not so bad," she smiled at him. "Last week I used this brush on LeBron James."

"Whaaat?" Smitty practically jumped out of the makeup chair. "Are you kidding me? Cause that's the sort of thing you can't kid about, lady."

"I'm absolutely serious."

DeMetri thought about that and slowly he sat up straighter in the chair. "Well, then . . ." he raised a single eyebrow in Cody's direction. "Take your time. I'll be telling this story the rest of the year. In fact," he nodded at Cody. "Pull out your phone and take a picture. I need proof."

Again Cody chuckled, and he realized he felt a decade younger than this morning when they'd boarded the plane. He snapped the picture, and another one once they were seated on the ESPN set, wired with microphones and waiting for the anchor to arrive.

"Even with all this, Coach, you know what it makes me feel?" He leaned close to Cody, his voice a loud whisper.

"What do you feel, Smitty?"

"Like I made the right choice — going to Liberty — following God's call on my life. I mean sure," he made a brushing motion toward the swanky set and then back in the direction of the makeup room. "I could get used to this lifestyle." He tossed his hands. "Who couldn't?" His expression grew more serious. "But this stuff is just the world. I'll

271

be working for the King of Heaven. That's gotta be better, right Coach?"

"Right." Cody hadn't heard DeMetri talk so much in all the past year. Before the kid could launch into another monologue, the anchor appeared. He shook hands with both of them and for the first time that day Smitty fell silent. This was the real thing, the anchor they all knew from watching *SportsCenter.*

"We're planning to run this interview the week between the conference championships and the Super Bowl. That's when we're in need of stories like this. And this is one of the best stories all year." He smiled at them, his enthusiasm genuine. For the next ten minutes he prepped them, running through the questions and assuring them that their answers should be brief. "Five minutes flies by. So let me lead."

They did and Cody had never been more proud of DeMetri. While the anchor started with Cody, reminding the audience how they might recall his face from the cover of *Sports Illustrated,* DeMetri sat quietly by, smiling and nodding in Cody's direction. For all his chattiness, when it mattered he was absolutely professional.

Not until the last couple minutes was DeMetri asked to respond. But his answer to the one question that came his way was one Cody would remember forever. It had to do with what motivated DeMetri and the guys, the reason they thought for even a moment that this season could be different from the three that had preceded it.

"That's easy." Smitty's grin was quick and sincere. "We started believing in miracles. And God started handing them out."

Cody chuckled, nodding in agreement. However long or short he might talk, he could never sum up the season better than that. The anchor seemed to love the answer too, because at the end of the interview he looked into the camera and gave a pointed message to the two teams contending for the Super Bowl that year. "I think if I were about to play the biggest game of my life I might take some advice from DeMetri Smith and start believing in miracles. You never know. God just might start handing them out."

With that the interview wrapped up, and the buildup of several months was over. The anchor thanked them and wished them luck in the coming season. He seemed surprised when DeMetri told him that he wasn't planning to make a career of football, but of preaching the gospel. "Well, then . . . good for you."

As they walked from the ESPN office to *Sports Illustrated* in the same building, Cody gave DeMetri a hearty pat on the back. "You made an impact on that guy. I mean it."

"You think so?"

"Yes." Cody smiled to himself, picturing the startled look on the anchor's face again. "I wouldn't be surprised if he started believing in miracles after meeting you."

Smitty nodded, satisfied. "That's what it's all about. Living for God. Believing His Word. Looking for miracles."

Whatever his professors taught him in the coming years would only be gravy, Cody thought to himself. DeMetri Smith was already wired to be a preacher.

He gave the same sort of answers at the luncheon with the *SI* staff. Hans Tesselaar welcomed them and introduced them to the other writers in the office. DeMetri entertained them with anecdotes from the season, and he finished with the same answer he'd given the ESPN anchor: that the team had merely started believing in miracles, and after that God started handing them out.

"I love this kid." One of the editors shot a look at Hans, then back at DeMetri. "If you ever need a magazine job, come here first."

Smitty laughed. "I better stick to Plan A.

That's the one that feels most right."

The men around the table and a few women laughed at Smitty's sincerity. The fact that he was so serious about the path God had called him to. When the lunch was over, Hans handed him an envelope. "This is from all of us. We want you and DeMetri to see a show, have dinner at one of our favorite Times Square restaurants, and then of course, the hotel vouchers are in there as well."

"Thank you." Cody felt honored. Certainly this wasn't the way they treated every cover story. Something about the boys of Lyle, the way God had worked among them, had touched the staff at *SI* in a special way. Cody wondered what sort of long-term impact the story might have on the staff — an eternal one, he hoped. It was something he and DeMetri would pray about later.

He didn't open the envelope until they were in the elevator. By then Smitty was practically breathing down his neck. "What show, huh, Coach? Tell me it's not *Mary Poppins*."

"Listen." Cody held the envelope at arm's length away from his player. "If it's *Mary Poppins* you'll be thankful, and we'll have a great time. That show really is one of the hottest on Broadway right now."

DeMetri backed up, hands in the air. "Fine. I'll be grateful. Just hurry and open the envelope already, Coach."

Cody did as he was asked, and the second the tickets came into view he felt his heart react. They were for *Hairspray*. Of course they were for *Hairspray*. Hans couldn't possibly have known that Cody knew someone in the *Hairspray* cast or that seeing these tickets would hit him like a truck. But God had known. And for some reason he was supposed to be at Bailey's show tonight.

"What is it?" Smitty peered over his shoulder and let out a squeal. "Are you kidding me? *Hairspray?*" He did a little dance, sort of an eighties move that made Cody worry the elevator might stop between floors. "*Hairspray,* Coach? That's like the ultimate black and white party! Have you heard of it?"

There was no reason to tell DeMetri about Bailey, about his past with her or the fact that she was in the show. He could tell him later if the subject came up. For now it was enough that he nodded. "Yes, Smitty. I've heard of it."

"I saw the movie. You saw the movie, right, Coach?" He didn't wait for an answer. "It's hysterical. Has this dude John Travolta." He paused. "You heard a' John Travolta, Coach?"

"Yes, Smitty. I've heard of him." The elevator opened and they stepped into the lobby. Out front the limo was already waiting for them. They climbed inside with DeMetri still going on about the movie version of the play.

"Anyway, this Travolta guy used to be some big stud, but in *Hairspray* like he plays a mom." He made a face at Cody. "I know, weird, right? But that's the way it always works with *Hairspray.* Some big dude plays the mom and that just makes it more fun. Plus," he paused only long enough to grab a breath, "did I mention it's like the best black and white dance party ever?"

"I know the storyline." He chuckled. "How about we get dinner? Then you can tell me everything you know."

"Everything?" DeMetri rolled his eyes in as exaggerated a fashion as possible. "That'd be the whole thing, Coach. I can't do that." He waggled his finger toward Cody. "You have to leave some element of suspense. I mean, this is our first Broadway show."

"It's our only Broadway show, Smitty."

"Well," he hesitated, gazing straight up as they entered Times Square. "That's probably true." He grinned back at Cody. "But a guy can dream, right?"

"Yes." Cody imagined seeing Bailey dancing in *Hairspray* in just a few hours. "A guy can certainly dream."

They ate dinner at Sardi's, a restaurant on Forty-Fourth Street in the heart of Times Square. The moment they walked up to the hostess desk, Cody could feel DeMetri was about to pass out.

"Coach!" His voice was the loudest whisper possible. "Look at this place. The waiters are wearing tuxedos!"

"Yes." He held his finger to his lips. "Let's get seated. Then we can talk about it."

DeMetri's eyes were almost completely round, his shock as obvious as the view through the glass walls that made up the dining area. "Look at that. There's like a million famous people on the wall. I mean, their pictures are on the wall. You see that, right, Coach?"

A quick look and Smitty quieted down. "The table. Wait till the table."

After they were seated the bursts of amazement continued to come from his favorite player. Their gift card allowed them whatever they wanted, so Cody ordered steak and lobster, and DeMetri chose a shrimp cocktail, filet mignon, and a flaming cherry soufflé for dessert.

"Tell me to stop eating the bread," he said

halfway through his meal. "I'm getting too full. But, Coach, this is the best bread I've ever eaten. Seriously."

"Stop eating the bread, Smitty."

"I can't, Coach."

"Fine. Then be full."

DeMetri burst into a big grin. "I can handle that."

Cody kept checking his phone, making sure they would leave the restaurant in plenty of time to reach the theater on the early side. He wanted to soak in the atmosphere, enjoy the fact that he was actually in Bailey's territory, in the place where she'd spent most of her time for most of the past year.

Finally, after DeMetri polished off his dessert and still had room for another soda, Cody decided to share the truth about Bailey. As much as Smitty needed to know, anyway. "Okay, so this play we're going to see . . ."

"It's called *Hairspray.* You've seen it, right Coach? You said you'd seen it."

"I've seen the movie. But not the Broadway show." Cody had seen DeMetri fired up before, but never like this. "Anyway, about the show . . . so there's this girl in the cast. Her name's Bailey Flanigan."

DeMetri raised one eyebrow. "You know a

279

girl in the cast?"

"She's from Bloomington. Where I grew up."

With a muffled gasp, Smitty pushed back from the table and rose to his feet. He only sat back down when Cody urged him to do so. "Your old girlfriend is in the cast of *Hairspray?*"

Cody wasn't sure how to answer that one. He shifted in his seat, angling himself toward DeMetri to buy a few seconds. "Well . . . I mean, I guess. I used to live with her family."

"Coach!" Shock mixed with a teasing sort of indignation. "You lived with her?"

"Not like that." Cody shook his head. "Very funny."

"Just kidding." Smitty crossed his arms, pleased with the situation. "So you lived with her family, and you fell in love with her. But then she left Indiana for New York City, and you found Cheyenne . . . and now you're here to see her on Broadway for the first time? Is that what's happening here?"

If only the kid knew how close he was to the truth. "You're missing a few details."

"But for the most part?"

"Well, yes. I guess so."

"So why didn't we plan to see *Hairspray* from the beginning? I mean, Coach, we just got lucky that's all. Otherwise you would've missed her."

He would've missed her. Cody let the thought work its way through him. *Like I've missed her so many times,* Cody told himself. "Yes . . . it must've been meant to be."

"Ooooh." DeMetri's eyebrows lowered and he looked suddenly worried. "What'll Cheyenne think? You seeing your old girlfriend tonight?"

Again there were things Smitty simply didn't know. "Chey's sick."

"I thought she was over it. Whatever it was."

"No." The truth about the gravity of Cheyenne's illness would come out eventually. For now it was enough that Cody didn't betray her confidence. "She's still pretty sick, Smitty."

"So . . . she's okay that you're here. That you might see this Bailey girl tonight."

Cody nodded slowly, picturing his last conversation with Cheyenne. "She told me to come."

"Wow." He gave an impressed shake of his head. "Not sure I could tell my girlfriend to go hang with her old boyfriend. That's pretty big of her, Coach."

"Chey has a pretty big heart." He checked

the time again. "Finish your soda. It's time to go."

DeMetri slurped down the rest of his drink, catching himself and quieting the process before he reached the bottom of the glass. "Ready!"

Whether he saw Bailey after the show or not, the next few hours would be some of the best Cody had experienced in months. They didn't need the limo to reach the show on time. The walk was only four blocks from the restaurant, and it gave them the chance to take in the enormous lit advertisements and craziness that could only be found in Times Square. "Would you look at that M&M guy up there?" Smitty stopped and shaded his eyes, squinting at the display above the three-story shop that featured exclusively M&M candy items. "It's the size of King Kong." He looked at Cody. "Don't you think, Coach. I mean seriously. Who puts an M&M man that tall on the top of their store?"

The running montage of exclamations continued the entire way to the theater, and only after they'd been let in and found their place in the third row, center, did DeMetri finally fall quiet.

"What . . . you don't have an opinion for once?" Cody whispered as they settled into the red velvet seats.

"Shhh." DeMetri put his finger to his lip. "You can't talk in the theater. Didn't your mama teach you anything?"

Coming from anyone else the idea of a mama comment might seem heartless. But both their mothers were serving time. Smitty's statement only made Cody smile. "You can whisper. It's okay. The show won't start for fifteen minutes."

Once he had permission, DeMetri began to comment on everything from the quality of the seats to the way *SI* had picked the best place in the whole theater for them to see the show. "Coach, I say try to win it all again next year. This is too nice for one time only. Those *SI* guys know how to do a night on the town right, you know what I mean?"

Finally, when DeMetri must've been nearly out of words, he settled in on the program and for the first time that night Cody had a few minutes to think. At the same time he texted Tara. He couldn't enjoy the next few hours without at least an update on Cheyenne.

We're at the theater . . . DeMetri's having the time of his life . . . How is she?

Her response came back almost instantly: *The same . . . sleeping. Don't worry about her, Cody. She wants you to enjoy your night with DeMetri.*

A flash of guilt came over him, like maybe he should mention that the next few hours wouldn't be just about him and his player. They'd be about Bailey too. But he let it pass. He would explain the situation later. After all, he didn't pick the show. The guys at *SI* did. He tapped out a quick response. *Will do. Thanks, Tara.*

"Hey, Coach." Smitty's tone was awe-struck again. He held up the program. "Is this her? Your Bailey girl?" He pointed to a black and white photograph, one Cody hadn't seen before. In it Bailey looked absolutely stunning. Her face and cheekbones, the way her hair fell. And her eyes . . . most of all her eyes. He steadied himself, not willing to let his feelings show in front of DeMetri. "Yes . . . that's her."

"Coach! She was in *Unlocked!* Why didn't you tell me that?"

"Sorry. She was in *Unlocked.*"

"That means . . . he did a quick calculation in his head. "She's the girl dating Brandon Paul."

"You know your pop culture trivia, Smitty. Gotta hand it to you."

"Coach, she's famous and she's hot." He dropped the program on his lap and held up both hands in a sign of mock surrender.

284

"I mean, don't take that wrong, Coach. Just saying."

"Yeah." He laughed quietly. "She's pretty."

He shrugged big. "Just saying."

Before Cody could respond, the lights went down and the audience erupted in applause. The house wasn't quite full, but the people in attendance were enthusiastic, for sure. Only then, as the curtain came up, did Cody notice something he'd missed before. Seated in the front row in what looked like a group of three people was — yes, it was him. It was Brandon Paul.

Cody felt the blood leave his face. After all this time he was finally at one of Bailey's shows and now . . . now the few minutes he might have with Bailey after the show would be awkward at best, with Brandon here too. Cody glanced at DeMetri. The kid's eyes were glued to the stage, oblivious to the fact that Brandon Paul was in their midst. Just as well. He probably wouldn't be able to focus on the show.

As the first scene got underway, Cody remembered the show a little better. If Bailey was in the ensemble, then her first appearance would happen at the end of this number. And sure enough that's exactly what happened. Despite the high energy of the number, Bailey came onto the stage moving in what felt like slow motion. He felt his lips open, felt the surprise work through his body, heart, and soul.

"She's really good." DeMetri leaned close and whispered. "And definitely hot."

"Shhh." They couldn't talk now, during the show. Not seated this close to the stage. "Later."

DeMetri flashed the okay sign and turned his attention back to the stage. Cody did the same and by the end of the scene the mix of emotions coursing through him was almost more than he could handle. First, she was a brilliant dancer. And that only made his next emotion more upsetting. Why had he waited until now to see her perform? He could've certainly found a way here before tonight. But instead she'd followed her passion and he hadn't seemed even remotely interested.

He was so angry with himself he had a hard time staying seated. Like seeing her now was enough to cause him physical pain — especially in light of all he'd missed, all the ways he hadn't been invested in her passion. No wonder she'd fallen for Brandon Paul. He was working in New York. So did that mean he came to every show? Cody had a feeling he knew the answer, and it only made him feel worse.

No matter how much he hurt, he had no right messing with what Bailey had found with Brandon, the way he clearly adored her. But partway through her next number, Bailey seemed to spot him. A minute later, she glanced his direction again and this time he was certain she'd seen him. Because she nearly tripped. For a brief instant, Cody considered leaving so he wouldn't cause her any more confusion. But he couldn't pull himself away, couldn't do anything but watch the entire show and then walk with DeMetri and the rest of the crowd to the stage door.

No matter how awkward the coming moments might be.

Cody couldn't tell her how she made him feel or that he still loved her or that watching her tonight made him fall in love with her all over again. None of those things would be right or fair. But Brandon Paul or not, Cody couldn't leave New York City without telling her at least this much:

She was absolutely perfect in *Hairspray.*

Fifteen

Bailey could only thank God that she hadn't fallen flat on her face when she spotted Cody in the audience. Not only was Brandon there in the front row, but Cody had never come to see her before. Why in the world would he be here now? She tried to ignore his presence, but clearly he was there with one of his players. The kid from the article — DeMetri, right? That was his name, Bailey was almost sure.

Again, why would the two of them be here in New York City?

She focused by finding Brandon in the audience instead. And each time, Brandon's belief in her, his love for her kept her from looking at Cody and carried her through the scene. But that didn't stop the fact that she was barely going through the motions, or the way her heart wouldn't drop the subject: Cody Coleman had finally come to see her perform on Broadway.

When the show finally wrapped up, despite Cody's presence she checked her emotions and realized something that made her relax a little. She was still most excited to see Brandon. The loyal way he had of being here every night, the way he'd opened his heart so completely to her. But she had to find a way to see Cody too. If he waited near the stage door anyway. And knowing Cody there was no guarantee he'd do that.

She wanted to tell Brandon that Cody was there, but in the rush backstage, there wasn't a perfect moment to have that conversation. She changed clothes quickly and together they headed out. They'd been doing this more often lately, and there was no denying one very real truth: Brandon's presence at the show each night, his willingness to sign autographs and take pictures with fans after the show had helped attendance.

"You were amazing." He hugged her and kissed the side of her head. "Let's get through this. I can't wait to be alone with you."

She opened her mouth to tell him about Cody, but as she did one of the girls from the cast came up and hugged her, and then Gerald and Stefano did the same thing. "Loved the audience tonight." Gerald's eyes looked happier than usual. "They loved us."

Stefano rolled his eyes. "I liked how the hairspray can wasn't on the prop table — always great to pantomime the biggest song in the show."

Again before Bailey could find even a single instant to say what she needed to say to Brandon, the two of them were shuttled out the stage door and immersed in the crowd. Bailey spotted Cody the moment the New York night air washed over her. He waited for her off to the right, a little before the actual start of the line to meet the show's cast.

Because of her role in *Unlocked,* and because she was dating Brandon Paul, she was always a favorite with the crowd. But Brandon was easily more popular than her. And now she touched his elbow and whispered near his ear. "I'll be right back. I have to talk to someone."

He nodded, and a bewildered look came from him for a moment or two. Then he squeezed her hand as they headed in opposite directions. Bailey held up her hand, letting the crowd know she would join Brandon in a minute. Then she slid past a row of people and worked her way toward Cody and the football player. She looked over her shoulder once and — in the fraction of an instant — she watched Brandon make eye contact with Cody. Brandon knew what he looked like, of course. Cody's face had graced the cover of *Sports Illustrated* just a few weeks ago.

Brandon shifted his look to her, and his expression told her all she needed to know. He was troubled and confused about why Cody was here. But he trusted her. He didn't need to say a word for her to know that much. She made a beeline toward Cody and finally she slid free from the crowd.

Despite the chaos and flashing cameras, regardless of the commotion that surrounded the stage door, in that moment it might as well have been just the two of them, her and Cody standing face-to-face. "Hi."

"Hi." Cody didn't look away, didn't seem to want to.

But beside him the football player coughed a few times and jabbed Cody with his elbow. "Coach . . . remember? You were going to introduce me?"

"Right." Cody tore his eyes from her and glanced at the kid beside him. "Bailey, this is DeMetri Smith. Smitty, this is Bailey Flanigan."

"Coach tells me you're his old girlfriend, but I find that hard to believe." The boy puffed his chest out. "Coach is a pretty smart guy, you know? If he ever had a chance with a girl like you I can't believe he'd find a way to blow it."

Bailey laughed out loud. "Yeah . . . my thoughts exactly."

"Great." Cody dug his hands in his jeans pockets and looked at her again. "Never thought my players would be critiquing my love life."

"Well, yeah!" Smitty gave him a disappointed look. "Seriously Coach. You don't leave a girl like this."

Again Bailey laughed, but Cody managed to give DeMetri a look that finally stopped him. "You know," DeMetri pointed at Cody. "I'm gonna go get Brandon Paul's autograph." He nodded at Bailey. "Pleasure meeting you, Bailey." His eyes flirted with her, then he shot another look at Cody. "I mean, really, Coach? Come on!"

"Go." Cody grinned at the kid, and after he'd walked away he looked at Bailey one more time. Again the moment felt like it was created for them alone. "So . . . you were amazing tonight."

"Thank you." She felt herself blush beneath his gaze, and she hated herself for it. "You should've come sooner."

"Yeah." He flashed her a sad sort of grin. "I guess I blew that too."

"Pretty much." She smiled, but only to hide the pain his words caused her. They couldn't spend another minute talking about what might have been. It was the story of Cody's life. One regret after another. "So . . . why are you here?"

"The state title." He explained about the luncheon with *SI* and the interview with ESPN. "DeMetri handled himself like a pro."

"Yeah, the kid doesn't hold anything back."

"No." Cody looked after his player and chuckled. "He'll make a great preacher someday."

"For sure." Bailey hugged herself, suddenly very aware that she and Cody hadn't come together in a greeting of any kind. With the paparazzi lurking at every backstage moment, that was probably just as well. A goodbye hug would be better than starting off that way. Already she could feel someone taking her picture. Which meant they were taking Cody's picture too. When she couldn't take looking into his eyes another moment, she looked down at the dirty pavement. Everything about her relationship with Cody was so wrong. Missed chances and lost opportunities. Fear and mistrust and doubt — negative emotions ruled the day when it came to him. The way they always had.

"Brandon's here." It wasn't a question.

She lifted her eyes to his. "Every night."

He nodded slowly. "I can see why. Watching you . . . it would never get old, Bailey."

She breathed in deep, not sure what to say next. "Cheyenne . . . how are things with her?" Bailey hoped he might say they were over — for the girl's sake more than anything else. Cody wasn't in love with her. She could easily see that much a month ago when they talked after the game.

"Not great." He shoved his hands into his pockets a little deeper and raised his shoulders a few inches. A different kind of pain fell over his eyes. "She's . . . she's been sick."

It wasn't the answer Bailey expected. "Very sick?"

"Yeah. Pretty sick."

Bailey didn't want to ask too many questions. "Related to her accident?"

"I think so." If there were more details to share, Cody wasn't telling.

"I'm sorry."

"It's okay. She'll get through it."

The moment was coming to an end, and there was nothing Bailey could do to prolong it. She wondered what had happened between Cody and Cheyenne to keep them together, but it wasn't her business. The moment passed and all they had between them was a silence as unfamiliar as it was uncomfortable. Bailey looked over her shoulder back at Brandon, and then to Cody once more. "Thanks . . . for waiting. You know, to say hi."

"You were the best dancer on the stage."

"Thanks."

More silence, and finally he smiled, but without the depth she was familiar with. "So, yeah . . . good seeing you."

"You, too." She didn't hug him, didn't do anything but hold her ground.

He took a step back and set his jaw, his teary eyes on some distant piece of sky. Then he glanced at her one last quick time. "Bye, Bailey."

"Bye, Cody." She didn't wait, didn't watch to see if he would be okay. Didn't consider going back to him again to hug him or comfort him. Brandon was waiting. She made her way through the crowd, head down, so people wouldn't notice her until she was at Brandon's side again. He was still busy, still signing autographs and taking pictures, a crowd of people gathered around him. As she came closer to him, Bailey was grateful. His distraction meant he wouldn't notice the one thing she didn't want him to see.

The rebel tears fresh on her cheeks.

The guy was Cody Coleman. Brandon knew it the moment he saw the way he looked at Bailey. The two of them had never met, and Brandon didn't see any reason to change that. But the whole time Bailey talked to him, Brandon did little more than go through the motions. In some ways he wanted to pull the guy aside and ask him how he could've been so careless.

Back when he and Bailey filmed *Unlocked,* Cody was all she could talk about. She wasn't interested in Brandon's flirting or attempts at luring her away. Her heart was undivided for Cody, for the guy she'd grown up loving. He would tease her about it, more because he was jealous than anything else. *Where is he, Bailey? Why doesn't he come by? What's the truth about your invisible boyfriend?*

She put up with him, but in the end Cody's lack of attention had given Brandon the chance he needed. The opportunity to show Bailey how she deserved to be treated.

"Brandon! Over here!" People screamed his name from the crowd, but even as he raced his Sharpie pen across dozens of programs, he didn't acknowledge them. Not really. He could only think of her — beautiful and talented and trusting him that this was a love he'd never known before.

God had worked out the timing, no question. Because when they met, Brandon wasn't ready for a girl like Bailey. Not at first. He would've seen her as just one more conquest, and when he realized her virtue he would've walked away, uninterested. Ready for the next fling willing to sleep with him.

The reality of who he used to be turned his stomach.

"Over here! Brandon, are you and Bailey dating? Tell us about it!" Voices called to him from every direction.

He smiled and waved and ignored the questions.

A girl like Bailey deserved to have someone fight for her. And since Cody never did that, as long as God would let him, Brandon certainly would. He glanced over his shoulder at her, trying to keep his concern to himself. She was backing up, pulling away from Cody. Headed his way once more.

Brandon felt himself exhale, and he wondered how long he'd been holding his breath. When she finally reached his side he literally felt whole again, like all was right with the night and the world. For the next thirty minutes they met with the crowd, and when Brandon's private SUV pulled up they made a dash for it.

They didn't say much on the way to her apartment, and not until they were sitting in the small sofa overlooking the city did Brandon feel himself unwind a little, feel his thoughts come together in a way he could talk about. Bob and Betty were already asleep, and Brandon was silently thankful. He and Bailey needed this time, and it was too cold for the roof tonight. For a long time he held her hands and watched her, reading the emotions in her eyes.

"That was Cody, the guy I was talking to."

He nodded. "I know." His heart thudded so hard, he wondered if she could hear it. "I recognized him . . . from *SI*."

"Right." She focused more intently on him. "He was in town for an ESPN interview. It was . . . the first time he'd been to my show."

Brandon wanted to say that was Cody's loss. But he kept his teeth pressed together, the words unspoken.

"What are you thinking?" Bailey looked worried, but not guilty. Definitely not guilty.

"I guess that depends on what *you're* thinking." He smiled, but deep inside he imagined how he would feel if in this moment she threw him a curve, if she admitted deep feelings for Cody. If she broke up with him. The thoughts hurt too much to consider, and he banished them from his conscious. He angled his head. "So . . . how was it? Seeing him?"

"Strange." She bit her lip and looked down at her lap for a moment. "For years . . . too many years . . . I thought God had Cody in my life so that he and I could be together." She allowed a sad laugh, maybe at the memory of the girl she'd been back then. "When he came home from Iraq I thought God saved him for me." She raised her shoulders and let them fall again. "But with Cody it's always been something. He didn't feel he was good enough, he didn't want to get in the way. Didn't want to get hurt."

"So he kept his distance." Brandon's voice was soft, meant to be the tender caress, the understanding her heart needed.

"Yes. Over and over again." She shook her head a few times. "I mean, it's still sad. Seeing him. Knowing what he walked away from. But . . . the feelings I had for him. They've changed."

Brandon did his best not to look alarmed. The change couldn't have been for the better . . . not when the two of them were so in love. "Changed?"

"Yes. When I hugged him on my porch that night after the game, it was like hugging a brother. Someone I cared about, but not someone I wanted to run off with." She winced a little. "Does that make sense?"

Light shone through the tightly closed shutters of his heart, the places where he was afraid of what this conversation might bring. "Yes. It does."

"To be honest . . . all I could think when I was talking to him was how," she released one of his hands and touched his face, her fingers like breath against his skin. "How much I wanted to be with you."

Relief filled him, but he kept his smile measured. He didn't want her to know just how worried he'd been, how empty and awful he felt signing autographs knowing that somewhere behind him Bailey was connecting again with Cody Coleman. He grinned, desperately wanting to lighten the mood now that his heartbeat had returned to normal. "So . . . you're saying I don't have to worry about Cody."

"No." Her answer was as sure as the love in her eyes. "You don't have to worry about him."

"Plus, if you measure us by how many times I've seen your show . . ." He brushed

300

his knuckles against the imaginary lapel of his wool sweater. "I win in a landslide."

"True." She laughed and the sound was like the most beautiful music. In a move that was as quick as it was cute, she bounced onto her knees and framed his face with her hands. She kissed him, still laughing. "Wanna know the truth?"

"Always." He felt himself falling once again into the trance that was Bailey Flanigan. He put his hand around her waist, keeping her close. "What's the truth?"

"You win by a landslide in every category."

"Really?" He made a dramatic face and wiped pretend sweat from his brow. "I'm glad to hear it . . . I mean, I really work at it. Training and the proper diet. All that stuff you don't think about."

Again she laughed as she plopped back down in the seat beside him. They talked for a minute about the growing crowd outside the theater, and Brandon was grateful. Glad beyond words that they'd moved past the discussion about Cody. The guy would always be a part of her past. But Brandon believed her. There was no concern Cody would ever be a part of her future.

Before he left that night, he worked the conversation back to the two of them, to the place where God was taking their relationship. "I'll be finished soon, headed back to LA."

Sadness flickered in her eyes. "I try not to think about it."

"And you . . . You'll still be here. Eight shows a week."

"Yes." She looked out the window. "Some of the cast thinks the show's doing a lot better." Her eyes found him again. "Probably because of you. People get two shows in one."

"Ha-ha." He put his hand on her shoulder, wishing they could share another few hours this way, together with the rest of the world shut out.

"Actually . . . I'm serious. Something's changed. We see Francesca in these meetings with the producers and it feels like we've turned a corner. Like the show might be given another year at least."

The realization sank like a rock in his stomach. "Hmmm." He couldn't let her see the way he felt. Couldn't let her think that maybe he wanted her show to close. "Whatever I can do to help." He grinned, but only to cover up the truth coming to light in his soul. By coming to see Bailey every day, he may have unwittingly helped prolong the run of the show. Which in turn would delay the two of them getting more serious than they were. Brandon's next two pictures filmed in LA. So the time they'd have together would be like before December: clandestine two-day visits and long Skype dates. Nothing more.

"I know what you're thinking." Tenderness filled her eyes. "Don't pretend around me, Brandon."

"What?" His quick response was one of pretend surprise, indignation. "Me? Pretend?"

"Come on. You don't want me here another year." She wasn't upset by the fact, just aware of it.

He let the charade fall away. "Okay, seriously? Of course I want you here, if that's where God has you." He waved to the city beyond the window. "Broadway . . . this is your dream, Bailey. I want that for you."

"But?"

"But in my heart . . ." He put his hand over his chest. "I wish you were in LA. With me." He gave her a sad smile. "Of course I want that."

"I guess . . . if that happened, I'm just not sure what I'd do there."

"You'd act." His answer came in a hurry. "My agent says he can get you ten auditions in the first week if you ever move to LA."

"Yeah, but . . ." She felt the strange nervousness well up within her again. "I'm not sure about Los Angeles. You know . . . if the life . . . the paparazzi and the insanity . . . if I could get used to it."

This was as deep as the two of them had ever talked about the subject. "What was it Katy said the other night? That it took her awhile, but in the end . . ."

"In the end, it was worth it." Bailey's smile didn't quite take the edge off the sadness of the moment. He was leaving soon and then there were no guarantees for either of them. "I guess I worry about it . . . like, what if I'm not wired like Katy Matthews?" She made a nervous face. "I mean, look how I handled the paparazzi the other night."

"That was the exception. We weren't expecting them."

"I'm not sure I could ever come to expect something like that. Crazy people running after us with giant cameras on a dark beach." She laughed quietly at the memory. "Never having normal . . . being the subject of all that craziness. I don't know, it makes me afraid sometimes, Brandon." The honesty in her tone cut him to the core. "Really afraid."

He wanted to cheer her on, insist that she was absolutely wired like Katy. Of course she could handle his public life. She had handled their time in New York City, right? She could certainly handle LA. But he didn't want to force the issue. In the end, she would have to make her own decision. It was the most terrifying part of being in love: that without a commitment to forever, separation was still possible.

"I guess we don't have to deal with every issue right now." He pushed his concerns aside. If he let himself think about all the possibilities he would make a case for Los Angeles here and now, fight for her and for them as if his next heartbeat depended on it. "Hey, we have a few more weeks, right? And we have tonight."

She studied him, as if something he'd just said baffled her. "You're really not afraid, are you?"

"Afraid?"

"About us . . . about where it goes from here or about whether we really have a future together."

He looked deeper into her heart. This was not one of those moments when he wanted to keep his thoughts to himself. When it came to their relationship, transparency was crucial. "Honestly?"

"Yes . . . of course."

"I'm terrified, Bailey." He ran his hand

down her arm, never looking away from her loving eyes. "I've never loved like this. Never known what love was until I met you." He shook his head slightly, overwhelmed again by the strength of his feelings for her. "But the fear of losing you doesn't make me run the other way." He slid his fingers between hers, holding tight to the connection between them. "It makes me run toward you."

His words must've been just what she needed to hear, because her eyes teared up, even though there wasn't a hint of sadness remaining in her smile. "That's why I love you. Because you run toward me."

"And I'll keep running. I'll fight for you until you tell me to stop." He pulled her close and cradled her head against his chest. "Love always involves fear. There are no guarantees about tomorrow for any of us. But in the meantime, while we're waiting for answers . . . while we're wondering what's at the end of this road . . . I want to walk it with you."

"Fearless?"

"Pretending to be fearless." He ran his hand over her hair, her back. "What does the Bible say about love? Perfect love?"

"It casts out fear."

"Right. So that's the way we have to live. When fear comes, we let our love send it packing."

"Okay." She wrapped her arms around his waist and held on tighter than usual . . . longer than usual. They didn't say much until ten minutes later when he finally had to leave. There was no need to rehash what they'd talked about. The reality was more complicated than the exchange of a seaweed ring on New Year's Eve along a Malibu shore. Their lives, their careers, and passions would prevent any long-term relationship, and until something changed no certain answers existed. Except one. The one that came from the Bible. When love was perfect, it would always cast out fear.

Again and again and again.

Sixteen

Jenny Flanigan felt moved to pray for Bailey more often lately, and even though she had no explanation for her feeling, she heeded it. Sometimes every hour of the day. It was Wednesday, almost halfway through January, and tonight Ricky's middle school church group was meeting at their house. The group took turns at different locations, and always when it was at their house the crowd seemed to swell. The Flanigans had more room, and so friends were welcome. It was a good chance to reach new kids.

She and Jim finished adding chairs to the circle in the living room, and she turned on the fireplace. It would take a few minutes for the flames to heat the room, and with the cold outside, Jenny wanted their meeting place extra toasty.

They were nearly finished setting up when Jim stopped and looked at her. "Did I tell you about Ryan Taylor?"

"No." Jenny leaned against the back of the chair she'd just moved in and blew at a wisp of hair that had fallen from her ponytail. "What about him?"

"The Colts made him an offer. This morning."

"Jim!" She shrieked her response and immediately put her hand over her mouth. She lowered her voice. "Are you serious? That's amazing!"

"I was going to call you on the way back from the practice field. But I forgot about it until now." He stood straight, his arms crossed. "The owners loved him when he came in for the interview last week. He'll fit in perfectly with the staff."

"That's the greatest news. I'll have to call Kari in the morning and celebrate with her." The Baxters had been friends of the Flanigans for years. Kari was the oldest of the Baxter siblings, and she'd been married for nearly ten years to Ryan Taylor. Ryan had some pro experience, but he'd coached Clear Creek for the last several seasons. Suddenly another question hit Jenny. "What about the head coaching job at Clear Creek?"

Jim laughed. "I was waiting for you to ask." He raised his brow. "What do you think?"

She sucked in a quick breath and held it. "Not Cody Coleman!"

"Why not?" Again Jim laughed. "Can you think of someone more perfect for the job?"

This time Jenny screamed out loud before she caught herself. "Jim, I can't believe it. I prayed about this exact thing. That Cody might return to Bloomington. Because he needs to be closer to family and he's spent long enough out there in Lyle. Plus our boys need to play for him, especially Ricky who hasn't even started high school." She rattled off five more quick reasons before she stopped and laughed at herself. "Cody's coming back to Clear Creek! I can't believe it."

"He only heard about the position this morning."

"So." Jenny laughed. "He'll get it. You and I both know that."

Jim came to her and wrapped his arms around her shoulders. "That's why I love you. Because you're so subdued, so subtle."

"Hey . . . I can be subtle when I want to."

"Subtle as a rifle." He kissed her, and his eyes told her he wouldn't have it any other way. "And listen . . . it's not for sure yet. Cody asked for time."

"Time?" Jenny tried to imagine a single

310

reason. "I figured he'd be halfway here by now."

"Not quite." Jim brushed the hair back from her forehead. "He's gotten attached to those kids at Lyle. It's a big decision."

Jenny nodded, understanding. "I'm sure they love him. Same as we do."

"Exactly."

They returned to getting the house ready for Bible study, and the whole time Jenny prayed for Cody, and for God's will with the Clear Creek football program. But that wasn't all. She prayed for Cody and Bailey too. She took a bowl of fresh apple slices to the sink and ran cold water over them. As she did, a picture came to mind: a memory she hadn't thought about in years.

It was Fourth of July and Cody had just returned from Iraq. He'd been a prisoner of war for months, and none of them had been sure they'd ever see him again. But that day, in the hours before the Flanigans' backyard picnic, they did know Cody was coming home — they just hadn't expected him for another week or so.

Jenny remembered the moment as clearly as if she were watching it play out again in front of her. Jenny had been upstairs when the doorbell rang. She moved to her bedroom door, ready to jog down and answer it. But before she could make a move, Bailey had appeared from the kitchen area and opened the front door.

And there he had been: Cody Coleman. Walking with crutches, and looking years wiser than he had when he left for training the year before. He came into the house and took Bailey into his arms. The hug they shared, the look between them, had made Jenny feel like an intruder. But even still she couldn't turn away. And she remembered thinking then a thought that stayed with her over the years: No one would ever love Bailey the way Cody Coleman loved her.

Jenny turned off the water and let the apple slices drain through the bottom of the colander. Lately she'd wondered about that thought, about Cody's love for Bailey. Images filled her mind, pictures she'd seen on Google, the ones the paparazzi caught every day or so of Bailey and Brandon. The way Brandon's eyes were always on her, no matter the picture. How there was no denying the adoration in his expression or the way he kept his hand at the small of her back, his arm around her shoulders. The love he felt for Bailey was so strong, so beautiful the whole world wanted a window to watch.

So maybe Cody's love was only a part of Bailey's past — the guy who taught her what it felt like to care so strongly. Maybe God had brought Brandon into her life for more than a distraction, more than a way to comfort her broken heart over the way Cody had walked out of her life.

Maybe Brandon was the guy God intended for Bailey all along.

"The kids are here."

She blinked and the thoughts left as quickly as they'd come. "What about Landon?"

"He's here too." Jim kissed her cheek. "Need help?"

"No, thanks." She wiped her damp hands on her jeans. "Apple slices and barbecue potato chips. I think we're set."

He glanced at the apples and gave her a doubtful look. "Wishful thinking, honey. Hope you have an extra bag of chips."

She laughed and finished setting the counter with the snacks. Landon Blake was their guest speaker tonight. His new role working with the sheriff department's drug intervention program was bringing him fresh purpose. Jenny had talked with Ashley about it yesterday.

"Ever since Christmas, it's like the old Landon is back." Ashley had sounded like she could cry over the change. "He's seen too many people overdose on drugs, been on too many calls where it wasn't a fire, but a lost life that caused them to respond. This new program . . . it's his way of saving people like he used to. Just without the smoke and flames."

Jenny loved that, loved the way God's plans for people sometimes changed, but no matter what the purpose remained. And it remained in a good way. Tonight the Bible study was on holiness. Being set apart from the crowd. Not giving in to the ways of the world. Landon would finish up by telling the kids what drug addiction looked like, how to recognize it in their friends, and how to report it if they were concerned.

In no time the study got underway, and after reading several Bible verses, Landon took the floor. "How many of you know that kids at Clear Creek are doing drugs?"

Jenny felt a flicker of discomfort from the place where she sat at the back of the room next to Jim. She'd like to think that none of them knew this, because none of the kids at Clear Creek were really using. But in the room of fifty kids, at least half of them raised their hands. Among them were Justin and Shawn.

"What?" She whispered. Her heart raced at twice its usual speed as she slid to the edge of her seat and watched. Beside her,

Jim squeezed her hand, clearly as troubled as she was.

"Okay, you can put your hands down." Landon took a handful of plastic Ziploc bags from the kit he'd brought with him. "Kids at Clear Creek are smoking pot." He held up a bag that contained a small sampling of what looked like marijuana. "They're doing cocaine." Again he held up a bag, this time with a small amount of a white, powdery substance. "They're doing ecstasy." The next bag held small white pills. "And they're doing heroin. Especially lately, because it's less expensive. People who used to do meth have switched to something cheaper." He lifted the last of the bags. "You'll see there's more than white powder in the bag. There's also a small end piece to a rubber balloon. If one of your friends has these lying around their car or in their backpack, you can be almost sure they're doing heroin. Because that's how heroin comes — tied in small pieces of balloons."

Jenny was horrified. This was all news to her. She liked the idea of having the kids' friends over, liked thinking of them working toward the next football season and getting excited about whatever school dance was coming up. The idea that their friends might be doing heroin was enough to make her sick to her stomach.

But even as she didn't want to believe it, she saw a few of the kids nodding along. They were as aware of the situation as Landon was, and the reality shocked Jenny like little had in a long time.

"Sometimes," Landon put the Ziploc bags back in his kit, "kids at school are involved in something and everyone sort of makes a pact. Like, don't ask . . . don't tell. Kids keep secrets for each other." He paused, pacing in front of them, making eye contact with some of the guys who had nodded earlier. "No one wants to tell on their buddy, right?"

The response was less obvious, but Jenny was still amazed. Landon had every kid's attention. As if all of them could relate in some way to what he was saying.

"But guess what, guys? Your silence could kill one of your friends." He waited, letting his words hit their mark. "That's right. When I was a firefighter, sometimes the calls involved drug overdoses. I'll tell you about a call we took last year after homecoming. The kids were in their early twenties, Clear Creek graduates, still home for the summer, not quite back to college. A group of them came to the game and left at halftime, looking for more action, more excitement."

Throughout the room, the kids were glued to the story.

"Around eleven o'clock someone brought over a bag of cocaine and a few balloons full of heroin. Some of the kids had used drugs before, but Darien had stayed away from it. Always at the party, but never doing the partying."

A few of the kids exchanged looks, and Jenny figured they could relate. If drugs were really that big of an issue, then lots of kids probably attended the parties where the using went down.

"Anyway, Darien decided — what with it being homecoming and all — that he would use a little heroin too. Just that one time. But the heroin made him feel sky high, and he figured maybe a little cocaine would make him feel even better . . . that, and a few beers."

Landon stopped, waiting until he was sure he had every student's attention again. "By the time his friends found him the next morning, Darien was blue. His skin was cold and he hadn't been breathing since maybe one or two in the morning." Landon folded his arms, his voice heavy with emotion. "Darien was a college athlete, a kid who had avoided the party scene year after year until that moment. He was the only boy in a family of girls, a kid with good grades and a dream of being a lawyer when he finished school."

Jenny heard a few of the girls sniffling, saw them wiping tears.

"He did drugs one time. Just once." Landon lowered his voice, respecting the fact that the story was hitting its mark. "He never called home, never asked for help. Never said goodbye to his parents or his sisters."

One of the girls uttered an audible sob, and she buried her head in her arms. A few of the guys were sniffling too.

"I talked to his mother at the hospital, and I'm pretty sure about this. The questions in her eyes will stay there the rest of her life. She kept saying the same thing over and over. 'Darien doesn't do drugs . . . I just don't get it. I don't understand.' "

Jenny felt two tears slide onto her cheek, and she wiped them quickly, blinking so she could see clearly as Landon finished his presentation.

"Here's the thing . . . Darien thought those guys were his friends. But they never really were. Because they gave him drugs. And his real friends — the ones who knew what Darien was getting into that night, the ones who didn't say anything or try to stop him — they can never go back and change it." Landon clenched his jaw, a controlled anger sounding in his voice. "I'd like to say this. Real friends . . . don't give you heroin and cocaine." He took a step closer. "And they don't stand by and do nothing if they think one of their buddies is doing drugs."

Landon explained that he would be there for half an hour after the Bible study was finished. "If you've seen something, if you have even the hint of a doubt about one of your friends, then come tell me. I'll follow up; I'll be the bad guy." He paused. "You be a friend. That sort of friend Darien could've used after Homecoming last year."

Jenny wasn't sure which she wanted to do more — break down and weep or give Landon a standing ovation. Whatever work he'd done saving people from burning buildings, nothing could've been more important than the talk he'd just given these fifty kids.

And later when she watched her own boys — Justin and Shawn — approach Landon and tell him about some of their friends, she could hardly wait to call Ashley. Because her husband had definitely found his purpose.

He was saving lives like never before.

■ ■ ■ ■

Cody prayed about the offer from Clear
Creek High, but in the end the decision was
easy. Clear Creek was where he'd first fallen
in love with football, and it was where he'd
first decided to coach the game. If God was
calling him back to Bloomington, he would
go. Cody had told the Lyle High administration, and already one of the experienced
middle school coaches was quietly being
asked to take over. The Lyle High leader-
ship was at peace with his decision.

Telling the guys in a month or so would
be much tougher.

His meeting that week with the Lyle
football players was one of the hardest in
Cody's life. Not because he was announc-
ing his departure — that would come in
March, after the administration was sure
about his replacement. Rather, the meeting
was difficult because Cody knew his goodbyes were looming. He knew and none of
his players had even the slightest idea.

Their time together that week was more
of a checkup, a chance to turn in equip-
ment from the month before and look
ahead to the off-season and spring training.
Six guys were graduating, among them

DeMetri Smith and Larry Sanders, along with Arnie Hurley. But there were new kids coming up, fresh faces all looking to him and to the program they'd built in just a year.

Cody was glad he had a little time before telling them good-bye. Especially now when Chey was so sick and Cody could hardly think about football.

He pulled up outside of the doctor's office and hurried up the stairs to the front door. Cheyenne was worse. They could no longer use words like stable to describe her condition.

Tara worked today, so Cody had dropped Cheyenne off at the doctor's and now — a few hours later — he would take her across the street for another MRI and a meeting with her oncologist. Even though Cody had a front row seat to watch Cheyenne be beaten down by her brain cancer, there were moments when he saw the gravity of her situation fresh again. As if it had been weeks since he'd seen her and he was only now realizing how sick she'd gotten.

Today was one of those days.

He walked into the chemo room and stopped in the doorway. A nurse was disconnecting her IV, giving her a sip of something, comforting her. And for a single instant

Cody didn't recognize her. He even glanced quickly around the room to see if maybe she'd switched beds. Because the girl sitting where he'd left Cheyenne looked almost skeletal. Her cheekbones jutted out and her bald head looked too big for her body.

Dear God . . . I can't do this . . . why won't You heal her?

Cody walked toward her.

My son, my grace is sufficient for you.

He set his resolve. There was a time long ago when grace held only a narrow definition for him. When it meant the way God forgave him for his past, for the way he had treated girls, and for his partying. And certainly God extended that type of grace. But lately he'd come to know the deeper meaning of the word. How God's grace didn't only pardon him from sin; it carried him through pain.

Pain like this.

Chey saw him, and with everything she had she tried to smile. "Hi."

"Hi." He wanted to cry, wanted to shout out loud that this wasn't fair. That a beautiful girl shouldn't be dealing with a disease like this. But instead he focused on the moment, how he could help. What little he could do. The nurse was about to help Chey into a waiting wheelchair, but Cody held up his hand. "Here. I'll do it."

The nurse stepped back, close by in case Cody needed help. She reached for an empty blue bag and waited off to the side.

"Here, sweetie . . ." He slid his hands beneath her armpits and moved her to the wheelchair. As he did he was horrified all over again, because she weighed almost nothing — like he was moving a bag of bones. "You okay?"

"I'm . . . fine." She put her head in her hands and breathed harder than before. "A little nauseated. That's all."

That was hardly all. Again Cody clenched his teeth. The battle was so fierce, so relentless. He helped Chey get situated. "Can I take her across the street? To her MRI?"

"Yes." The nurse handed him the white-ringed blue bag. "You might need this."

He didn't want to take it, didn't want to need it, but he had no choice. Not in the way Cheyenne was feeling or the futility of his efforts or the fact that even now she couldn't just come home and rest. None of this was the nurse's fault. He managed a smile in her direction. "Thank you. I'll take her now."

The trip across the street was interrupted twice because Chey felt dizzy moving along in the wheelchair, like she was going to throw up. But she managed to avoid being sick while they made it up to the fourth floor, and while the technician performed yet another MRI. The results would come within an hour, so another nurse put the two of them in an examination room to wait.

Cheyenne seemed a little stronger than earlier. She asked him about his meeting with the Lyle football players. "I bet they can't wait for next year."

This should've been when he told her about the call from Ryan Taylor, the offer waiting for him at Clear Creek High. But he couldn't bring himself to say a word. "The guys are good . . . anxious for another season."

"I bet." She looked off. "You'll do great, Cody. I know it."

He hated this, the way she couldn't say that, yes, she too was looking forward to another season. "They told me . . . to tell you hi." A rush of emotion made it hard for him to find his voice. He cleared his throat, fighting with himself. "They . . . want you in the front row again. Like last year."

"Hmmm." She looked at him, her eyes distant and unsure.

Again he wanted to shout out loud, tell her to keep fighting. But there wasn't anything realistic about the idea. This battle was far beyond her ability or his. Only God could save her life now. Without a miracle, she couldn't look forward to much more than the next day.

Conversation between them was limited, so Cody was grateful when — for once — the doctor didn't take forever to find them with the results. From the moment the man stepped into the room, Cody knew the report was bad. Doctors could only hide so much. He moved to his place beside her wheelchair, ready to support her whatever came next.

"I'm sorry to have to tell you this . . ." The doctor was an expert in his field, someone Tara had connected them with. If anyone might see a glimmer of hope in Cheyenne's battle against brain cancer it was this man.

But the words that came from him now blurred together in a series of terrible fragments, like shrapnel from a losing firefight. *Not responding to treatment . . . more fingers from the tumor . . . the brainstem under attack . . . quality of life had to be considered.*

Cody did everything he could to focus, but he was more concerned about Cheyenne, who seemed to slump a little more in her wheelchair with each bit of information from the doctor. Even still, she was clear-minded enough to ask the question that stood like a mammoth in the middle of the room. "So . . . you're saying there may not be any point . . . in continuing treatment?"

"It's a question we need to ask." The doctor took a step closer and put his hand on her shoulder. "Cases like yours make me wish we were two decades down the road in our research. But today . . . I really don't have any answers."

The air around Cody became hot, and he could almost feel the sand swirling between them. Bombs dropping all around, and he could see Art beside him, watch him hurled to the ground, bleeding from his head and chest. He closed his eyes and willed the images to leave him alone. This wasn't his battle . . . this wasn't Iraq. Cheyenne needed him.

Please, God, clear my mind. Jesus, let me focus on Cheyenne.

Immediately — as soon as he said the name Jesus — the images left and he turned his eyes to the doctor. "If she continues treatment . . . will it . . . will that buy her time at least?"

The man pursed his lips, his expression knit together with frustration and futility. "I can't promise that. So far she's had almost no response to the treatment." He angled his head, clearly hating what he was about to say. "If it were me . . . I'd go home and spend the rest of my days outside buildings like this one."

He explained that Cheyenne could go home now and let the office know what she decided. "We can arrange for hospice at your home, if you should choose that."

Hospice? Cody struggled again to stay in the moment. How could it be that a few months ago Cheyenne was dealing with an occasional headache and now they were talking about hospice? He thanked the doctor, and without saying a word he wheeled Cheyenne out of the room, down the elevator, and out into a freezing cold snowstorm.

"Take me . . . over there." She pointed to a spot out of the way of foot traffic around the corner. "Please, Cody . . ."

He moved her wheelchair as quickly as he could, and she managed to wait until they were alone at the far end of the building before she threw up. He held her up as she heaved again and again, emptying her stomach of whatever little it held. As she dropped back down to the wheelchair, she gasped for breath. "You . . . you shouldn't . . . have to do this."

"Cheyenne, don't." He spoke the words quietly, near the side of her face so she

wouldn't miss his tone. "I'm not going anywhere."

"They . . . can get me hospice. You
shouldn't . . . be here. You don't . . . need
this."

"I need you . . . I need to be with you."
He crouched down beside her wheelchair,
his arms around her thin shoulders. "I'm
not going anywhere. I told you that."

She struggled to her feet and threw up
one more time. As she did she started to
sob, deep waves of hysterics coming up from
her grieving soul. She wiped her mouth and
turned to him, too weak to do anything but
collapse in his arms. "Don't leave me . . .
Please, Cody . . . don't leave."

"Shhh . . . it's okay. I won't leave." His
heart pounded. He still had no idea how
he'd do this. How God expected him to
walk this amazing girl to Heaven's door.
When she quieted down, when she had
some form of control, he spoke the words
once more. "I won't leave."

Whatever happened from this point, however many days or hours Cheyenne had left
on earth, one thing was sure: The words
he'd told her, he meant with everything in
him. He would stay and fight this battle with
her, whatever that meant. Wherever they
wound up.

Because only death could make him leave her now.

SEVENTEEN

Bailey walked through the doors of Starbucks that Wednesday morning, and what she saw made her hesitate half a beat. Gerald was already there, sitting at their familiar table, his Bible open, lost in study.

Who would have thought; she smiled at the picture he made alone there.

God, You're working on his heart. I can see that. Please . . . give me the words. Help me show him Your love.

Bailey stepped into line.

Love, my daughter . . . love in grace and truth.

She was convinced she would do just that. Whatever questions Gerald still had, God would direct her to the right Bible verses, the right approach so that he felt loved both ways: with grace, of course, and with truth — truth that was sometimes easy to forget in today's culture.

Gerald's drink was a double cappuccino

with a pump of caramel. Bailey ordered that and an Americano for herself. Not as heavy as coffee, and less filling than a latte. She took the drinks to the table and Gerald looked up, surprised.

"I lost track of time." He slid over to make room for her. "I thought I still had fifteen minutes."

"I'm early." She handed him the drink. "The others won't be here for a little bit."

"Oh . . . good." He seemed distracted. Like he was still thinking about whatever he'd been studying. He thanked her for the drink and turned his eyes again to the open Bible on the table.

Bailey glanced over. From the looks of it Gerald was reading Romans 12. She sat back and allowed the comfortable silence between them. There wasn't much she could add to whatever God was already saying to her friend. After a couple minutes, Gerald looked up. His eyes shone with layers Bailey had never seen in him before. "Ever feel like God wrote a part of the Bible just for you?"

She smiled. "Every time I read it." Her heart pounded for what was at stake here. "People get freaked out about the Bible . . . like it's something to be used against people. A literary, spiritual hammer." The expression on Gerald's face told her he was tracking with her, not feeling nervous or judged. She put her fingers on the edge of his Bible. "God wants us to see this as His love letter to us. Everything we need to live a life free of the bondage of sin, all we need to experience that abundant life of faith and purpose and closeness to Him."

"Mmm." Gerald closed his eyes for a moment. "Sounds wonderful."

"It is." She chose her tone carefully. "It is for everyone who trusts Him."

Gerald nodded slowly and looked back at the Scripture. "Do not conform any longer to the pattern of this world." He lifted his eyes. "The pattern of this world? The pattern of life here in New York City . . . on Broadway?" He laughed, but the sound was sadder than anything Bailey had heard in a long time. "That pattern is pretty set. Everyone's popping pills and partying . . . sleeping with whoever . . . guys and guys . . . guys and girls . . . whatever."

Her heart ached like it hadn't in a long time. Gerald was right. Living here — regardless of any knowledge of truth — the temptation to feel comfortable was very real. The pattern of the world. "I remember a long time ago . . . my mom made curtains for our TV room." She shifted her gaze, allowing herself to go back to that time when she was fifteen and her brothers were all younger than that and life had seemed so simple, so predictable. "They hung on every window. Six windows. So it was definitely the first thing you noticed when you walked in the room."

Gerald winced. "Let me guess. Bright orange? Or aqua blue?"

A ripple of laughter accompanied the memory. "Close." She made a face in Gerald's direction. "Orange and blue plaid. Seriously."

"Oooh." Gerald shook his head. "Not good."

Bailey's laughter let up, and she was back there again, standing alongside her brothers — speechless as they took in the way the curtains changed the room. "I'll never forget it." She paused. "My mom tilted her head one way, then the other, and finally she shrugged and said. 'If you look at the pattern long enough, you don't really see it.' "

Depth of heart was never an issue for Gerald. He was deep and kind and passionate, and instantly he saw the connection. "Wow . . . that's it, right? Exactly." He narrowed his eyes. "Look at the pattern long enough, and you don't really see it. The pattern of the world."

"Yes. I think about those curtains whenever I read that verse in Romans 12. Do not conform to the pattern of this world." She rested her forearms on the table. "Like God's urging us to get rid of the ugly curtains. Because if we surround ourselves with the wrong patterns long enough . . . we won't even see them."

"Scary." Gerald breathed in slowly through his nose. He lifted his chin, as if he was mentally facing some unseen giant. Ready to take on the pattern of the world. "I like the rest too. Be transformed by the renewing of your mind." A sad smile lifted the corners of his lips. "My grandma used to say, 'Garbage in, garbage out.' "

"I think my grandma used to say the same thing."

Gerald's gaze was off in the distance somewhere, focused on his personal giants — whatever they were. He blinked a few times, but his gaze didn't shift. "I've been . . . a part of the pattern. God's made that really clear." When he looked at her, his eyes were damp. "I'm not sure how to change. I've spent my whole life believing things were okay, things that go against God."

"A lot of us do that." Bailey was treading a slippery path here. "God puts His truth in our hands and then it's up to us. Keep conforming . . ."

"Or be transformed." Gerald's eyes shone with an understanding that hadn't been there before. "I can't see tomorrow. If . . . God will help me be attracted to girls. Or if —" His voice cracked. The tears spilling quietly onto his cheeks. "Or if He'll make it so He's enough. All I need."

Bailey reached out and took hold of Gerald's hands, running her thumbs along his palms, letting him talk — whatever she could do to hide the shock flooding her veins. In all her time in New York she had never dreamed of a moment like this. Her lack of faith made her feel ashamed. How crazy that she'd been willing to read the Bible with her castmates, but never imagined that reading God's Word would really bring about this sort of life-changing response. She felt humbled by the moment, mesmerized by it. God had never been more real in all her life.

"He is, right, Bailey?" Unshed tears filled his beautiful green eyes. "He's enough for me, right?"

"Yes." Bailey didn't realize her own tears until then. She blinked, wiping at her wet cheek with her shoulder. "He's enough. He'll show you the life He has for you. One day at a time, Gerald. Hour by hour."

Gerald nodded, relieved. He eased one of his hands from Bailey and covered his face. For a long moment, quiet sobs got the better of him. The slaying of the giants well underway, the pattern recognized. Bailey had no idea why the others weren't there yet. They were easily five minutes late. But whatever reason, she believed completely that God was behind the delay.

So that this divine moment might have a chance to play out.

He wiped his face and grabbed a quick breath. Despite the very great conflict that had to be raging in his heart, Gerald seemed utterly unaware of the other people in the coffee shop. Not that they were very noticeable with the chaos of Times Square happening all around them — both inside and outside the Starbucks. But the entire street could stop and watch, and it wouldn't have changed the moment for Gerald.

His focus was complete. When he seemed able to talk again, he looked at her once more. Red cheeks and bloodshot eyes, his nose a little runny. "Will you pray with me? So I can have Jesus and His salvation? Please, Bailey?"

She swallowed a few unexpected sobs, blinked back her tears and nodded. "Yes.

Of course." She looked around. The place was busy, but in their corner table the whole world seemed to exist for this moment. "Here?"

"Yes. Here. In the middle of Times Square. Center stage." The sound that came from him was mostly a cry. "I just know I can't go another minute without asking Jesus to save me."

There was nothing she could do about the steady stream of tears on her cheeks now, and she didn't care anyway. She put her hands on Gerald's shoulders and bowed her head close to his. "If you agree with what I'm praying, just repeat the lines of the prayer after me, okay?"

"Okay." Hope filled his tone. "I'm ready."

Bailey had never done anything like this. Sure she'd talked to girls in college about finding faith, and she'd led Bible studies. She'd even played a part in helping Brandon Paul find faith in God. But this? The immeasurable change in Gerald's heart? Bailey felt less than able, but even as that thought crossed her mind God breathed the truth behind it. Bailey wasn't bringing about the change happening here at the worn wooden table in a Starbucks on Broadway.

God was.

She sniffed and found her composure.

Never mind that her tears kept falling. At least she could talk. For now that's all God asked of her. "Dear God, I come to You asking for Your mercy."

Gerald hesitated, and gradually it dawned on him that this was the prayer . . . the one he should repeat if he believed it. He jumped into action the moment the realization must've clicked in his mind. "Dear God, I come to You asking for mercy."

"I admit I'm a sinner . . ."

"I admit I'm a sinner . . ."

"That left to my own ways I would choose death through any number of sins over the life You freely offer."

"That left to my own ways . . ." He hesitated. Then, "I have chosen death through a number of sins over the life You freely offer."

Bailey understood what was happening. Gerald was choosing to edit the prayer to fit him exactly how he was feeling this moment. She felt her hands shake and she tightened her hold on her friend's shoulders. "But now I know the truth, and I ask You to forgive me for my sins." Bailey waited while Gerald repeated the line. "I believe Jesus died on the cross to pay the price for my sins . . . And I ask You to come into my heart and be my Savior for all time." Gerald's voice was heavy with sorrow as he repeated that line. "Right here . . . right now . . . I surrender the old me . . . and I ask You to make me new again. With new life in Jesus Christ."

Gerald put his hands over Bailey's. "Right here . . . right now . . . I surrender the old me." His voice gave out and another few sobs filled in where he could no longer speak. He grabbed a couple fast breaths. "I completely surrender the old me. And I ask you to make me new again. With new life in Jesus Christ."

When the prayer ended, Gerald flew into her arms and the two of them stayed that way for a long time — until finally Bailey felt someone tap her shoulder.

"Uhhh . . . okay, that figures." It was Stefano's voice. "We're late one time . . . one time, and we miss something like this."

Bailey felt the smile on her lips. She opened her eyes and turned in time to see him throw his hands up in the direction of a few of the girls, all of them regulars in the Bible study. The three of them looked from her to Gerald and back again. Their expressions made it clear they were almost afraid to ask what had just happened.

Before she could think of where to begin, Gerald was on his feet. He held his arms out to the sides, his teary eyes all lit up. "I did it! I gave my life to Jesus!"

"You did?" Stefano's shock rang loud in his question. "Are you serious?"

"I am!" He wrapped his arms around each of the girls, and then he hugged Stefano. "I want it all, friends. Hope and redemption and salvation. Eternity!" He looked back at Bailey. "I don't want the pattern of the world another minute longer."

All three of their castmates stood motionless, eyes wide, lips slightly open. But just when Bailey wondered if they might mock Gerald or tell him to rethink his newfound decision, Stefano's eyes welled up. "I'm . . . I'm happy for you." He crossed his arms in front of him. "Maybe . . . maybe that'll be me someday."

"Someday soon." One of the girls touched Stefano's shoulder. "We've been talking about it. How reading the Bible was doing something inside us. Changing us somehow." She looked straight at Bailey. "What you said . . . how all of us are born with a sin struggle, and how God wants us to keep looking to Him to fight that sin — whatever it is . . . that's really stayed with me."

Again Bailey was so surprised she could've dropped to her knees here in Starbucks. Instead, Gerald motioned for the others to get their drinks. "We're in Romans 12 today . . . hurry up. It's too good to miss."

An hour later they finished, and as they left the coffee shop Gerald walked beside her. "I already checked. The Times Square Church is having a baptism service this week." His tears were gone, his eyes clearer than ever. "I want to go." He hesitated, joy radiating from his expression. "Would you come, Bailey? It would mean so much."

She could do nothing to stop the fresh tears that sprang to her eyes. She laughed so she wouldn't cry. "Yes. Of course. I'll be there for sure."

Then — as if to further prove the change that had happened in his heart — Gerald positioned himself in front of the other three and invited them also. "I want us to all be there. The whole Bible study."

It was more than Bailey could take in. They still had five hours before they would meet up again for that night's show, and when she was finally back at Bob and Betty Keller's house she went to her room, sat on the edge of her bed, and pulled out her phone. Brandon would be filming, but she couldn't wait another minute. As fast as her fingers would fly across the miniature keyboard, she texted a message she wasn't sure she'd ever send.

God worked a miracle, Brandon. Gerald gave his life to Jesus. He's a believer! Right there in Starbucks!! (This is me crying because I can't believe it!) He's getting baptized this weekend. I know . . . remind me to breathe. I love you . . . see you tonight.

When she'd sent the message, Bailey covered her face with her hands and let the sobs come. Because she was grateful God had used her today despite her lack of knowledge or experience at this sort of thing, and because she was humbly aware of her own desperate need. For a Savior she didn't deserve and a salvation she hadn't earned.

Tears filled her heart and overflowed onto her face and jeans — tears for all the ways she was thankful and all the ways her heart was breaking. Because the pattern of the world was so ugly and deceiving, and because that very pattern had trapped so many countless people. And because despite the longing in the soul of mankind for a rescue, the pattern of the world was easy to get used to, like a room full of bad curtains. The world could talk about love and life, goodness and grace . . . and miss the calling God had for every person on earth. Every single person. Regardless of their sin struggle.

The call to be transformed.

EIGHTEEN

Bailey expected the show to be one of the best ever, especially after a morning like they'd just shared at the coffee shop. And she was right. From the time they gathered at the theater, the cast could sense something different, something special about this night. Gerald couldn't stop talking about Jesus and the Bible and how God was working a miracle in his life. Most of the cast didn't know what to make of him. But everyone was kind, all of them happy because he was happy — even if they didn't quite understand.

The show seemed to fly by, and Bailey remembered after the curtain went up that this was a late night for Brandon. After filming, the crew was meeting to look at the daily footage, make sure they were capturing what they needed to put the movie together. Brandon had told her he couldn't be there till eleven o'clock or later. She didn't hear from him until she checked her phone between acts and found a response from him in her text messages.

Bailey, that's amazing!! Seriously!! I'm SO proud of you for caring about your cast . . . for caring about everyone. I can't wait for later to hear about Gerald. Love you too . . . now dance your heart out for Him.

Before the second act, Gerald pulled her aside, still glowing from places in his soul she doubted he'd known existed before today. "Let's go out after the show — the whole cast. We can celebrate, and I'll tell them about Romans 12. How about that?"

She laughed, overflowing with joy at his heartfelt enthusiasm. "We might want to start with just a verse or two."

Gerald thought for a moment and then grinned. "You might be right."

"But I like the idea of celebrating." She hugged him, letting the highlights from earlier that day play in her heart again. "Maybe the Stardust Diner down the street?"

"Perfect!" Gerald stayed, and the moment between them became deeper even as the rest of the cast hurried back onstage for the second act. "About earlier, Bailey . . . thank you." He put his hand on her shoulder and gave it a gentle squeeze. "I always felt like . . . no matter what I decided about the Bible . . . you loved me anyway." He leaned close and kissed her cheek. "Thanks for that. I . . ." He shook his head, looking somewhat amazed. "I never met a Christian like you before."

His words stayed with her as she took the stage . . . with every beat of music that remained and every dance move she poured herself into. For months at a time she hadn't thought her contribution to the *Hairspray* cast was worth anything at all. She'd taken the criticism of many of the cast members and her director, and she'd struggled with defeat and great loss after Chrissy died. More times than she could remember she'd gone home and poured out her thoughts in her journal, in her prayers, asking God to show her why He'd brought her here. What her purpose in this season of her life really was.

After Gerald's talk she didn't have to ask anymore. She knew.

The tremendous and exhilarating high that filled her soul as a result convinced her that this was, indeed, the best show of her entire time on Broadway. She'd never sung better, never danced cleaner . . . never believed more that this stage and this cast and this moment was right where she was supposed to be.

As they filed off the stage after curtain call, she could hardly wait to find Gerald, to help round up the others for the celebration he wanted all of them to share. But before she could find him, as she was still taking her last few steps off the backstage steps, she heard Francesca Tilly's voice. "Everyone listen up." Bailey couldn't see her, but she would've known the voice anywhere. "I need everyone to meet in wardrobe. Immediately, please."

What in the world? The wardrobe area was the one place backstage where they could all gather. Any other space would've been too small. But they had no meeting scheduled tonight. Bailey hadn't even known Francesca was in the building. Wednesdays were usually just the cast and the stage manager.

The dancers fell quiet except for nervous glances swapped between them. Still wiping sweat from their foreheads, still dressed in their costumes, they filed silently to the wardrobe area. "This can't be good," one of the girls whispered.

For the first time it occurred to Bailey that the meeting might not be about a change in choreography or a call to excellence. Her throat felt dry, and she wished she had a bottle of water. She wound up next to Gerald in the second row. Francesca stood at the far end of the wardrobe area, watching them, arms crossed.

When they had all filed in, Francesca allowed a flicker of sorrow in her expression. Proof that whatever was coming was different than anything she'd said to them before this moment. She cleared her throat. "I don't have good news. The producers have cancelled our show."

Soft gasps came from the cast and a couple guys hung their heads. Bailey felt the shock come over her like a sudden downpour.

Francesca was going on. "Whatever financial formula they use, we didn't cut it. We have ten days — through the end of January. After that you'll all be released." She hesitated, her lips pinched together. "We've had a good run here, people. I'm sorry. I wanted you to know as soon as I did."

Bailey couldn't feel her feet, couldn't tell if she was breathing or not. What had the director said? They were finished? The show was over? This wasn't really happening. Everyone said they were doing great; they were filling the seats, right? That was the last report . . . it could be a year or longer before this moment might come. Francesca was saying she'd be there for the last few shows and something about closure. But everything about her announcement felt surreal, like a bad dream or a not-funny joke. Their show was finished? Bailey felt herself begin to shiver. She could barely hear over the pounding of her heart.

Gerald and the cast agreed that a celebration now would fall flat for sure. Instead, he invited everyone to watch him be baptized. He found her and hugged her before they went their separate ways. "I'm not afraid of this . . . God will show me what's next."

"Right." Bailey smiled at him, grateful for his response. "That's what I hoped you would say. I was just reminding myself of the same thing."

They didn't talk long, and the theater emptied more quickly than usual, everyone shocked and needing time to grasp their new reality. Not until she was home at the Kellers' and she could finally talk to her mom did the truth set in. "It's over, Mom . . . they've cancelled the show." In the end she hadn't even lasted a year on Broadway. And with the feedback she'd gotten from Francesca, she had two choices: Take dance classes and work hours every day, all while hitting one audition after another . . .

Or she could ask God what was next.

"How do you feel? Other than shocked . . ." Her mom's voice was kind, gentle. Bailey loved how steady she was.

"I'm . . . not sure." Bailey found a Clear Creek High sweatshirt in her bottom drawer and slipped it over her head. Between the cold outside and the chill of the unknown, Bailey was desperate to be warm again. "I guess I'll get a copy of *Backstage* magazine . . . see which shows are auditioning. I need to get back on a show as quickly as possible, for sure." She hesitated. "I know that . . . and I know God has a plan. It's just a little hard to see."

"I'm sorry." There was an ache in her mom's voice. "I didn't see this coming."

"Me, either." Her teeth chattered a little. "Anyway . . . my morning was amazing." She caught her mom up on the development with Gerald, the baptism they'd attend that weekend.

"That's wonderful." She sounded unrushed, taking Bailey's disappointment slowly without any pronouncement about Broadway being a hard place or God moving her on or where He might be taking her next. "All we really know is that Gerald's decision out-shadows it all. That, and you'll be absolutely ready for the next dance audition."

"I hope so." Bailey exhaled. She wasn't cold anymore. "I love how you look at things, Mom." She was about to explain how the cast had been secure in their show run for another year when another call came through. She glanced at the Caller ID and saw Brandon's name. "Hey, Mom, can I call you back?"

"Definitely." She hesitated. "It'll be okay. I know it will."

Bailey felt herself nodding in agreement. "Thanks . . . I believe that. Deep down, I really do. I love you."

"Love you too."

Her mom's voice reassured her, but she needed to talk to Brandon, needed to tell him the news. A part of her didn't want to take his call, didn't want to tell him because of their conversation about distance and how the show kept her here, away from him in LA. She switched to his call, not sure if he was still there. "Hello?"

"Ahhh . . . there. I'm okay now." He gave an exaggerated exhale. "Baby . . . you have no idea how badly I needed to hear your voice."

"Thanks." She smiled despite her sadness. "You too." She bit her lip, wondering if he could hear the hurt in her tone.

"Okay, so I can't stop thinking about Gerald. I need all the details . . . tell me everything."

"It was great." She touched on the highlights, but her enthusiasm wasn't what it would've been. "He's so happy, Brandon."

"Hmmm." Admiration filled his tone. "I knew God was going to do something amazing with that Bible study."

"Thanks." She was quiet, not sure how to break the news. Besides, as soon as she told him, the reality would hit. She was losing her job. Her dream role was about to be a thing of the past.

"Bailey . . ." He was quiet for a few seconds. "What's wrong?"

She closed her eyes and exhaled. "There's no easy way to say it."

"Say what?"

"It's the show." Another long sigh. "We're done, Brandon. All of us. Ten more performances and the run's over."

"What?" He took a few beats and then groaned. "I can't believe it. Oh, baby, I'm sorry. I thought . . . things were going well, right?"

"They were." The producers' decision still didn't make sense. "We had an average of twenty more seats sold every night last week. One of the guys had the numbers."

"So . . . are they sure? I mean . . . it's not just a warning?"

"No." She loved this about him, the way he responded to her loss. Never mind that it opened doors for the two of them to be together more. Brandon only cared about her pain. She opened her eyes and looked out the window. "It's not a warning. The show's been cancelled."

He sighed, his frustration and shock evident. "I can't believe it. The show's so good." They were both silent, letting the reality sink in. "This is so weird, the timing."

"Why?" She stood and walked to the window, looking up at the slice of sky between the buildings across the street.

"You're not going to believe it." His laugh was one of disbelief. "My agent called today. He has a part he wants you to read for in early February. A lead in a big picture they'll film in LA later this spring." Even still he didn't sound happy about the situation. Amazed, but not happy. "I told him it wouldn't work . . . you were busy with *Hairspray*. But now . . ."

Bailey felt her whole world tilt. "Really? That's crazy . . ." Her feelings instantly stretched in opposite directions. "I mean, I really appreciate that. But I sort of thought . . . I mean, I figured I'd audition for a few more shows in New York. You know . . . because I just got here, Brandon. Not even a year ago."

This time the silence was his. "So . . . you want to stay in Manhattan?"

"Well, yes." She hated how this sounded, but she could do nothing to change the fact. "I've wanted to dance on Broadway all my life. I mean . . . I won't stay here forever . . . but for now. Yes. If I can stay, I will."

"Oh." More quiet, this time longer than before. "Well, then . . . I guess I can tell the casting director you aren't interested."

Bailey's heart pounded. "I'm interested. I just . . . I really want another Broadway show. If I can win a part, anyway."

"Don't worry about it . . ." He chuckled, but she knew him well enough to hear the hurt in his voice. "Do what you have to do . . . I believe in you, baby."

The call ended sooner than usual, and Bailey felt the distance between them more than ever. When they were off the phone, Bailey stayed at the window for a long time. Thinking about her time in New York, the Bible study . . . the nights of performing. Gerald's decision. She'd grown up this past year in Manhattan, learned how to live out her faith and find her way in the big city.

Learned much about who she was and what mattered most and how to never let a day go by with regrets about the people God had placed in her life. She longed for the next opportunity, the next audition. Because of course she needed to stay in New York and pursue the next show. Brandon would understand.

This was where God had placed her.

NINETEEN

Cody climbed into the back of his pickup truck and grabbed hold of the last of Cheyenne's furniture — an old office chair she'd used at the desk in her apartment. He slid it to the waiting hands of the guy from Goodwill and then dusted the snow off his gloves. The man seemed indifferent about the items — an old sofa and end table, a small dining room set, and a few lamps. A couple oversized Hefty bags full of summer clothes and dresses she'd never wear again.

The guy didn't say anything. He gave Cody a receipt and that was that. Cody climbed back in his truck cab and realized he was shaking. Was it so easy, getting rid of the things that surrounded a life? He had worked cleaning out Chey's apartment since early that morning, but it wasn't that hard. A cleaning service would be through later today. His part was to clear out her furniture, pack up her extra clothes, and gather the couple boxes of personal items that sat on the seat beside him.

Her apartment manager was buying her bedroom set in exchange for the past month's rent. Another easy transaction. But every movement, every one of her belongings he lifted into his truck that morning and dropped off at Goodwill was like ripping away another piece of his heart. Each minute of this awful day just another reminder. She didn't have long. Sure, she'd been more stable the last few days, but the end wasn't far off.

Cody set his eyes straight ahead and drove out of the Goodwill parking lot and back toward Tara's. It was the last Saturday in January and the doctors were on board with Chey's decision. She would stay at home in Tara's guestroom until God took her to heaven. They'd refused hospice for now. Tara had taken a few weeks off work, and Cody was able to come every day after school. The doctor had warned they'd need hospice eventually. It would be better for all of them. But Cody didn't want to call for help until it was absolutely necessary.

When he got back to her, Tara was asleep on the couch in the front room. Exhausted like they all were. Cody found his resolve and headed down the hall to the room where Cheyenne was staying. The drapes were open, sunlight streaming in through a break in the clouds. Much of the time lately Chey slept, tired from the cancer and a combination of the drugs she was taking to lessen her constant pain.

But right now she was propped up in bed, a peaceful look on her face. She turned at the sound of him and smiled — the sort of smile he hadn't seen in too long. "Hi." Gratitude shone in her eyes. "You're already finished?"

"Yes." Cody came into the room and took the chair beside her bed. "Everything you asked."

"You found the boxes?" She sounded content, like they were merely having a conversation about a trip to the grocery store and not the elimination of all her earthly belongings.

"I did. They're in the living room." He wanted to cry, wanted once more to shout out loud that they couldn't possibly be doing this, talking about cleaning out her apartment because she would never go home again. Instead he clenched his teeth and studied her, waiting. "You have enough clothes here, right?"

"I do." She searched his face, her great appreciation apparent. "Thank you, Cody.

What you did today . . . it means a lot."

"Not a problem." Cody didn't know what else to say. He wanted to talk about something else, anything else. "You . . . look good." He angled his head, giving her a smile he hoped didn't look as sad as he felt. "Feeling better?"

"I am." She breathed in slowly, more full of life than anytime in the past week. "I saw you pull up. I thought maybe . . . we could talk."

He nodded and reached for her hand. For a long time he only held it, trying not to notice her bony fingers or the way her skin felt thinner, dryer. "What's on your mind?"

She waited, letting the question sink in. "Heaven." She smiled. "You. Your trip to New York." She uttered a quiet laugh. "A lot, I guess."

"Well . . . I don't really want to talk about heaven." He managed a crooked grin. "If that's okay."

"For now." She laughed once more, light and breathy. The sound was another reminder of her weakness. "We can talk about that at the end."

He breathed in sharp through his nose. "I thought I told you about New York."

"You told me about the interview and DeMetri's loquaciousness. And about seeing *Hairspray.*" Her eyes danced at the memory. But just as quickly the light faded some. "But you didn't tell me about Bailey Flanigan." She paused. "Did you see her?"

Cody released her hand and leaned over his knees. For a few seconds he stared at the beige carpet. "She's in the show, Chey." Then he lifted his eyes to her, more tired than he'd felt before. "Yes. I saw her."

"But you didn't tell me about it. Whether you talked to her."

"I did. Not very long. She was with Brandon Paul . . . and she had to meet with the fans."

Cheyenne nodded slowly. She looked out the window again, in no hurry to get to the next part of the conversation. Finally she looked at him, and again her smile reached all the way to her soul. "You still love her."

She had done this before, uttered a statement about Bailey that held not even a hint of questioning. As if the truth of the words was a given. "Cheyenne . . ." he whispered her name, then looked at the floor again. After a long time he raked his hand through his short dark hair. "Why do you say things like that?"

"Is it uncomfortable for you?" She reached for his hand.

"Yes." He hesitated, but he took her

fingers in his. "Very uncomfortable."

"Because it's true."

A long breath rushed from him, and he worked to keep his frustration at bay. "Do we have to talk about this?"

"It's okay, Cody. I understand." Her eyes found the blue sky outside her window. "You know how I feel about Art."

Her comment should've hurt at least a little. But it didn't. Further proof that his feelings for Cheyenne were friendship. That they had always only been friendship. But maybe if she hadn't been in the car accident, if she hadn't gotten sick . . .

"I think . . ." he began, "I think you and I . . . we had a chance."

"We did." Again there wasn't a hint of doubt in her voice. "If life had been different, I could've loved you. Really loved you." She faced him, her smile colored by a knowing he'd never seen before. "But if I'm honest with myself, nothing we could've shared ever would've been exactly like Art and I had together."

Cody tried to understand why she was doing this, why she felt it so important to tell him how she'd always loved Art more. Why she wanted to talk about Bailey. Maybe because she didn't want to face death feeling anything but glad for whatever was next in Cody's life. Didn't want to head to heaven with even a hint of jealousy. Cody wasn't sure. He released her hand again and sat up straighter, wanting to change the subject as badly as he wanted his next breath.

But Chey wasn't ready yet. "The thing is, I saw the way you looked at her that day. At the football game." Her smile stayed, proof of either her great inner strength or her sincere peace with the topic. "When the two of you looked at each other, there was no one else in the stadium. No one."

"She has a boyfriend."

"I know." Chey brought her fingers to her brow and massaged her temples. She winced and sucked in a sharp breath.

"What is it . . . what can I get you?"

"Nothing." She shuddered slightly and shook her head, as if to tell her body she wasn't willing to let the pain have the upper hand. Not now. "I can't take anything else for another hour."

Cody sat back, amazed at her strength. She was in the final stages of brain cancer. Certainly if she wanted more pain medication she could have it. But she wanted these days to be lucid and as normal as possible. So pain was a regular part of her life. "There's a reason why I bring this up."

He wasn't sure he wanted to hear it. "It's sort of pointless. She lives in New York and she's in a serious relationship."

"This isn't about her." Her expression relaxed, the pain wave subsided for now. "It's about you." She focused her eyes intently on his. "When I thought about this moment, this conversation . . . I always thought I would tell you to find her. After I'm gone . . . or before, if you wanted. Find her and fight for her and tell her how you feel."

It was exactly the direction Cody figured this was going. Her statement confused him, and he knit his brow together. "That's not what you're going to say?"

"No." The concern and caring in her eyes doubled. "Being sick, I've had time to think about you. How much love you have inside you . . . how much you have to give." She reached out and took his hand again. "So much love."

He felt the sting of tears, but he willed himself to be strong. He needed to hear her out, understand what she was getting at. "My real question, Cody, is why? Why did you leave her?"

"Bailey?" His heart picked up its pace. Wherever this was headed, he was pretty sure he didn't want to go there.

"Yes." She grimaced a little, but somehow found the ability to ignore the pain again. Outside the sun disappeared behind another bank of clouds, casting gray shadows over the bedroom. "You were there for me . . . because you walked away from her."

How would he ever explain this? He felt frustration well up inside him and he sucked in a deep breath and held it. "It's a long story."

"Not really." She ran her fingers along his, loving him, her voice the picture of patience. "When you love someone . . . like you think you love Bailey . . . you never walk away. Not for any reason."

"She . . . she deserved someone better than me." He squeezed Chey's hand and stared at the floor again. "I was the bad kid, the guy her family helped out. She was . . . she was this ideal, this perfection. I was never good enough for her."

"There it is." Cheyenne released his hand and helped herself sit a little higher in the bed. Her tone grew more intense. "How many times have you walked away from that girl?"

Cody wanted to run, wanted to leave Cheyenne and get in his truck and drive as far and fast as he could from here. His relationship with Bailey was none of her business. No one had the right to ask him about this, about the times he'd walked away. "I always had a reason."

"You weren't good enough? Really, Cody?" She laughed, but the sound was beyond sad. "You're a war hero, for heaven's sake. You would've laid down in front of a bus for me . . . and I'm sure you would've done that for her too. You watched her grow up and your eyes say you still love her." Cheyenne narrowed her eyes. "But you always ran." She held his gaze, gathering her strength. "So . . . that tells me that deep inside, I'm not sure she's the right girl for you, Cody."

"She's not." His tone was nervous, desperate to change topics. "She's dating someone else."

"That's not the point. If you wanted to be with her, you would've demanded she come talk to you in New York City, and you would've told her you weren't leaving until you shared your feelings for her. If you wanted her, you would've never walked away that Thanksgiving . . . just because she was filming a movie with some Hollywood star." She lowered her chin. "You think I haven't put the pieces together. But I have. The two of you were dating, and you just left her, Cody. You walked away."

He clenched his jaw. Why was she doing this, taking him back to that time? The walls felt like they were closing in around him, and he closed his eyes. "What's your point, Chey . . . why are you saying this?"

"Because I think God showed me something. I think you're in love with the *idea* of Bailey Flanigan more than you're in love with *her.* If a girl makes you feel like you're not good enough, then maybe you never will be. It's not her fault . . . not your fault. But maybe with her you never could've been the amazing man of God, the selfless friend, and the romantic strong guy you could be . . . with someone else."

Her words crushed him, pushing in around his heart and suffocating his soul. He wanted to shout at her and tell her she was crazy, that she couldn't possibly know him that well, and that the reason he'd left Bailey time and again was because he was young and immature and he hadn't known how to handle her, hadn't understood that he could deserve a girl like Bailey.

But he couldn't say it, couldn't refute her. He closed his eyes for a few seconds and a voice resonated in his heart.

Listen, my son . . . wisdom is precious . . .

He blinked and looked again at Chey as the realization in his heart took root. Because along with the heaviness on his chest was something he hadn't expected to feel, a voice he didn't want to acknowledge.

The voice of Truth.

"Maybe . . . maybe you and Bailey will find your way back together." Cheyenne didn't sound threatened by the idea. But she didn't sound okay with it, either. "But when I picture you years down the road . . . I picture you with someone better." She didn't hesitate more than a few seconds. "Not better than Bailey, but better for *you*. Someone who makes you feel good about yourself, whose love makes you feel . . . ten feet high."

He felt the tears again. "This . . . the way I ran so many times . . ." He struggled, try-ing to find his voice. "It was never Bailey's fault. She tried to make me stay."

"I'm not blaming her. I'm just saying . . . if she was the right girl, you wouldn't be sit-ting across from me right now." She crossed her arms, her voice sadder than at any point in the conversation. "I would just be a girl you met at a dinner party once at Tara Collins' house. A girl whose name you prob-ably wouldn't even remember. Because you'd still be in Bailey's life. And she never would've started dating Brandon Paul . . ." She let her voice fall quiet, to almost a whisper. "If Bailey was the right girl."

Cody couldn't fight the crushing sorrow another minute. He dug his elbow into his knee and pressed his head against his fist. Bailey was the right girl. She had been the right girl all of his life, right? From the time he'd met her. And his leaving, his running had never been her fault. She had tried to tell him that too many times to count. But somehow . . . in some way Cody hated to admit, Cheyenne had to be at least partly right.

Because in the end, Cody left Bailey. He always left.

Whether that was because he still saw her as a little girl, a younger sister . . . or if it was because he couldn't hold his head up around someone so pure, Cody wasn't sure. The only thing screaming at him were the basic truths, the fact that Cheyenne had to be right about some of what she said.

After all, he was sitting here.

"I'm sorry." She leaned toward him and put her hand on his shoulder. "I didn't want to upset you. I guess . . . no offense to Bailey . . . but if you can't feel ten feet high with her, there's someone else, Cody. Someone who will make you feel like the amazing, tremendous guy you really are."

Cody dragged his knuckles across his

cheeks, drying the few tears that had slipped. He didn't want to talk about this, not before and not for another minute. But he had one question for her: "So, when you think about my future, you want me to let go of Bailey Flanigan, is that it? You think there's someone out there better for me?"

"Yes." A perfect peace filled her eyes. "That's what I'm saying." She tilted her head. "You're not a runner, Cody. You're a fighter. You saved your whole unit when you were a prisoner of war and you found a way to live, to come home again." She hesitated, never looking away. "You stayed here with me when any other guy would've bolted. Through the accident . . . through the cancer. You're loyal and faithful and committed."

Her words were like a balm to his breaking heart. She was right. He would only run in war if there had been no possible way to take on the battle. If a fatal outcome was practically certain. The way it had felt with Bailey. The fact that she thought so highly of him made the pain lift enough so he could breathe.

Cheyenne shrugged one shoulder. "But with Bailey . . . you ran every time." Her smile told him she wanted him to understand her motives, her intentions — and that they were only for his best. "The look in your eyes when you see her, it's like you've convinced yourself she's the only one, the only girl you could ever love." She still spoke slowly, deliberately. As if she'd saved an entire day's strength for this moment. "I guess . . . I just think you're wrong. Otherwise you wouldn't have run."

It was so much to think about. Cody sniffed and steadied himself, grabbing onto the resolve he needed to not break down at the enormity of what she had just said, the possibility she had only just opened up to him. "You said . . . you said you wanted to talk about heaven?"

A giggle passed over her lips and the sound released air into the room again. "There's not much to say there. I guess . . . I'm excited." She breathed in slowly, a full cleansing breath as if even now she could almost see a glimpse of heaven's gate. "I get really excited thinking about it. Being whole and well . . . having an eternal purpose of some kind." Her voice wavered just a little, and her eyes grew watery. "Seeing Art again. I'm not afraid." She laughed like a kid looking forward to Christmas. "I can't wait, Cody. When I go . . . I don't want you to be sad."

His tears were back. He couldn't watch

her waste away, couldn't grasp the fact that in her dying days she was concerned about whom he would love, and he didn't know how to think about her death without feeling pain. But here . . . his tears weren't for her; they were for himself. She cared about him more than he had understood before today.

"Hey . . . you're not supposed to be sad." She still had her hand on his shoulder. "That was the whole point. I'm ready, Cody . . . I'm not afraid at all."

He nodded, refusing to break down completely in her presence. "I don't like it . . . thinking about you gone."

"I won't be gone. I'm just going first. We'll both be there eventually."

"Yeah." Cody laughed because it was one way to keep from crying. "I'll probably want about a hundred years in heaven to catch up with Art."

"Hmmm." She looked happier than she had all afternoon. "Me too." She yawned and withdrew her hand again. "I should probably sleep. But . . . I've prayed for you so much, Cody." She met his eyes once more. "I couldn't leave . . . without telling you what He'd put on my heart. That maybe . . . maybe it's time to let go of Bailey. Time to acknowledge that she was never really more than an ideal, an image of the life you wanted to live."

The truth — if there was truth to what she said — grated against his heart and still made him want to run from it. But he believed her, that this was something she had to tell him. It was that important. "Thank you. For making it a priority. For caring that much."

"I had to." She blinked back fresh tears, despite her smile. "I love you. I want the best for you."

He stood and took her slowly in his arms, holding her frail body and willing strength into it. There were no words, nothing he could say to change where they were at. Whatever impact this conversation might have on him in the days and months to come didn't matter as much as one obvious truth: In Cheyenne, God had given him a very rare gift. A gift he wouldn't accept from Bailey Flanigan — whatever the reason.

The chance to feel ten feet high.

TWENTY

The baptism of Gerald Gear Fontinni was one of the brightest highlights of Bailey's time in New York City. In attendance at church that afternoon was nearly every member of the *Hairspray* cast and of course Brandon, there beside her, holding her hand and understanding exactly what the moment meant to her.

Bailey loved Gerald's attitude, that he truly had no earthly idea how he was going to leave the lifestyle he'd created for himself or how God was going to change his heart and passions. He didn't need the answers. His trust in God was absolute. And as he went into the water, Bailey could hear him again, see him again the way he looked at Starbucks that past Wednesday morning. When he had looked at her with teary eyes and asked in a breaking voice whether God was really enough, really all he needed to take this step of faith.

The pastor talked to them about baptism, about the picture it made of being dead to the old self and alive to the new self — the one Jesus had died to set free. Bailey leaned in close to Brandon as Gerald nodded, as he publicly made a confession of the faith he'd grabbed hold of that week. Some of their castmates shifted nervously, uncomfortable with what they were witnessing. But none of them looked away. And Stefano watched the entire scene with tears streaming down his cheeks.

Bailey had a feeling he might be next to surrender to Jesus' calling on his life.

"I remember this," Brandon whispered close to her face. "Your dad . . . baptizing me in your backyard. My life's been different ever since."

She slipped her hand around his waist, feeling his strength the way she hadn't felt it before. When she met Brandon, he was as far from being a believer as Gerald had been a year ago. After he gave his life to the Lord, he still didn't have the sort of faith she could draw from, the strength of character she could lean on.

But he had it now. Bailey didn't know when that had changed, but it had. She looked up to Brandon and relied on him and trusted him. More than she had understood before this day. She laid her head on his shoulder and together they watched as Gerald was dipped beneath the water.

When he came up out of it, he raised both fists in the air and shouted out loud: "New life! I have new life!"

Bailey couldn't stop her tears. She brought her fingers to her lips and laughed quietly, overwhelmed by the joy of it all. Never mind that their last show was in a few hours. This was real life, and for Gerald the run of show had just begun.

Even the castmates uncomfortable with what had just happened gathered around Gerald once he had dried off and changed back into his clothes. Anyone who didn't know him would've thought Gerald was high on some crazy upper, or that maybe he'd had five too many cups of coffee. But when Gerald hugged her he was practically bursting with the chance to tell her how he felt. "It's the Holy Spirit, Bailey . . . I feel Him working in me. It's the best feeling ever."

She wanted to tell him to be careful, that the feeling wouldn't always be there, and that being a Christian oftentimes meant walking through dark places in the journey and living only on an unseen, unfelt faith. But this wasn't the time. Wherever she wound up, whatever show on Broadway, she would stay close to Gerald, and along the way he would continue to grow. For now she only returned his hug and said the one thing he needed to hear. "I couldn't be happier for you, Gerald. Everything about your life will be different after today."

"I know." He shivered a little, the happiness almost more than he could bear. "I can hardly wait!"

When the service let out, the cast ate an early dinner at the Stardust Diner where the wait staff took turns singing show tunes and popular hits from the past fifty years. Some of the workers were friends of the cast, and more than once during dinner one of the staff would pull a *Hairspray* cast member out onto the floor to sing along.

The two hours there were unforgettable. Half the songs found the whole cast singing along from their tables, and even Brandon sang some. "I told you." He laughed after one of the songs. "I always wanted to do live theater."

"Well." She kissed his cheek. "This is your chance."

It didn't occur to her until after they finished the meal that Brandon hadn't been interrupted by fans throughout the entire dinner. Certainly people must've recognized him, but maybe seeing him as part of such a large group of singers, fans were content simply to take in the moment. Catch a clip of video on their phones or a quick photograph from a distance.

Bailey was grateful. Because this wasn't only a celebration for Gerald, it was a goodbye party. After tonight this group would never have a reason to gather again, never have the bond that for this moment they still shared.

The show that night was everything any of them thought it would be. The notes rang a little clearer, their voices sounded a little more connected. Every dance move was in sync. Brandon sat in the front row again and when the final curtain call came, his eyes shone with tears just like everyone in the cast. The audience knew it was the cast's final performance, so the standing ovation began the moment the show ended. Bailey was surprised to see some of the people in attendance crying too — like everyone there that night understood what was at stake and how painful the goodbye, how final the moment.

When they finally cleared the stage and filed into the wardrobe area, the hugs and picture-taking and promises to keep in touch lasted another hour. Francesca came by for a little while and thanked them for their work, their professionalism. She said she hoped to work with them all again at some point, and she encouraged them to continue in their Broadway careers. To never give up on their dreams.

Bailey thought about all the years she'd longed for a chance to perform on Broadway. How her high school boyfriend Tim Reed had won a part a year before her and how hard she'd worked to get cast in *Hairspray*. She had been honest with Brandon. News of her show closing had brought to the surface just one thought: She needed to find another show.

But since then she'd looked through *Backstage* magazine, same as her castmates, and found nothing. No musicals auditioning for replacement ensemble parts. No new shows in town. She could always come back when something was casting. But for now she had made up her mind about the immediate future.

She would go home for a few weeks, and then set out for Los Angeles. Until she spent a season living in Brandon's world, she couldn't live in fear of it. The audition he'd told her about was still an option — though it wasn't a given. Several talented actresses were up for the same part. Either way, she would live with Katy and Dayne and pray every day that God would show her whether living in Brandon's world was something she could handle.

Brandon stayed during the goodbyes, keeping to himself, off to the side to give her this time — as long as she needed. When Bailey was finally ready to go, she took Brandon's hand and smiled into his eyes. "Thank you . . . for waiting."

"You needed this." He leaned close and kissed her forehead. "You ready?"

She nodded. "I am."

The night was warmer than it had been all winter — nearly forty degrees. And since they'd both worn their winter coats, Brandon didn't even have to ask about the rooftop. He merely stepped into the elevator with her once they reached her apartment building, shared a look with her, and pressed the button for the top floor. There was no wind that night, so when they stepped out onto the roof, the air was pleasant — as if God had created this moment just for them.

He led her to the far side, to the patio where they had danced more than two months ago. "You were beautiful tonight." He allowed himself to get lost in her eyes, his expression that familiar one, where he looked half dizzy just being with her. "Maybe you should look for another show."

"No." She felt a rush of sadness, but the feeling didn't change what she knew to be true. "I followed my dream, and I was incredibly blessed to have this chance. But I can take a break from Broadway." She put her arms around his neck, an easy space between them. "Nothing's casting in the near future." She smiled. "Broadway's not my dream right now."

"Mmm." He swayed gently with her. "What's your dream now, Bailey?"

"Maybe . . . my dream is you."

He smiled in response and it took up his whole face. "I sort of hoped you might say that."

She steadied herself. "Seriously . . . I don't need New York right now. I've done this, and now it's time for something else. At least until the right show comes along."

He nodded, searching her eyes. "The LA audition?"

"Yes." She nodded, certain. "I've prayed about it. I'll go home for a few weeks and then I'll go to LA. It might be a long shot, but I need to try. To see if God is opening doors for me to act, to work in movies."

"You mean . . . do life together?" He framed her face with his hand. "Even with the relentless paparazzi."

"Even with that." She brushed her cheek against his. "As long as I can be with you."

"You're serious?" He stopped swaying and took a step back. His eyes locked on hers. "How long have you known this?"

She laughed. "I called Katy Matthews this morning. Before the church service. I told her I wasn't sure how long I'd need a place, but for now I'd like to live with them."

Brandon turned away and raised both hands to the sky. "Thank You, God!" he shouted the words, turning in a fast circle as if he wanted the whole city to hear him. "Bailey Flanigan is moving to LA! Whoo-hooo!"

"Shhh." Bailey went to him and pulled him into a hug. "Someone'll call the police."

"Good!" He was still loud, but he turned his focus to her once more. "They can celebrate with us." For a moment he bent over, his hands on his knees. "I mean, give me a minute to catch my breath, Bailey. I'm sitting in the audience tonight wondering if you'll ever consider working in LA . . ." He straightened again and held his hands out. "And now you're moving there? You're serious? You're moving in with the Matthews?"

Bailey loved the way he made her laugh. With Cody life always seemed serious, like she was forever talking him into staying or trying to convince him she was telling the truth or wondering why he had run away again. With Brandon — though they had their share of serious moments — for the most part she was always laughing.

This was one of those times.

He took her hand and led her along the entire perimeter of the building, the length of the paved path all the way back to where they started out near the far patio. "That's me trying to keep my feet on the ground." He exhaled and laughed at the same time. "Okay. Now that I have a grasp on this new reality . . ." He settled down some and came to her, pulling her close and looking deep into her eyes. "Tell me this, Bailey . . . how am I going to survive two weeks without you?"

Bailey hadn't thought about that. She was still laughing, because after his last few minutes it was a little hard to take him seriously. "You're still going to be here, right? Finishing the movie?"

"Yes." He grew quiet, studying her, his mind clearly racing. "Unless maybe you can get a room here at the Ritz and come with me to set every day and we could leave here at the same time."

"Brandon . . ." She put her hands alongside his face. "I need to go home. I have to figure out what to do, and spend time with my family." She brought her face close to his. "Plus, I'll see your eyes every night on Skype."

"Mmm." He groaned, as if the distance might be more than he could take. "Two weeks though —"

"Then we'll be in LA . . . for who knows how long."

"Hey, wait a minute." He was lost in her eyes, that much was obvious. "*I* know how long." He kissed her, just long enough for her to know the depth of his feelings. "Ask me."

"You're crazy." She swallowed another wave of giggles, doing her best to be serious. "Okay, fine. How long will I be there?"

"That's easy." He slipped his arms around her waist and swayed with her again. "Forever, Bailey. You'll be with me forever."

"In LA?" The idea scared her more than she was willing to talk about. Deep down it was the one thing she wasn't sure about. Whether she could see herself living in LA, being a California girl when Bloomington was still so deeply rooted in her heart. "You see me in LA with you forever, huh?"

"Not in LA." He didn't blink, didn't laugh. Bailey could sense that Brandon had never been more serious in all his life. "Wherever you are, Bailey. That's where I'll be. As long as my heart's beating."

There was nothing to say, no need for words. Brandon had said the only thing that mattered, the words that stayed with Bailey long after he left and she returned to her room to start packing. Brandon didn't need LA and she didn't need New York. They only needed one thing to feel like they were home.

They needed each other.

Bailey held onto the thought then and through her final days in New York as she shared a teary goodbye with the Kellers and thanked them for opening their home and their hearts. She would always be better for the lessons she'd learned living with the kind and giving couple.

The goodbyes continued, and the thought of Brandon sustained her while she spent a final morning with the friends in her Bible study. All of them agreed to keep in touch, and Bailey was encouraged by their news that day. The group planned to join Gerald at his new church's Bible Basics small group.

Finally it was time for Bailey to leave New York. The day before her flight home to Indianapolis, she went to the rooftop alone and looked out over the city. God had brought her here, and He had been faithful to grow her in a season where she had lived out her dream. The dream of dancing on Broadway. Now though, her dreams had changed. And God would go before her to LA, she was sure of it. As she breathed in the city air one final time, she felt peace about the move and a familiar thrill.

She could hardly wait to see what He had next.

TWENTY-ONE

Cheyenne's breathing was labored and she hadn't sat up in two days. She was losing consciousness and every moment was more than Cody could bear. He sat at her bedside, and Tara sat across from him in a second chair. "Dear God . . . we can't do this. Please . . . if she's ready, take her home."

Cody wasn't there yet, couldn't pray that way. He still wanted God to work a miracle, give Chey another chance at life. Heaven would always be there. This was the only time she'd have to be young and alive and a part of God's plan on earth. The idea that this was the end for her was still something he couldn't believe. When Tara prayed that way, that God would take her home, all he could do was clench his fists and lean on his knees and stare at the ground.

"Maybe . . . maybe I should get her some water." He stood and walked to the door. "Do you think she'd drink some? If I brought her a glass?"

Tara's cheeks were tearstained, her body weary from standing by in Cheyenne's fight. The answer was in her eyes, but she must've known that Cody needed a purpose, a reason to leave the room. "Yes, that'd be good." She leaned over the bed and took Chey's limp hand. "Cody's going to get you water, baby. Okay? You need some water?"

Cheyenne rarely responded. She'd been this way since the weekend, and now it was Wednesday, the eighth of February. A hospice nurse had been by earlier and the news was worse — the way it was always worse. Cheyenne didn't have long. There was no way to tell whether she'd ever open her eyes or talk or sit up again.

"Yes, Cody . . . she might want some." She patted Chey's hand, and turned to face him. "Why don't you get her some water?"

All his days at war had not prepared him for the battle they'd waged alongside Cheyenne, the battle against brain cancer. It was one thing to see death and destruction moment by moment. But this long, slow fade . . . this cutting of the ties to earth one string at a time . . . Cody wasn't sure how much more he could handle. Every time Cheyenne went to sleep he wondered if he'd see her one more time, or if she'd have one more time to open her beautiful brown eyes. Whether he'd ever hear her voice again. As it was, they hadn't been able to rouse her in nearly forty-eight hours.

He got the water, stopped to add ice, and then rethought the idea. If she would take a sip, then she didn't need ice cubes. The water would be enough. Water and a straw — the kind with the bendable top. So if she was thirsty she could sip it without having to lift her head. Yes, that was the best way.

Even before he stepped back inside her room he could smell it. Nothing about the smell was familiar to him. Again, in Iraq death was quick and merciful. Injured soldiers who could be saved were operated on and sent to recovery. Death never had a smell the way it did here.

Inside the room he walked slowly to the side of Cheyenne's bed. Tara leaned back, giving him space to work, to try to reach her. "Chey? Sweetie can you hear me?"

No response.

Cody gritted his teeth, holding the glass of water steady. He brushed his free hand against her cheek, soft and tender. "Cheyenne . . . I have water. Are you thirsty?"

For the first time that day she made a sound. Nothing loud, no audible words. But a soft moan that told him at least this much:

She could hear him. A ray of hope cracked the darkness and splashed a birthday candle of light on the moment.

"Try again. I think she's thirsty." Tara folded her hands, her body tense as she watched. "Please, Cody . . . keep trying."

"Cheyenne, it's me, Cody . . . I have water for you."

Gradually, in a way he was almost sure he would never see again, she moved her eyelids, struggling for the chance to open them.

"Come on, honey, that's it. I'm here. I have water for you. Are you thirsty, Chey? Can you take a drink?"

She worked her eyelids again, and Cody had the feeling that in all her life she had never exerted such effort. With everything in her she clearly wanted to open her eyes, to look at them and give them what they all wanted. One last time to connect. Finally, when watching her effort was enough to make him sick to his stomach, Cheyenne actually did it. She opened her eyes just enough to see him.

"Cheyenne!" Tara was on her feet. The room was dimly lit, but now she turned the bedside lamp up a notch. So Chey could see them clearly. "Sweetheart, you're awake!"

"Mmm." Chey squinted, trying to focus. She looked from Cody to Tara and back again. Barely, she parted her lips and suddenly Cody remembered why he was standing at her bedside and what was in his hands.

"The water." He brought the cup to her, holding the straw to her lips with his other hand. "Here, sweetie . . . you can drink now. Take a drink, Chey."

She nodded, at least he thought she did. It could've been her body suffering another little seizure, the mini-strokes the hospice nurse had said would be normal at this stage. Either way, she pursed her lips around the straw and sucked back some of the water. Not much. Not enough to make a difference. But it was progress, a sign that life still screamed to be heard despite the losing battle at hand.

Cody didn't realize it until then, but he was crying — tears streaming down his face as he held the water to her lips. "Chey." He forced himself to stay strong, to keep his feelings from getting the upper hand. "We're here. We've been here the whole time."

She stared at him, straight at him. Nothing else about her looked even remotely like the girl she'd been just two months ago. Her hair was gone, her cheeks sunken, and her limbs little more than skin and bones. But her eyes . . . her eyes were absolutely familiar. Cody held onto them as long as he could, refusing even to blink for fear of missing a moment.

Tara stood beside him, and now she put her hand over Cheyenne's. "It's good to see you awake, sweet girl. We've been praying for you."

With a slow shift, Chey turned her eyes to Tara. In what could only be described as a miracle, the corners of her mouth lifted and her eyes danced with what life remained. "I know." Her voice was barely audible, hoarse and weak. But she had talked. The connection filled the room with electric hope.

"Could you hear us . . . when your eyes were closed?" Cody needed to know.

She turned her eyes to him and nodded. Again, the movement was barely perceptible. But it was there. "I . . . hear you, Cody. Every . . . word."

It was her — the way she would talk, her determination to speak his name, and make sure he understood her. She was here and she was lucid and she understood him. The knowledge gave him the strength he needed, the ability to stay here beside her until she drew her last breath. His principal had given him a sub all this week and the next if he needed it. And now he knew the one thing he had hoped might be true: She could hear him.

"Chey . . . are you in pain?" Tara brought her face close to Cody's, probably so Chey wouldn't have to work so hard to shift her attention between the two of them. "Are you afraid?"

"I'm . . . not afraid." She smiled with her eyes, and her breathing sounded more labored than before. As if every effort took its toll on her. "I'm . . . going to see Jesus." Even cancer couldn't keep her eyes from dancing. "And I'm . . . gonna see Art."

Tara began crying, quiet sobs shook her as she nodded and she brought her free hand to her face. "I'm sorry, honey . . . I'm just, I'm so happy for you. You'll be fine in a little while."

Again Cody could feel the tears on his cheeks. How surreal it was that in a very short time Cheyenne would be walking the streets of heaven, catching up with Art and basking in the presence of Jesus. He let Tara do the talking, since he was pretty sure he couldn't say a word if he wanted to.

"Chey, will you do me a favor?" Tara was still crying, unable to stop the sobs, unwilling to let them stop her from saying what was on her heart.

"Yes, Mama." She managed to slide her hand over Tara's, bringing comfort to the older woman, thinking about others even in her final moments. "Tell me."

"Can you . . . when you see Art," her voice cracked. "Can you please . . . tell him how much I miss him. Tell him . . . I'm counting the days. Till we can be together."

Chey smiled again, her eyes dry and full of light. "I'll tell him."

"Okay." Tara reached for a tissue from the nearby table. "I'm sorry, baby girl. I'm not good at this." She shook her head as she blew her nose. "I don't know how I'll do it . . . with both of you gone."

"You'll . . . have Cody." Cheyenne smiled at Cody, the hint of a smile, but it was her smile nonetheless. "Take care . . . of her."

"I will." Cody had thought about it before, but only in a subconscious sort of way. The idea that after Cheyenne was gone Tara would be alone. She'd have her job and her home and her routine, but the people who had mattered most to her would be gone. All except for him. No matter where life took him, Tara would remain. He would include her for holidays and stop by on certain Sunday nights. Cody put his arm around Tara's shoulders and kept his eyes on Cheyenne. "She won't be alone. Don't worry."

Again she nodded, but this time her eyes flickered and her eyelids seemed to lose the fight for a few seconds. When she fought to open them again, Cody knew she wouldn't be awake more than a few heartbeats longer. "Love you . . . Cody . . . Mama."

"I love you, sweet girl." Tara leaned over the bed and kissed Cheyenne's head, framing her face with both hands. "We're staying right here. As long as you keep fighting."

As she drew back, Cody took his turn. "Chey." He put his hand alongside her bony face. "You know how I feel. I love you." He didn't bother hiding his tears. As long as he could talk, he barely noticed them. "You tell Art . . ." He swallowed, searching for his voice. "Tell him it's not the same without him."

She nodded, just barely, and gradually her eyes closed. Her breathing slowed, and her hand went limp again. Suddenly Cody had the strongest sense that this was her last time, the last time they would connect with her this way. He couldn't stand it, couldn't stay here looking at her, watching her slip away. He stepped back from the bed. "I . . . I'm going out back. I need air."

Tara didn't blame him, didn't ask him to stay. They each had to handle losing Cheyenne in their own way. She nodded at him, as if to say she understood. The moments they'd just been given were a gift. If he needed time to savor what they'd shared in the last few minutes, so be it.

Cody couldn't leave her room fast enough. Like by getting out of there he could find a place where she was still vibrantly alive, still laughing and teasing him and telling him exactly how she felt — even if it wasn't what he wanted to hear. But as he walked through the house he was reminded that every place, every seat and room and doorway, was empty of her presence, because she'd never fill them again. He stepped out into the cold and sat in the nearest frozen patio chair.

Dear God . . . I don't understand . . . I can't do this.

Cody hung his face.

My son . . . you can do all things through me . . . I give you strength and grace, exactly as much as you need.

Really? He covered his face. *Are You sure . . . is that You, God?*

This time there was no answer, but he was seized with an overwhelming urge, a thought he hadn't had once since Cheyenne began this battle. As soon as it came over him it made complete sense. It was something he should've done sooner, but he hadn't had time to think about it, to act on the thought until now. The feeling was this: He needed to call Jim Flanigan, the man who had been more of a dad than anyone in Cody's life. He needed to talk to the man as badly as he needed to leave the room where death was winning.

Without hesitating, despite the tears still streaming down his face, he pulled his cell phone from the back pocket of his jeans, found his list of favorite numbers and there — where it would always be — was the Flanigans' home number. He tapped it lightly, held the phone to his ear while it began to ring, and waited. The whole time he had just one thought.

Why hadn't he done this sooner?

Twenty-Two

Bailey had been home for ten days, and everything about the trip had been more than she had expected. She'd been to two of the boys' basketball games and had coffee dates with her mom nearly every morning, the two of them sitting at the kitchen counter and catching up on all the little details of her life in New York, details there hadn't been time to share over Skype or on one of her trips home before this.

She and Brandon had connected every night — usually on Skype, but once with just a phone call. "Have I told you lately that I miss you?" he'd said last night. "Two days feels like two years without you."

Bailey had smiled, wishing she could hold his hands, touch his face through the phone lines. Before shooting his movie in New York, they would go weeks without seeing each other and think it was normal. Now, she felt the same way he did. That the time apart seemed like forever.

It was strange, really. Because Bailey had been home long enough to think about Cody, to contact him if she wanted to, but she had no interest. Her mom had even asked about it the other day, whether she'd heard from him. "No." She wondered when her mom would finally accept the reality of Cody's disinterest. "I never hear from him." And Bailey still felt a slight frustration at the reality.

"Of course, he knows you have Brandon." This reminder came often from her mom, as if once more she were still pulling for Bailey and Cody somehow.

"Yes, but, Mom . . ." Bailey had kept the moment lighter than a conversation like this would've felt a year ago. "Remember what you told me? I'll know it's the right guy because he'll pursue me like a dying man in the desert pursues water."

"Yes." Jenny had nodded, her eyes thoughtful. "I did say that."

"I'm not married, after all." Bailey had held up her left hand then and pictured the seaweed ring that'd been there on New Year's Eve. "I have no ring on my finger."

"Not yet, anyway." Her mom's smile was genuine, proof that she really did like Brandon. Even though they'd all known

Cody so much longer. "So you're saying he could at least call."

"At least!" Bailey had uttered a frustrated laugh. "He could text or write or stop by the house. I mean come on, he could call, right?" She'd raised her hands and then let them fall by her side again. "I mean, Mom, let's be real. This is how Cody's always been."

"Not always." Her mother still cared about him, clearly. "You were the first person he came to see when he came back from Iraq."

"That was like a million years ago."

"I know, but he cared about you. I believe he still cares."

"Right." Bailey had chuckled. The truth hurt less than before. "He's just not that thirsty."

The subject of Cody hadn't come up since then. There were too many other things to talk about. The reality of her move to Los Angeles, and whether she could handle life in the limelight — the chase of the paparazzi. The way it was so different from the life she'd been raised with. Some nights she and her mom stayed up until well after midnight talking about the what ifs. Like what if Brandon took a movie that paired him up with someone edgier, the sort of actress the studio wanted for him.

"Girls in Hollywood can be pretty forward." Her mom wasn't trying to discourage her from loving Brandon. Bailey understood. She only wanted her to be realistic.

"I'm not worried about Brandon falling for someone else. It's more the movies, the sorts of films he might have to make. The scenes they might have him do." Bailey felt sick even talking about that. "If I worry at all, I worry about that."

Now it was Wednesday, late afternoon, and Bailey was sorting through the clothes that still remained in her closet. She hadn't taken many summer clothes when she went to New York. Katy had already promised to take her to some of the best stores along Third Street Promenade in Santa Monica. But she didn't want to overlook the clothes in her closet.

Her brothers were at basketball practice, still at school, so the house remained quiet. But she wanted to show her mom an outfit she'd found in her top dresser drawer. She slid into the shorts and top and jogged downstairs. "Mom! You around?"

"She's in her office." Her dad's voice came from the kitchen. "On deadline for a magazine article."

Bailey reached the bottom of the stairs,

which put her across from the kitchen. Her dad was standing at the stove stirring a pan of what looked like ground beef. He raised his wooden spoon in her direction and grinned. "I'm making dinner tonight. Be prepared for a treat."

She giggled and raised her eyebrows. "You know it." Her dad loved cooking dinner, but he was a little too creative. Always added a few too many spices or an unusual ingredient like artichoke hearts or cayenne pepper or horseradish. They had at least a dozen funny stories of the nights when their dad made dinner, and tonight's dinner would probably join the list.

"So . . ." She did a quick twirl. "What do you think? Too high school? Can I still pull it off?"

"Too high school?" Her dad blinked, wide-eyed. "You're still in high school, right? Or was that last year?"

"Daddy!" She laughed and gave him a tender look. He was always doing that, seeing her the way she'd been as a much younger girl, finding nostalgia in their everyday moments together. She was about to cross the kitchen and hug him, the way she'd done more often this last week at home. But before she could head his way, the phone rang. "I'll get it." She nodded to the pan on the stove. "You're a little busy."

"Are you kidding?" The contents of the pan sizzled louder in response. He made a face and adjusted the burner. "Really, sweetheart. This is a breeze."

"Yeah. I can see that." She hurried over to the far kitchen counter and picked up the phone on the third ring. "Hello?"

At first the caller on the other end was quiet, all except a muffled sort of sound. Almost like the connection was bad. "Hello?"

Again there was no response, just the subtle noises. Whoever it was, the call wasn't clear enough to stay on the line. She was about to hang up, when she heard a voice. "Bailey?"

She held her hand over her other ear. The kitchen was silent except for the sizzling meat, but even so, the caller was almost impossible to hear. "Yes? Who is this?"

"I'm sorry," he coughed. His voice was a mix of tortured sorrow and maybe a little anger. He was crying. That much was obvious. It was the reason she could barely understand him. She was about to ask again who it was when he cleared his throat. "This is Cody. I . . . I need to talk to your dad. Is he there?"

Bailey felt her heart hit the floor. "Uh . . .

hold on." She could tell her mom she was over Cody and laugh at his lack of effort where she was concerned. But when he called crying on the other end of a phone line her heart reminded her. She still had feelings for him. Still cared about whatever had upset him this badly. She walked the phone to her dad and swapped a look with him. Silently she mouthed the words: "It's Cody . . . he's crying." She hesitated, not wanting to hand the phone over so quickly. "Cody . . . is . . . is everything okay?"

"No." He was still crying, still fighting for the strength to talk. "I'm sorry, Bailey . . . I need your dad. Please . . ."

His tone caught her by surprise. Whatever had happened, it must've been bad. Maybe something with his mom . . . or maybe he'd started drinking again. Some situation so bad he could only talk to her dad. "Okay. Here he is." She shrugged as she handed the phone over. Again she whispered, "He's really upset."

Her dad's teasing from earlier disappeared instantly. He handed the wooden spoon to her, took the phone, and stepped aside. "Cody. Hey, what's going on?"

Bailey watched her dad through the entire conversation. His face grew more alarmed in the first few seconds of the call. "Oh,

Cody, why didn't you tell us sooner? Man, I'm so sorry. That's awful."

Her mind raced, trying to imagine what could've happened. The call didn't last long before her dad took it into the next room. After that, all Bailey could hear was the hushed tones of her dad talking, maybe even praying with Cody. Fifteen minutes later he returned to the kitchen, his face several shades paler.

"Dad, what is it?" She set the spoon on the counter beside the stove and turned the burner off. The dinner could wait. "What happened to him?"

"Not to him." He gripped the counter and hung his head for a moment before looking at Bailey again. "It's his girlfriend . . . Cheyenne." Her dad didn't hesitate, didn't make her wonder any longer than necessary. "Bailey, she's dying. She has brain cancer. It could be any time."

Bailey felt like her dad was talking about someone else. She blinked and shook her head. "She had a car accident a year ago . . . she's much better now." Bailey crossed her arms and leaned her hip into the counter. Her mind raced in time with her heart. "We saw her at the football game. She was fine."

"No . . . remember? She went home early. With a headache."

The realization caused a faint feeling to come over her. Her dad was right. That's exactly what had happened. It was the reason Cody could come talk to her after the game. Because Cheyenne had gone home sick. "So she must've . . . he probably found out . . ."

"About that same time. He said she was put in the hospital that night. They got word sometime in the few days after."

Bailey couldn't get her arms around the emotions crashing in on her. Why hadn't Cody told her when they saw each other in New York City? Or at least called her dad sooner? Here all this time . . . all this time she had written him off, believing he didn't care, that he couldn't be bothered to call or text. She had assumed he'd dealt with his lack of feelings for Cheyenne and broken up with her by now. But instead . . . instead he'd been walking with her through a terminal illness. "Dad . . ." She took a few steps and fell into his arms. "How could this happen? She's been through so much."

"No one knows for sure." The gravity in her dad's tone was something she rarely heard. "The tumor happened at the exact spot of her brain injury from the accident."

The truth was more awful than anything Bailey could've guessed. She squeezed her eyes shut and pressed her face into her dad's chest. "Poor Cody . . . I can't imagine."

"To think he's walked this path by himself. I told him I'd drive out there tomorrow morning after meetings at the Colts' facility. Just so we can pray, so he knows he's not alone."

"The older woman, Tara . . . Is that where she's staying?"

"It is. I guess Cheyenne was going to marry Tara's son. But he was killed in Iraq. He was part of Cody's unit."

"I know." Bailey thought about the times when she'd been frustrated that Cody had left her for Cheyenne. But now she couldn't hold that against him. Clearly the girl had needed Cody. God must've known that.

"What's happening?" Her mom came to them, her expression dark with worry. "Who was on the phone?"

"Cody Coleman." Her dad put his arms around each of their shoulders pulling her mom close. "His girlfriend Cheyenne . . . she has brain cancer. It's terminal."

"She doesn't have long." Bailey felt the tears in her eyes, the sadness in her heart. She'd come full circle in her feelings for Cody, because despite their pasts, she was comfortable wanting to help Cody without any of the usual emotional complications.

He was a friend to her now. Nothing more. She was supposed to leave for LA in two days, but she might have to postpone the trip. All that mattered was the heartache Cody was going through. And the reality that they needed to be there for him — whatever that meant.

However that looked.

TWENTY-THREE

Brandon couldn't wait to set his plan in motion. He had a ring picked out, but he wanted to know for sure it was the type and style she liked. The plan was for Bailey to go shopping with Katy Matthews, and while they were looking at clothes, Katy would randomly take her into a jewelry store — pretend it was an impulsive move, something spur of the moment.

Then they'd look at engagement rings, and Katy would dream with Bailey — ask her what she liked and even have her try on a few. Just for fun. Then Katy would report back to him by the twelfth and sometime before Valentine's Day he would buy it.

Then, on February fourteenth, he would do what he'd wanted to do since Christmas Eve: He'd ask Bailey Flanigan to be his wife.

He was sitting on his balcony overlooking the Pacific Ocean and running the plan over in his mind that morning when his phone rang. The sight of Bailey's name made him smile and he answered it quickly. "Hey, how's the packing?"

"I'm getting there." She sounded quieter than usual, defeated even. "I might stay an extra day or so."

"In Bloomington?" Brandon thought about his plan. He stood and walked to the balcony railing, the ocean breeze cool against his face. "Like over the weekend, you mean?"

"I'm not sure." Again he heard sadness in her tone. "Something's come up . . . with Cody."

"Okay." Brandon sucked in a breath and held it. The ground beneath his feet shifted, the way it always shifted when he heard Cody's name. He tried to keep his voice even. "So what is it? With Cody?"

"Not him, actually. His girlfriend." Bailey sounded like she might start crying. "Brandon, she has brain cancer. She's dying."

Brandon exhaled and felt his shoulders sink. He turned his back to the ocean and leaned against the railing. "Bailey, that's terrible."

"I know. He called here to talk to my dad." She hesitated. "I wanna be here for him. If he needs me."

A part of him wanted to know if this

changed anything, if it meant Bailey might stay in Bloomington even longer than the weekend. Like through Valentine's Day, even. He didn't want to ask, didn't want to come across callous. Instead he'd waited for her to explain the situation more fully. "My dad's going to see him . . . to pray with him." Bailey sighed, the sorrow still evident in her tone. "That's about all he wants right now. So it might not affect my flight. I'll have to see."

Again Brandon was sorry about Cody's girlfriend. But he was secretly glad Bailey didn't think she needed to stay, didn't feel she had to be part of helping Cody through this terrible time. She had an audition in LA, after all, a life to get started. Cody was a part of her past — even if he was still connected to her family.

Their conversation ended with Bailey promising to get back to him as soon as she knew anything. Brandon finished his coffee and headed for the studio. He had meetings scheduled all morning, high-powered discussions about the offer on the table. The details were coming together; the lawyers from his agent's office were almost finished looking over the document.

His agent and manager still couldn't believe a major studio was willing to sign him to a seven-movie deal. It was the sort of gargantuan contract actors today just weren't offered. And the price tag per picture would put him in rare air, for sure. The discussions were about creative control and movie genres and leading ladies. No one asked Brandon whether he'd be willing to take the deal.

That much was assumed.

He stopped in the coffee shop on the first floor afterward, a place where even though people recognized him, they'd leave him alone. This was where he worked when he wasn't on set, after all. The entire place was full of actors and directors and producers. The staff at the coffee shop had no real reason to overreact to his presence.

As he crossed the lobby toward the corner, he thought about the deal again.

God, Your blessings are amazing. Nothing about this contract is from me or my efforts. It's from You, all from You.

Bailey often talked about the silent prayers she would utter, and how God would put a response in her heart. A quiet whisper or a reminder of a Bible verse she'd read earlier. That happened to Brandon once in a while, but not here. He didn't have time to think about the reason, because as he walked into the coffee shop he immediately spotted

Dayne Matthews. He was talking to another producer, someone else in the world of faith films — from what Brandon remembered. Their conversation looked like it was just about over.

"Hey." Dayne spotted him and waved. "Brandon, come here. I'd like you to meet someone."

Brandon took the quickest path past a few other tables and gave Dayne a quick hug. Then he turned to the other man. "Hi. I'm Brandon."

"Yes." The man laughed lightly as he shook Brandon's hand. "I know who you are."

"Jared's one of the producers I'll be working with over the next few years." Dayne grinned at the guy. "Lured him away from one of the biggest studios on the planet."

"I had to make a change. Wanted to be on a team that turned out movies I could take my daughter to see." He looked at Dayne. "I figure there's this tremendous interest in faith films and investors looking to make it happen." He turned to Brandon again. "Dayne has the right idea. All we need is quality movies."

The exchange was easy and lighthearted. Not meant to be a slam at Brandon or at the movies he was about to agree to make.

But the words hit him like so many darts, poking at his comfort level, and making him question himself for the first time since talks about the new contract came up. He dismissed the thoughts. There was room in the industry for those who made family-friendly or faith films, and at the same time room for Christians to star in more mainstream pictures.

Jared had to go, so he shook Brandon's hand once more and gave Dayne a light slap on his shoulder. "Great ideas, man. We're going to take over the industry."

"Absolutely."

Again Brandon felt like he was on the wrong team. He took a quick breath. "You headed home?"

"Not yet." He glanced at the time on his phone. "I have another meeting in an hour."

Brandon wanted to ask what the big deal was, why the sudden spate of meetings, and how come he was only just hearing about big investment dollars being slated for faith films. But it didn't seem the time. "Has Katy heard from Bailey?"

"A few times. She should be here before the weekend, right?"

"Yeah." He laughed, but he didn't feel at ease for some reason. "I wish it were today. I can't wait to see her."

Dayne pointed to the closest table, the one in the corner, far from anyone else at the coffee shop. "Why don't you get a coffee and talk for a few minutes. If you have time."

"I do." The idea sounded perfect. "Want anything?"

"I'm good." Dayne acted like his fingers had the jitters. "Too much coffee already."

"Okay. Be right back." Brandon slipped into line and ignored the whispers between the girls behind the counter. He was too busy thinking about the timing, how God must've planned for him to run into Dayne. He got his coffee and headed back to the corner table.

"So, how are things? With Bailey . . . with life?" Dayne leaned back, his tone casual.

"Good." Brandon took a sip of his coffee. Dayne was someone Brandon wanted to know better, a guy who had once been where Brandon was, and who had allowed his faith to lead him even in his professional life — that and Bailey would be living with him and his wife. The two of them, Brandon and Dayne, were bound to get closer. "Like I said, I can't wait to see her."

"You two have been dating for a while now. What? Almost a year?"

"Almost." Brandon couldn't believe it had

been that long. The time had flown by. "That makes me feel better about my plans for Valentine's Day."

Dayne crossed his arms in front of him, curious. "What plans?"

"Didn't Katy tell you? About the engagement ring?"

"What?" Dayne allowed his voice to raise a few notches. "No, she did not tell me about any engagement rings." He tossed his hands. "I'm always the last to know."

Brandon laughed, glad again for the time with Dayne. "Yeah, Katy's taking Bailey shopping when she gets in tomorrow. And Katy's going to take her into a jewelry store — just like all casual and everything — and she'll find out what sort of ring Bailey likes. Then I'll go back to the same store on the thirteenth and buy it for Valentine's Day —" He snapped his fingers. "Then I'll be ready to ask her."

"Wow . . ." Dayne chuckled, but he had lost the lighthearted look from earlier. "Katy's in on that plan?"

"Yeah . . . of course." Brandon felt a slight hint of awkwardness. "What . . . you think it's too soon or something?"

Dayne didn't look uncomfortable. "Actually . . . I do. All things considered."

His words kicked Brandon in the gut. "I

414

don't know." His laugh was a cover for the insecurity he felt. "Like I said . . . we've dated for almost a year. I've known her longer than that."

"I get it." Dayne smiled, a deep kindness in his expression. "It's not you, man. You're ready . . . I believe that. But you need to think about her."

Brandon pictured him and Bailey kneeling in the sand on New Year's Eve, wishing he had a ring so they could make their desires official. "We've talked about it." He still wasn't clear why Dayne felt this way. "I think she's more ready than she might let on."

"Possibly." Dayne slid his hands into the back pockets of his jeans, still calm. "The thing is, she just lost her job in New York and now she's moving to LA for the first time, thinking about an acting career." He made a face that said he could be wrong, but he doubted it. "Girls need time to settle in."

"Did Katy need time?" Brandon only knew what he'd seen in the tabloids back when the two of them were dating. Bailey had never talked about what went on behind the scenes with the couple.

Dayne chuckled and gave a single nod of his head. "Yes. She needed time. She almost left me because of the business."

A strange feeling made Brandon's soul feel uneasy. "Hmmm."

"And remember Bailey's reaction to the paparazzi on New Year's? She certainly didn't take it in stride."

"But we can work on that, find ways around the media." Brandon still didn't see what that had to do with his desire to marry her. "We'll always have to work on that issue. Waiting longer wouldn't make a difference."

"I don't mean a lot longer. Just give her time to settle in." He chuckled again. "I mean, man, she'll barely be off the plane on Valentine's Day. Maybe give her time to unpack."

Again Brandon could tell from his tone that Dayne meant no harm by his advice. As much as it wasn't what Brandon wanted to hear, he had to admit there might be wisdom in it. "So maybe later this spring?" The disappointment weighed heavy in his voice.

"Yeah, something like that." Dayne's face turned thoughtful, pensive almost. "So word on the street is you're looking at a new contract."

Brandon was glad for the change in topic. He grinned. "It's amazing. Biggest contract this studio has ever offered." The reminder made him feel dizzy. "It's just a blessing . . . I mean, no one deserves the sort of money and marketing and attention this is going to get."

"Attention?" Dayne sat back, clearly curious. "You mean when they announce it?"

"Right, it's crazy." He leaned on his forearms, excitement brimming from deep inside him. "They're planning a red carpet party, everyone in the business invited. Catered, the whole deal." Brandon laughed, still amazed at the details that came out of the meeting he'd just had. "A few of the top acts in music will perform at it. Justin Bieber . . . Rascal Flatts. Like, bigger than I ever could've dreamed."

Dayne nodded, listening, his smile easy. "Wow . . . I haven't heard of that for a contract signing before. Will they announce the scope of the deal?"

"Not really." This was a point Brandon had been adamant on. "They'll announce it one film at a time. And since box office incentives are built into the contract the amount could vary each time. So yeah, that makes more sense. But they'll talk about my cut for the first film. So, seven films in four years . . . people can do the math and get a pretty good idea without us coming out and saying what the contract's worth."

"Pretty big money."

"I can't even think about it." Brandon rarely let the numbers weigh on his mind. "When I do, I just ask God what He wants me to do with it all, like build a school for an African village or start up a ministry here in the inner city. Something big."

Dayne was quiet. "Have they talked about the sort of films you'll do?"

It was the first point in the conversation where Brandon felt the slightest disapproval from Dayne. The cafeteria was getting busier around them so they moved to a quiet booth where they could keep talking. "They have. It was a big sticking point for me." He nodded, trying hard to look like the competent businessman he wanted to be — as best he could for a guy in his early twenties. "My agent helped work that out with the lawyers. Making sure I'll have a right of refusal if they bring me a project I don't like or something that compromises my faith."

"Really?" Dayne seemed surprised. "Usually with a big studio contract they keep most of the control. So did you tell them you didn't want to do anything rated R?"

Brandon blinked. "Not so much by the rating . . . like my agent said, some movies are rated R for theme, and really there's a lot of redemptive storytelling that takes place."

"Yeah." Dayne winced. "I could see an agent saying that."

Brandon's frustration grew a little more with every minute. "Hey, Dayne, you've been this route." He was careful to keep his tone from sounding rude. "If something about my contract's bothering you, just tell me."

"Okay, I'll be honest." Dayne sighed and crossed his arms again, his attention completely on Brandon. "The studio doesn't care about your faith, man. They care about making money. And if they think that means you need to be more of a bad boy, they'll do everything in their power to make you a bad boy. And I mean everything. Force you to attend the wrong parties, the ones they think are right. Set girls up to flock around you so the paparazzi will make it look like they caught you doing things you're not even thinking of doing." He didn't laugh. "Believe me, Brandon, the studios don't invest that kind of money without getting their own way when it comes to movie selection, image, leading ladies. Whatever they think will put people in the seats."

Brandon nodded. Deep down he knew

this, right? He'd known it from the beginning. But he'd never thought of it that way, that some of the situations he'd been in might've been set up by the studio. Allowed, maybe. Approved of, even. But set up by his employers? The possibility that the paparazzi pictures from a night on the town could in some way be the doing of the marketing department of one or another film he'd been in?

Dayne must've seen how surprised Brandon was. "Picture it," he continued. "You're done filming, ready for a night out. You get a call from your agent or someone at your management company. They tell you about a party — an exclusive, an invitation from another celeb. They tell you where and when to go, and they make it seem like they're doing you a favor." He paused, his eyes locked on Brandon's. "Right? Isn't that how it works?"

"Well . . ." Brandon felt sick, like he wasn't sure he could stand if he wanted to. Again he hated looking at those moments in this exact light. "Sometimes. Yeah, that's happened. But that was before."

"Before your last two movies, maybe. But with this contract it'll be every time." Dayne frowned. "Remember, Brandon. I was you just a few years ago. A puppet in the hands of a studio, thinking I was running my own life. In the end there was only one way out." He shrugged one shoulder. "Just wanted to share that with you. Since they're offering such a big contract."

Brandon didn't know what to say, how to respond. "I guess . . . I never thought about it like that."

"I mean, I know you're thinking of Bailey and engagement rings . . . but this contract could change your life. Have you had your own lawyer look at it?"

Confusion added to the mix of emotions smothering him. "My own? You mean the one from my agent's office?"

"No." Dayne was more serious than he'd been throughout the entire conversation. "Your agent will make a fortune off this contract. I'm talking about a lawyer *you* hire, someone independent who will tell you what you're really signing. What it'll mean for you."

"Oh." Brandon felt stupid, like a kid who had inadvertently let the adults in his life make all the decisions. "I guess I hadn't thought about it that way."

Dayne took his wallet from his back pocket and pulled a business card from inside. "My brother, Luke Baxter, is an entertainment attorney. I'm sure he'd love to take a look at it." Dayne slid the card across the table. "Give him a call. At least then you'll be protecting yourself."

Brandon nodded. "Thanks, Dayne . . . I mean it. I need someone like you, helping me out. Especially where God's concerned." The frustration he felt was nothing to his gratitude. "The Lord must've arranged this meeting, huh?"

"Not just this one." Dayne's face relaxed and he grinned. "The one before it. Where you met Jared James."

He wasn't sure he was tracking with Dayne. "The guy doing Christian films with you?"

"Absolutely. Look up his work. He's one of the most talented moviemakers in the business." Dayne's face held a knowing, as if he was absolutely confident in whatever dots he was privately connecting. He gave another casual shrug. "At least you know you have options, Brandon. For now, any-way." Dayne looked at his phone again. "I better run." He stood and gave Brandon a solid hug. "I hope I didn't say too much." He took a step back. "I care about Bailey . . . and I care about you. There's a right way to go about the next five years, and there's a wrong way. Pick the wrong way and I think you could lose more than your reputation and witness. You could lose the girl too." He hesitated. "I'll be praying for you, buddy. Really."

Brandon couldn't do anything but nod, unable to move or speak in response. Instead he watched Dayne go, took what was left of his coffee, and headed outside to the waiting car. Discouragement grabbed at him from every angle. Dayne had pretty much shot down the idea of a Valentine's Day engagement and then made him doubt the very contract he was about to celebrate.

Brandon settled into the plush seat, and he remembered the last thing Dayne said: He'd be praying. Brandon believed him. And if he prayed too, then the answers would eventually be clear on every point.

As the driver headed for his beachside home, he slipped the business card Dayne had given him in his back pocket. He didn't need to bother the guy. The contract signing wasn't for another month or so. Besides, he would read through the document himself first. How difficult could it be? Brandon understood Dayne's point. Brandon could always do Christian films exclusively. The idea wasn't a bad one, but Brandon had bigger plans, grander ideas.

If he could take his faith into the mainstream world of major motion pictures, he would have a greater impact, right? Whether the film was an action movie or a thriller or a drama, if it had the scope and marketing the studio was planning to bring to his next seven pictures, he would reach far more people. Brandon felt convinced, and by the time his driver dropped him off back home, he was at peace with his decision. Dayne meant well.

Unless he spotted something troubling, there was no reason to have Luke Baxter look at his contract.

Twenty-Four

Bailey was nearly packed, ready for her flight in four hours, when the house phone rang. For the past two days she'd thought often of Cody, what he was going through and the heartache he must be feeling. But she hadn't reached out to him. After all, he hadn't wanted to talk to her, and that was okay. She understood. In a situation like this, the last person he'd want to talk to would be her, his old girlfriend.

From up in her room Bailey couldn't hear whatever conversation might be happening downstairs. After a few minutes she went to the top of the landing and heard her mom walking up from the kitchen. Bailey waited, and when her mom came into view she knew. The tears on her cheeks told the story. The call had to be from Cody.

"Cheyenne has maybe an hour." She wiped her tears and sounded stronger than she looked. "Cody says it'll be anytime."

Her mom hugged her. "Bailey, he sounded so sad." She drew back and gave a few shakes of her head. "I asked if there was anything we could do, and he said no. He just wanted us to pray."

Bailey felt her heart breaking for Cody. "Mom, that's awful." She wished they could all be in heaven now, with no more death or dying or worries about which career path to take, which guy to love. "Life can be so hard."

"It can." Her mom took hold of her hands. "It's why we need God so much."

She closed her eyes and nodded. "Let's pray for Cody."

Her mom led the prayer. "Father, we ask that You be in that room where Cheyenne is about to go home. Fill it with the presence of Your Holy Spirit and comfort Cody and Tara. Give them strength, Lord, to be there for Cheyenne, to love her and hold her hand as she goes from this life to the next." Her mom's voice trembled. "Most of all we ask You to comfort Cody. Father, life always seems to be hard for that young man. Please . . . as Cheyenne goes home we pray You will bless Cody with sunshine in the days to come." She sighed. "Thank You for Your truth and Your salvation. So we don't for a minute have to worry or wonder about where Cheyenne is headed. Because heaven is real. In the powerful name of Jesus, amen."

Bailey released her mom's hands and dabbed at the tears beneath her eyes. "Thanks, Mom. That was perfect."

Her mom looked intently at her. "Do you think maybe you should stay another few days? Be there for Cody?"

The idea hadn't hit Bailey, but now it seemed almost obvious. "Do you think so?"

"Sort of." Her mom lifted one shoulder, her ambivalence evident. "I mean, our family is like his family. And this is bound to be one of the most difficult couple days he's ever faced."

Times like this Bailey wondered again if her mom didn't still hold out hope that somehow she and Cody would find their way back together, that he would be a regular part of their family once again. Bailey tried to keep the issues separate — her past with Cody and his potential need to see her family in the next few days. Maybe even her. "I'm not sure he'd want to see me." She bit her lip, weighing the options. "He didn't want to talk the other day."

"Only because he was crying. He needed Dad that night."

"I know, but . . . what good could I really do?"

Her mom waited for a few seconds, giving serious thought to the possibilities. "Maybe it isn't so much that you'd see him. But just him knowing that you had stayed, that you didn't leave for LA the day his girlfriend died."

Put that way, Bailey easily saw the right answer. How callous would she appear if she blithely hopped on a plane in the hours after Cheyenne went home to heaven, as if Cody's pain and heartache were of no concern to her. She nodded slowly. "You're right. I need to call Brandon." She had no choice really. "He'll understand."

"I'm sure you can get a flight out tomorrow or Sunday." Her mom hugged her again. "I think that's the right choice, Bailey. I'll let you go make your call."

When her mom was gone, she slipped back into her room, sat on the edge of her bed, and dialed Brandon's cell. Usually she would text first, see what he was doing. Especially since he was filming today and he'd have his phone off. But she wanted him to hear her voice as she left the message. "Brandon . . . something's come up with Cody. I won't be going to LA until probably Sunday." She paused. "I'm sorry, baby. Believe me I wanted to be on that plane." She stood and mindlessly played with the zipper on her suitcase. "Call me back."

Then — so that he'd know how much he still mattered to her, and so he'd know that his loss meant something to her — she texted Cody. She doubted he had his phone on in this last bit of time with Cheyenne. But whenever he looked, she wanted him to see her message.

My mom told me about your call. I'm heartsick about this, Cody. I'm so sorry. I cancelled my flight to LA so I could be here. In case you need anything. Please . . . let me know. My mom and I can bring meals or make phone calls — whatever. I'm here for you.

That was all. And if her mom was right, then what she'd said and done was enough. Now it was up to Cody if he needed her in any real way over the next couple days. And if all the message did was remind Cody how much she cared, then it was still the right thing to do.

For the next hour, Bailey responded to fans on Twitter and Facebook. Ever since she and Brandon had been more public about their relationship, she had a ton of girls following her on both sites. Some of them were angry she was dating Brandon

Paul. But most of them seemed to know she was a Christian. They had questions for her about whether a guy should treat them a certain way or talk to them a certain way, questions about their relationships with their mothers and their friends.

The aching void among teens touched Bailey more with every passing day. At first she would only check for comments from fans once in a while. Now she didn't even like using the word fan. The people who clamored for her advice and attention were friends. She cared about them as much as if they had stopped by her house to share the troubles on their hearts.

Not until four o'clock that afternoon did she hear back from Brandon. By then she'd called the airlines and booked a flight out for midmorning on Sunday. That would put her in Los Angeles at just after two in the afternoon with the time change in her favor. She took Brandon's call in her room, so she'd have more privacy.

"Hey, I got your message." He sounded hurt. "Would it be okay if we Skype? I need to see you."

"Of course." She crossed the room and opened her laptop on her computer desk in the corner. "Give me a minute or two, okay? You back at your room?"

"Yes." Again he sounded down, defeated. Very unusual for him. "I'll be ready when you are."

They hung up and Bailey worked quickly to sign onto Skype. Then she checked her look in the mirror and adjusted her hair into a loose side ponytail. She didn't wear any makeup, but that didn't matter. Brandon knew the real her. She tapped a few last buttons and instantly her own face appeared and then reduced in size as his face filled the larger part of the screen.

"Hey . . . hi there." She hated that he sounded hurt.

"Hi."

She smiled. "It's good to see you."

He smiled, but his eyes looked flat. "You don't know how much."

One thing was certain. Bailey hadn't imagined what she heard. "You look upset."

"Well, yeah. I was counting down the hours." His smile proved he wasn't angry. "What happened?"

She took a deep breath and kept her answer short. "Cody's girlfriend . . . she's going to die today sometime. He called and talked to my mom."

"Wow . . . I'm sorry. That's . . . that's too sad." Brandon felt sick for Cody, but he was still confused at how the guy's very great loss affected Bailey's flight out. "So . . . you're not coming till Sunday?"

"It was my mom's idea." Bailey wished they were in person, so she could touch his hand or his shoulder. "We've pretty much been all the family Cody's had. So maybe I should stay around, in case he needs us."

A hundred thoughts seemed to flash in Brandon's eyes, but he only clenched his teeth for a minute. "You think in the hours after his girl dies he'll want to see you?"

"I don't know." She tried to keep the whole issue very matter-of-fact. "My mom just thought it might seem a little heartless to fly to LA right now."

Brandon wasn't going to understand. His expression made that very clear. But rather than fight with her, he found his smile again. The tenderhearted smile Bailey loved so much. "I can't say it makes sense to me." His tone rang with hurt, but he clearly meant whatever he was about to say. "But if that's what you need to do, you have my support."

Bailey felt herself breathe out, and she realized she'd been more than a little worried about how Brandon would react. She wasn't sure staying made sense to her either. "I want to be with you. Not here. You believe that, right?"

"I do." He didn't hesitate. "Will you . . . go to him?"

She shook her head. "I don't plan on it. I texted him and told him I was staying. That if he needed anything he could call."

"That was nice." Brandon's voice lacked even a little sarcasm. He was obviously trying to see this her way. "You haven't heard back?"

"No. I doubt I will. But I think my mom was right." She returned his smile, grateful for this time, for the chance to talk to him face-to-face. "Staying here is the kind thing to do."

Brandon nodded. He leaned his face on his fist and allowed the look in his eyes to lighten a little. "I guess I'll have to switch up my countdown clock."

She giggled, and it felt wonderful. Especially in light of the heaviness of the afternoon. "Me too." She looked deep into his eyes, past the issues at hand. "I can't wait, Brandon. I miss you like crazy."

"Well . . ." He grabbed a full breath and sighed. "That makes two of us."

They talked for a few minutes about his day, his filming, and then he let her go. "If you're staying at home another few days, you might as well hang out with your family."

"Thanks." She told him she'd call later, and then they ended the Skype session. Bailey was glad that at the end of the conversation Brandon turned the attention to her family. She wondered if it was his way of saying that he trusted her, that this time apart wasn't going to be about her and Cody.

Just about her doing an act of kindness for an old friend.

The goodbye took longer than even the hospice nurse had expected. For the last few hours Cheyenne's breathing had slowed dramatically, with long breaks between her in and out breaths. But still she held on. Now the afternoon was wearing down and evening was coming. Cody couldn't imagine another night of this, sitting beside her with no way of helping, wondering if every heartbeat was her last.

He sat in the same chair, the place where it felt like he'd been sitting for the past month. They took turns standing over her, talking to her, praying for her. Right now it was Tara's turn. Sometime yesterday they both had sensed a change, a peace in Cheyenne as if she wanted them to know she was ready. It was time for her to go. And so they no longer urged her to hold on, to fight the cancer and stay with them.

Tara ran her fingers over Cheyenne's sweaty forehead. "Go ahead, baby . . . go home to Jesus. He's waiting for you, honey." She wasn't crying today — like at some points in the last week — wasn't fighting God's will in the situation. And by now His will was very clear. Cheyenne was almost on the other side. "Art's waiting for you, sweetie. Run home, baby girl."

Even now Cody wanted to weep for the sadness of the situation, the life Chey was going to miss here on earth. But when it was his turn to stand over her and pray for her and talk to her, he could do nothing but echo Tara's message. She needed to let go. Tara sat down after fifteen minutes, and he stood, running his hand over her bald head, whispering close to her face. "I know you can hear me, Chey . . . and I agree with Tara. We want you to go. It's okay to release everything here, honey. Jesus has His arms open wide for you. Art, too. You gotta tell him for me . . . when I get there he and I are gonna do some intense fishing. Probably a little football, too." He paused, his eyes damp. "Okay, sweetie? You tell him that for me."

In response, her breathing seemed to slow even more until he could count on two hands the number of breaths she took in a minute, and then on one hand. Tara joined him on her feet, as if she sensed the moment was almost upon them. "Dear Jesus, be with us . . . walk her home, Jesus . . . walk her home." For the first time that day Tara started to cry. "We can feel You here, Lord . . . take her hand and take her away from this. Please, God . . ."

Another breath and after several seconds another.

Cody watched, not sure whether he was breathing either. Ten seconds . . . fifteen . . . twenty. Chey gasped one final breath and then, in a moment they would remember forever, she exhaled and smiled at the same time. The exact same time.

And that was it.

Her chest didn't rise again, and no air passed over her lips, in or out. Tara spoke first. "She's home!" She turned and fell into Cody's arms. "She's with Jesus. She's with my Art again." Her tears were a mix of unearthly sorrow and otherworldly joy. She pulled back and stared out the window at the winter sky. "You're home, baby girl . . . you give my boy a hug, okay?"

Cody looked at Chey, at the strong woman she was . . . at the friend she had been. For all the death he'd seen in Iraq, he'd never seen anything like this. A homegoing. Watching Cheyenne die was exhausting and all but impossible. But it was also beautiful, because very clearly she was no longer in the body that lay still on the bed. She was free and whole and well and happy.

Forever happy.

He stepped back from the bed and ran his hand over Tara's back. "You okay, Mama?" It was the name Chey had called her, the name Art had called her. Now that it was just him, he would call her that, too. Always. "I want to go outside for a bit. You okay?"

"I am." She wiped at her eyes and sniffed. With gentle movements she reached out and stroked Cheyenne's hand. It was still warm, no doubt. But not for long. "I'll call the morgue and stay with her. You go ahead."

Cody didn't want to stay with the body of his friend. He wanted to be outside, in the fresh air where the idea of heaven was so much more real. Without wasting another moment, he hugged Tara again and then left the room. When he was outside on the familiar patio chair, he closed his eyes and breathed in deep. Out here he could still hear Chey's voice in the wind, still feel her beside him, her hand on his shoulder assuring him she wasn't afraid.

God . . . help me know how to do this . . . I

miss her so much.

Almost as if by answer, he pictured his buddy Art. The big smile and bigger laugh, the way he would've stepped in front of a bullet for Cody or anyone else. He imagined Cheyenne coming into the kingdom, being greeted by Jesus and a host of people who had come to meet her. And he thought about that moment when she would see Art again, when they'd run into each other's arms and hug for the longest time.

A smile pierced the sadness in his heart. If he could hold on to that picture, he'd be fine. Even when it felt like every heartbeat required effort. Cody looked into the winter sky and remembered their last real conversation, when she'd talked to him about two things pressing on her heart. Heaven, of course.

And Bailey Flanigan.

From then until now Cody hadn't wanted to think about her message, the strength of her feelings. But now . . . with her gone . . . he had no choice. Chey meant nothing harmful by her observations, and she spoke them with no sense of jealousy or manipulation. It wasn't for herself that she feared Cody might run to Bailey in the season after her passing.

It was for him.

Her point was a simple one: Maybe he and Bailey had never been right for each other. Not all first loves were forever loves. The idea only added hurt to his heart. Whatever way he chose to believe after this, Cheyenne's wisdom would remain. He might need weeks to sort through the implications, and longer than that if he decided she was right. For now he couldn't think about it. He wanted to hold onto Cheyenne, the life inside her, the love. But even as he dedicated his entire existence to her memory, he remembered his cell phone in his back pocket.

He had called the Flanigans earlier today, but he hadn't checked his phone since then. The air was cold, more snow in the forecast for later that day. He pulled out his phone and clicked the front button. Sure enough, he had two voicemail messages and a text. He checked the text first and felt his lungs fill with a quick breath. It was from Bailey.

My mom told me about your call. I'm heart-sick about this, Cody. I'm so sorry. I cancelled my flight to LA so I could be here. In case you need anything. Please . . . let me know. My mom and I can bring meals or make phone calls — whatever. I'm here for you.

He pictured her, sitting in the home she grew up in, the home he grew up in, waiting and wondering. Trying to decide whether she'd made the right choice by going to LA two days later. The way he'd talked so short to her the other day probably made her wonder whether he cared at all for her.

Fresh tears poked pins at his eyes and he closed them against the chill of the winter wind. He didn't need casseroles or phone calls or errands run for him. He needed just one thing. No matter what Cheyenne had told him a few days ago. Suddenly he needed her more than he needed the morning. He let his fingers tap out the message, straight from his heart to hers.

I need you, *Bailey. only you.*

TWENTY-FIVE

Bailey received the text just before dinner. She read it a dozen times thinking through the different ways he might've meant the words, or how she should best respond in light of the fact that she had a boyfriend. A boyfriend she loved very much.

Finally she allowed herself to settle on the explanation that made the most sense. She had offered her help, offered to be there however he might need her. And he had taken her up on her offer. They had known each other since she was a freshman in high school. If he wanted to see her now, to grieve with her and draw strength from her, then she was ready to be there for him.

On her way down to help her mom with the meal, she answered his text. First there was the obvious: Cheyenne was gone. And in the painful time after saying a final good-bye, Cody had finally checked his messages. There was no need asking how she was.

Bailey was sure about that. She poised her fingers over her phone's keyboard and thought for a long minute.

Dear God, please give me the words. It's always so complicated with Cody. But this time it's not about me or about us . . . this is for him. So give me the right words . . . please.

The answer spoke peace to her heart.

Daughter, I am with you . . . love as I have loved.

God wanted her to love Cody, the way He loved Cody. The way she might love anyone who needed her help. Whatever other complications their past added to the mix, she would set them aside for now. She stared at the blank text box and began to type.

I told you I was here for you, and I am. Just tell me when and I'll come to you. Again . . . I'm so sorry, Cody.

She reread her message and then sent it. A minute passed while she stared at their conversation, hardly believing that this was really Cody Coleman she was talking to, and knowing once more that God didn't want her to think about him that way. Not during this season. Just when she was going to put her phone away and head downstairs, his response appeared on her phone screen.

I'll come to you. I'll pick you up tomorrow morning at nine o'clock and we can go to the lake. We'll have about an hour. Then I need to talk to your dad about a few things. Is that okay?

Yes . . . I'll see you here. And hey . . . I'm praying for you.

This time his answer came more quickly. *Thanks. I can feel it.*

After dinner she told her mom about the conversation. "He's taking me to Lake Monroe. Then he wants to talk to Dad."

"We'll be here." Her mom's eyes filled with peace. "This is good, Bailey, that the two of you are going to talk. That he's making the effort and coming here to pick you up."

Bailey almost always agreed with her mother; the two of them saw things the same way often. But something in her mother's tone bothered her. "It's not a date. You know that, right?"

"Of course." Her mom looked a little hurt. "I'm just saying I like that it matters enough for him to come to you. Even though you were willing to go to him."

Even after they finished talking and Bailey headed up to her room, she wasn't convinced — as if secretly her mom hoped tomorrow would be a turning point for Bailey and Cody, and they might find in the wake of tragedy that they loved each other again. But the idea was ridiculous. Even if she still had feelings for Cody, this wouldn't have been the time for him to pronounce a newfound love for her. He was grieving, and he needed someone who knew his heart.

Nothing more.

Once she was upstairs she called Brandon and gave him the update. The call was brief, and Bailey knew that deep down Brandon wasn't happy about tomorrow's meeting. But he trusted her. That reality spoke louder than anything either of them said.

By the time Saturday morning rolled around, Bailey's stomach was nervous about whatever lay ahead. Sure, she could tell herself she was only meeting him as a friend, only helping him grieve. But that didn't change the fact that for so many years of her life she'd been in love with Cody Coleman, that she'd waited for him when he went to Iraq and longed for him every day after that. Right up until this last year.

She was sitting outside in a short winter jacket when he pulled up. His pickup was the same one he'd had the past several years, and something about seeing him stop in the circle at the front of her house made her feel like she was nineteen again . . . or twenty . . . or twenty-one. Back when she lived for moments like this.

There was no reason for him to get out, so she jogged down the walkway and slid into his passenger seat before he could kill the engine. The cold air, combined with her nerves, made her sound breathless as she buckled her seatbelt. "Hi." She was careful to keep her tone subdued. The reason she was here was at the front of her mind. "I'm sorry." She faced him, still catching her breath. "She was way too young."

"She was." He leaned over and hugged her. His eyes were dry, but clearly he hadn't gotten much sleep. As he sat up and faced the wheel, he glanced at her again. "Cheyenne's safe. I know that. It's just . . . she said some things. I couldn't get past them until I talked to you."

Bailey nodded and the fear inside her tripled. Chey had said something to him in the days before she died? Was that what he meant? And was the conversation somehow about her, because why else would Cody want to talk to her in light of that very same discussion? *Be patient, Bailey,* she told herself. *God, help me be patient.*

They said very little as he drove to the lake, as he parked in their same parking spot adjacent to the trailhead and climbed out of the car. Bailey wore several layers beneath her coat and at the last minute she decided to leave it in the car. She didn't want to be too warm. And she had no idea how much walking Cody had in mind.

Again she didn't wait for him to get her door. The less this felt like the past, the better. They walked fifty yards or so to their rock, the enormous boulder that sat at the edge of the trail and overlooked the lake. "Up here okay?"

Bailey nodded, glad she'd left her jacket behind. Once they were both seated at the top, side by side, their eyes on the cold gray lake far below, Bailey quietly repeated what she'd told him earlier. "I'm sorry . . . I really am."

"It's not your fault." Cody looked like he'd been up all night, and his eyes proved he'd been crying.

"I didn't think you'd call." She kept her eyes on the lake, not looking to make a connection or renew a connection now. "Didn't seem like you wanted me to be a part of this, of the heartache you've been going through."

"It wasn't that." He seemed to know what she was talking about. "That night I just needed your dad. The way I would've needed my own dad if he were in the picture." Cody didn't seem particularly open. He set his jaw and stared straight ahead. But after maybe a minute of sitting in silence, he sighed and turned his eyes to her. "I have two things I'd like to tell you."

Bailey felt her heartbeat quicken. Whatever it was, he had thought this through. There was a point to their meeting.

"That day on your parents' front porch . . . I didn't tell you everything." The doors in her eyes were open and he walked straight into the rooms of her heart — where only he had ever been. "Remember I told you that I ran from you because I was trying to survive? Because that's what I was trained to do when the situation looked hopeless?"

"Yes."

He folded his hands tightly together, as if that was the only way to keep from reaching out to her. "Well . . . I was wrong. That's why I'm here. Because for one thing, I had to tell you that."

His admission took seconds to work its way through her. She searched his eyes. Hadn't she always wondered if this was how he'd felt back then? Whether he regretted his decision? "You're saying . . . you should've stayed?"

"Yes." The word was a raw whisper, agonizing and heavy with regret. "If it killed me." He watched her, waiting for her response.

She folded her arms in front of her, aware again of the cool lake air. "I might need a minute."

"I couldn't go another day without telling you." His tone, his face made it clear he wasn't sorry he'd finally been honest. "Don't be upset with me."

"I'm not." Her teeth chattered again, and she willed herself to resist the cold. "It's just . . . it's too late. I mean, where does that leave us?"

"That's the second part." Cody studied her, the closeness from a few minutes ago still there between them. "Cheyenne said something about you, in one of our last conversations. Something that made me see the two of us . . . I don't know, differently."

Bailey pulled one knee up and hugged it. "What did she say?"

"Well . . . Chey watched me, she watched us . . . how we looked at each other that night before the game."

Bailey knew what was coming. Cheyenne was a very special girl from everything Cody had ever said. She probably wanted to give her blessing that after she was gone Cody should find Bailey again, pursue his first love again. She waited . . . wondering what she would say in response, how hearing those words would make her feel.

"She told me . . . in her opinion my feelings for you were really only for the *ideal* of you. That it would be a mistake to try to make things work with you again."

The rock beneath her seemed suddenly made of foam rubber. "She said that?" Bailey's head began to spin. How could Chey know? Because she'd seen how they looked at each other at a football game? And just like that she could proclaim that in her opinion the two of them weren't right for each other? Bailey was in love with someone else, and even she still struggled with the way they had looked at each other that night.

"I know what you're thinking." He sounded tired. He looked out at the water again. "That maybe she was jealous, or — I don't know — if she couldn't have me, then she didn't want anyone else having me." His eyes caught hers again. "Especially not you." He shook his head. "But that wasn't it. Actually . . . what she said made sense in a sort of sad way." The water caught his attention again. "That's why I needed this time. To see if maybe you agreed with her."

Bailey felt faint, like she was stuck in some bad dream or being tossed on a stormy sea with no sure sense of where the ground was. "I . . . I guess I don't get it."

For a long time, Cody rested his forearm on his knee and let his head fall on his wrist. "I'm tired. I'm sure I'm not making sense."

She had to agree, but she waited. Of all the things she thought he might talk about, the idea that she wasn't the right girl for him was probably last on the list.

He slumped a little, obviously worn out from all he'd been through. "But it was that other part Cheyenne pointed out." The pain in his eyes made it clear that none of this was easy for him. "That deep down if I kept running from you, then you probably weren't the right girl for me. And I probably wasn't the right guy."

Bailey thought about that for a moment, and gradually the truth in Cheyenne's thinking dawned in her heart. "I hadn't . . . thought of it that way before."

"Yeah, me either." Cody straightened his shoulders.

Again Bailey waited. The air was warming, the sun breaking through the storm clouds from last night. But the cold inside her remained.

Cody put his hand on her shoulder. "It's true in a way. When I ran so many times, when I left for the Army, and when I left for Indianapolis while you finished up your movie with Brandon Paul . . . I always said the same thing. That you deserved someone better . . . that I wasn't good enough for you."

She nodded, clenching her teeth to keep from shivering. It was still hard to believe this was really happening, that she was sitting here along the snowy edge of Lake Monroe talking to Cody Coleman about the past.

The sunshine felt warm on their faces, as if God, Himself, was shining a light of understanding between them. Cody removed his hand from her and wrapped his arms around his knees. For a long time he looked out at the lake as if by doing so there might be a way back to yesterday, to a time when this understanding might've made a difference for both of them.

"My mom . . . when you left after that summer. She told me I'd know love was right because . . . the right guy would pursue me like a dying man in the desert pursued water." She sniffed, and felt the knowing look in her eyes. "You never did that."

"No." He squinted against the glare of the sun and then lifted his face to the sky and closed his eyes. "I didn't."

"So why tell me now?" She felt the beginning of tears in her eyes, and she slid away from him, her legs tucked beneath her. "Why tell me that Cheyenne didn't think we were right for each other?"

"She thought it was my fault." He looked broken, like he was aware he'd probably said too much and now he would've done anything to take back at least that part — the part about Cheyenne's feelings. "I thought you should know . . . because . . . well, because maybe she was right."

"That we were never meant to be?" Anger fanned a flame in her soul. Her voice grew louder, tears choking every word. "You thought I'd want to *hear* that?"

"Maybe not. But it was my fault. I can see that now."

Bailey stood and turned her back to him. The rock was icy and it occurred to her that if she slipped she'd fall halfway down the hillside. Before that was even remotely possible, Cody was up and at her side. "Come on . . . let's get down."

"No." She jerked her hand from his and as she did, she felt her feet fly out from under her. Before she could scream, he grabbed hold of her. Caught her beneath her arms and pulled her to the other side, back to the path and to safety.

He was out of breath, more from the close call than the effort it took to save her.

"You're crazy!" he yelled at her. "You could've killed yourself up there."

She didn't say anything, didn't know if she could if she wanted to. Her heart pounded out the fact that he was right. If he hadn't been there . . . She swallowed hard and put her hands on her head, struggling to catch her breath.

"Bailey . . ." He reached out and waited. "Please . . . I don't want to fight."

For a few seconds she turned away from him, leaving him standing there. What right did he have to take her hand now, after all he'd told her? All the ways he'd opened old wounds in her heart? She blinked back another wave of tears and finally . . . when she wasn't strong enough to resist him a moment longer, she turned and gradually reached out to him.

He didn't slip his fingers between hers. That would've been too intimate, too confusing given the conversation, and given the fact that she had Brandon. But he held her hand the way an older brother might've held it, as a way of telling her everything was somehow going to be okay. "I guess . . . what I want to say is that . . . I should've treated you like a real girl."

"Real?" She thought about pulling away again, but she waited.

"Instead of some picture of perfection on a pedestal." He took a step closer, his eyes locked on hers. "Chey was right; I treated you like an ideal. Like you were this unattainable figure. And every time I got close enough to love you, I ran away."

She was still breathing hard, but again she felt the fight leave her. Somehow in the past few seconds a dawning happened in her heart, as if for the first time she could see clearly her love for Cody and the relationship they'd shared over the years. He was an ideal for her too. "You were my first love. I thought you were bigger than life."

"You did?"

"Yes." Her tone whispered to him in a way that was kinder than before. "You were the big man on campus, the football hero of Clear Creek High, and you looked out for me. You never would've let anything happen to me."

"Hmmm." Cody looked surprised. Like this was the first he'd understood how Bailey felt back then. "And I thought you were perfect."

A sad laugh sounded on her lips. "We were both wrong."

"Yes." He gave her hand a gentle squeeze. "Your mom is right about the guy in your life. He should pursue you like that." The

454

sadness in his eyes was back again. "The way I never did."

They were talking in circles, and suddenly Bailey only wanted one thing. To get home again, so she could call Brandon Paul. "You have my past, Cody. You'll always have that."

He released her hand and held his arms out. "Come here, Bailey."

She looked at him and in that moment she saw the guy she'd loved for so many years when she was a young girl. The guy she thought would hold her heart forever. She went to him willingly and they hugged for a long time.

The hug of two old friends, nothing more.

The realization gave her a glimmer of hope that maybe . . . maybe someday they might actually be friends again. The way they'd been in the beginning. Cody didn't mean any harm by bringing her out here today and telling her what he'd told her. She held him a little tighter. "I'm sorry, Cody. About Cheyenne. I can't imagine."

"Thanks. I needed this . . . being with you today. You're family to me, Bailey. You always will be."

"The way it should be." For the first time, Bailey was convinced of one very powerful truth: Cody had made a transition. He didn't see her as the ideal anymore, as the girl he was in love with.

He saw her as a friend, as family.

She eased back and took his hand again. "Let's go." She smiled. "My dad's waiting."

On the path back to his truck, she told him about the audition she had next week, and how she was ready to live in Los Angeles for a year.

"Timing is always so weird when it comes to us." Cody grinned at her, but the sadness in his eyes remained. "Clear Creek is offering me the head coaching position."

"Really?" Her family hadn't told her. The irony was as bold as the blue sky over Bloomington that morning. Cody coming back to Clear Creek High the same season she would set off for LA. She asked about how he thought his kids back at Lyle would handle him leaving and he explained that many of them were graduating. The others were close enough that they'd be fine, whoever replaced him as head coach.

In no time they reached his truck and after a few more minutes of catching up they pulled up in front of her house again. Cody followed her inside so he could find her dad, and before she returned to her bedroom, they shared one last hug. "Thanks, Bailey . . . for making time for me."

"Of course." She eased back, looking

straight at him, into his familiar heart. "I'm glad you talked to me. I think . . . I think Cheyenne was very wise."

"Me, too." His smile grew sad again. "Even though I didn't want to hear her opinion at the time."

"Well . . ." Bailey took a step back. "I hope . . . down the road . . . we can have more days like this. Really, Cody."

He nodded, and his expression told her he was willing to believe such a time was possible. That maybe they would finish the way they had begun — the best of friends. Bailey walked quickly to her room, sat down, and pulled her phone from her purse on the table beside her bed. And as she called Brandon, she realized that — for the first time in forever — she had spent time with Cody and she didn't feel angst or confusion or pain.

She felt peace.

Cody found Jim Flanigan and the two of them prayed together and read the Bible — from 1 Corinthians — about having hope regarding death, that for the believer it was life to life. No taste of death was even possible. The time in God's Word lightened Cody's heart and convinced him the Flanigans would always be his family.

As he drove back to Indianapolis that afternoon, as he went over the plans he had to meet Tara at the mortuary and make arrangements for Cheyenne's memorial service, he replayed his time with Bailey once more. Maybe it was selfish, asking her to meet with him. Sure, he'd wanted to tell her the two things he'd shared with her earlier today.

But there was more.

Cheyenne had challenged him with their talk that day, telling him that he should look for the person God had for him, and that maybe Bailey wasn't that person. Cody knew only one way to find out if she was right. And that was by spending time with Bailey.

Being with her was a mix of the wildest emotions imaginable. Yes, he still had feelings for her, still caught his breath over the beauty in her blue eyes or the way she held his heart whenever she was near. But he finally understood what Cheyenne meant — though he had no idea how in the little time she'd known him she'd been able to see it. When he looked at Bailey he saw the high school girl she'd been, almost more than the woman she'd become. The innocent girl who had given him his first understanding of a life outside the one he'd been raised in, outside the one he'd been living. Pure . . . sweet . . . unattainable.

One-in-a-million.

He remembered on the drive home something she'd said to him a year ago November, when he came to her house to tell her he was leaving for Indianapolis. She'd told him he could go, but he couldn't force her to say goodbye.

"You can't make me stop loving you, Cody Coleman," she'd shouted at him. "You can't."

Cody would remember that as long as he was breathing. But was that a good thing? Should a girl have to yell that at the guy who loved her? Poor Bailey . . . he'd made her work so hard for even a single good moment between the two of them.

And today he'd done that same thing again, right?

Bailey had told him only briefly about heading to LA and reading for a part next week. His response should've been one of interest and investment. *What movie was it? What part?* He could've asked her to read her lines for him, and he could've looked for ways to build her up and compliment her for the effort she'd put into memorizing the scene. In his heart, he was that kind of guy . . . he cared that much.

Instead he hadn't done any of that, hadn't asked her a single question or learned more details about the audition or asked her to share even one thing about the part — the way he would have if he were really pursuing the girl he loved. Cody was at peace with the revelation in his heart. The truth Cheyenne had spelled out that he had always loved the idea of Bailey more than he'd loved the girl. After today he would let go of the possibility of Bailey's love, but he felt certain he would gain something in the process.

The reality of her friendship.

TWENTY-SIX

Brandon woke up early that Valentine's Day and took his coffee out on the balcony overlooking the beach. He hadn't slept well last night, realizing that today would've been the day he proposed to Bailey were it not for his conversation with Dayne. Brandon set the hot cup on the balcony railing and stared out at the faint pinks over the Pacific. The sun was up, but it wouldn't clear the mountain behind him for another half an hour. It was the time of morning Brandon liked the most.

He breathed in, loving the way the ocean air felt in his lungs. In the days since meeting with Dayne he'd done a lot of praying. Spent more time than usual reading 1 Timothy and Philippians and Hebrews and Romans. About being surrounded by a great cloud of witnesses and not wanting anyone to cut in on the race he was running, wanting to push ahead with endurance.

Eyes on the cross.

Brandon took a sip of his coffee and let his eyes settle on the horizon, the perfect straightness of it. In the journey of life ahead, he wanted nothing more than to be that straight line. Perfect in dependability, always unyielding to the temptations of the world, the darkness in it. But Scripture had only underscored the message in Dayne's words that day. More than anything in life he wanted a stronger faith, a deeper relationship with the Lord. And he wanted a deeper connection with Bailey Flanigan.

Sure they'd had fun. He'd taken her on crazy dates and he'd shown her that he meant what he'd said back when he started chasing after her a year ago. He always had a plan . . . and he was determined to fight for her. But marrying her would mean a whole lot more. He needed to be a spiritual leader for her, someone she could look to whatever storms came their way.

One thing hadn't even occurred to him until the two extra days Bailey spent in Bloomington. If he was going to marry her, he needed to ask her father first. He hadn't been raised that way, but she had. She deserved a guy who would take time to make sure her dad, her parents, were on board with his desire to propose.

"I have a lot to learn, right, God?" His voice was a whisper, mixed with the breeze and the distant sound of the surf. "But I'm ready . . . You can test me, Lord. It's okay. I want to grow."

That was something else the Bible had taught him. The fact that time and again God's people needed to spend time on the threshing floor in order to be refined. That fire was a part of the process for anyone desiring a strong relationship with God. What testing had Brandon been through? In some ways he didn't want to ask God to test him, because there was no telling how the Lord would accomplish that.

One thing was sure: Bailey would love LA. He stared at the sea, at the beauty in his backyard. But he believed this: God had his best interest in mind. For that reason, he was excited about their date tonight at Katy and Dayne's. He planned to pull Dayne aside at some point and ask about having weekly Bible studies, a way Brandon might be challenged on a regular basis, a way he might grow because of the wisdom Dayne had already gained along the way.

And now that he'd read through his new contract thoroughly, now that he'd found sections he was unsure about, he was going to do something else today as soon as possible.

He was going to call Luke Baxter.

Bailey helped Katy cut the vegetables for that night's barbecue. They were doing shish-kabobs on the grill, something that never would've been possible in Indiana tonight. But here, the sun was shining across the ocean out back and the day hadn't been any cooler than seventy degrees.

Another reason to fall in love with it, right, Lord? She'd been keeping an ongoing dialogue with God since she'd arrived in Los Angeles. The timing was perfect. Her time in New York behind her, any thoughts of Cody firmly put to rest. Now with her audition tomorrow she was ready for this next season, believing that the Lord had her here for a reason.

"I forgot to tell you." Katy rinsed off the knife she'd been using to cut chunks of onion. "I'm following you on Twitter now."

"You are?" Bailey lit up. The time she'd invested in Twitter and Facebook while home in Bloomington remained a priority. Like a whole generation of girls needed a reason to do the right thing, encouragement that believing in God was still in vogue, still the only way to true joy. "I've been a lot more into it lately. A lot of teenage girls are looking for someone to follow."

"And the cool thing is, you'll lead them to follow the God they really need — you're telling them not to settle for anything less."

"I hope so." Bailey loved that Katy had noticed. It made her feel the way she used to feel years ago when Katy lived in their family's upstairs apartment and led Christian Kids Theater. Back then Bailey would walk on clouds for a week if Katy caught her doing the right thing or improving in some way. "It's funny . . . *you* were that person in *my* life. I mean, my mom and I are so close. Of course. But I needed a girl to look up to, someone close to my age."

"And now you can be that for these girls." Katy pulled a few zucchini from the refrigerator. "I can't believe how many people follow you."

"It's because of Brandon." Bailey rolled her eyes, her laugh lighthearted. "Let's be honest."

"But still . . . I try to picture all those people filling up a couple of major college football stadiums. It's a lot of influence." Katy gave her a quick side hug. "I'm glad you take it seriously."

"I do." In the other room, she could hear the guys laughing with Sophie, playing tennis on the Wii. "We're almost done here."

"I can finish the rest . . . you go hang out with Brandon." She smiled at Bailey. "That boy's crazy about you."

"I know." She lowered her voice. "For the longest time . . . I sort of thought he was just a friend, someone who made me laugh. You know, that Cody was the right guy for me." She glanced toward the other room, making sure the guys couldn't hear her. "Not anymore."

"No." Katy shook her head, a smile dancing in her eyes. "Cody Coleman? That boy missed his chance. And you definitely gave him chances."

"Yeah . . ." She didn't feel hurt about the past anymore — another benefit of the talk she'd had with Cody just a few days ago. "I'll always care about him. Just not like that." She absently found the tiny engraved heart that hung from her necklace, the one Brandon had given her. "I want to be adored, appreciated. I want a guy who'll fight for me."

"I'm pretty sure that's him." Katy pointed her knife toward the family room. "Sitting out there."

"I know." Her heart sang inside her. "I feel that way more every day." She had already told Katy about the seaweed ring and the fact that Brandon wanted to propose. The other day when they'd gone shopping for summer clothes, Katy had even taken her into a jewelry store to see which rings she liked.

"Because a girl has to dream," Katy had told her.

But in the light of day, away from wedding rings — seaweed or solid gold — the idea of getting engaged still felt a ways off. Like she and Brandon had life to figure out first. Big things like whether she could work and live here, and whether the contract he was about to sign would change anything between them.

Now Katy lowered her voice another notch or two. "Do you think he's still planning a proposal? At some point soon?"

"I'm not sure." Bailey felt a ripple of nervousness. "I wouldn't mind waiting a little while. You know, see how things work out here." She didn't like to think about his looming contract, and the publicity it would likely cause. "We have time. There's no rush."

The guys drifted into the kitchen, laughing over the Wii game they'd just played. "You should see Sophie." Brandon came up to Bailey and put his hand around her waist. "She's a better tennis player than anyone on the circuit." He nodded, his eyes alive with laughter. "I'm serious."

For the next fifteen minutes the guys helped thread the skewers with pieces of chicken, pineapple, and vegetables until they had enough to get started. Brandon helped Dayne at the barbecue, and Bailey made a peanut butter sandwich for Sophie. "You're pretty." Sophie stood right beside her, casting adoring eyes in her direction. "You can stay in my room, 'kay, Bailey?"

Across the kitchen Katy laughed out loud. "I knew she was going to do this. She's been talking about you living with us nonstop."

Bailey smiled at the little girl, and for a moment she tried to imagine how wonderful it would be to have a daughter of her own — a blue-eyed angel looking into her eyes and adoring her. The way she had adored her own mother. The way Sophie was looking at her now. The moment passed and she patted Sophie's head. "Tell you what, sweetheart. I'll be right across the hall, okay?"

"And we can have sleepovers, right?"

Out at the barbecue, Brandon leaned his head in through the patio door and gave her a look that was part flirty, part teasing. "Sleepovers can be fun."

"Yeah." Dayne poked him with the barbecue tongs. "Especially when you're married."

"Of course." Brandon gave Dayne a look of exaggerated innocence. "That's what I meant."

They all laughed except Sophie, who busied herself getting situated at the table and asking Bailey to put extra strawberry jam on her sandwich. "Please," Katy reminded her.

"Please." Sophie looked happy with herself. She smoothed out her ruffled skirt and fixed her long curls so they fell just right over her shoulders. "Sometimes I feel like a princess. Don't you, Bailey? Sometimes feel like a princess?"

"That's it." Katy pointed at Dayne. "You need to stop reading her that book — *The Princess and the Three Knights.* She's starting to believe she's royalty."

"That's all right." Dayne winked at Sophie and then grinned at Katy. "It's good for little girls to believe that."

"I guess." Katy laughed as she crossed the kitchen and gave Sophie a kiss on her cheek. "You're always a princess, baby. Don't forget that."

Bailey could almost see herself at that age, her mom bending down and kissing her cheek, telling her she was a princess much the way Sophie believed it now. All teasing aside, Bailey had to agree. It was the way her parents raised her, to believe that she was special, set apart. One-in-a-million. If Sophie grew up that way it would make it easier for her to follow God's calling. Easier to resist the pitfalls of the world. Because she would want to act in keeping with her place in life. The place of a princess.

The dinner that night was perfect. Bailey sat by Brandon, and something about him seemed different, deeper. Bailey couldn't put her finger on it. He didn't say anything unusual or let on that he was thinking something more intense than the light conversation around the table. It was simply a feeling, a connecting between them at a different level.

Whatever caused the change, Bailey loved it, and she loved the way he made her feel cherished in his presence. After dinner, Dayne and Katy offered to do the dishes so the two of them could take a walk, and Bailey was grateful. It was dark outside, and she needed alone time with Brandon, needed it more during these early days in LA than she'd let on. Because a part of her missed Bloomington more than she had admitted even to herself. Snowy, freezing days and all.

Like other nights when they'd hung out together, Brandon's driver had done an elaborate job of leading the paparazzi on a chase, keeping the photographers away for the night. Mock reservations had been made at a local restaurant, one where celebs often hung out. The manager was in on the ruse, though he didn't know where Bailey and Brandon were really going to end up on Valentine's Day. He was happy to get the buzz going, spread the word in quiet ways that Hollywood's hottest young couple were going to share the holiday at his establishment.

An hour ago, Brandon's driver had pretended to leave Katy and Dayne's house with the couple in the back. Instead he had two caterers who had helped bring dessert to the Matthews' house. He took them to the restaurant and ushered them in through the back door — giving the photographers who had chased him little chance to actually make out the couple's faces. Once inside, the caterers went their separate ways, their cars waiting out front.

Meanwhile, Brandon and Bailey were left at the Matthews' house without a single pair of eyes looking for them to walk out the back door.

This time they were both fairly certain

they'd be left alone. Brandon took her hand and led her quietly across the empty stretch of sand to the water's edge. "We spend a lot of time here, have you noticed that? Walking along the beach."

"I love it." Bailey stood close to him, looking out at the moon on the water. "This was the site of the famous seaweed ring, after all."

"Mmmm." He put his arm around her shoulders and held her close, his body warm against hers. "How could I forget?"

The air between them was easy. "Thank you, by the way." She turned her back to the water and faced him.

"For what?" He brought his fingers to her face and slipped a section of her hair back behind her ears, so he could see her face despite the ocean breeze. "Dayne gets most of the credit for the shish-kabobs."

She laughed. "Not that, silly. Thanks . . . for not proposing to me tonight. I mean," She caught her hair in her hands and pulled it to one side. "This is Valentine's Day, but instead of something all serious, you wanted to hang out with Katy and Dayne." She smiled deep in his eyes. "Thanks for that."

"Oh." His face fell, but she knew him well enough to know he was teasing. "So . . . go ahead and keep the ring in my pocket? Is that it?"

"Quit it." She backed up a few steps until the surf churned around her ankles. Then she bent down and flicked a few drops of foamy water at him. "You're such a tease."

"Me?" He ran lightly into the water, catching her by the waist and threatening to drop her into an approaching wave. "Look at you, Miss Splash-Whenever-I-Want-To."

"Sorry!" She released a quiet scream. "I didn't mean it!"

He started to let go, like he really might let her get drenched in the cold water out here this late at night. But then at the last moment he stood her back on her feet. "Of course . . . ruin my proposal. You deserve to be dunked."

"Brandon!" She was laughing harder, so hard she couldn't possibly be serious with him now. "There was no proposal tonight. You wouldn't have brought me here."

His grin went a long way to hide his thoughts, whatever they might be. But again she felt that new, attractive depth about him. Like he was growing into a man who would not only love her, but take care of her. When they were back up a few feet from the water, he looked at her, letting the silliness settle for a minute. "You feel less ready . . . is that it?"

She looked at him and saw that despite his smile, his wide open eyes, he wasn't teasing. She folded her arms in front of her and looked out at the farthest points of the dark sea. "It's different . . . living here." She lifted her chin, letting the breeze dry the drops of water on her face. "I guess I need to be sure . . . that I can make this my home."

"Because sunny Februarys are hard to get used to." He slipped his arm around her shoulders again. "Right?"

"No . . . but if I fall any harder for you, there won't be any looking back. And I still love Bloomington." She'd thought about this a lot lately. "I never pictured getting married, raising a family here in LA, at the beach. I don't know; it just doesn't seem the same."

Brandon nodded, his expression thoughtful. "I understand. It's a big decision."

This was one more thing she loved about him, the way he had of giving her space and time, knowing that she couldn't be rushed. She was about to thank him again when suddenly they heard the sound of pounding feet. "Not again."

"Run, Bailey." Brandon took her hand and led her. "Don't turn around."

Did this always have to happen? Even after the extensive plans they'd made to find time alone? Would they have to stay shut up in Brandon's beach house or locked in some other indoor place in order to find time alone? Bailey ran as fast as she could, but she could sense the people behind her gaining ground.

"Bailey! Brandon! Turn around. Come on . . . we know it's you!" the man closest to them shouted, his voice intense.

Bailey suddenly felt the familiar fear grab her around the throat, making it hard for her to catch her breath. It wasn't the presence of the paparazzi . . . it was the permanence of them that made panic course through her veins. "I . . . can't run . . . that fast, Brandon."

"You can do it. Please . . . keep running." Brandon wasn't out of breath. He had already slowed his pace so she could keep up with him.

What was wrong with her? At home she could run twice this fast on the track at Clear Creek High. And she'd been working out more than usual, having danced for hours on end during *Hairspray* rehearsals and performances. Her cardio ability should've put distance between the heavy-footed paparazzi and them. She pushed herself, but even as she did, she knew the problem. It was her fear. She couldn't draw a breath because her panic was moving faster than either of them or the photographers.

Dear God . . . please . . . give me Your peace. Slow my racing heart.

Katy and Dayne's house was only a hundred yards away, but it might as well have been a hundred miles. Bailey felt the defeat hit her. There was no way they could outrun the paparazzi all the way to the Matthews' back staircase.

"Just a few pictures!" The voice was closer, the feet behind them gaining ground quickly.

"They won't hurt you." Brandon looked back at her as they kept running. "Just don't turn around. It's okay."

But suddenly, before Bailey could respond or will herself to believe him, she felt a hand grab her from behind. The jolt stopped her sharply and dropped her to the sand.

Brandon wheeled around and moved to her side.

"I'm okay . . . it's my ankle. It turned." She closed her eyes, held her hand over her face even as the man who had made her fall began taking pictures.

The anger and rage that came over Brandon's face was unlike anything Bailey had ever seen. He rushed at the photographer and grabbed the man's camera. Another ten photogs ran up a dozen yards behind him, but they stopped short when they saw what Brandon was doing. They all lifted their cameras and began taking pictures at rapid fire. Even in the dark of night, Bailey figured they were getting something they could use. She was still sprawled out on the sand, more worried for Brandon than herself. "Brandon! Stop."

"No!" He didn't look back at her. "I saw him grab you! I won't let him do that."

The man before him was squaring off at him, his fists raised, his camera now untangled from around his neck and down on the shore, half immersed in the surf. Brandon loomed over the man with an intensity and strength Bailey hadn't known he was capable of, and before the guy could take a swing, Brandon punched him square in the face. As the man fell to the ground, Brandon stood over him, ready to hit him again. "If you *ever* . . . ever touch her again," Brandon seethed, his voice raised, body shaking, "you'll be sorry." He looked like he might kick the man, but then he backed up. "You hear that?" He shouted straight at the others, disregarding the fact that their cameras were still shooting at him, still capturing every moment. "Don't touch her again!"

From where she lay, Bailey was giddy with his show of protection. She eased herself to her feet and tested her ankle. It hurt, but it wasn't sprained or broken. Even if it was she couldn't take her eyes off Brandon, still glaring at the paparazzi.

On the ground, the man was writhing, holding his nose. "I'll sue you, Brandon Paul! Mark my words, I'll sue you."

"Go ahead." Brandon brushed his knuckles on his jeans and made a fast approach at the laid out photographer once more. He hissed in the man's face. "Ever heard of self-defense? Call a lawyer, and I'll have you thrown in jail for assault."

This time he took a step back and shouted at the guys. "Get off this beach . . . now." He waited, backing up so he could take hold of Bailey's hand. "You heard me, go."

The photographers didn't know what to do. They were used to being the pursuers, the ones in control. But not now. Sheepishly they waited for the downed photog to grab his wet camera and scramble in the opposite direction from Brandon. Then, as if they'd had enough of this crazed version of Brandon Paul, they headed as a group down the beach, back to wherever they came from.

Brandon looked at her, put his hands to

her face, and searched her eyes. "Are you okay?"

"Yes." She felt dizzy, but not because of the paparazzi or her breathlessness. Her lungs worked just fine. "That was amazing."

"What?" His knuckles were bleeding and he wiped them again on his jeans. "I meant it, Bailey. No one better ever touch you again."

"I know . . ." She smiled and brought his hand to her lips, kissing the scraped areas near his bleeding knuckles. "No one's . . . ever done that for me."

Brandon looked upset with himself, guilty somehow. "I'm sorry . . . I lost it. I've never done that before and it was . . . it was wrong."

He was right about that, but she understood. "You didn't mean to punch the guy. It's okay." She touched the side of his face. "You defended me."

"I had to." He was still breathing hard. "I mean, what was I supposed to do? Someone touches you they'll have to deal with me." His face relaxed some and he kissed her lips, kissed her tenderly and gently. "I've got you, Bailey . . . no one's ever going to hurt you again." He was out of breath. "But I can't go around punching paparazzi, either."

He kept his arm around her shoulders, glancing back every few seconds to make sure no one followed them. As they made their way back to Katy and Dayne's, Bailey's heart had never been more full. Because Brandon Paul didn't only love her. He would die for her. Defend her. And though she hadn't meant it literally, Brandon had done something no other guy had ever done. Even Cody Coleman. Something she had only dreamed a guy who loved her might do.

Brandon had fought for her.

Twenty-Seven

Jenny Flanigan hung up the phone and stared out the window for a long time. Jim must've realized the call was over because he walked up behind her. "That sounded interesting."

"It was." She turned and hugged him for a long while. "Bailey had quite a night." She explained about the dinner at Katy and Dayne's and the walk she and Brandon had taken on the beach and the crazy paparazzi chasing after them. "I guess one of them grabbed Bailey's wrist and she fell to the ground."

"What?" Jim took a step back, angry. "That's not okay."

"Brandon didn't think so either." She raised her brow. "He drew back and leveled the guy. Threw his camera down and punched him square in the face. Told the others they'd be sorry if any of them ever touched her again."

Jim's eyes grew wide and a smile filled his face. "Brandon did that?"

"Yep." Jenny knew what her husband had to be thinking. "If you ever worried whether Brandon could take care of her, I guess that settles it."

"But . . ." Jim came close again, kissing her forehead, his eyes full of compassion. "He's not Cody Coleman."

"I know." She released a long sigh. "You could always read my mind."

"Not always . . ." He tilted his head, patient with her, kindness filling his tone. "Let's go sit in the living room. The kids are asleep. We can talk out there."

"Not very romantic . . . talking about our kids on Valentine's Day." Jenny had promised herself that tonight would be about just the two of them, the love they shared, the romance that still marked their marriage now more than ever. But she hadn't counted on the call from Bailey.

"Not romantic?" Jim chuckled. "Watching you figure out our kids is very romantic. Makes me beyond glad that God brought you into my life." He kissed her again and then took her hand, leading her into the next room. "I definitely married up."

"Jim . . ." She loved when he did this, showering her with compliments she didn't actually deserve. Because deserved or not she loved him for being the kind of man who knew exactly what she needed.

When they were seated on the sofa, she exhaled again. "I have a confession."

"I sort of figured." He put his hand on her shoulder, and ran his fingers along her arm. "About Bailey?"

"Yes." She drew another deep breath and let it out again.

"Keep that up and you'll need a paper bag." He raised his brow at her. "This is me, remember? You can talk about it."

She laughed at the mental picture of herself hyperventilating rather than simply saying what was on her mind. "Last weekend, when Cheyenne died, I encouraged Bailey to stay a few days. So she could be there for Cody."

"Hmmm." Jim didn't sound critical or judgmental. Just puzzled. "I wondered why she stayed. He was reaching out more to me than her."

"I know. But I told her . . . it would be callous to rush off to LA. When maybe he would need her."

"And . . ." Jim didn't need to say more than that. They knew each other too well.

"And I never believed anything of the sort. I just figured . . ." She shrugged, embarrassed by her own actions. "I figured if Cheyenne was gone, then maybe once Bailey and Cody had a day together, he would use that time to tell her how he's always felt about her."

"So . . . you're convinced about Cody. That he's the guy for her, is that it?"

She exhaled again, but when she caught his pointed look again she laughed out loud at herself. "It's all about that long ago Fourth of July. I got my mind stuck on something back then, and I can't see it any other way."

"You?" Jim brushed his free hand in her direction and made a silly face. "Never!"

"I know . . . it's true. Every once in a while." She nodded, sheepish, and grateful for the way he had of keeping the moment light. Even when her confession really was a serious one. "You remember that Fourth of July?"

"When Cody came back from the war." He didn't have to ask; he was tracking with her as if he knew her thoughts before she spoke them.

She went on to describe what she'd seen that day. "I've probably told you this before."

"Probably."

"Anyway . . . I'll tell you again because it

sets up my confession."

He smiled at her. "Of course."

She explained once more how Cody had walked through the front door and hugged Bailey. "And I told myself no one . . . no one would ever love her like Cody loved her."

Jim's smile softened a little. "I remember feeling like that."

"Right . . . see?" She allowed another hard exhale and caught herself again. "At least I'm not the only one."

"But? Because there's a *but* here. I can feel it."

"But that Cody Coleman . . ." She shook her head, still frustrated with him. "He didn't cooperate. A year ago summer I thought their love story was all but written. And not for a minute did I think some . . ." She waved her hand in the air. "Some playboy Hollywood hunk would sweep our girl off her feet. Not when Cody had been there for so many years loving her, waiting for her."

"Waiting for her?"

"Well." She made a face. "That's the thing. I thought he was waiting. That he wanted her to have her college days . . . and then that he was backing off so she could follow her dreams. But, Jim, that boy has backed himself right out of the picture."

"Yes." Jim's face was more serious than before. "He certainly has."

"And so here's the confession."

"I knew it was coming."

She laughed, and it felt good. The truth she was wrestling with was not a funny matter. But at least Jim didn't think she was terrible for where she was headed with this. "I think with Bailey I always thought I could sort of hold the pen to her story. I'd see the people she should stay away from, the people she should run to — like Katy Hart back in the day."

Jim nodded, his eyes locked on hers.

"And when Cody came into our lives, well, to be honest at first I didn't like him. I thought, you know, over my dead body was a kid like Cody Coleman going to come into our home and fall for our daughter."

"I felt the same way."

"Right." She felt herself relax a little, felt the intensity of her story soften. "But he changed, and he became this . . . this amazing guy. And when he came back from war I took my little pen and wrote that part of Bailey's story. Cody would love her. And they'd live happily ever after."

For as strong as Jim was, as focused as he could be on defensive schemes and play-breakers, and for as much football trivia as his brain somehow managed to draw from, he was also one of the most sentimental men ever. The tears in his eyes now reminded Jenny of the fact.

"Anyway . . ." She felt the sadness in her smile. "I think . . . God is asking me to set the pen down. That He and Bailey should have the chance to write this story."

Jim nodded slowly, thinking for a long while about what she'd just said. "That seems fair."

"I mean . . ." She looked out the window again. It was snowing, but she could only see the stretch of sandy beach where an hour ago Brandon Paul stood up for her precious daughter. She turned back to Jim. "I like Brandon. I really do."

"He loves her."

"Yes." She could hardly deny that much. Not now, especially. "He's attentive, always. I look at pictures of the two of them and . . . well, seriously, he can't take his eyes off her."

"So . . . you were the reason Bailey met with Cody the other day." He raised his brow in her direction again. The way he might look at the kids when they'd forgotten to take out the trash.

"Yes." She felt the guilt in her expression. "I really thought it might be good for them."

"And was it?"

"No. Everything went horribly wrong. He told her he didn't think they were right for each other. Some crazy thing like that." Her confession was overdue if she were honest with herself. Her heart had known all along that she'd made a mistake pushing for Bailey and Cody to be together. "Anyway, God's been waiting for me to admit I was wrong. I should probably tell Bailey too."

"In time. She's fine for now." Jim wasn't angry with her. He understood she only wanted the best for their kids. Especially Bailey, in this season of her life.

"You forgot one other thing about Brandon." Jim ran his hand along the side of her face. "As long as you've laid your pen down."

"Yes?" She smiled and a light bit of laughter came from her. It felt so good to be real with him, and to know that he loved her anyway.

"He's pursued her."

"I know, I know . . ." She looped her arms around her husband's neck. "Like a dying man in the desert looking for water."

They both laughed and kissed and remembered a dozen more reasons why they still loved each other, still enjoyed the romance between them. And when they turned in that night Jenny was grateful for her time of confession. She would always love Cody, always care about him. But that didn't mean he was the right guy for Bailey. Because she meant what she had said. For the rest of time, where Bailey's story was concerned she would lay her pen down and do what she should've done a year ago.

Let God be the Author.

READER LETTER

Dear Friends,

As you know if you've followed the journey of Bailey Flanigan, not all stories take a direction we expect. For the first time since I started writing novels, I found the characters of this series bossing me around, dictating the next part of the plot and the authenticity of their decisions.

From the beginning, I was Team Cody . . . the way so many of you are. And I can promise you, I still love Cody. But Brandon certainly has grown on me. He seems determined to grow in his faith and to prove to Bailey that his feelings aren't shallow or fleeting. Of course, Bailey and Cody and Brandon will take this story to another level in the coming book: *Loving* — the final piece of the Bailey Flanigan Series.

I hope along the way you've thought about what ways you long for God's wisdom and the ways you long to connect with the people in your life. Our days should be marked with passion and concern, with a determination to make our lives and relationships the best they can be. If nothing else, I pray that walking alongside Bailey and Cody and Brandon has helped you feel strongly about that.

As always, I look forward to your feedback. Take a minute and find me on Facebook! I'm there at least once a day — hanging out with you in my virtual living room, praying for you, and answering as many questions as possible. On Facebook I have Latte Time, where I'll take a half hour or so, pour all of you a virtual latte, and take questions live and in person. A couple hundred thousand of us hang out and have a blast together, so come on over and be my friend on my Facebook Fan Page. You all are very special to me.

Also visit my website at *www.KarenKingsbury.com.* There you can find my contact information and leave me a message on my guestbook. Remember, if you post something on my Facebook or my website it might help another reader. So thanks for stopping by. In addition, I love to hear how God is using these books in your life. He gets all credit, and He always will. He puts a story in my heart, but He has your face in mind.

Only He could do that.

Also on Facebook or my website you can check out my upcoming events, such as Women of Faith and others. You can find out about movies being made based on my books and become part of a community that agrees there is life-changing power in something as simple as a story. Post prayer requests on my website or read those already posted and pray for those in need. If you'd like, you may send in a photo of your loved one serving our country, or let us know of a fallen soldier we can honor on our Fallen Heroes page.

When you're finished with this book, pass it on to someone else. By doing so, you will automatically enter my "Shared a Book" contest. Email me at *contest@Karen Kingsbury.com* and tell me the first name of the person you shared with, and you'll be entered to win a library of signed books! In addition, everyone who is signed up for my monthly newsletter through my website is automatically entered into an ongoing once-a-month drawing for a free, signed copy of my latest novel.

There are links on my website that will help you with matters that are important to you: faith and family, adoption and redemption. Of course, on my site you can also find out a little more about me, my faith and my family, the writing process, and the wonderful world of Life-Changing Fiction™.

Also, follow me on Twitter! On Twitter I have an ongoing "Tweet a KK Quote" contest, where you can tweet a quote from one of my books. Be sure to include my Twitter name — @KarenKingsbury — and the book title. I retweet many of these throughout the week, and give away a signed book to a winner every Monday.

Finally, if you gave your life over to God during the reading of this book, or if you found your way back to a faith you'd let grow cold, please know I'm praying for you. Tell me about your life change by sending me a letter to *office@KarenKingsbury.com.* Write, "New Life" in the subject line. If this is you, I encourage you to connect with a Bible-believing church in your area, pray for God's leading, and start reading the Bible. But if you can't afford one and don't already have one, write "Bible" in the subject line. Tell me how God used this book to change your life, and then include your address in your email. My wonderful publisher Zondervan has supplied me with free paperback copies of the New Testament, so that if you are financially unable to find a Bible any other way, I can send you one. I'll pay for shipping.

One last thing. I will donate a book to any high school or middle school librarian who makes a request. Check out my website for details.

Again, thanks for journeying with me through the pages of this book. I can't wait to hear your feedback on *Longing!* Oh, and look for Bailey Flanigan's final book — the fourth in the series — in stores in March. Until then, keep your eyes on the cross.

And don't forget to leave the lights on.

In His light and love,
Karen Kingsbury
www.KarenKingsbury.com

DISCUSSION QUESTIONS

1. What team do you find yourself on with Bailey? Team Brandon or Team Cody? Why?

2. Has your opinion changed during the Bailey Flanigan Series so far? Why or why not?

3. Did you have a first love? What happened to him or her?

4. Do people sometimes grow up in different directions? Explain this.

5. What did Bailey's mom mean when she told Bailey that the right guy would pursue her like a dying man in the desert pursues water?

6. Does Cody or Brandon pursue Bailey this way? Explain.

7. What is Bailey longing for in this book? Explain.

8. What is Brandon longing for in this book? Explain.

9. What is Cody longing for in this book? Explain.

10. Jenny Flanigan had somewhat of an agenda in *Longing*, in that she felt Cody was the right guy for Bailey. Have you ever tried to hold the pen in the story of your life or the life of someone you love? How did that work out?

11. Cheyenne is a very wise character in this series. What were some of the revelations she experienced?

12. Hard times were a regular part of Cheyenne's life both before we met her in this series and up until the end of her story. How did Cheyenne deal with her hardships?

13. How have you dealt with hardships in your life? What did you learn about suffering while reading this book?

14. In *Longing,* Bailey quotes Romans 8:28 from the Bible. Look up that verse and write it out here. What did that verse mean to Bailey?

15. What does that Bible verse mean to you? How have you seen the truth in that verse come alive in your journey?

16. In her final days, what revelation did Cheyenne have for Cody?

17. Do you think Cheyenne was right in her assessment of Cody's feelings for Bailey? Why or why not?

18. Landon's announcement at the Baxter Family Christmas party brought much joy to Ashley. What was the announcement and why was it important?

19. Have you ever experienced a change of career that happened against your will? How did God use that time to grow you?

20. If you could write the ending to Bailey's story, how would you write it? Explain.

ABOUT THE AUTHOR

New York Times bestselling author **Karen Kingsbury** is America' favorite inspirational novelist, with over fifteen million books in print. Her Life-Changing Fiction™ has produced multiple bestsellers, including *Learning, Leaving, Take One, Between Sundays, Even Now, One Tuesday Morning, Beyond Tuesday Morning,* and *Ever After,* which was named the 2007 Christian Book of the Year. An award-winning author and newly published songwriter, Karen has several movies optioned for production, and her novel *Like Dandelion Dust* was made into a major motion picture and is now available on DVD. Karen is also a nationally known speaker with several women's groups. She lives in Washington with her husband, Don, and their six children, three of whom were adopted from Haiti. You can find out more about Karen, her books, and her appearance schedule at www.KarenKingsbury.com.